KU-226-138

HER FESTIVE FLIRTATION

THERESE BEHARRIE

AN UNEXPECTED CHRISTMAS BABY

TARA TAYLOR QUINN

MILLS & BOON

First Published in Great Britain 2018
by Mills & Boon, an imprint of HarperCollins Publishers,
1 London Bridge Street, London, SE1 9GF

Her Festive Flirtation © 2018 Therese Beharrie
An Unexpected Christmas Baby © 2018 TTQ Books LLC

ISBN: 978-0-263-26543-9

1118

MIX
Paper from
responsible sources
FSC® C007454

This book is produced from independently certified FSC™
paper to ensure responsible forest management.

For more information visit: www.harpercollins.co.uk/green

Printed and bound in Spain
by CPI, Barcelona

HER FESTIVE FLIRTATION

THERESE BEHARRIE

For Grant,
who makes every Christmas the best day of the year.

And for my family. I love you.

CHAPTER ONE

'Ma'am, I can't let you go in there.'

'But—'

'No "buts".' The man turned back to where smoke obscured the eco-estate where Ava Keller's home was. 'There's no way you're going into that.'

Ava gritted her teeth. She hated him. Though she'd never met the man before, she hated him.

The rational voice in her head told her she was projecting. That coming home from work to find her home covered in smoke had upset her. That being upset had manifested itself in her short tone and strong emotions. Like hatred.

Yes, the rational voice said. She was definitely projecting. But then, she'd never prized rationality in stressful situations. That was why, when she'd been left at the altar a year before, she'd attended the wedding reception. She'd eaten the cake. She'd gone on her honeymoon.

Rationality wouldn't make her feel less stressed. Nor would it make her less emotional. And rationality wasn't going to save one of the only things in her life that was still important to her.

So when an idea occurred to her and the rational voice warned against it, she knew she was going to do it. And though it was a bad idea—a *terrible* one—she would do it anyway.

Heaven help her.

She turned, walked a few steps away from the wall of

men blocking the path to her house, and let out a blood-curdling scream.

They hurried towards her, and later she would think that they must have made quite a picture. Those huge, muscular men in their official uniforms—some firefighters, some police—hurrying over to her as if they were lions and she were fresh meat.

She would also later think that at least ten men hurrying over to her had been overkill. But right now she was pretending to be a damsel in distress, and she was certain that merely the *idea* of that caused men to flock.

Really, her duping them was their own fault.

And that of her excellent acting skills.

Unfortunately, being a copywriter for a cybersecurity company didn't often allow her to illustrate how dramatic she could be.

'I think… I think I just saw a *person*.' She gripped the shirt of the man closest to her. 'Right there—down the path at that bush.' Now she injected a layer of panic into her voice. 'It's so close to the fire, Sergeant. And it looked like my neighbour. An old man with no teeth.'

There was a beat when she wondered whether she'd gone too far. She *had* laid it on a little thick. Mr Kinney was barely fifty. He had all his teeth and he wasn't in danger.

To make it more believable, she let out another tiny little screech. And when the man who'd blocked her from getting near her house moved forward to comfort her she cried, 'No, no, not me. Help *him*. *Help him!*'

If the fire didn't do the job first, Ava knew she was going to burn in hell.

But it worked, and three of the men ran down the pathway while the others moved forward, bodies tensed, ready to help if necessary.

It was all she needed. Without a second thought for how irrational she was acting, Ava bolted up the incline of the road she'd been blocked from earlier, and didn't stop until she was so far from the men she'd left behind she could barely see them.

Nor could she see in front of her.

When panic crept up her throat, she ignored it. Told herself to remember all those nights she'd spent unable to sleep and Zorro had comforted her. To remember that it was only when she was looking after him that she felt capable. Able. And not as if some of her personality traits—her honesty, her bluntness—meant she somehow couldn't be a partner. A *wife*.

But all thought fled from her mind as her body adjusted to its new environment. The smoke seemed to be stuck in her mouth. Clogging her lungs. Burning her eyes. She pulled off her shirt and tied it around her nose and mouth, trying to keep her eyes open.

It didn't make much difference. The smoke was so thick she could barely see her hands in front of her. And the more she tried, the more her eyes burned.

So she wasn't entirely surprised when she walked right into a wall.

The force of it stunned her. But after a moment she realised it wasn't a wall. Not unless this wall had suddenly grown hands and gripped her arms to keep her from falling.

She was pretty sure she'd walked into a human. A human *man*.

As opposed to an alien man?

Clearly the smoke was doing more damage than she'd thought.

She heard a muffled sound coming from the man. He was obviously trying to tell her something, but he was wearing a firefighter's mask and she couldn't make out a single word. She shook her head and then, deciding that this interaction was taking precious time from her rescue mission, she pushed past him.

But she'd forgotten he had his hands on her arms, and they tightened on her before she could move.

'What are you *doing*?' the man asked now, wrenching off his mask.

She still couldn't see him. Which, she thought, was probably a good thing, since his voice didn't indicate that he felt any positive emotion towards her.

'I have to get to my house.'

'Ma'am, this area has been evacuated. The fire could reach us at any moment.'

'So why aren't you out there, making sure that it doesn't?'

'Are you serious?' The disbelief in his tone made his voice sound familiar. 'You *have* to leave, ma'am. Your property is not as important as your life. Or mine.'

'It isn't about my *property*,' she said, her voice hoarse from smoke and desperation. 'My cat is in there. I have to... I have to save him.'

Something pulsed in the air after she'd finished talking, and she could have sworn she'd heard him curse.

'Where's your house?'

Stunned, she took a moment to respond. 'It's not far from here. I can show you.'

'No. Just tell me the number and I'll make sure I find the damn cat.'

'Seventeen.' She hesitated when he handed her his mask and turned away. 'Wait! Don't *you* need this?'

'Yes,' he ground out. 'But you're going to need it more. Just put it on and go back to where you came from. I'll find you.'

It was a few seconds before she realised he wasn't there any more.

'Check under the bed!' she shouted at her loudest, and then she put the mask on and retraced her steps back towards the men—no easy feat with the smoke even thicker now.

She was immediately swarmed, but she ignored them—ignored the complaints and chastisement—and kept her eyes on the clouds of smoke in front of her.

She only realised she hadn't taken off the mask when someone gently removed it from her. A paramedic, she thought, as it was replaced by an oxygen mask and she was asked to breathe in and out as the woman listened to her heartbeat before gently checking her body for burns.

Rationality won out now. It reminded Ava that she'd put her life in danger. That she'd put someone else's life in danger, too. And, even though the thought of losing Zorro sent pangs of pain through her body, she couldn't justify that.

So when the paramedic told her she needed to sit down, to drink some water, to get her heart-rate down, she obeyed, not voicing any of the protests screaming through her head.

A cat. *A freaking cat.*

That was what he was risking his life for. That was what he was abandoning all the rules of his training for. He could see the headlines now: *Volunteer firefighter Noah Giles dies trying to save a cat.* Smoke blurred his eyes, grated in his throat, his lungs, but somehow he made it to number seventeen. Smoke shrouded it, much as it did the other houses on the estate. When he'd been making his final rounds, checking that humans and pets had been evacuated, he hadn't expected to find anyone.

They'd had the entire day to evacuate the area, and it had been erring on the side of caution, really, just in case the veld fire should spread.

Except now he wasn't being cautious, he thought, coughing as he pushed open the door—in any other circumstance, he'd probably be annoyed that it had been left unlocked—and leaned against the wall. His head felt light, and it was pure determination that pushed him forward.

Determination spurred on by the emotion in the woman's voice when she'd told him about the cat. It had been familiar, somehow, and had hit him in a place he hadn't known existed. As if he cared that someone loved a cat as much as this woman loved hers.

And since he was risking his life for this cat, clearly he *did* care.

The damn cat had better be the most intelligent cat in the

entire world, he thought. He'd be pretty annoyed if he died for any other kind. Just before Christmas, too, when he was planning to tell his father that after seven years of restlessness he was finally ready to put down some roots.

But only in terms of where you live.

He grunted. Then chose to ignore the unhelpful voice in his head and focused on checking the entire house systematically. Being inside protected him from the smoke somewhat, but he knew he couldn't stick around for long.

When he got to the bedroom, something told him to look under the bed. Beady eyes stared back at him when he did so, and air gushed from his lungs. How could he be this relieved at finding a pet that wasn't even his own? He shook his head, refusing to think about it, and then belly-crawled under the bed and gently pulled the cat into his arms.

It gave a low *meow*—a warning, he thought—but he didn't pay much attention to it. His goal now was to get back to safety.

He was already back at the front door before he realised he couldn't let the cat go out into the smoke. And shortly afterwards he realised the same thing about himself.

He knew that the cat—which was already wriggling in his arms—would run away the second he put him down. And so, taking a deep breath—and once again rethinking all his decisions in life—Noah stuffed the cat inside his open jacket before buttoning it up.

There was some struggling—and a sharp pain as the cat's claws stuck into his belly—but eventually the cat stilled. He looked around for something he could use to cover his face before he braved the smoke again, but instead his eyes rested on a picture that stood on the mantelpiece. A picture of all the people he'd cared about growing up.

And among all their faces, his own.

If she'd ever wanted to discover how to upset a paramedic, she'd found out that evening.

'You *have* to go to the hospital.'

'No.'

'Ma'am—' The woman cut herself off and hissed out a breath. 'Look, your heart rate is still high, and one of the things that can happen with smoke inhalation is—'

'Cardiac arrest. Yeah, I know. I watched that TV show, too.'

'It's not from a *show*.' The paramedic wasn't even trying to hide her annoyance now. 'I'm a medical professional and I know that—'

Ava didn't hear the rest of the woman's speech. She'd stopped listening the moment she saw a man emerge from the smoke. Ignoring the now protesting woman, she stood and pushed forward.

And then stopped when she saw who the man was.

'Noah?'

She watched as he tossed aside a cloth—no, not a cloth; the throw that had once been over her couch—and then bend over and brace himself on his knees.

'Hey, paramedic lady!' Ava said, turning around in panic. But the woman was way ahead of her, and brushed past Ava with the oxygen mask and tank Ava had been using minutes before.

Just as they had with her, the men rallied around Noah. Though this time, of course, it was because Noah was their colleague, and not some foolish woman who'd run into the line of fire—literally—to save a cat.

She watched helplessly as they guided Noah towards the ambulance, and then, when they were there, tried to get him out of his suit. But he shook his head and made eye contact with her.

It jolted her heart. Had the poor thing sprinting as if it were in a life-and-death race it *had* to win.

So, nothing's changed in the seven years since you've seen him, then?

Clearing her throat—her mind—she took a step forward, her legs shaking though her strides were steady.

When she reached him, he pulled the oxygen mask from

his face, coughed, and then said, 'Are we going to have to talk about why you decided to run into a fire to rescue a cat, Avalanche?'

His words were said with a crooked half-smile, and then he began to unbutton the jacket she'd only just noticed was moving to reveal a squirming Zorro.

There had been a pause before she'd even realised it was her cat. And that pause came because she'd been distracted by the muscular chest under the white vest Noah had just uncovered.

No, she thought. It had been *years* since she'd seen Noah. *Years* since she'd even thought about the silly crush she'd had on her brother's best friend. Or about the kisses they'd once shared.

There was no way any remnants of that crush were still there. She'd been in a five-year relationship since then. She'd almost got married.

But you didn't *get married*, a voice in her head said enticingly.

So clearly, there *was* a way.

CHAPTER TWO

Ava REACHED OVER and pulled the cat into her arms. Noah noted the squirming stopped immediately. *Go figure.*

'No one calls me Avalanche any more.'

It was exactly the kind of thing he'd expected her to say. And even though he didn't know what to do about the nostalgia surging in his chest, he smiled.

'You used to love it.'

'I *never* loved it.'

'Why would I keep calling you that if you didn't love it?'

'I've asked myself that question for most of my life.'

He smirked. Then heard the next words come out of his mouth before he could stop them. 'I've missed you, Avalanche.'

Her eyes softened, and she reached out and placed the oxygen mask back over his nose and mouth. 'It's nice to see you, too, Noah—'

Her voice broke and he frowned, pulling the mask away again.

'Has someone checked you out?'

'I'm fine.'

'I told her she needed to go to the hospital,' said the paramedic he hadn't even realised was still there. 'But she doesn't believe me.'

'Why? What's wrong?'

'Nothing,' Ava said with a roll of her eyes. 'I'm fine.'

'Elevated heart rate,' the paramedic told him.

'She's at risk for cardiac arrest?'

'I am a healthy twenty-five-year-old,' Ava interrupted as the paramedic was about to give an answer. 'I have a healthy heart. In fact, I had a check-up at the doctor's last week and she confirmed it.'

Twenty-five. The last time he'd seen her she'd been eighteen. A kid, really. *Not that that stopped you from treating her like a woman.*

He clenched his jaw. Told himself to ignore the unwelcome voice in his head. But when his eyes moved over her—when they told him she was very much a woman now—the memories that voice evoked became a hell of a lot harder to ignore.

He shook his head. 'Smoke inhalation is dangerous.'

'Which is why *you* should be going to the hospital and not me. I was in there a fraction of the time you were.'

'But my heart rate is okay.' The paramedic nodded when he looked over, and he gave Ava a winning smile. 'See?'

'Smoke inhalation is dangerous,' she replied thinly, with a smile of her own, though hers was remarkably more fake than his.

It made nostalgia pulse again, but memories of the way things had been before he'd left made him wonder if nostalgia was really what he was feeling.

But she was right about the smoke inhalation, and because of it—and because he knew his team wouldn't let him work unless he got checked out—he agreed.

'Fine. But if I'm going, you're going, too.'

She opened her mouth, but he shot her a look and she nodded.

'Okay. But we're stopping at the veterinary hospital first. I need to make sure Zorro's okay.'

The fierceness of her voice softened as she said the cat's name, and he watched as she pressed a kiss into its fur. It stumped him—one, that she could show more affection to a cat than she could to a man she'd basically grown up with and, two, that she could show affection to *that* cat.

It was the ugliest cat he'd ever seen.

He assumed Ava had named him Zorro because of the black, almost mask-like patches on his face. And he supposed in some way those patches *were* cute. But he couldn't say the same for the rest of the cat's body. The orange, brown and white splotches looked as if the cat was the result of a scientific experiment gone wrong.

He'd never really been one for cats, and perhaps he was just biased against them. But, he thought, eyeing the cat again, he didn't think so.

He would never have said the cat was ugly as he looked at Ava, though. Her brown eyes were filled with emotion— love, affection, he couldn't quite tell—and her tall frame had relaxed.

And he realised that if he wanted her to get checked out he was going to have to agree to take the ugly cat to the veterinary hospital.

'He's sitting in the back.'

Five hours later they'd both been checked out. Noah had been put on oxygen for a portion of that time, while they ran tests, and when he'd met Ava in the waiting room later she'd told him the same thing had happened with her.

Though the test results had shown nothing alarming, they'd been given strict instructions to rest, and to return if any potentially dangerous symptoms emerged.

'You didn't have to wait for me,' Noah told her as she got up and joined him.

'I know. But I… I wanted to know that you were okay.' She ran a hand over the curls at the top of her head. 'I'm pretty sure Jaden would kill me if I were responsible for the death of his best man.'

'That's all I am to you?' he teased, though it came out a little more seriously than he'd intended.

'No, of course not.' She paused. 'You're also my only way to call the vet and ask about Zorro. My phone's died.'

He laughed, and it turned into a cough.

'You're sure you're okay?'

'Fine.' He waved a hand. 'Just normal after-effects.'

She bit her lip. 'I really am sorry. I didn't mean for you to get dragged into this.'

'I'm glad I was the one who *did* get dragged into it,' he retorted. 'At least I have training.'

'Ah, yes—one of the thousands of things you can do when you have family money.'

He winced. 'How did you go from apologising to insulting me?'

She grinned, and his mind scrambled to figure out why his body was responding. He'd given himself a stern talking-to when he'd left all those years ago. Hadn't spoken to Ava since then. His body had no business reacting to her smile.

'It's one of my unique talents.'

What are the others?

Now his mind froze, and when Ava didn't say anything else, he wondered whether he'd said it out loud. But her expression didn't change, and he put down the strange thought to the after-effects of inhaling smoke. There could be no other explanation.

Sure, keep telling yourself that.

'So, can I call the vet?' she asked after a moment.

He blinked, then handed her his phone and took the seat she'd vacated as she made the call.

He watched as she spoke to the vet. Watched as she set a hand on her hip and then lifted it, toying with her curls again. She'd cut her hair into a tapered style that somehow made the oval shape of her face seem both classic and modern.

He supposed those terms would work to describe her entire appearance. He'd always thought her beautiful—with an innocent kind of beauty that was much too pure for him—but with the haircut, and the clothes she wore that suited that cut, she *was* an enticing mix of classic and modern that made him want—

He stopped himself. Frowned at the direction of his thoughts. He couldn't think of his best friend's kid sister as *enticing*. He couldn't think about wanting anything when it came to her.

She was just Ava. Little Avalanche. The girl who'd run in circles around him just for the fun of it when she was six. Who'd snorted if she laughed hard enough up until she was fourteen. Who'd asked him to be her first kiss so she could practise, and who'd eagerly responded when he'd kissed her a second time—

Nope. *No*. That line of thinking was going to get him nowhere.

But when she turned and smiled at him—and his body yearned to get *somewhere*—he realised that Jaden's wedding was going to be more complicated than he'd expected.

CHAPTER THREE

HE HADN'T CHANGED one bit.

No, Ava thought as Noah stood, her eyes flitting over him. He *had* changed. Though she now remembered how greedily she'd taken in his muscles earlier, she'd forgotten about them between then and now.

Possibly because he was wearing one of his colleague's ill-fitting T-shirts.

Probably because she'd been too distracted by his face.

It had happened before, too many times to count. And Ava didn't even blame herself for it. How could she? Objectively, Noah had the prettiest face she'd ever seen. And though the word didn't seem to fit with the rest of him— not any more, since the strong, muscular body he had now was more rugged than the lithe one he'd had when they were younger—she couldn't deny the perfect lines and angles of his face *were* pretty.

But just because she couldn't blame herself for it didn't mean she didn't find it annoying. It was. Because if he hadn't been so pretty she might not have found herself *still* having this absurd crush. *Years* later.

And then he walked towards her, rubbed a hand down her arm, and said something in that deliciously deep voice of his. And the voice in her head that had called her a liar when she'd put her crush down to just his looks laughed and laughed.

Damn it.

'Avalanche?'

'Hmm?' She shook her head. 'Oh. You said something?' If only she could remember what. 'Yes.'

'Yes?' His hand dropped. 'What do you mean, *yes*?'

Double damn it. Clearly her guess had been wrong.

'I mean, yes—' She exhaled sharply when she couldn't think of an appropriate cover-up. 'Yes, I have no idea what you said and my attempt at hiding it has failed miserably.'

He stared at her, and then he laughed. 'Clearly you're the same old Ava. Honest even when it doesn't benefit you.'

'Would it kill you to not be so blunt? No one needs you to be this honest.'

'Yes, that's me,' she said brightly, hoping it would banish the darkness of Milo's voice in her head. The memories that voice inevitably evoked. The pretence of the rest of her wedding day. The weeks after, when she'd looked in the mirror and asked herself why she couldn't be different. Better. *Easier.* 'Would you repeat what you said?'

'I asked where you'll be staying tonight?'

'Jaden's,' she said automatically. But then she shook her head. 'No, Jaden isn't here. He and Leela are staying over at the vineyard their wedding is going to be at. They want a better idea of what their wedding will feel like.' She rolled her eyes. 'As if it will change anything. The wedding's two weeks away. What are they going to do if it doesn't "feel" right?' She sighed. 'I guess I'll be staying at a hotel.'

'Why not your mom and dad's?'

'They're with Jaden and Leela at the wedding venue.'

'Sounds horrific.'

'Yes,' she agreed with a small smile. 'I can't imagine anything worse than a wedding at Christmastime.'

She knew that because *her* wedding had been at Christmastime. And not only had her day been spoiled, but her entire festive season. She was still not prepared to spend the first anniversary of her being jilted at another wedding. With the same guests. And the same whispers.

But she had no choice. Her brother was getting married.

'Of course, the fact that this isn't exactly a romantic weekend for Jaden and Leela sucks, too. My parents and Leela's parents are there, so Jaden and Leela probably had to get separate bedrooms.'

It hadn't occurred to her before, but it amused her now.

'Oh, no,' Noah said with a frown. 'Your parents can't think—?' He broke off when she gave him a look. 'Apparently they can.'

'Unfortunately, my parents can and will believe whatever they want of their children.'

Like the way they thought the collapse of Ava's wedding had been because of Milo's faults and not Ava's. And how they still didn't see anything wrong with how grumpy she was—or wonder how much easier she could have been—even after a broken engagement.

'Anyway,' she continued, 'no one's there. And my access to all those places are locked in the drawer next to my bed.' She closed her eyes briefly. 'So, yes, a hotel.'

'What about Zorro?'

She lifted a brow. 'Are you still looking out for him?'

'I'm looking out for *you*.'

She thought she saw him hesitate before he continued.

'You're my best friend's sister. There's an unspoken moral code that requires me to help you when your brother can't.'

'I'd like to think that moral code comes from the fact that you and I were friends once, too,' she said slowly. 'It doesn't matter anyway,' she added, when the thought had her stomach twisting. 'The vet wants to keep Zorro overnight. He wants to make sure he's okay.'

'Are you okay with that?'

'Of course I am.'

'Sure,' he said easily. 'So there's no part of you that's worried about him?'

When her spoken agreement got caught by the emotion in her throat, she sighed. 'There's a *big* part of me that's worried about him. But he's in the best place to make sure he's okay.'

He studied her. 'He'll be okay,' he said quietly, and then, as if he understood that she wouldn't be able to hold back the tears if they kept on talking about it, he said, 'You should stay with me.'

She stared him. 'What?'

'You should stay with me,' he said again. 'At my place.'

'What place? Your dad's?'

'I'm a big boy, Ava,' he said dryly. 'I have a place of my own.'

'I meant,' she said deliberately, when his words sent thrills down her spine, 'that you've been away for seven years. How do you have a place of your own?'

'I invested in property.'

'Of course you did,' she muttered. 'No, thanks, Noah. I think I'll just get a hotel room.'

'You don't know how long it'll be before you'll be able to go home.' He paused. 'You might have to spend a couple of nights there.'

'I'll survive.'

'What about Zorro?'

She narrowed her eyes. 'I told you—'

'Yes, he's staying at the vet's tonight. But what happens tomorrow, when they call you to tell you he's fine? That he can come home?'

'I'm sure I'll be back in my own house by then.'

'But what if you're not?' He waited a beat. 'I have a pet-friendly home.'

'Noah—'

'Ava.'

Their gazes locked. Her brain said, *No, Ava*; her body said, *Yes, please*. The juxtaposition fluttered on her skin, and she blamed her gooseflesh on that and not on how sexy and serious Noah's eyes looked. Or on the memory of how that was exactly how they'd looked before he'd kissed her all those years ago...

'No, Noah.'

She said it with a sigh of regret. She hoped he wouldn't hear that, but her filter wasn't working properly. She was too tired. Her throat ached. Her lungs pained. Her body reminded her that she'd done a full day of work before she'd arrived home to find the place full of smoke. Not to mention the swirling in her head at the unwelcome feelings and memories being in Noah's presence evoked.

'I've already put you out way too much tonight. I'm the reason you're here. You should go home by yourself—' Had she *really* just said that? '—and get some rest. Besides, I have to call my family now, before they hear about the evacuation, freak out and start driving back here in the middle of the night. And I do *not* want to tell them—specifically, Jaden— that I'm staying at your place tonight.'

'Ava…' he said softly, and walked closer to her.

Something pressed into the backs of her legs, and she realised it was one of the seats in the waiting room. Because when he'd moved closer to her she'd moved back.

Stay.

She straightened. 'Noah—'

'Let me speak,' he interrupted, and the tone of his voice— seductive, commanding—silenced her. 'It's been a difficult night. We're both exhausted, and it's going to take more energy than either of us has to find you a hotel. I'm not leaving you alone to arrange all this,' he said when she opened her mouth. 'And I'm not even mentioning clean clothes, proper toiletries, a warm meal. Stay with me.'

'What do I tell my family?'

'Whatever you like. It's the easiest option,' he said with a smile, as if he knew she was already starting to formulate the lie she was going to tell them. 'You'd do the same thing for me, Ava. We're family, too.'

She nearly laughed. 'I haven't seen you in seven years, Noah.'

'Doesn't change anything.' He paused. 'I've only seen Jaden three times during those seven years. All three times it was because he'd come to see me. Because he considered me to be family.'

'You're his best friend.'

'Family,' he said firmly. 'Friends come and go. And I

went. If we weren't family I wouldn't be back here at Christmas, preparing to be best man at your brother's wedding.'

'You're…stubborn,' she said, when defeat washed over her.

'I like to think of it as persistent.'

'Well, you better hope persistence will help us if Jaden ever discovers the truth about the lie I'm about to tell him and our parents.'

'Noah, you know I appreciate you offering me a place to stay, but—' Ava broke off, wondering how to tell him. But then she remembered that he already knew she was honest. 'But it looks like Father Christmas and the elves threw up in here.'

Noah chuckled. 'That's not a bad description, actually.'

He stood next to her and she held her breath, as if somehow it would make her less aware of him.

'I had a company come in and decorate for Christmas before I got here. They got a bit…carried away.'

She took in the tinsel that hung on every flat surface, the Christmas stockings that accompanied it. The Christmas lights that were draped around pieces of furniture that should not have lights around them. And, of course, the gigantic Christmas tree next to the fireplace.

'I think that's an understatement.'

'Probably.'

He took the handbag and coat that been draped over her shoulder and arm respectively, and hung them on a coat rack she hadn't noticed.

'I've been meaning to do something to make it less… *this*—' he nodded his head at the decorations '—but I haven't had the time.'

'Christmas season is fire season in Cape Town.'

'Yeah. And this season's been particularly bad. Hence the fact that I—a mere volunteer—have been fighting fires for pretty much the entire two weeks since I've been here.'

She took a seat at the counter in his kitchen, accepting

the glass of water he offered her. 'Is that why I didn't even know you were back here?'

'I told Jaden. It must have slipped his mind.'

'Must have,' she said softly.

But she didn't think that was it. Jaden hadn't been entirely forthcoming with her since he and his fiancée had announced that their wedding would be at the same time of year hers had been, almost one year later to the day. In fact, he was avoiding her. More so since Leela had asked her to be a bridesmaid.

So she would put down Jaden's neglect in telling her Noah was back to that, and not to the fact that he hadn't wanted her to know. Things had moved on since Jaden had caught them kissing that one time. It probably had nothing to do with the anger he'd felt towards both of them back then.

Probably.

'You okay?'

She looked up to see Noah's eyes steady on her. 'Perfect. This place is amazing.'

She looked around at the light green walls, the large windows that offered an incredible view of the mountains and the hills, the stone-coloured furniture. She took in the marble countertops, the sleek, top-of-the-line appliances, the white and yellow palette that brightened the kitchen.

And then her eyes rested on the sexy man who looked so at home in all of it. And although her heart did unwanted cartwheels in her chest, she forced calm into her voice.

'I mean, what I can actually see underneath all this tinsel is amazing.'

'Oh, ha-ha.'

She grinned. 'So, how about you show me to the shower, Mr Festive?'

CHAPTER FOUR

WHEN HE'D STUDIED photography after school it had been because he'd had a passion for it. He'd enjoyed the challenge of seeing things in new ways. In ways others didn't. He'd created a website to show off his work, and when he'd received that first enquiry to use one of his pictures he'd realised he could use his passion to make money.

Soon his photos had garnered more attention. And then a photo editor for a popular nature magazine had reached out to him about a job in Namibia. And suddenly he'd realised he could use his passion to give in to his wanderlust.

He supposed his surname had given him a push that most twenty-year-olds didn't get. The Giles name was still synonymous with the media empire his great-great-uncle had created. The empire that had been passed down to his grandfather, when his great-great-uncle had died childless, and then down to his father.

Having an empire and money behind him had meant he could take only the jobs that interested him. That he'd been able to use his skill and passion for jobs that *meant* something to the world. That he'd been able to use the money he didn't need to invest in properties back home in South Africa and wherever else his heart desired.

All while avoiding the pitfalls of settling down. The trap he'd seen his father fall into over and over again since his mother had died. But he couldn't deny that it felt good to have a place of his own. Not somewhere he just stayed, but somewhere he *lived*.

He'd only been back in Cape Town for a fortnight, but it was a source of pride for him. And never more than at this moment, as he showed Ava to his spare bedroom.

When she'd disappeared into the bathroom he went to his own room and put some of the spare clothing he had there in hers. And then he went back to the kitchen, to start on the meal he'd promised her. Which, he thought even before he reached the kitchen, was a stupid idea. On his best days he could manage to fry an egg. And it would usually end up deformed. Edible, but deformed.

It would definitely not be the kind of warm meal he'd promised Ava, so he called the twenty-four-hour deli up the road. He was almost out through the door to go and fetch the food, too, before he realised he looked like crap. He'd changed out of his firefighter's uniform before going to the hospital, but he was still sweaty and grimy. And fairly certain he would not have wanted to meet himself, let alone hand over food to someone looking like he did at that moment.

He went to his room, threw off his clothes and headed to the shower. He heaved a sigh when the water hit his body. It kneaded muscles he hadn't realised were tight and painful. It also reminded him that he'd stuffed a cat into his jacket and the cat had *not* appreciated it.

He washed his hair, his body and then, feeling faintly human again, put on clean clothes. But before he put on his top he realised he should probably put something on the scratches on his stomach. They were deeper than he'd first realised. So he grabbed his top, heading to the kitchen where he kept the first-aid kit.

'I thought they fixed everything at the hospital.'

He was halfway through putting salve on the scratches when she spoke. He glanced back, and his throat dried when he saw her in his clothes.

They were too big for her, but they looked better on her than they ever had on him.

'Uh...they did. But they also took me at my word when I told them I had no external injuries. I forgot about these.'

She walked around the counter and he got a whiff of the fruity scent of the shower gel he'd put in his spare bathroom. It smelled a hell of a lot sexier on her than it did in the bottle.

Oh, boy.

'Which external injuries?' she said, and then, though he tried to angle his body away from her, she sucked in her breath. 'Oh, crap,' she said on an exhale. 'Did Zorro do this to you?'

'No,' he said dryly, struggling for normality. 'It was some other cat I put next to my stomach.'

'I'm sorry,' she said, and then she took the salve from him and began to smear it gently on his scratches. He felt his torso tremble—saw it, too, though he tried to ignore it—and hoped Ava wouldn't notice.

'I'm sorry,' she said again. 'Is it painful? It's a lot more enthusiastic than I'd expect from Zorro.'

'It's fine.' He gritted his teeth as her hand moved lower, down to the scratches near the waistband of his pants.

'Clearly it isn't.'

Her touch was still light, still gentle, but when she moved lower still he grabbed her wrist.

'It's fine, Ava.'

The words were said in a harsher voice than he'd intended, and her eyes widened. But that was better than having her move any lower and having his body respond in an unpredictable way—or a very predictable way. He was only just clinging to his control as it was.

'I'm—I'm sorry.'

'Don't be.'

He was still holding on to her hand, but he softened his voice. And then she looked at him and his world tilted.

Uh-oh.

What the hell was she *doing*?

She'd acted without thinking. Or she *had* been thinking,

but not about how it would feel to be touching Noah's bare torso. No, she'd been thinking about how her cat had hurt him. How her cat had hurt him because of *her*. Because Noah had gone back to save Zorro so she wouldn't have to.

But she wasn't thinking about that now either.

In fact, she couldn't be sure that she was thinking at all. Because now she was caught in Noah's gaze when she was pretty sure she shouldn't be. He was so close she could see the grey flecks in his blue eyes. She could see the emotions there, too.

The caution. The interest. The *desire*.

It had her remembering that he still had her wrist in his hand. And that realisation sent a heady heat slithering from the contact, up and around her arm, settling much too close to her chest. To her heart.

Her other hand was still braced on the lower half of his body. Much too close to his—

'Um…' she said, pulling her hands from his body and stepping back. 'It's probably okay now.'

'Yeah,' he replied in a hoarse voice. He cleared his throat. 'It was fine before you came in.'

'Of course.'

There was an awkward beat of silence, but Ava took solace in the fact that it came from both of them. She hadn't been the only one acting stupidly. She hadn't been the only one affected.

But thinking about it like that didn't comfort her as much as she'd hoped.

'Could you pass me my top?' Noah asked after a few moments.

'Yeah, sure.' She paused. 'Where is it?'

'Behind you.'

When she turned back to hand it to him there was a slight smile on his face.

'What's so funny?'

'Nothing,' he said, pulling on his top.

Disappointment sailed through her as she said goodbye to his abs.

'I was just thinking it's going to be an interesting wedding.'

'That's one way to put it.'

'You don't think so?'

'I think that I need to get through it in any way that I can. Which,' she said, considering, 'might involve alcohol.'

'Ah. You're old enough to drink now, aren't you?'

She cocked an eyebrow. 'You say that as if *you* weren't the one who handed me my first beer.'

His smile widened. 'See—interesting.'

'You and I have *very* different definitions of that,' she replied, and walked back around the counter. Her breath came out a little more easily now that there was space between them.

'Probably. But I think it might have the same results.'

Which was precisely what she was worried about. Because after the short, but very eye-opening interaction they'd just had, she was beginning to think her crush was no longer a secret.

Or perhaps she was more concerned that this unexpected flare-up of her crush was no longer a secret. Because if she'd managed to keep it secret after she'd asked him to kiss her for the *first* time, she certainly hadn't after she'd thrown herself into their second kiss.

But in the seven years since they'd last seen one another— years during which she hadn't even *heard* from him—she had managed to hide her feelings. And if what had just happened between them meant that Noah shared those feelings—

Noah? Sharing her feelings?

She nearly laughed aloud at the ludicrousness of it. She'd always known the reason he'd kissed her the first time had been out of pity. And the second kiss had just happened because he'd been heartbroken and hadn't known *what* he was feeling.

Anything they'd shared was in her imagination. Back then

and now. No one wanted Ava. No one wanted someone who spoke before she thought. Who was prickly for most of the time and defensive for the rest.

Just because Milo said it doesn't make it true.

But it does, she corrected the voice in her head.

Milo hadn't wanted to marry her after being with her for five years. He was the best person to know the truth. And if he hadn't wanted her Noah sure as hell wouldn't either.

The sooner she realised that, the better.

He was back from the deli in less than fifteen minutes. Ava had graciously allowed him to leave without commenting on the fact that he was buying their food. But maybe it wasn't grace. Maybe she just needed space to deal with what had happened between them, just as he had.

It was a natural reaction to being around a beautiful woman, he'd told himself on the way to the deli. He hadn't dated in so long he couldn't remember. His body had just been reminding him that he had needs; his mind just responding as any person who had needs would.

But when he returned and saw Ava sitting on his balcony, staring out over the mountains visible to most residents of Somerset West, he faltered. Had she looked this forlorn before? This defenceless?

Now she seemed nothing like the spitfire who had tried to save her cat from a blaze and everything like that little girl he'd once saved from being bullied. And when his heart turned in his chest and his arms ached to pull her into his arms, Noah worried that his reaction to her earlier hadn't just been natural. That it had been...*more*.

It didn't help that when her eyes met his—brown and steady—he instinctively knew she *wasn't* that little girl who'd needed saving. Her gaze wasn't as innocent, as trusting, as that little girl's had been. It was weary, cautious—as if she were ready to defend herself at any moment.

'This place is just as beautiful on the outside as it is on the inside,' she said into the silence.

Grateful for the distraction—his thoughts bothered him more than he'd thought they should—he nodded. 'This particular view sealed the deal for me.'

'I can imagine.' She pushed out from the table she'd been sitting at. 'I'd love to enjoy it some more, but I'm hungry. Like, *really* hungry. What do you have in there?'

He swung the deli bags out of her reach when she tried to peek inside them, and thought about how similar this was to how they'd been before he'd left. How similar it was to how *she'd* been before. And how it didn't make him feel like he needed to protect her.

'You'll find out when I serve it.'

'Spoilsport.' She followed him to the kitchen. 'Can I help?'

'No.'

'Excuse me?'

He smiled at the disbelief in her voice, and then took his time removing the takeaway dishes from the plastic bag and placing them on the kitchen counter.

When he saw her hovering, he said, 'Have a seat.'

'You're really refusing my help?'

'Yes.' He opened his fridge, showing her different drinks one by one until she eventually nodded at the fruit juice he took out. 'I didn't ask you here so you could help me cook, Ava.'

'I think you're using the word *cook* wrong,' she commented dryly, and then took the glass he offered her and went to the couch.

He could almost see her body sag into its softness. He was glad he'd refused her help.

'You know, the last time I was at your house—and this was when you still lived with your father—you didn't know what "cook" meant then either. I think you gave me and Jaden leftovers from the night before.'

'How do you know I didn't cook the night before?'

'Because it was delicious.' She smiled brightly at the look he gave her. 'And because your father's made me a few more of those pasta dishes since you left and it was definitely not *your* cooking.'

His hands paused. 'You've seen my father since I've been away?'

He saw her cheeks pinken. 'Yeah… I mean, occasionally…' She cleared her throat. 'I've been helping him with some stuff. We're…friends.'

The pink turned into a deep red, and if Noah hadn't been so perplexed by the whole thing—if his heart hadn't been racing in his chest—he'd have found it charming.

'So, just to check that I've heard you correctly,' he said slowly, when his brain refused to process what she'd told him, 'you say you're *friends* with my father?'

'Don't make it sound so outlandish, Noah,' she said with a roll of her eyes. Her embarrassment seemed to have worn off. 'Your father is incredibly interesting. And he's young for his age. I can barely tell he's in his sixties.' She sipped her juice. 'And, while we're at it, I might as well tell you that by "occasionally" I actually mean at least every two weeks. More often if my schedule—and his—can manage it.' She lifted her shoulders at the look on his face. 'We enjoy each other's company, Noah. There's nothing wrong with that.'

All the blood seemed to drain from his body.

'Ava,' he said, his voice strangled. 'Are you trying… Are you trying to tell me that you're in a relationship with my father?'

CHAPTER FIVE

AVA STARED AT him for what felt like for ever. And then she choked back a laugh and used the opportunity.

'I'm sorry, Noah,' she said solemnly. 'We didn't want you to find out this way.'

His jaw dropped, and it took every bit of her self-control not to show her enjoyment.

'But...but...how? *Why?*'

'I don't think I have to explain *how*,' she said matter-of-factly. Man, she was really getting to use her acting skills today. 'I mean, I know for a fact that *you* know how to kiss. And, sure, there's some other stuff which I'd be happy to—'

'Ava.'

His voice had taken on a quality Ava had never heard before.

'Please do *not* allude to your sex life with my father.'

She bit her lip so hard she was afraid she'd draw blood. 'We're all adults, Noah.'

'No, we're not. You're still a *kid*.'

He was angry now, and Ava tried not to let him thinking of her as a kid bother her.

'You've been gone for a long time, Noah. I'm not a kid any more.'

'My father,' he repeated in a daze. 'My *father*.'

'Yes.' She paused. 'You asked me why earlier. I've already told you some of it. He's interesting. And kind. And he's got such a sweet heart. And an impressive—'

'Do *not* finish that sentence.'

'Why not?' she asked innocently. 'I was only going to say he has an impressive…' she dragged out the pause for as long as she could '…personality.'

He stared at her. 'You've got to be kidding me.'

She contemplated whether she should just say yes, she *was* kidding him. But there was one more thing she wanted to say first…

'You know, Noah, you not being at home has been really hard on your father. And, as your possible stepmother, I wanted—'

'Ava!' he barked, his expression stricken.

And, because she'd done what she wanted to, she grinned at him. 'You are *such* a sucker, Giles.'

There was a long silence before his features relaxed. Only slightly though, she noted.

'You were joking.'

'I was.'

Another stretch of silence. 'What made you think that joke would be *funny*?'

She laughed. 'The entire time I kept it going?'

She laughed harder when he threw the empty juice bottle at her, and she caught it triumphantly.

'You're going to have to try better than that.'

'Yeah, well, let me first get over the heart attack I've just had.'

She chuckled to herself as he prepared their food, still muttering, but when he brought over her plate—chicken, a portion of lasagne, potato salad, coleslaw—she gaped.

'Who do you think you're feeding? The South African army?'

'You said you were hungry.'

'Yeah, but I meant for a normal human-sized person.' She dug into the meal anyway, almost hearing the food echo as it dropped into her empty stomach. 'Thank you,' she said gratefully.

'Yeah, no problem.'

A companionable silence fell over them as they ate, and for the first time Ava realised how tired—and hungry—Noah must be. She saw the dark tint under his eyes, the slight creases around them.

'You should go to bed,' she said softly. 'You look exhausted.'

'Thanks.'

He gave her a small smile that had her heart flipping over.

'You don't look too great yourself.'

'Ah, I've missed this insult-for-insult thing we've always had.'

'Hmm…' he said, non-committal, and took another bite of lasagne, watching her all the time.

She refused to shift in her seat. Refused to look away. Even though she desperately wanted to do both. Tension ticked up.

'You didn't say it before,' he said after he'd swallowed.

'What?'

'That you missed me.'

'What do you mean?' Now she *did* shift. 'It's not just something you say when you see someone after a long time.'

'It's *exactly* the kind of thing you say when you see someone after a long time.'

'Yes, well…'

She left it at that, unsure of what else to say. The conversation was wading into dangerous waters and she, for one, had no interest in swimming. She just wanted to stand safely in the sand and frolic on the beach. She just wanted to feel the sun on her skin and *maybe* put her toes in the water.

But swimming held no appeal to her.

'Is it because—'

'Noah,' she interrupted with a half-smile. 'We've been through enough today. I think we should probably leave this conversation for another time.'

He studied her, and again she refused to let him see how uncomfortable it made her.

'Sure,' he said, and then he nodded at her plate. 'Are you done with that?'

Noah woke to a house that was significantly less festive than the one he'd gone to sleep in. But, he thought, as he took in the tinsel that now hung only over his fireplace—along with the stockings and the lights—and the significantly fewer Christmas-related items around the house, it was perfect.

He didn't know what to say when he found Ava by his Christmas tree. She had tinsel over each shoulder, draped around her neck, too, and was taking some of the ornaments off the ridiculously overdone tree.

Just as he had the night before, he watched her. She was muttering to herself, occasionally bopping her head as if she were listening to music only she could hear. It was so homely it was almost enticing, and he had to step back, out of her range of view, to deal with how that made him feel.

He wasn't interested in *homely*. He'd thought he'd once *had* homely—until he'd been old enough to realise the man he'd seen in his parents' bedroom when he was younger hadn't been his mother's *friend*. It hadn't been his father either. But by the time he'd been old enough to realise that his mother had passed away and his anger had seemed pointless.

Not that that had stopped the anger from finding a home, he thought, as he remembered the women who had come in and out of his life—of his father's life—after his mother's death. The women who'd never stayed long but had always left his father with that sad look on his face.

The same look his father had had when he'd confirmed that Noah's mother *had* cheated on him the one time they'd spoken about it.

If that hadn't put Noah off *homely*, his own attempt at it had taught him a lesson. A lesson his heart and his mind still hadn't forgiven him for.

So what was wrong with him now? Why did he feel drawn to the image Ava was creating by that Christmas tree?

He'd been back all of two weeks. He'd been reunited with her all of twenty-four hours. *Barely* that. Maybe that was why he felt as if something were wrong. Because it *was*. There was no possible way he could want something he'd never wanted before after only two weeks. There was no possible way he could want it with a woman he'd only been back in touch with for barely twenty-four hours after seven years.

What about the eighteen years before that? And what about that kiss?

His spine stiffened. Ava had told him last night that she didn't want to talk about the kiss. Not explicitly, but he'd got the picture. And he couldn't blame her. The only reason he'd even brought it up was because he'd thought *she'd* want to talk about it.

But, no. It seemed they were going to pretend it hadn't happened.

He took a moment to compose himself—it took longer than he would have liked—and then strolled into the living room.

'Mrs Claus?' He forced a cheer he didn't feel into his voice. 'Is that you?'

'Why, yes, little elf, it is.'

She turned to him, eyes twinkling, and he was immediately drawn back into the memory he'd just tried to suppress...

'Jaden is taking for *ever*.'

'His speciality,' Noah replied. 'He and Monica are probably making out somewhere.'

Ava's face twisted in disgust. 'Why would you put that image in my head? I'm perfectly happy thinking about my brother as a monk.'

Noah snorted. 'Jaden is *not* a monk.'

'Stop it.'

'You're an adult now, Ava,' he said with a smirk. 'At least, almost.'

'I'm *eighteen*.'

'Like I said—*almost* an adult.'

She narrowed her eyes at him. 'Just because I don't want to hear about my brother's sex habits doesn't mean I'm not an adult.'

'You're *eighteen*.'

She rolled her eyes. 'Yeah, and you were *such* a kid when you were eighteen.'

He had been, he thought. He'd made all kinds of stupid decisions between the age of eighteen and now. Most notably falling hard and fast for a woman who had no intention of committing to him. Worse yet, a woman who had shown him he was at risk of following in his father's footsteps.

'We should probably head to the pools without him,' Noah said after a few more minutes. 'We don't want to get there and have them turn us away.'

Ava nodded and walked ahead of him along the path to the pools. It was going to be thirty-eight degrees Celsius that day, and they'd decided—Noah, Jaden, Monica and Ava—to survive the heat by going to the natural rock pools near Noah's house.

They weren't private pools, but because they were situated in an ecologically sensitive area that the government only allowed twelve people access to per day. There were already four of them, so they'd got up extra early to take the short hike to the rock pools.

Or at least that had been the plan before Jaden hadn't shown up.

'You'd have thought he'd have told you he'd be late,' Noah commented.

'He doesn't do things just because we think he should,' Ava said with a sigh. 'He told me last night that he'd meet us at the starting point. His excuse then was that he needed to fetch Monica.'

'Why didn't you go with him?'

'Because he was meant to be spending the night at *your* house.' She gave him a look. 'Even though my brother is two years older than me, he still isn't an adult.'

'That lie was more for your parents,' Noah said, automatically defending his friend, even though Jaden was the reason Ava had taken that jibe at him.

'Yeah, well, he could have at least had the decency to pitch up on time.'

They didn't speak for the rest of the trip. In fact the only communication they had with one another was when Ava missed a step on an incline and called out, and he pushed forward to help steady her.

His hands rested on her hips, just above her butt, and long after he'd let go his fingers could still feel the softness— the plumpness—of her there. It made him *want* her—which was ridiculous. She was Jaden's *sister*. And he'd just dodged a massive bullet with Tiff. The last thing on his mind was wanting anyone—let alone the girl he'd once seen smell her armpits to test whether she needed to start wearing deodorant.

It was ridiculous, he thought again. Except his eyes dipped to the rounded curve of her butt in her cotton shorts. To her thighs, which were thick and strong and made him think things he shouldn't be thinking about his best friend's little sister.

It put him in a mood, which kept him silent until they reached the entrance of the pools and were told they were the first there.

'Yes!'

They high-fived each other, and then Ava turned to the guard. 'Is it okay for us to keep places for my brother and his girlfriend? They're slower than us, so we went ahead to could get spots for all of us.'

She smiled widely at the man, and Noah watched as he blinked and then nodded. Sympathy pooled in his stomach. He didn't think *he'd* be able to resist that smile either. It was the kind that could make anyone feel blinded. Combined with Ava's naturally husky voice, its effect was potent.

But he *had* resisted that smile, he told himself. And he still did. All the time. In fact he barely noticed that it made her eyes crinkle. Or that it softened her features, making her look like some kind of mythical creature.

Man, what had Tiff *done* to him?

'Noah?'

He blinked, his gaze zooming in on her.

'You didn't hear a word I said, did you?'

'Er...yeah, of course I did.'

'Liar.'

His lips curved. 'You want to know whether this is a good spot to sit in.'

She narrowed her eyes. 'That's a logical deduction. It's not because you were listening to me.' She tossed her head back. 'So, is it?'

His smile widened. 'It's perfect.'

They set up the blankets and umbrellas they'd brought, but by the time they were done Jaden and Monica still hadn't arrived. Neither had anyone else.

'Screw this,' Ava said after a moment. 'I'm hot, I've walked further than I generally do most days, and I deserve a swim.'

She was pulling off her top and wriggling off her shorts before he could say anything to stop her. And by the time he could he found that his voice was gone. Stolen by how beautiful her body was.

She's off-limits...she's off-limits...she's off-limits.

He repeated the words inside his head, over and over again, hoping it would drown out the other voice in his head pointing out how beautiful the brown skin of her body was against the white of her bikini. How the rounding of her breasts, her hips, was the stuff of fantasies. How they would be the stuff of *his* fantasies in the future.

She's off-limits...she's off-limits...she's-off limits.

She gave him a smile he didn't understand, and then she threw her clothes at him. The pile landed against his chest, his hands barely lifting in time to keep everything from fall-

ing to the ground. And then she turned and his heart ham-
mered, his body tightening as he got a better view of the butt
he'd been admiring earlier.

With one sly look over her shoulder, Ava ran and dived
into the water.

It took all the time she was under the water for him to
realise that she'd been trying to seduce him. But his mind
rejected that explanation even as it pointed out all the ways
her actions had been an attempt at seduction.

Before he knew it he was pulling off his T-shirt and following her into the water. When he emerged, he found himself a short distance from her.

'Cooler now?' he asked, surprised at how steady his voice
was.

'Never been cooler.'

Her eyes were twinkling, her expression teasing, but there
was a seriousness there, too, somehow, and he wondered if
that could be more seduction.

'This isn't in my head, is it?' she asked him softly.

'I don't know what you're talking about.'

She gave him a small smile. 'So maybe we should keep it
like that, then. We'll pretend like you aren't looking at me the
way you are now. That I didn't say anything about it—about
us—at all.' She paused. 'We can pretend it didn't happen—
just like after the first time we kissed.'

'You asked me—'

'You could have said no,' she interrupted him. 'In fact,
you *should* have said no. I'm your best friend's sister. You
had no business kissing me.'

'I know.' Somehow he found himself even closer to her.

'Why would you want to be my first kiss, Noah?'

'You asked me to be.'

'And now I'll always have the story of how my brother's
best friend kissed me for the first time.'

'You were sixteen. Too old not to have been kissed.'

She laughed—low, husky—and it vibrated through his
body. 'Is there a timeline for that I don't know about?'

'Yes.'

'Like the rules about who your first kiss should be with?'

'Honestly, I don't care.' And in that moment Noah thought he'd lost his mind. 'I don't care about the rules and the ages.'

'Because you *wanted* to kiss me.'

'Yes.'

'Just like you do now.'

He didn't answer her. Only slid a hand around her waist and pulled her against him as their lips met.

CHAPTER SIX

'WHAT?' AVA ASKED, when the silence extended much too long for her liking. When the expression on Noah's face went from easy to tight and the emotion rippling across his features made her stomach tremble.

'Nothing.' His voice was hoarse.

'Are you okay?' She dropped the ornament she held in her hands to the couch and moved forward. 'Should I take you to the doctor? Back to the hospital?'

'No.' His voice was stronger now. 'No,' he said again. 'I'm fine. I just got a little…distracted.'

The air moved more easily into her lungs. 'By what? I thought you were about to have a heart attack.'

'Sorry,' he said. Still, she heard the strain. 'This looks great, by the way. You didn't have to do it.'

'I know,' she said, and picked up the ornament she'd dropped, putting it with the others. 'But it was the least I could do after you took such great care of me and Zorro yesterday.'

He studied her, and as the seconds ticked by Ava tried not to wriggle under his gaze.

'You couldn't sleep, huh?'

She laughed, but the words jolted her. How had he known? 'I slept fine.'

He arched a brow.

She hissed out a breath. 'Fine. I slept okay for the first bit, and then I woke up and my mind started thinking about everything that happened and everything that's going to happen and I couldn't go back to sleep.' She forced a smile. 'At least it's the weekend.'

'Hell of a time to have to think about your house burning down.'

She shrugged, though sadness wove through her. 'I haven't had the heart to check.'

'I'll call the station.'

Ava continued removing the ornaments from the Christmas tree while he went outside to make the call. As she did so, she wondered why she hadn't told him that her house had been at the bottom of the list of things she was worried about. At the top of the list was whether Noah was okay and whether Zorro was.

Because early that morning she'd realised again how much danger she'd put him in by having him go back for Zorro. The smoke could have had a worse effect than she'd imagined. Because, of course, as that thought had occurred to her she'd done an internet search on smoke inhalation and found out the most horrific things. Things even that TV show hadn't prepared her for.

Which had got her thinking about Zorro. And how, though she hated it that she'd put Noah in danger, she couldn't bring herself to regret it. She'd thought about all the times she'd cried and Zorro had curled up near her. Not anywhere close to her body—he was still a cat—but close enough that she'd understood he was offering her as much comfort as a cat could.

She'd thought about how he'd helped her stave off loneliness when it had threatened to overwhelm her. When thoughts of how much she needed to change had kept her up at night. When the hopelessness that she wouldn't be able to change had done the same. As had the fear that no one would ever love her. Zorro had kept her calm through it all.

And then, of course, she'd thought about the wedding. And the fact that she was being forced to participate in it when it was the last thing—the *very* last thing—in the entire world she wanted to do.

She was fully aware of the resentment that had come along with that thought. Fully aware that it had spilled over too many times during the planning of Leela's bachelorette party, which—thankfully—was now behind her. She had worried that during these last two weeks her resentment would spill over in ways she wouldn't know how to clean up.

'Well, the fire is still ongoing,' Noah said as he walked back into the room. 'But the wind's shifted, which means the direction of the fire has changed.'

'Away from the estate?'

'Yes,' he said, and started helping her remove more decorations from the tree. 'They're waiting for the smoke to subside and then they'll check everything out. It might still be a while before you can move back in, though.'

'Oh. *Oh*...' she said again, on an exhale. 'That makes me feel better than I thought it would.'

He frowned. 'I thought you were worried about your house?'

'I was. I *am*.' She stood on her tiptoes to get to the higher parts of the tree. 'But there are other things, too.'

'Like what?'

'Oh, you know...' She didn't elaborate, and though the silence that fell between them felt expectant—as if it wanted Ava to elaborate too—they both let it extend.

'I know you were pulling my leg about you and my father yesterday,' Noah said after a while.

His tone was casual, but Ava knew he was fighting to achieve it.

'But before that conversation went so terribly wrong, I did get the impression you were friends with him.'

'I am.'

With most of the decorations off, she reached up for the angel at the top of the tree. It was higher than she could reach, but she managed to touch the bottom of it. Thinking she could tip it over, she jumped and tried again. Except that did nothing except make the branches of the tree rustle.

'Here.'

It was the only warning she got before Noah's hands were on her hips, lifting her.

Her breath whooshed from her lungs and heat spread through her body. It felt intimate, this completely innocent gesture of his, and it charged the air around her. Around *them*, she thought, when she glanced down and saw the expression on his face.

She reached up for the angel quickly, thinking that as soon as she got it down they'd go back to being easy around one another. Except when he put her down and she turned to put the angel with the other decorations she was faced with his chest. And though it was covered by his T-shirt, she could still see the muscles of it.

Which wasn't a surprise, since a picture of him without his top on had been seared into her brain the day before. No, she thought immediately. A *long* time ago. Specifically, the day he'd followed her into that water and she'd had the opportunity to run her hands over every glorious inch of it…

Her fingers itched to do it again. His body was different now. Bigger. Stronger. And she wanted new memories that could replace the ones she visited on particularly hard days. Which also made her think that she'd lied when she'd told herself that her relationship with Milo had stopped her from thinking about Noah.

'Excuse me,' she said softly as the thought shook her.

She put the angel on the couch and took another step back, suddenly thankful Noah hadn't closed the door after he'd made his call and a slight breeze was blowing through the house.

'So,' she said very deliberately, 'I know putting a Christmas tree up is a sacred thing, but—'

'It isn't.'

'What?'

'Sacred.'

She frowned. 'Of course it is. It's a pivotal part of mentally preparing for Christmas.'

'Okay,' he agreed. 'But it's not sacred.'

'Noah,' she said with forced patience. 'How many times have you helped us put up our tree? You know it's sacred. We do it and we have dessert and fruit after, along with whatever cold drink we desire.' She frowned. 'You *know* this.'

'I know that's how *you* celebrate it, Avalanche.'

He lowered himself to the couch, and something about the movement made her think he hadn't slept well either.

'But my dad usually did our tree on his own. I'd get home and it was already done.'

'So you came to celebrate with us?'

'No, I just visited.' She gave him a look and he smiled. 'So I came to celebrate it with you. So what?'

She thought about it for all of two seconds. 'Get dressed.'

'What?'

'Get dressed. We're going to the shop. First, to buy me something a bit more presentable for being out in public,' she said, frowning down at his clothes which she still wore. 'And as soon as we've done that we're going to buy something nice for breakfast. Chocolate croissants, eclairs…maybe a fruit platter so we don't feel entirely guilty about our life choices. And then, dear Noah, we're going to decorate your tree.'

'This wasn't such a bad idea after all,' Noah said an hour later, when they were back from the shops and were taking a pre-tree-decorating break on the balcony.

Ava shot him a look. 'Oh, please. You complained from the moment I suggested it. And now that we have this delicious spread—' she gestured to the breakfast they'd bought, consisting mostly, if not completely, of the kind of food she'd suggested earlier '—you're changing your mind.'

'I'm an adult,' he said mildly. 'I can change my mind as and when I see fit.'

She grunted and popped a piece of croissant into her mouth. He grinned at the inelegance of it. He might not be prepared to think about the more uncomfortable moments or memories being around Ava brought, but he still enjoyed spending time with her.

'Okay, so,' she said after a moment, 'it might seem like I'm dodging your question about your father, but I'm not.'

'Hence you bringing it up now?'

'Exactly.' She gave him a winning smile. 'A couple of years ago Jaden asked me to drop off something you'd sent for your father after the last time the two of you had seen one another.'

'It was the magazine my pictures were in.'

'Yeah. A small magazine with, like, a ten-person readership.'

It had been an international magazine with thousands of readers. He smiled.

'Anyway, something came up, but Jaden had already promised your dad he'd bring it over. So I took it, and Kirk invited me in for a drink—completely platonically,' she added dryly, 'and we started talking. And became friends.'

Noah sat back, his coffee in his hand. 'Sounds simple.'

'Don't make it sound like there was some *thing* that had to happen for us to be friends.' She tilted her head. 'Or wait—maybe there was. He'd just finalised his divorce—'

'His fourth.'

'And he wanted some company,' she finished, as if he hadn't interrupted her.

'What do *you* get out of it?'

She sighed. 'I don't know. Like I told you yesterday, he's a lovely man. And he's wise.'

'Not wise enough to stay away from marriage.' Anger and resentment rippled through him.

'Noah,' she said in a low tone.

It sounded like disappointment. He wasn't sure why that stung. Or why it felt worse than anger.

'Besides, I guess that other than that it was a way for me to get away from wedding planning. It takes up your entire life and makes you feel worse than you can imagine.' She rolled her eyes. 'And it's supposed to be the best day of your life.'

'What are you talking about? Leela and Jaden weren't even engaged two years ago.'

'Yeah, I know.' She stared at him. 'You don't remember, do you?'

He frowned. 'Don't remember what?'

'Or maybe you don't even know,' she said softly, almost to herself.

And then she laughed, but the sound of it was strangled and it had his stomach turning.

'I'm sorry, I hadn't realised.' Her eyes met his, and there was pain and a sick kind of amusement in them. 'I'm talking about *my* wedding, Noah.'

CHAPTER SEVEN

'*YOUR* WEDDING?' HE REPEATED.

'Yes,' she said calmly, but she broke off flakes of crust from her croissant, undermining the tone. 'I was supposed to be married now.'

The thought of it had his mind spinning. A sick feeling stumbled through his stomach. An ache echoed through his chest.

'Clearly I'm missing something here. Why don't you start at the beginning?'

'There's not much to tell,' she said, in a way that made him think there was. 'I started dating a guy about a year after you left.'

A light blush spread over her cheeks, though he wasn't sure why.

'We were together for four years before he proposed. And we were engaged for a year before he left me at the altar.'

'He—' If he'd thought his mind had been spinning earlier, it had nothing on what was happening inside of his head now. 'A guy you were in a serious relationship with for five years left you at the altar? What the—'

'I appreciate the sentiment,' she interjected, with a smile that was half amused, half sad. 'I shared it. Still do some days.'

She went quiet for a moment, and when her eyes met his there was pain there that illogically he wanted to fix.

'But I'm over it.'

She'd never been a good liar. 'I'm sorry, Avalanche.'

'Thank you.'

A beat of silence passed. He wanted to say something about how relationships weren't worth the pain. Or point out that this was the exact reason why he didn't want to get involved with anyone. But it didn't seem like the right thing to say, especially when part of it was a lie.

He didn't want to get involved with anyone because he was terrified that history would repeat itself. And Noah had no intention of living his life in the same way his father lived his.

'You were going to get married and you didn't invite me?' he said, deciding on a more innocuous route.

But as soon as he'd said it, and emotion tightened in his chest, he realised it wasn't so innocuous after all.

'I was going to get married and I *did* invite you. I just never got a response to my email. Just like with all the others I sent.'

He opened his mouth to ask what email, but froze as dread filled him. The night after they'd kissed—after he'd felt things he never should have for his best friend's younger sister...after he'd been *caught*—he'd blocked Ava's email address.

Pre-emptively, he'd thought back then, because he hadn't wanted her to ask him why he was leaving without saying goodbye. Why, after they'd kissed, he'd decided to take advantage of an opportunity he'd been avoiding deciding on for a month. He hadn't wanted her to ask him whether that decision had anything to do with her. In fact, he'd wanted her to think it had *nothing* to do with her and everything to do with how things had ended with Tiff.

A stupid hope, he knew.

Just like the stupid decision he'd made when he hadn't known any better. Because of it he'd missed out on seven years of Ava's life. He hadn't heard from her and hadn't wanted to contact her. Hadn't thought he'd had the right to in case she was avoiding him purposely.

'Ava, I'm so—'

'Nope. *No*,' she said, in a tone that was a little too bright, with a smile that was a little too bright. 'Don't apologise. You were travelling around the world. Photographing new and exciting things. You don't have to apologise for not replying to my emails.'

'I do.' He braced his wrists on the table. 'I blocked your email address.' Shame rose in his throat as he took in the expression on her face. 'After the…er…the kiss—' *real mature, Noah* '—I blocked it.'

'You *blocked* my email address?' she repeated. 'After you kissed me, you blocked my emails?'

Her voice had gone thin, and it felt like a warning. But he had to face the fact that he'd made a mistake. It was the only way he could redeem himself.

'It was a stupid thing to do. I was an immature kid, and—'

'After you kissed me.' She slammed a hand on the table. '*You* kissed *me*, Noah.'

'I know.'

And now his shame had nothing to do with how she was responding and everything to do with how he'd crossed a boundary with her—with Jaden—that he'd never be able to erase.

'I'm sorry.'

She tossed her head back and looked up. If he didn't know any better he'd wonder if she was crying. But Ava didn't cry. He hadn't seen her cry since that girl had bullied her. It had been a watershed moment for her, he thought. The girl had *wanted* to make her cry; Ava had refused to give her what she wanted. And since then Ava had refused to cry in front of people in general.

He knew because he'd asked her about it. Long before the day they'd kissed. Which was why he knew that the betrayal and hurt on her face after Jaden had caught them—and Noah had then ignored her—would be the worst she'd let him see. He'd respected her for it, even as disgust had pooled inside him.

Exactly like now.

But, unlike then, when her eyes met his now they were clear of emotion. 'It's okay. We were both kids. It was a mistake.'

Was it?

He didn't ask. It wouldn't have been fair.

'Besides,' she continued, 'I got the information I needed from Jaden. That you were safe.' She answered his silent question. 'And when I started hanging out with your father I got it from him.' She paused. 'Life goes on.'

He didn't reply to that. The morning had been an overload of information that he wasn't ready to dwell on. But even as he thought that questions sprang to his mind.

She'd been engaged? She'd invited him to the wedding? Why hadn't Jaden told him? Why hadn't his father? She was friends with his father? Why did he feel betrayed? Confused? Raw?

The thoughts were unwelcome, as were the emotions. Acknowledging either was bound to lead him down a path he had no intention of travelling. The path of examining his past. Of facing his mistakes. Doing it with Ava about blocking her emails was enough for that day.

Except the universe seemed to have another idea.

'Tiff's going to be there, you know. At the wedding.'

Immediately after she'd said it she regretted it. Partly because she knew Jaden had wanted to tell Noah that the woman who'd broken his heart would be part of the wedding. Mostly because the stunned, strained expression on Noah's face wreaked havoc on her heart.

You're hurt and now you're lashing out, hurting other people in the process.

She squeezed her eyes shut—trying to ignore the voice that confirmed she was a terrible person—and focused on the upside. She'd done the right thing. Jaden should have told Noah about Tiff coming ages ago. He should have given Noah the opportunity to opt out of being his best man as soon as he'd known Tiff was going to be a bridesmaid.

'I'm sorry, did you just say Tiff is going to be at this wedding?'

'*In* the wedding. She's the maid of honour.'

He swore and shook his head. 'How the hell did *that* happen?'

'Because the world is cruel and does things like this all the time.'

'Your ex isn't going to be there, too, is he?'

She laughed at the incredulity of his tone, and relief rippled through her when it broke some of the tension.

'No, thankfully not. But Jaden *is* getting married almost to the day when my wedding was supposed to happen last year, so I still think the world is cruel.'

'He's—' Noah broke off with a shake of his head. 'What the hell happened? It sounds like Jaden thought about what would hurt the people he loved the most, and then decided to do just that.'

'It's not entirely his fault,' she said in his defence, though she'd been blaming him for a while. 'He was outnumbered. Leela wanted to get married close to Christmas, and the venue only had this date available. Tiff is also one of Leela's friends,' she added. 'I hate to break it to you, but she's responsible for introducing Jaden and Leela.'

'How?'

'Jaden bumped into Tiff at a restaurant and was forced to greet her. She was with Leela, and there was enough of a spark between the two of them that they exchanged numbers. So...' She considered. 'Not entirely his fault.'

'He still should have told me.'

'Absolutely. Which I kept telling him. But he said he wanted to tell you in person.'

'A heads-up over the telephone—or even an email— would have been appreciated.'

'Maybe we should give him the benefit of the doubt.'

Noah made a low sound in his throat and, taking in the look on his face, Ava giggled.

'It's not funny.'

'Oh, absolutely not,' she said, and laughed some more. 'But I can't keep being mad about this, Noah. It's *exhausting. I'm* exhausted.' Her laugh turned into a hiccup of despair. 'See what I mean? I'm tired of this. And of feeling this way. So I'm going to laugh and try to get through this *stupid* wedding, where every member of my family is going to look at me with sympathy, or ask me why I haven't moved on yet, or how my year has been. *Urgh.*'

She tilted her head back and tried to gain some semblance of control over her emotions again.

'Tell them it's none of their business,' Noah said after a moment. 'And then ask them about the most inappropriate thing you've heard about them.'

'What?'

He was grinning when she looked at him. 'You know how we keep hearing things about our family members? Like my uncle has two kids no one talks about. *Two.* So, my suggestion is, if someone asks you about how you've been doing, or makes some reference to the wedding, you ask about the two kids no one's talking about.'

She stared at him, and then grinned. 'That is the most brilliant thing I've ever heard.'

CHAPTER EIGHT

'WELL, THEN,' HE SAID, on a roll now, 'prepare yourself for something even better.'

'Not possible.'

'Oh, but it is.' He waited a beat. 'I don't think I'm going to like this wedding any more than you're going to.'

She narrowed her eyes. 'Continue.'

'And since I don't have any family there to embarrass— except maybe my dad, and he's as open as they come about his mistakes—maybe you and I should make a little wager.'

'A wager?' Ava sat back and rested her legs on the chair in front of her. 'You intrigue me, Mr Giles. What are the terms of this wager?'

'If you're going to try and put your family members on the spot, you'll have to do it in front of me. I'll give you points for how well you do it.'

'And in return?'

'You entertain me.'

'Oh, no. No, no, no,' she said with a laugh. 'That's not a *wager*.'

'It is. I'll bet you that you can't get a thousand points.'

'How dare you? Of *course* I'll get to a thousand points.' She paused. 'We'll discuss the determination of points later. But first I have to point out that I'm not really getting any- thing out of this bet. And, no, entertaining you doesn't count.'

'Okay, fine,' he said with a grin. He was enjoying this process almost as much as he was enjoying seeing the light back in her eyes. He hadn't realised until it was gone how much he cherished it. 'What do you want?'

'Hmm…let me see. Money would be too easy for you.'

'I'm fine with money.'

'No,' she said, with a smile that made his body ache. '*I'd* like to be entertained, too.'

The thought gave him visions of the two of them in that rock pool again. He shook his head. He was still recovering from his first memory. And from the feel of her waist under his hands. And from the way she'd looked at him after-wards, when she'd turned and he'd been so tempted to kiss her. And then from the reminder that he had no business being tempted by her, especially after what she'd just told him she'd gone through.

'I propose this,' she said, interrupting his thoughts. *Thank heaven.* 'We both try to entertain each other. It can come in the form of me saying inappropriate things to my family, or you doing something silly like…singing a song during the reception. Just an idea,' she said with a grin when he opened his mouth to protest. 'Whoever reaches a thousand points first, wins.'

'I'm *so* proud of how much you've grown into this,' he said with mock pride. 'I accept your proposal. I do, however, want to know how the scoring is going to work.'

'We have to witness the other person doing things in order to give points.'

'Fair.' He paused. 'The points are given in tens. From ten to one hundred.'

'One hundred is the maximum?'

'Unless there's a spectacular opportunity to take it all.'

'Take it all?' she repeated. 'As in win?'

'Yes.' A ripple of excitement went through him. 'Like doing a song during the reception.'

'I like it.' She bit her lip. 'Okay, but before we continue, this *can't* ruin Jaden and Leela's wedding. So, sadly, no sing-ing. Unless, of course, we've received permission.'

'I completely agree.'

'So how are we going to score points?'

'Ah, that's harder.' Leaning in, he said, 'How about dealer decides? It'll be open for discussion, of course, but we each decide how much we want to give the other.'

'Fine, but there should be ranges. Ten to fifty points if we do something to defend ourselves. The two secret children thing, for example.'

He nodded.

'Sixty to a hundred points if we do something to defend the other person.' The side of her mouth curved. 'So, if Tiff says something about how you look, for instance, I'll just mention how much *she's* changed.'

'Into a decrepit old woman?'

She let out a sparkling laugh. 'Fifty points to you. But, no, just how much better she looks as a brunette than a redhead.'

'Sixty points. Seventy if the delivery was good.'

'Perfect,' she said, and leaned forward, stretching out her hand. 'Do we have a deal?'

'We do.' He started forward, but paused. 'Wait—when is the start, and when is the finish?'

Just as she opened her mouth her phone rang from where it was charging in the kitchen. She ran inside the house and a few minutes later reappeared.

'That was Jaden.' She blew out a breath. 'After I reassured him—again—that I'm fine, he wanted to know if I could meet him at the Stellenbosch Christmas Market. Apparently their visit to the venue has encouraged them to spend more time with the wedding party. They want us there.' She rolled her eyes. 'I expect you're going to get a phone call, too.'

Seconds later her prediction proved true. The conversation was quick, and when Noah hung up Ava said, 'I guess we're starting today.'

'And the winner will be declared at the end of the wedding. Deal?'

'Deal.'

They shook hands.

* * *

Ava knew how significant her deal—wager, bet—with Noah was. By agreeing to it she was making sure she wouldn't be alone during the wedding, or during the run-up to it. And, while it had started out as a way to distract them both from the wedding, having an ally would do more than just distract Ava.

It would help with the loneliness she'd felt during this process, since she was the only one who wasn't looking forward to the event. It would help her keep up the pretence that she was fine. Unhappy about the wedding, but completely fine within herself.

Which was a lie, but no one had to know that. Hell, at the best of times she managed to ignore it herself.

At the worst of times she tried to figure out how she could turn herself into someone more palatable. And then she'd wonder if being more palatable meant she'd find someone who would actually want her.

But now, with Noah at her side, the wedding would fall into one of the best times. She was sure of it.

She left Noah's house before he did, telling him they needed to arrive separately so that they could avoid any questions. In the car park she put on some make-up, and then looked down at the yellow floral dress she'd bought earlier that morning with Noah. She liked how bright it was against her skin. Liked that it made her feel like sunshine even when darkness still tumbled around inside her.

Taking a deep breath, she went to find her brother and future sister-in-law at the market. It was enthusiastically decorated for Christmas, and the prerequisite Father Christmas was in a cordoned-off area for kids to have their pictures taken with him. She smirked as 'Father Christmas' was handed a screaming child, before spotting Jaden and Leela at a large table.

'Ava.' Jaden got up and pulled her into a hug. 'Are you okay?'

'I'm fine,' she said brightly, before brushing a kiss on

Leela's cheek. 'Like I told Mom and Dad *and* you on the phone last night, I was evacuated in time.'

'We wanted to come as soon as you called.'

'I know. But it made no sense. Your wedding venue is over an hour away, and it was late. I didn't want any of you driving when I was fine and I'd booked myself into a hotel. Again, I *told* you all this last night.'

'We were worried.'

She softened. 'I know, but I really am okay.'

'I heard the fire's changed direction, though,' Jaden said. She nodded. 'Have they told you when you'll get to move back?'

'Probably this evening.'

She said it even though it wasn't the truth—or at least she didn't know if it was. But she'd managed to temper their worry—though not as much as she'd first thought, she considered, looking at her brother. Still, convincing them to stay at the vineyard the night before had been no mean feat. They'd hovered over her since her wedding day—although, true to the tradition of her family, none of them had actually *asked* her about it.

But that didn't mean their concern for Ava had disappeared. And if she'd told them she'd had to go to the hospital—that Zorro had had to, too, and that he was still there—they'd have overreacted. She wasn't in the mood for that. Less so since she'd probably have to tell them *more* lies to hide the fact that she'd stayed at Noah's the night before.

If she couldn't move back to her house this evening she'd figure something out. But for now she had to distract her brother, so he wouldn't pry any more than he already had and become suspicious. Insults were the quickest—and easiest— way to do so.

'You need to get a life, Jaden. You can't be this worried about me after I told you I was fine.'

'Forgive me for caring.'

'Is that how you apologise to someone you care about?'

He rolled his eyes. 'I'm sorry that you're the most annoying little sister in the world.'

'Are we handing out apologies?' Noah asked, joining their group.

Jaden's face split into a grin and they did a little handshake and back pat, before her brother introduced Noah to Leela. Noah forewent another handshake and pulled Leela into a hug, and then they all settled at the table.

'So, where is it?' Noah asked.

'What?' Jaden replied, with a wider smile than Ava had seen on him in a long time.

'My apology?' When Jaden frowned, Noah said, 'I've heard there are some things about this wedding you haven't told me.'

Jaden's expression immediately dimmed, and Ava caught Leela's eye and gestured that they should get up. 'We're going to get some drinks,' she said, putting an arm through Leela's. 'We'll give you two a chance to catch up.'

'He feels bad about it,' Leela said when they were far away from the table. 'About the Tiff thing. About *your* thing, too.'

Ava blinked, and then let go of Leela's arm. This was the first time either Leela or Jaden had referred to their wedding being so close to the anniversary of Ava being jilted.

Ava had always assumed that it was out of a desire for self-preservation. That neither of them wanted to face Ava's potential wrath. But Ava had no desire to engage over it now. There was nothing any of them could do to change what was happening.

'I'm sure everything will be fine,' she said soothingly. 'Why don't you tell me about your trip? How did everything go?'

As she'd known it would, talking about the wedding distracted Leela. She went from serious to animated in seconds, and for a moment Ava wondered where Leela got her excitement from.

Ava had never been excited about her own wedding. Nervous and anxious, yes, but not excited. In fact, those nerves, that anxiety, had built and built until finally she'd been standing at the altar. She wondered now whether those emotions had been because she'd anticipated that Milo would leave her there.

Even now she couldn't figure it out. But she didn't think too hard about it. The memories of that day had gone on a shelf at the back of her mind—deep in her memory storage cupboard—along with the memories and emotions of Noah seven years ago. Memories and emotions that were best left alone.

She paid the bartender for their drinks, and then she and Leela made their way back to the table. Things didn't seem too tense, but that didn't keep Ava from asking as she settled in next to Noah.

'All sorted?' she said under her breath as Jaden said something to Leela.

'About as much as it can be.'

'You have the moral high ground now,' she told him. 'But the moment he finds out I stayed at your place last night—'

'Don't even say it,' Noah muttered. 'He might hear, and I'm still begging for forgiveness for the last time something happened between us.'

'From him or from me?' she asked, before she could stop herself, and then she shook her head. 'Forget that. I don't have the energy to go down that road. No!' she said when he opened his mouth. 'If you try to talk to me about this I'm going to deduct points from you.'

'Against the rules.'

'There *are* no rules.'

'There's one rule now.' His eyes didn't leave hers. 'No deductions.'

'Fine.'

They stared at each other. But when it turned into something more than just defiance they both looked away.

Directly into the eyes of her brother.

CHAPTER NINE

'I TOLD YOU,' Ava said after a moment.

But the look on Jaden's face didn't change. It was almost as if he hadn't heard his sister.

Noah swallowed, and wondered whether it was too late to back out of the wedding. He didn't *have* to deal with these looks, or the reminder that Jaden had once thought Noah had taken advantage of Ava. Or that he sometimes believed that himself.

Ava nudged him with her elbow under the table, and then repeated her words. 'I told you, Noah. He was going to tell you.'

'Er...yeah. Sure...'

'What are you two talking about?' Jaden asked.

'Well, I ran into Noah yesterday,' Ava said easily. 'He was part of the team dispatched to the estate to deal with the fires. Anyway, I asked him about Tiff by mistake, and he didn't know.' She tilted her head. 'Even though he's been here for over *two weeks*, Jaden.'

'He was fighting fires,' Jaden said defensively. 'And why would you mention it anyway, if you weren't sure I'd told him?'

'Oh, I don't know.' She leaned forward. 'Maybe it was the surprise of seeing him at all, since you didn't even tell me he was here already.'

Jaden opened his mouth, but just then two other people joined their group. One Noah didn't recognise, though Jaden told him it was a colleague he'd grown close to. The other he recognised all too well.

He stood when the rest of them stood, and gave himself permission just to look at her. Ava was right; Tiff had dyed her hair. But other than that she looked the same as she had seven years before. Tall, smooth brown skin. Perfect features. One of the most beautiful women he'd ever seen.

But she'd changed the course of his life. He couldn't be drawn in by beauty any more.

'Noah,' she said, and surprised him with a hug. 'You look good.'

'Thank you.' He didn't bother telling her she looked good, too. She already knew. 'It's a…a surprise to see you.'

'But a *good* surprise?' she asked teasingly.

He opened his mouth to reply, but was interrupted by a snort coming from beside him. When he turned to look at Ava she widened her eyes in innocence. It immediately eased some of his tension.

'Ava,' Tiff said, in a tone that suggested she wasn't Ava's biggest fan. 'Such a treat to see you again.'

'Treat…inevitability…' Ava lifted her shoulders. 'To each his own, I guess.'

'Delightful, as always.'

Ava offered Tiff a smile, and he wondered if she thought the smile was sweet. It wasn't. It was terrifying. But it seemed to do the trick, because Tiff moved to sit at the opposite side of the table and not next to him, as he'd thought she'd initially intended to. Jaden's other groomsman—Ken—sat next to Ava.

'Sixty points,' Noah whispered as they took their seats again.

'Really?' Ava pulled her face. 'It hardly deserves that much. I was barely trying.'

'The rules are the rules.'

'Fair enough.' But her hand found his under the table and squeezed.

If someone had asked him how the afternoon would go

after that moment, he wouldn't have been able to answer. Not coherently anyway. He was much too aware of the two women at the table who represented such different things in his life.

He'd fallen so hard for Tiff that he wasn't surprised he still had the bruises to show for it. He'd met her during the second year of his photography course and had asked her out, considered getting his own place so that they could move in together, and had even been planning on proposing to her all in the space of a year. *One year.*

It hadn't seemed strange to him that their relationship had moved so fast. He'd only been thinking about that feeling in his chest when he was with her. How it made him feel invincible.

But he wasn't. Neither was their relationship. And when it had crashed and burned he'd seen nothing *but* how fast it had been. He'd seen that pace over his entire life, in his father's relationships—had witnessed it, had judged it—but he hadn't seen it in his own life. It was his biggest regret. And, though he'd never tell his father, his biggest failure.

His relationship with Tiff had changed him. Had changed the way he saw relationships. Changed the way he saw his father. How could he blame the man for falling so hard and fast when Noah had experienced it himself? So easily, too. It was worse because Noah knew his father's behaviour somehow linked back to what had happened with his mother.

But Noah's behaviour had come *before* he'd discovered Tiff cheating on him. He could only imagine what would have come after if he hadn't stopped himself.

He'd practised tight control in his dating life since then. He'd gone out occasionally, but he'd never invested too much of himself. He was too afraid of being sucked into that emotion again. Emotion that would lift him high enough that he'd *want* to experience it even after it had plunged him back to the ground.

That was how his father started his cycle; Noah refused to let it become his own.

And now, sitting opposite the woman who'd started it all…
It shook him more than he cared to admit.

As if sensing his thoughts, Ava bumped her shoulder against his. When he looked over she winked at him, and rolled her eyes in an exaggerated way before stifling a yawn. He smirked, and then full-out grinned when he felt a movement under the table and heard Ava hiss in response. Jaden sent her a pointed look—to go along with the kick under the table, Noah assumed—and again some of his tension faded.

Ava had always had the ability to do that. Which might have been why he'd ignored all his newly made resolutions the day he'd kissed her. There had been no control in that, and it had confused their relationship even more.

He'd had no idea what their relationship had been when they were growing up. He *still* didn't. He couldn't quite call them friends. Not in the way he'd call Jaden a friend. Nor was their relationship like that of family, no matter how much he'd tried to convince her—and himself—of that.

If it was, he was going to hell for all the improper thoughts he'd had about a family member. And so, just like he had before—before that kiss, at least—he would ignore the fact that those thoughts existed. Because although he couldn't define their relationship, he knew that it came with boundaries.

Unspoken ones at first, and then, after Jaden had caught them kissing, clearly outlined ones. In hard tones, loud volumes, and even louder disappointment.

He'd felt ashamed that he'd kissed her even as he'd done it. He hadn't needed Jaden to tell him he should have been. So when he'd moved away and hadn't said goodbye, he'd thought it for the best.

Except, he thought, remembering how Ava had looked when he'd told her he'd blocked her email address, maybe it hadn't been.

But it was in the past now. And that was where he needed to leave it all. His relationship with Tiff. The way he felt about relationships as a result. Whatever he'd once shared with Ava.

The way he was going to get through this wedding was to stay in the present. No matter how much the past called to him.

She'd sensed the change in him the moment her brother had joined them.

No, she thought. It had happened when her brother had caught them in that strangely intense look they'd shared. The easiness between them had slipped behind a barrier she only now realised had been there when they were younger, too. The kindness—the softness in his eyes when he'd look at her—had changed into something else. Something more... *polite*.

If she hadn't hated politeness before—the insincerity of it—Noah's reaction would have ensured it now.

And then Tiff had swooped in with her perfect beauty, and Ava had felt the Noah she'd been talking to—*engaging* with—since they'd reconciled slip even further away from her.

The tension had built inside her so much that at the first opportunity Leela gave them to leave the table, Ava jumped up and exited the tent that enclosed the market.

There was no one else in the field behind the tent, and it eased the weight that was on her chest. Until she heard the rustling of the grass behind her.

'Ava! Ava, wait!'

Her legs kept moving, though she wasn't completely sure why. Did they want distance from this stupid wedding and its stupid planning? Or were they running from the man who didn't have to do much to turn them into jelly?

'Hey,' Noah said, catching up to her.

She didn't stop.

'You okay?'

'Fine.'

'Ava? Ava, *stop*. Stop walking.'

She stopped—but not because he'd asked her to. They were far enough away from the market now that the live band who'd been singing songs about the festive season was muted. Plus, they'd reached the side of the field where a row of trees provided shade.

'What's going on?'

'Nothing. I just needed a break from…everything. The wedding.'

He studied her. 'Okay, fine. Let's pretend like I believe you. Which I don't.'

She didn't respond.

'Why did you agree to be in this wedding when you clearly don't want to be?'

'Have you ever tried refusing when a bride asks you to be a bridesmaid?'

He gave her a look.

'Or a groom asks you to be best man. Whatever. You know what I mean.' She took a breath. 'Not only did Leela ask me without any warning—I'm still working on forgiving my brother for *that*—she did it at Sunday lunch in front of both my family *and* hers. As much as I wanted to, I couldn't say no.'

'Surely they would have understood?'

'Surely Leela should have known that having her wedding exactly a year after mine *and* asking me to be in her bridal party wasn't a good idea? And yet here we are.'

He shoved his hands in his pockets, but Ava could have sworn he'd wanted to reach out to her first.

'I'm sorry.'

She waved a hand. 'Why should you apologise? You're in as much of a mess as I am.' She forced the next words out of her mouth. 'How was it? Seeing Tiff again?'

'Strange.' He kicked at the grass in front of him, watched as the dry golden-brown blades flattened. 'But fine.'

She snorted. 'Yeah, *right*.'

'If you can lie about what's going on, I can, too.'

'Touché.'

They stood like that for a few moments, and then Ava sighed. 'We should probably get back.'

'Why? So Leela can talk us into finding things to add to the wedding favours at the market?'

'Technically, that's what we're supposed to be doing now.'

'There are other people in the bridal party.'

'Yeah. And they've been doing the majority of the work for the past year. You weren't here, and I've been about as helpful as this conversation has been in working out our frustrations.'

He smiled. 'You have such an elegant way of describing things.'

'Of course I do. I'm a copywriter. I have to find wonderful ways of describing boring things all the time.'

'Should I be offended that you're calling me boring?'

'Not you. Or this conversation, really.'

She angled her body and he began to walk next to her at the sign. But their pace was slow, giving them plenty of time to avoid their duties.

'It's easier not to talk about things.'

'About the wedding?'

'About all of it.' She sighed. 'But even though I haven't spoken about it people still—'

She cut herself off. Revealing it to him felt as if she was confiding. She didn't *confide*. Confiding meant making herself vulnerable. Exposing herself, flaws and all. And she wouldn't do that when she was determined to keep those flaws to herself.

But she'd already said too much.

'People still treat you differently?'

She nodded. 'They treat me differently, and then they try to cover it up—which, again, makes them treat me differently. It's annoying. I mean, they were annoying before, but now they're *super*-annoying.'

'I know what you mean. Not about the annoying part,' he said when she shot him a look. 'At least not *entirely* about the annoying part. But, no, I meant about my father.'

Ava stopped herself from sucking in her breath; holding

it in at the information he'd offered. Noah didn't ever speak about how his father's actions made him feel.

Or maybe he just didn't ever speak about it to you.

And why would he? she wondered in response to that inner voice. They'd never had the kind of relationship where they'd bare their souls to one another. Well, *she* had. But that was because she'd been young and foolish. Because she'd thought Noah was just as much her friend as he was Jaden's.

But their kisses had drawn lines in the sand. They'd managed to ignore the first line because they'd ignored the fact that the kiss had happened at all. And the second line...

Well, they'd never had to deal with that until now. She could feel that they were approaching it. But she wouldn't cross it.

If it was going to be crossed *he* would have to be the one who did it.

'It was worse when I was younger and didn't understand it. The only thing I knew was that whenever my father brought a new "friend" home, people would look at me in a certain way. The same way. When I was older I realised it was with sympathy.' He paused. 'They'd never say anything about it; they'd just give me sympathetic looks. And when he got married there were fake congratulations. When he divorced, fake consolation. It drove me mad.'

'I never realised.'

'Yeah, well... I became a pro at hiding it.' He gave her a slanted look. 'You, not so much.'

She laughed lightly, though it wasn't really funny. 'You'd be surprised.' But again, because that felt like confiding, she continued. 'It's never been my aim to hide it. Except maybe with my parents. They believe—' She cleared her throat when emotion stuck. 'They believe that I'm better than I am. I don't want to disappoint them. Not any more than I already have.'

Noah stopped, reaching out and grabbing her hand, forcing her to stop, too. 'You've *never* disappointed them.'

'You don't think their daughter being jilted in front of all their friends and family was a disappointment?' The words spilled from her lips unfiltered. 'You don't think realising there's something wrong with their daughter disappointed them?'

'Ava!' He said her name in both warning and surprise. 'Where is this coming from?'

'It's always been there,' she said flatly. 'I'm pretty sure you've experienced it yourself.'

CHAPTER TEN

NOAH HAD NO idea what Ava was talking about. Or where her words were coming from. Had he missed this side of her? Or had she just changed since he'd last seen her?

The latter, he thought, when his mind reminded him of who she'd been back then. Confident in her decisions. Brazen in her efforts. Fearless in her mistakes. The insecurities she was showing him now had come after. And the thought of it had his blood boiling.

'Who *is* this man?'

She blinked. 'What?'

'The man who left you. Who is he?'

'Why?'

'Because I'm going to kill him for doing this to you.'

She stared at him, her hand slackening in his. 'I don't—I don't understand.'

'The last time I saw you, you weren't this person. *He* did this to you.' The venom in his voice surprised him.

She shook her head. 'Don't be an idiot, Noah.'

'He broke your heart and made you doubt yourself.'

'He didn't break my heart.'

But she didn't say he hadn't made her doubt herself. The absence of those words echoed loudly between them.

'I'm going to make it painful,' Noah said after a moment.

'Noah, stop it.' She let out a harsh breath. 'It doesn't matter. It's over.'

'And you're fine with being like this now?'

'I've always been like this.'

'This is *not* who you've always been.'

'How would you know?'

'Because I know you.'

'You *knew* me. Or you thought you did.'

'No.'

'Yes. Because *I* didn't really know myself then either.' She pulled her hand from his completely. 'It's been seven years, Noah. Seven years and things have happened and I've changed. I've got to know who I really am. It has nothing to do with him.'

She walked ahead now, leaving him staring at her back. He had no idea what had just happened. He didn't know where her fierce response had come from. Nor the fierce protectiveness in his chest.

He hoped what she'd said wasn't true. Knew that there was enough of the old Ava there to give that hope life. Because if there wasn't he'd have to wonder if he'd had anything to do with it. If his walking away—walking away after kissing her—had been part of what had caused her to change so drastically.

But that wasn't possible. It was too vain for him even to think that. And it told him he needed to re-evaluate the power he'd thought he had in a relationship he couldn't even define.

It bothered him for the rest of the afternoon. Bothered him more than having the woman who'd broken his heart sit across from him. More than having to listen to her make conversation as they went through the market, trying to find things to add to the favours to give the Keller wedding more of a festive feel.

He ignored Tiff for the most part, and breathed a sigh of relief when she seemed to get the picture. But there was no relief from the situation with Ava. And by the time Leela gave them updated information about the rehearsal dinner, happening in a few days' time, he still hadn't figured it out.

'Are you coming?' Jaden interrupted his thoughts.

'Where?'

'To my place for drinks.' Jaden frowned, making it clear that Noah had missed the invitation. 'To end the day.'

I can't think of anything I want to do less.

He didn't say it. Instead he looked at Ava, and she gave an imperceptible shake of the head. She wasn't going. And since she was still staying with him—he assumed—he'd pass, too.

'Nah. I'm still not feeling great after the fire yesterday. I should probably get some rest or I might be out for longer than I want to be.'

'What fire?' Tiff asked.

'It's a little too late to be concerned about my well-being,' he replied flatly. Being out of sorts with Ava had destroyed his filter. He felt bad almost immediately, and added a weak, 'But thanks for asking.'

'You sure you're okay?' Jaden asked as his frown deepened. 'Should I come over to your place for a catch-up?'

'No,' he said—a little too intensely, he thought, when he saw the surprise on Jaden's face. When he saw the smirk on Ava's. 'No, it's fine. We'll catch up another time. Go have fun.'

Giving him a suspicious look, Jaden nodded. 'Ava?'

'Oh, no. I can't imagine anything more terrible.'

She gave her brother a smile, and Noah saw Jaden's annoyance soften.

'But thanks for asking.'

She aimed a sweet, slightly mocking smile at Noah, and he couldn't help the way his lips curved in return. But when Jaden narrowed his eyes at them Noah sobered immediately. Thankfully Jaden didn't say anything about it, and then he and Ava were alone.

'I thought that would never end.'

'Me, too.' He paused, and was about to say something about what had happened between them earlier when she spoke.

'Forty points for that jibe against Tiff. You could have got fifty, but then you said thank you and it kind of spoilt it for me.'

'I felt bad.'

'You shouldn't have. She broke your heart.'

'Yeah, but we were kids.'

'You're defending her? After what she did?'

He quirked an eyebrow. 'How much do you know about that?'

'Nothing.' Her cheeks went pink.

'Jaden told you, didn't he?'

'No.' When he didn't reply, she sighed. 'I swear he didn't.' Then she mumbled something.

'What?'

She mumbled again.

'Ava,' he said exasperatedly.

'*You* told me, okay? Inadvertently. That night you and Jaden were sitting out on the balcony, talking about it.'

He remembered the night in question. It had been the day after he'd found Tiff half-naked with another man in the driveway of her house. He'd worked through most of his shock at that point. Mainly because Tiff had tried to explain it away—although why she'd even tried made no sense to him—and he'd accepted that things were over.

He'd been in the first stage of trying to figure out what that meant when he'd told Jaden.

'Where were you hiding?'

Though her cheeks darkened, she answered him. 'On the veranda underneath the balcony. Pretending to read a romance novel so my parents thought I was being productive. Which I *was* being. At first.' She wrinkled her nose. 'But you weren't really keeping your voices down.'

'It was a private conversation,' he said sternly.

'I know. I'm sorry.'

He waited a beat. 'No, you're not.'

'No, I'm not.' She lifted a shoulder. 'It's the reason we can have this conversation, isn't it?'

'You say that as if it's a *good* thing.'

'Well, I told you that my fiancé left me. Think of it as an equal exchange of information, if you like.'

'I'm not sure I do.' But then he shrugged. 'It was a long time ago. Much further back than what happened to you.' He paused. 'You'll get over it.'

'But it changes you. It changes you in general, I mean,' she added hastily when he frowned.

'It wasn't too bad in my case.'

She narrowed her eyes, but then her features relaxed. 'Sure.' She paused. 'Do you want to get out of here? I mean, it's pretty and all, but the live Christmas jingles are getting to me. And Father Christmas keeps looking at every pretty woman who passes in a way that's threatening to ruin my childhood memories.'

'Yeah, fine.'

But he didn't trust the change in her mood.

It was early evening as they headed for the car park, and the light was dim enough that the market's Christmas lights had been switched on. He couldn't deny it gave things a festive feel. The kind he'd only ever really felt in South Africa.

It was strange, considering he'd been all over the world. He'd spent Christmases in America, in the UK, in other African countries. He'd seen Thanksgiving and snow— things that made it clear Christmas was on its way.

Comparatively, there wasn't much in South Africa that did that. But there was a *feeling* here. When the Christmas carols started playing in stores late in November. When the decorations went up and Christmas trees could be found in the strangest public places around the country. When Christmas lights went on and families got together.

The feeling was so much more special now, since he'd been away for such a long time. And it made him realise how bad it must have been for his father to be away from South Africa at Christmas time.

Kirk loved Christmas. Once, when Noah had asked why, his father had told him he wanted to make sure Noah got the experiences he hadn't had growing up. But Noah knew that wasn't it. Not when his father's zeal for Christmas seemed to have started the year after Noah's mother had died. And since then Noah and his father had never spent a Christmas apart.

So maybe it wasn't so much Christmas in South Africa that Kirk loved as it was spending time with *Noah* during Christmas. Which was the kind of long-term commitment that Noah hadn't seen in any of his father's other relationships.

Noah, a voice in his head said in warning. It sounded disappointed, and it reminded him of how Ava had said his name when he'd mentioned his father's disregard for marriage earlier. It stung now, as it had then, but almost immediately resistance surged inside him.

He couldn't just *forget* how Kirk's relationships had affected him. How they had caused him to have the mixed-up belief that because of his father's relationships he'd attract the same kind in his own life. How a part of him didn't believe it was all that bizarre, since his first serious relationship had ended with him being cheated on just as his father had been.

'It's not that bad.'

He blinked. 'What?'

'The lights.' She looked back at the market, at the trees that surrounded it, the lights that adorned them. 'It's quite festive.'

'I agree.'

'So why are you scowling?'

'I was thinking about my father.'

He heard her unspoken question and realised it was the second time he'd brought his father up with her that night.

'He loves Christmas.'

'Yes.'

He lifted his eyebrows. 'You know?'

'For as long as I've known you, I've known Kirk loves Christmas. And we're friends now, remember? I decorate his tree with him.'

He hid his surprise. 'Do you make him buy food, too?'

'Yes, actually.'

She smiled at him and he angled his body towards her, as if to catch that smile.

'But the whole thing is much more successful with him. We actually decorate the tree, for instance.'

'Isn't that what we're going to do at home now?'

She gave him a strange look, and he realised his body was now completely facing hers. He also realised he'd spoken about 'home' as if he had one. As if the years he'd been a vagrant, photographing anything from fauna to civil wars, hadn't been an attempt to figure out whether he *wanted* a home.

'I should probably find somewhere else to stay.'

'Or you could stop resisting my help and just come to my house until you can go back to your own,' he said. 'You can't stay with your family unless you want to explain to them where you stayed last night. And we've already been through why a hotel won't work.'

She turned to face him, the distance between their bodies minimal now, and suddenly his thoughts stepped into dangerous territory. *Forbidden* territory, only ventured into once before. No, twice, he thought as Ava's eyes met his.

He didn't give much thought to the first time they'd kissed. Ava had told him she'd wanted to know what it felt like; he'd agreed. Because if it hadn't been him it would have been someone else. That had been a given, but he'd known what kind of mood she'd been in that night. She wouldn't have cared about *who* she'd got to kiss her.

At least with him she'd been safe.

He'd brushed off the stirrings of his body back then. Told himself it was just hormones. Sexual frustration. And when she'd given him a bright smile, declaring it had never happened as she bounced off, he'd set it aside.

But now he remembered those stirrings. Because they were back, and more acute now than they'd been then. More acute now than they'd been when he'd kissed her the second time. The time that had nothing to do with familiarity or safety. The time that had been about danger and unsafe territory.

Just like now.

'Fine. But only because I need to help you with your tree. Because I owe you.' Her voice was husky.

'You don't owe me anything, Avalanche.' He lifted a hand and brushed at the hair curling over her forehead. 'If you did, you've already repaid me.'

'No,' she denied.

She took a step closer to him, though he didn't think she was aware of it. At least not fully. Just as he wasn't fully aware of his other hand lifting and resting on her waist.

'How could I have?' Her voice was breathless now. 'I did nothing.'

'You saved me from Father Christmas and the elves throwing up in my house. You helped set up my tree. Or you will. And you saved me from the humiliation and emotion of seeing my cheating ex-girlfriend again.'

'I didn't save you from anything.'

'You did,' he said, and felt the mood shift from flirtatious to serious. To intense.

The air sizzled around them.

'Noah...'

She said his name on a sigh; half defeat, half frustration. But there was more in her tone, and he couldn't quite figure it out. Because he couldn't, he took a step back.

Before he could speak, her phone rang.

'The vet,' she said, her face tightening into an expression he almost felt in his stomach. But her voice was steady when she told him, 'I'll meet you at your place later.'

She'd answered the phone before he could reply.

'I'm *so* sorry, my sugar plum,' Ava murmured to Zorro as she snuggled him. She could feel his displeasure, but he didn't claw his way out of her embrace. Which he would have done if he hadn't missed her just a tiny bit.

Eventually she let go of him, setting him on her lap and

waiting to see what he wanted to do. He gave her a look that confirmed he wasn't happy, but settled into a sitting position. She supposed it was the lesser of two evils. He didn't want to go back into his carrier, and the rest of her car seemed equally unappealing. She had no doubt he'd run far away from her the moment they got home.

It took her a second to realise that she wasn't sure *when* they'd get home—she hadn't heard anything about the state of her house yet—and she dropped her head back against the headrest and evaluated her life choices.

She'd managed to call the vet that morning, but the receptionist had said the vet had been called in to an emergency operation and would return her call that afternoon. She'd completely forgotten about Zorro after that. She'd been too enamoured with her childhood crush. Too busy playing games with him that would have no winner. Not if she kept going the way that she was.

The moment they'd shared as they'd left the market had been a clear sign that going back to Noah's would be a mistake. But her options were limited—just as Noah had pointed out. No family, no hotel. And the fire *had* changed direction. Surely it wouldn't be long before she'd be able to go back home? It wouldn't kill her to stay at Noah's for one more night.

Maybe they could just focus on decorating the Christmas tree. And they could keep the conversation neutral, like talking about their jobs.

But then she remembered what had happened when she'd needed to take the angel off the top of the Christmas tree. And how talking about her writing career earlier had led to her almost confiding in him.

She let out a breath. She didn't have much choice, and she could hardly stay parked at the end of Noah's road for ever. So, like her cat, Ava chose the lesser evil and made the short trip back to the house of temptation.

CHAPTER ELEVEN

'EVERYTHING OKAY WITH ZORRO?'

'See for yourself.'

Ava lowered herself to her haunches, opened the door of the carrier, and out came the ugly cat. He immediately drew himself up as he looked around, realising he wasn't at his own house. Noah almost held his breath when the cat aimed its creepy, unblinking stare at him, but quickly realised that was ridiculous and let out the air in his lungs.

If only he'd been able to shake off the unsettled feeling he'd had since leaving the market as easily.

'I'm going to be honest with you. I'm not entirely sure what I should be looking for.'

She laughed softly, almost hesitantly. 'The vet said he's fine. He's on anti-inflammatories, but they didn't think it was serious enough for antibiotics. Which once again proves how much I owe you.'

'You don't owe me anything.'

Zorro gave a loud meow, and Ava quirked a brow. 'Humour me.'

'Fine,' he said, mostly because he was tired of arguing. 'What will it take for you to think we're even?'

'A flat hundred points?'

Not expecting that, he leaned forward. 'I'm not sure I can accept. This isn't a part of the bet.'

'So let's *make* it a part of the bet.'

'No,' he said after a moment. 'That blurs the lines too much.'

'It blurs the lines of the imaginary game you and I set up?'

He shrugged, and she let out a breath.

'How about supper, then?'

'I feel *so* appreciated.'

'Noah.'

He smirked. 'I have to eat.'

'Yes, you do.' She went to the kitchen, opened a cupboard door. And then did the same for each of the other cupboards. 'There's nothing here.'

'There are eggs.'

'Nothing,' she repeated. 'How do you feed yourself?'

'The deli. Plus, there are still croissants from this morning left over.'

'I'm not feeding you croissants for supper.' There was a beat before she continued. 'Watch Zorro. I'm going to the shop. I'll be back before you can get weird about babysitting a cat.'

True to her word, she left before he could protest.

'Your owner has a habit of leaving before I can argue with her,' he told the cat after a moment. 'Should I interpret that as a sign of her approach to life?'

The cat jumped onto his kitchen counter and gave him a level stare, as if to say, *You're on your own here, buddy. I'm not saying a word about her.*

'Loyalty,' he commented. 'I guess I can respect that.'

Not wanting to examine how he felt about calling a cat loyal, he got himself a beer. His body groaned when he lowered himself on the couch shortly after, and he realised it hadn't entirely been a lie when he'd told Jaden he needed rest.

His throat felt significantly better, though there was still the occasional cough. But he'd survive, he thought, and brought the beer to his lips.

He just wasn't sure he'd survive having Ava stay another night.

Things had become uncomfortable at the market. Probably

before that, he realised, remembering how she'd responded to his 'I blocked your emails' news. It annoyed him, but there wasn't much he could do about it. Talking about what had happened would only make things worse. And clearly ignoring it did, too. But he had no energy to try and figure out how to make things better. So he'd let things sort themselves out.

He set the beer on the table, kicked off his shoes and made himself comfortable on the couch, switching the TV on. With some undemanding Christmas movie playing, he settled back and told himself to relax.

Clearly he'd listened to himself, too, because when he opened his eyes again there were people on the TV screen he didn't recognise from before, and his house smelled of an enticing array of spices.

He shifted, and then frowned when he felt pressure on his chest. When he saw why, he wasn't sure how he'd missed that Zorro was sitting on his chest. The cat was giving him that blank, staring look, and this time it seemed to say, *Sit up. I dare you.*

Not appreciating being taunted by a cat, Noah shifted, and Zorro gave him a look of disgust—or disappointment—before gracefully leaping off his chest.

'Oh, you're awake,' Ava said as she moved a pot from the stove to the counter.

'I didn't realise I'd been asleep.'

'I figured. Your beer was only half-drunk when I got back from the shop.'

'How long ago was that?' he asked, standing before doing a quick stretch. He felt his body crack, heard it sigh, and then shook his arms out.

When he met Ava's eyes again, she blushed.

'Not too long,' she said, though it sounded forced. 'An hour? Hour and a half?'

'I must have been tired.'

'Clearly.' She paused. 'You didn't sleep well last night. Why?'

'Sometimes a fire sits with you.'

'Did this one sit because of me?'

He was going to deny it, but then figured he had no reason to lie. 'Partly. But it's never easy to think about the people who are going to lose their homes. And the damage to the area.' He shrugged. 'Part of the job.'

'I didn't realise.' Her expression twisted in sympathy. 'Why would you want to volunteer, then?'

'You're asking me that *now*?' he said with a smirk. 'I did the training when I was eighteen. You know that.'

'Yeah, I guess I'm just delayed in asking about it.' She took plates from his cupboard. 'Doesn't change the fact that I want to know.'

He grinned at her sass. 'Sure. My dad told me to find something I could do to help people. We used to make sandwiches and give them to the homeless every Tuesday. Every second Thursday we'd volunteer at the soup kitchen.'

She frowned. 'Really? Why didn't I know that?'

'It's not something we advertised. It wasn't about that for my dad. And he taught me that, too.'

'So even though you could afford to donate to charities who did things like that, you chose to do it yourselves?'

'We did both. It's part of the responsibility when you have more than others.'

He lifted a shoulder, though it felt as if he carried weight there. But he ignored it—just as he ignored the guilt he felt at the resentment he held for his father when Kirk had made such an effort raising him.

'In any case, after the fires in Kayamandi we were at the station, trying to figure out how we could help, and I heard one of the guys saying they wished they had more volunteers. I knew it was something I could do.'

'Sounds like a noble decision,' she noted quietly. 'Though you were so scrawny back then.'

He laughed, unoffended. 'I guess. Things started to change after I took the training. I tried to do more.'

'And then you left.'

Was that a hitch he heard in her voice? 'Yeah, but I trained

as much as I could while I was away. Found stations to volunteer at if I stayed anywhere long enough. When I got back,
the station put me through the final test again and brought
me in when I passed.'

He accepted the fresh beer she handed him before dishing up their food.

'They needed as many hands as they could get.'

'Volunteer firefighter, silent philanthropist, photo-
journalist…'

She gave him a plate and he realised why what she'd made
smelled that good. Biriyani. *Biriyani.*

'That's quite the CV, Mr Giles.'

'Yeah, but it doesn't include the ability to make biriyani.'
He inhaled appreciatively. 'How did you manage to make
this so quickly?'

She laughed. 'I became a pro when I realised I didn't care
for the commitment of more than two hours for cooking. It
probably doesn't taste as good as those ones, but you'll survive.'

He took a mouthful and groaned. 'This is just as good as
any other I've tasted.'

She reached over the counter and patted his cheek. 'Oh,
poor, naïve Noah. I do appreciate your inexperience.'

He snorted, but didn't reply. Not only because the food
was genuinely amazing, but because her touch had seared
his skin. And he couldn't do anything about it. Couldn't say
anything about it. He was sure that if he did the easiness
they'd somehow got back would disappear.

'I'm sure your dad is looking forward to having you
around for the next few weeks.'

'Yeah.' He frowned. 'But it isn't for a few weeks.'

'No? He told me—' She broke off when he gave her a
look. Again, a pretty blush stained her cheeks. 'He likes
talking about you.'

'Does he? How much?'

'Every time I visit.'

Needing time to digest that information, he ate more food, and then took his time drinking his beer.

'I know we've spoken about it, but this friendship you have with my dad is weird.'

She laughed softly and settled next to him with her own food. But she didn't start eating. Instead, she ran her fork over the rice, ruffling it as she did so, over and over.

'I used to think so, too. And so does Jaden. And my parents.'

'They're probably worried he's going to rob the cradle. What?' he asked when she gave him an unhappy look. 'It's happened before. It'll happen again.'

'He's *lonely*, Noah. Your mother died when you were four. Can you imagine the loneliness that follows losing the love of your life *and* having to raise a four-year-old by yourself?'

'That loneliness has nothing to do with my mother dying.'

'Of course it does. Your father's love for your mother—'

'Made him weak.' Bitterness controlled his tongue. 'She cheated on him and he forgave her, even though I know how much she hurt him. That's when the real loneliness started.'

He ran a hand over his mouth, then pressed it to the counter.

'And then she died, and he started jumping from one relationship to another. But that had nothing to do with loneliness. He was—*is*—just running from his weakness. From her. From the memory of her.'

When she didn't respond he looked over at her, and winced when he saw her face.

'You didn't know.'

She shook her head slowly.

'I'm sorry, I thought—'

'Don't,' she interrupted. 'You have nothing to apologise for.'

'I thought… You're friends with him… Or Jaden…' He didn't know what he was saying. Or why he still felt as if he needed to apologise.

'Jaden wouldn't have told me,' she said after a long pause. 'He wouldn't have broken your trust like that. And your father...' She took another pause. 'My friendship with your father started because I didn't want to...to talk about things.'

She cleared her throat.

'About being left at the altar. About how it messed with—' She broke off, gave a quick shake of her shoulders. 'My point is that your father never asked me about any of it. And, yeah, neither did *my* family, but your father's silence about it didn't come with expectations. He didn't... He didn't *need* me to pretend that I was fine when I wasn't.'

'But your family did?'

'It was better for us all if I pretended. That way they could move on with their lives and I could...*deal* with things.' Her face tightened, but she continued. 'And even though your father didn't ask me anything, he let me ask *him* things. And he answered, even though some of my questions were inappropriate.'

His heart thudded. 'What did you ask him?'

'How he could deal with the failures. With the broken relationships. With the brokenness.' She lifted her hands and he knew she was referring to herself. As if *she* were broken. 'He told me I needed to move on. Move forward. And that was it. That was about as deep as we got. He wouldn't have told me about it either.'

He didn't reply. Tried to process what she was saying.

'I think,' she said slowly, 'that, for him, moving on— moving forward—meant pretending like your mother didn't cheat.' She hesitated on the last word. 'I'm sorry.'

'Don't be. It makes sense.'

And because it did, he couldn't find the words to break the silence that fell over them. He ate the rest of his dinner, but didn't taste it. And then he excused himself and went to do the dishes.

A part of him knew that his feelings about his father were irrational. And that somewhere in those feelings there was an anger he'd transferred to his father after his mother had died. After he'd realised the truth of what she'd done, of what he'd seen. After his father had confirmed it.

Because how could he have been upset with his mother? His life had gone on in the same way it had before he'd seen his mother with another man. Even when, as an adult, he'd thought back to the few memories he had of before she'd died, Noah couldn't remember his parents acting any differently because of what had happened. It had only been after her death that things had changed. And he couldn't blame her for that.

But he did blame his father.

All Noah had seen growing up had been a steady influx of women in his father's life. Some stayed longer than others. Some were kinder than others. And sure, those who'd been kinder *had* stayed for longer.

But as the father of a young child, shouldn't his father have protected him from witnessing that? From experiencing the instability? From the consequences Noah now saw in his own life because of it?

Or had he wanted his father to protect him from what his mother had done?

He paused as the thought stumped him. As it had him wondering if his father wasn't the only one running from the memory of his mother. Whether Noah's stance on relationships was just as much because of his mother's cheating as it was because of his father's behaviour.

Was *he* weak, too?

'Noah?' Ava said softly, and he started when he saw her standing in the kitchen with him. 'Are you okay?'

'Fine,' he lied, though he didn't think he did it particularly well. Not when the uneasiness in his chest was reflected in his tone.

Had he been judging his father too harshly?

There was a long silence as she studied him. As he dried his hands off to give them something to do because her looking at him made him restless. And then she stepped forward and slipped her hands around his waist, laying her head on his chest.

In that simple movement the war inside him settled. As if

her body against his—her body in his arms—had brokered some kind of peace treaty. Pieces mended that he hadn't known were broken before. And one particular piece—one he'd known about but had ignored—clicked into place.

He couldn't run from her. He'd never been able to.

He tightened his arms around her and then stepped back, afraid of what he might do now that he'd allowed himself to acknowledge that he felt something for her. Afraid of what it meant that he'd let himself acknowledge it *now*, after discovering that his relationship fears extended more deeply than he'd thought.

It had thrown everything he knew about himself, about their relationship, into a hurricane he could feel inside him. And facing it would bring that hurricane's destruction into his life. Into their lives.

He couldn't do it. He wouldn't.

She sensed the shift before she saw it. On his face. In his body. His eyes.

But then, what did she expect? He'd just told her his mother had cheated on his father. And *she'd* told him that maybe his father had chosen not to remember that fact so that he could move on with his life. So that he could move on from Noah's *mother*. So that he could move on *with other women*.

Milo was right; she *did* have a knack for saying the worst things at the worst times. It had been one of the many things he'd told her when he'd listed the faults which made her unsuitable for marriage. Faults that had had her remembering every single failure in her life and how they'd somehow been a result of those faults.

'You're too honest.'

'You say the wrong things all the time.'

'You make light of everything.'

'You're so prickly.'

It sickened her that she still heard his voice in her head. That the insecurity she'd felt since then was almost a daily occurrence. But the doubt didn't leave her just because she was annoyed it had come courtesy of her ex. Though she wished it didn't have her regretting simple things, like offering someone she cared about a hug because she wanted to comfort him.

To avoid thinking about it, she walked back around the counter and forced herself to finish her meal. She handed Noah the dish once she was done, and as he washed it, she went over to the couch where Zorro had made himself comfortable.

But her thoughts still buzzed in her head, like a fly caught in a room looking for an escape.

Suddenly determined to quieten them, she stood and got her phone. She scrolled to the appropriate song, linked her phone to Noah's Bluetooth speakers, and a few seconds later Christmas carols filled the room.

Zorro looked up in confusion at the sound, and Ava's lips twitched when, seconds later, she saw the same expression mirrored on Noah's face.

'Care to explain?' he asked as he joined her in the living room.

'We are *not* going to get sucked into the drama of this wedding and this season and our pasts,' she told him fiercely. 'So we're going to decorate this tree and have fun doing it.'

CHAPTER TWELVE

IT *WAS* FUN.

He hadn't expected it to be. He'd expected tension after their conversation. After their hug. But it was almost as if Ava had closed the door on anything that might have prevented them from having a good time. And somehow he found himself following suit, refusing to let himself dwell on the darkness of his realisations.

She'd always had the ability to do that. To make things seem…lighter. And whether that was because she joked about them or because she put her unique brand of I-don't-care on it, she never failed to make him feel better.

Which, he supposed, was part of his problem.

'Do you remember that year Jaden went through his goth phase?' Ava handed him a twinkling ball and pointed to where she wanted him to hang it on the tree.

'I do. Fondly. Although, as soon as it was over he vehemently denied it had ever happened.'

'And we'd believe him,' she said, eyes twinkling, 'if it weren't for photographic evidence.'

'You have *photos*?'

'*So* many photos.' She handed him another ball, waving her hand to indicate that he could put it anywhere. 'The goth one is my favourite. Especially because it happened over Christmastime, and the contrast between our Christmas tree and Jaden's all-black clothing is hilarious. Well, that and the fact that I get to use it for my slideshow at the rehearsal dinner.'

His eyes widened. 'They're letting you do a *slideshow*?'

'*Letting* is not quite the word. I'd say forcing.'

She stretched up to put the last of the ornaments at the top of the tree, revealing the smooth skin at her belly. Noah swallowed.

'Leela wanted to include me. Again, I couldn't exactly say no. The upside is neither could Jaden. Though he's begged me to keep it "appropriate".'

'Which, of course, you'll ignore.'

'Of course,' she agreed, smiling winningly at him.

His heart pattered. 'An unfair advantage for our game.'

Something tightened on her face, but then she relaxed. 'Perhaps. But you have your best man's speech, so—'

'Oh, no.' He groaned.

'Oh, no?' she repeated with a smile, and finished putting tinsel around the base of the tree. 'Did you forget? Please tell me you forgot. It would make my night.'

'I *did* forget.' He rubbed a hand over his face, and then sank down into a chair. When he felt it dip behind him, he realised he'd almost sat on the cat. 'Sorry,' he said absent-mindedly, and then shook his head. 'Jaden didn't tell me.'

'I'm sure he didn't think he had to. It's a well-known responsibility of the best man. Which you should have known, considering...' She trailed off with a wrinkled nose, but he couldn't tell if it was because of their earlier discussion or because she was making fun of him.

'Yeah, well, my dad didn't once ask me to make a speech. He must have known I might have said something...un-filtered.'

'Or maybe he just didn't care about tradition.'

She smiled, and he realised it was a peace offering. An apology of sorts in case she'd offended him. But other than the fact that he had to take a moment to figure out whether she was right—she *did* seem to understand his father better than he did—he hadn't been offended. And she should have known that.

'Look, I don't want us to tiptoe around each other because of—' he waved a hand '—everything. My relationship with my father is complicated. More so, I think, because I've never told him how I feel. About what happened with my mother or about his relationships after.'

There was pulse in the air, and Noah's heart dropped.

'I thought you said you didn't talk about deep things,' he said.

'I also told you we speak about you a lot,' she replied sympathetically. 'I mean, I might be wrong, but he's always spoken as if he knows about your disapproval. At least about his relationships after your mother.' She paused. 'Again, I know this is probably really weird for you, and I'm sorry. In fact, if I'd known you'd be coming back and we'd be having this conversation, maybe I wouldn't have become his friend.'

'You didn't think I was coming back?'

'You didn't,' she pointed out. 'For seven years you didn't come back.'

He straightened in his seat. 'It bothered you?' When she shook her head, looked away, his heart ached. 'It *hurt* you.'

'It's not… I'm fine. I'm *fine*,' she said again as he stretched out and took her hand, pulling her towards him so that she could sit down next to him.

He put his arm around her waist—gently, loosely—so that if she wanted she could pull away from him.

'I didn't realise. I should have, but I didn't.'

'Why should you have known? We weren't friends.'

'But we were *something*.' Unable to resist, he lifted a hand and cupped her cheek. 'I don't have the words to describe it, so I'll settle for that. Something. We were something.'

'Something?' she repeated, and lifted a hand over his. 'It's describes this—us—perfectly.'

He smiled, and then felt it fade. 'I am sorry. I shouldn't have blocked you. I should have tried to contact you.'

'Why didn't you?'

His hand fell to her lap and her own followed quickly, tangling with his. As if she wanted to tell him that her question hadn't been an accusation. As if she wanted him to know that her hurt didn't matter.

And, because it did, he answered her truthfully. 'I was scared. I was scared that I'd messed it up with that kiss.'

'How could you have messed it up when it had been fine before? After the first kiss.'

'Because before—' He sucked in a breath. 'Before you were just sixteen. You didn't know any better, and I… I made excuses.'

Her eyes widened, and when he realised how deep a hole he'd dug himself he tossed the shovel aside and dived in.

'I told myself anything I had to to make sure things wouldn't change—just like we agreed.'

'And the second time?'

'The second time… Well, the second time, there wasn't an opportunity for excuses. There was just accusation. Just guilt.'

Her hand tightened, and it felt as if she were pulling away from him. But he held on.

'It was easier to feel that way than to feel something else, Ava. And I was scared of losing my friendship with Jaden.'

'But what about *me*?'

He couldn't answer that question. Didn't know if he could tell her that his guilt had been about more than just his friendship with Jaden. It had been about taking advantage of her. Taking his broken heart out on her.

'I made a mistake,' he said softly.

'It wasn't a mistake. It was a choice. You made a choice.'

When she lifted her eyes to his, what he saw there stole his breath.

'Just like you chose to cut all contact with me.' She blew out a breath. 'You chose Jaden. I don't blame you for that. At least, I try not to.'

'I couldn't stay in touch with you and keep believing it was a mistake.'

He'd surprised himself with that, and when silence followed his words, he didn't know how to break it. Eventually she nodded, and then patted his hand with hers.

'Come on,' she said, her voice sounding as if she were fighting for the easy tone. 'We still have to put the angel on top of the tree.'

'Sure,' he said, determination lighting inside him. 'But first, I need to make another decision. We both do, actually.'

'What are you talking about?'

'I want to kiss you, Ava,' he said softly. 'But because it's going to complicate our lives, without a doubt, I need you to make that decision with—'

She pressed her lips to his.

She'd heard nothing more after Noah had said he wanted to kiss her. Which was probably why she was still kissing him, even though somewhere vaguely in her mind she knew he'd been warning her about something.

But who cared when his lips were on hers? When this gorgeous, sexy, *beautiful* man was kissing her?

In that moment she forgot that she'd been left at the altar. She forgot that even on her best days the fact that she had been left at the altar took something from her.

But not now. Oh, no, not now.

Now she was thinking that she was whole again. That Milo had been a fool to leave her. That *he* had been in the wrong. That *he'd* been the reason things hadn't worked out.

Because it was hard to think of herself as anything less than perfect when Noah Giles was kissing her.

He was the kind of kisser who did everything intentionally. Every touch of his tongue, every movement of his lips—all intentional. And all with the intention of making her—Ava Keller, the woman he was kissing—feel as if she were the only woman in the entire world.

She let him sweep her away with it. Let herself enjoy the way he knew which plunge of his tongue would give her goosebumps. Let herself lean into the way his fingers brushed over her body, the way his hands kneaded and squeezed.

She felt powerful when she heard him moan. Felt a healing warmth pool in her heart just as she felt it pool low in her stomach. She didn't complain when he pulled away from her mouth and pressed kisses on her jaw, on the slope of her neck. Heard herself moan when his mouth claimed hers again with a passion—a *need*—she didn't think she'd ever felt from a man before.

This kiss was nothing like the ones they'd shared before. It wasn't inquisitive, nor desperate, though there was both curiosity and desperation in the mating of their lips now. But the overriding emotion Ava felt as she kissed Noah was the sense that it was *right*. That this was where she *belonged*.

It was a terrible thing to feel. And it would no doubt keep her awake long after it had ended. But for now, in this moment, she let herself feel right. She let herself feel whole. And when he shifted and pressed his body over hers she let herself be seduced.

'We probably shouldn't—'

Ava cut him off by pulling his head back to hers, and Noah smiled against her mouth, letting her kiss him.

He didn't want to be the one who stopped them. Knew that if he did he'd regret it. But then, he thought, maybe he'd regret it anyway. More intensely once he realised that he *was* kissing her. That he was *enjoying* kissing her. That he wanted nothing more than to *keep* kissing her.

'Ava,' he said with a sigh, leaning his forehead against her. 'This is turning into something that—'

'Something that both of us want and one of us *desperately* needs to get out of her head?'

He chuckled lightly, and pressed a peck to her lips. 'Yes. Both of us for both of those things.'

'Then why are you stopping?'

'Because it's too fast.'

'Hmm…' she said, and shifted under him.

He got up, and for the first time noticed the cat watching them from the opposite coach. He wasn't even sure when Zorro had moved. He'd been too…involved.

'Fast used to be your pace.'

'And look where *that* got me.' *And my father.* 'So I suppose the more important question at this point it why you're so determined to go fast.'

'I'm not—'

'Ava,' he interrupted gently.

She sighed. 'Maybe I think that if we go fast we'll outrun the reasons this is a bad idea. Or forget how poorly it could turn out.'

He stared at her, and then laughed. 'Well, you *do* have a point.'

Her mouth curved. 'I generally seem to.'

'And yet you still doubt yourself,' he said. 'You shouldn't.'

She opened her mouth, but nothing came out. She closed it again and nodded. 'I suppose. So,' she continued after a moment, 'I guess I should go to bed. Alone,' she said on an exhalation of breath that was as much disappointment as air.

He laughed. 'Or you could stay here and we could put the angel on the tree. And then,' he said, taking her hand, 'we could kiss some more.'

'But I thought you said—'

'Not going fast doesn't mean we can't stay in the same spot, Ava.'

He took the angel from the chair and put it on the top of the tree before pulling Ava back into his arms.

It was fine. It would all be fine. Fine. *Fine.* All completely fine.

Ava groaned as she made her way down the path that led to Leela's parents' house. Their property was gorgeous: beautiful green hills, tall trees and an incredible view of the Helderberg Mountain. And that didn't even include the view of the house: the tall white building that looked more like a showpiece than somewhere people lived.

But she barely saw it with her mind whirling around the way it was. Because this was the first time she'd see Noah since they'd spent that entire night making out. It had been an immensely satisfying evening, the kind she hadn't experienced in ages. But they hadn't slept together, and now, with the benefit of hindsight, Ava took solace in that fact.

Though it didn't help her feel any less guilty. And she knew that seeing Noah now, a week later, would be strange.

Still, she kept telling herself that it was fine.

Noah had helped her clean her house of soot the day after their night of making out, when she'd been allowed back onto the estate, and that had been fine. Granted, there had been touches and kisses, and maybe a half an hour of making out before he'd left, but things had been *fine*. Just as her work week—which had been so busy she hadn't had time to talk with him—had been fine.

It was all fine. Fine, fine, *fine*.

Which is why you're acting like a complete fool right now.

Ava paused, blew out a breath. And then inhaled deeply and exhaled for the same length of time. She was freaking out because of Noah, yes. But she knew it was also because this was the first wedding event where she'd have to face *people*. People who'd seen her fiancé walk away from her at her own wedding. People who'd seen the shock and hurt on her face.

She couldn't be surly. It would only prove to them that she'd had as hard a time about it as they believed. Besides, the time to be surly was over. It had been fine when they'd been planning. But now, with the rehearsal dinner, Leela and Jaden were actually starting their journey to committing to one another. She couldn't be surly about that.

And, in truth, she wasn't surly about *them*. She *wanted* Jaden and Leela to marry. She wanted them to be excited about their future together. She just hoped that neither of them would ever find out how it felt when all of it came crashing down around them.

Yeah, you're going to be completely fine.

Grunting at the stubborn voice in her heard, she squared

her shoulders and walked into the house. It was beautifully decorated. Tables were decked with the wedding colours—blue and yellow—though not overly so, so that it looked like as much of a wedding celebration as a festive one. There was a Christmas tree in the corner; lights draped across the room. The sliding doors were open to the pool with the mountain view just beyond it.

Even Ava had to admit she was impressed.

'Are you ready?'

The voice sent a thrill down her spine, and gave her the opportunity to school her face before turning to face its owner.

'For what?'

Noah's eyes swept over her—she felt almost naked when she saw the greed there—but he only smiled. 'To lose.'

'To— Ha!' she said, though her heart was still thumping. 'Try again, Giles. I'm already leading in this game.'

'By twenty points. Don't think that's a head start you'll be able to keep.'

'I'm not worried. You're much too nice for your own good.'

His lips curved, and then he leaned over and brushed a kiss on her cheek. 'You look amazing.'

Again, his eyes swept over her. This time he kept the perusal slow, steady, as if he were actually undressing her. She shifted her weight between her feet, resisting the urge to brush a hand against the blue-and-white polka dot dress she'd worn for the event.

She'd made an effort with her looks—she'd even put a yellow ribbon in her hair, for heaven's sake—because she'd known that good behaviour wasn't a guarantee. The dress was long, but the neck plunged between her breasts, and she hadn't been able to wear a bra.

She regretted it immensely.

'I appreciate your compliments, but if you don't pull yourself together people are going to ask if we need a room.'

'Not a bad idea.'

'What isn't?'

Jaden joined them with a frown, and both she and Noah straightened.

'Doing my speech for Ava later tonight,' Noah said easily. 'So she can give me some pointers.'

Ava kept her eyes on Jaden, but she could feel her face warming. Noah's words had sounded dirtier than he'd intended. Or perhaps *as* dirty as he'd intended. She couldn't tell with him.

'I'm not sure that's a good idea,' Jaden replied, and Ava let out her breath. 'Ava's not the best public speaker.'

'Well, had I known that's what you think about me I wouldn't have agreed to this stupid slideshow.' Ava tilted her head. 'But now that I know what you think about me I suppose it gives me a certain freedom. Maybe I should talk about that holiday in Zanzibar when you—'

'Ava,' Jaden said with a wince. 'Would you please not talk about my past relationships at the rehearsal dinner of my wedding?'

'But it's part of the fun,' she teased.

'Just wait until you—' Jaden's eyes widened as he realised what he was about to say. 'Ava, I'm sorry. I didn't mean—'

'Oh, look, it's Uncle Cyril,' she interrupted him brightly. 'I think I'm going to talk to him about our cousins.'

She left before Jaden could apologise again.

Before she could see more sympathy in his eyes.

CHAPTER THIRTEEN

'SHE'S JUST SAID she's going to talk to our uncle about the children he's estranged from.' Jaden groaned. 'Barely ten minutes in and I've already freaked her out.'

'I think that happened a long time ago,' Noah commented quietly, watching as Ava greeted the older man and began talking. He watched as the man put a hand on Ava's shoulder, saw her face blanch before she forced a smile and then said something that made the man frown.

She was playing the game by herself, he thought with a smile, and tried to figure out how he could make his way over to her without arousing suspicion.

'I don't know if that's true,' Jaden said, watching Ava, too.

Which, Noah thought in hindsight, was probably a good thing. He didn't know if his face held any of the lust—or those other pesky emotions—their kissing had brought to the surface.

'She hadn't been herself long before my wedding came along.'

'Really? Or is that just what you're telling yourself so you feel better about doing this at *this* time of year? Not to mention asking her to be in your wedding party after what happened?'

Jaden turned to him, his eyes narrowed. 'When did you become my sister's defender?'

'Since you've seemed to have abdicated the position.' As anger lit inside him Noah took a deep breath. 'But you can't even answer my questions, Jaden, which makes me think you *know* how hard this has been for her. And don't even try arguing with me. You know I'm right.'

Jaden lifted the side of his mouth, though it wasn't in a smile. 'I don't like it that you're taking her side over mine.'

'Man, are you *listening* to yourself?' Noah grabbed a glass of champagne from a waiter to distract himself from the annoyance that had taken his anger's place. 'This isn't about sides. This is about you supporting your little sister through a tough time.'

Jaden blew out a breath and then stole Noah's champagne, downing it before Noah could complain.

'Wait,' Jaden said. 'How do you even know about all this? How do you know this is tough for her?'

'She…er…she told me.'

'She *told* you?' Jaden repeated.

Realising he was losing the higher ground, Noah ran a hand over his hair. 'Yeah, but only because we were talking about the wedding after the fire on Friday—' He stopped too late.

'Exactly *when* after the fire did you speak with my sister?'

'Round about the same time she told me about Tiff being a bridesmaid.' He wasn't proud of it, but his ex had walked in and given him the perfect opportunity to regain control.

'Look, about that—'

'It's fine,' he interrupted when his guilt immediately flared. 'I mean, what could you have done? She introduced you to the woman you're going to spend your life with. Ava,' he answered Jaden's unspoken question.

'She really ran her mouth off with you,' Jaden said with a frown. Then he shook his head. 'I should have told you.'

'Yeah, you should have.'

'I'm sorry.' He paused. 'I've been caught up with this wedding. Maybe too caught up, since I've been ignoring what Ava needs from me.' He set his empty champagne glass on a passing waiter's tray, and then patted Noah's back. 'But that doesn't mean you have free rein with my sister.'

'Wh—' Noah stopped, wondering how the conversation had turned pear-shaped again.

And because he didn't understand how—and because Jaden seemed to be in a strange mood and so did he—he didn't say what he wanted. That Ava wasn't an inanimate object. That she was a person with feelings. With agency.

'I don't know what you're talking about.'

'Yeah, you do.' Jaden said it easily, but there was a warning in his eyes. 'You know now and you knew it seven years ago, when you kissed her. She deserves more than what you've given the women who've come after Tiff.'

Jaden slapped him on the back again and walked away. It took Noah a few moments before he could figure out what had happened, and another few to process how he felt about what his best friend seemed to think of him.

But Jaden was right. Hadn't Noah himself thought about the control he exercised in his dating life not too long ago? The relationships he'd had after Tiff couldn't even be defined as such. There had been no emotions involved, on either side, and so no potential for hurt.

Still, Jaden's reaction had stung. More so because it was fair. And because now, after his conversation with Ava about his father—his mother—Noah knew his stance on relationships was more complicated than simply not wanting to repeat his father's mistakes.

He didn't want to repeat his father's pain.

He'd known it since the day Ava had told him about his father's advice to her to move on. But the more Noah thought about it, the more he'd realised that Kirk hadn't chosen to move on by forgetting about his wife's cheating, like Ava had said. No, Noah had been right when he'd thought his father was running.

But had he really thought that made his father weak? Because, if so, Noah was weak, too. Because though he'd chosen a different way to deal with it than his father had—choosing few to no relationships over a constant flow of them—Noah's motivations were the same. Except he didn't think he'd ever outrun the pain. His father's or his own.

It turned his stomach. And strengthened his resolve that he couldn't fall for Ava. Not any more than he already had. Not when he didn't know if his pain would allow him to give Ava what she needed.

Jaden was right: Ava deserved more than what Noah could give her. Especially while he figured out what exactly that was. But when his eyes settled on her, Noah felt everything inside him yearn. And he knew his resolve wouldn't be easy to follow.

'If it wasn't against the rules I'd deduct all your measly forty points for leaving me alone for half an hour. *Half an hour!*'

'I'm sorry.'

'You sound sincere, but I can't help but think that you did it on purpose. So that you wouldn't have to reward me handsomely for all my efforts.'

'That bad?'

Ava took a glass of champagne from a waiter and gave him a look. 'It's bad enough that I'm going to drink this glass of champagne instead of the sparkling water I'd intended on drinking tonight.'

She downed it and reached for another.

Noah put a hand on her free hand when she moved the glass to her lips again, and there was understanding in his eyes when he said, 'You don't want to get drunk tonight, Avalanche. You want to be here for your brother and future sister-in-law. You want to give a funny, yet charmingly embarrassing speech with your slideshow for all these guests. And then you want to go home and pretend it didn't happen.'

She gritted her teeth. Forced herself to relax when he squeezed her hand. And then told herself not to cry.

'This is…harder than I thought it was going to be.' She sipped from the champagne to hide the tears prickling in her eyes.

'I'm sorry.'

'Don't be.' She forced a smile. 'It's not your fault.'

'No. But maybe if I'd stayed you wouldn't be going through this.'

She gave him an even look, ignoring the thrill going up and down her spine. 'If you'd stayed, Noah, I think I would have been in a lot more trouble than I am now.'

Her eyes shifted to behind him, and something tightened inside her when she saw her parents. And then she saw Noah's father just behind them, and that something loosened slightly.

'Ava?' Noah said when she pulled her hand from his.

She nodded her head in the direction of the new guests, and felt him straighten beside her.

'Aunty Ruth… Uncle Sam,' Noah said, giving them both hugs before doing the same with his father.

It was so familiar that it sent a pang through her for all the years they'd missed. But, putting it aside, she kissed her parents and hugged Noah's father. Kirk gave her an extra pat on the back, signalling his support, and she smiled with a slight nod.

She hadn't had to tell Kirk how being in Jaden's wedding had made her feel. But when she'd made her way to Kirk's house after Leela had asked her to be a bridesmaid—eyes dry and heart aching—he'd patted her on the back just as he had now. And then he'd told her some innocuous story about work and she'd listened, refusing to think about real life for the rest of the day.

Somehow Kirk had known that being in the wedding would bring all the memories back. The memories of inadequacy. Of disgrace. Of failure. Somehow Kirk had known, and not even her own family had. But then, Kirk's experiences put him in a unique position to understand. And, since her family hadn't had those experiences, how could they know unless she'd told them?

You told Noah.

But Noah didn't know all of it. There was both a comfort and a despair in that.

Because she couldn't reconcile it, she sipped her champagne and chatted with her parents. And ignored the concerned looks both Noah and Kirk sent her.

Tonight wouldn't be one of those moments when she gave up her control. No matter how stressed she was, she would get through her slideshow. Even with her insides quivering at the weight of keeping it together, she would get through it.

She *would*.

Ava was suffering. It was in the slight shake of her hand when she brought the champagne flute to her lips. In the way she smiled at her parents but her eyes remained cautious. How the corners of her eyes were crinkled with strain. How her lips thinned whenever she wasn't fake smiling.

He didn't understand how the others couldn't see it. Or, if they could, how they didn't care. And, since he'd specifically told Jaden about it, Noah had to believe his friend was *choosing* not to care. It bothered him so much he didn't know what to do with the anger vibrating through his body.

When it was announced that Ava wanted to say something about the happy couple, he almost snorted. There was no *want* in this situation. She'd been forced to say something. And, as miserable as she was about all of it, the fact that she'd agreed reinforced that she was determined to make the rest of her family believe she was okay. And make them feel better about themselves as a result.

Even at the cost of her own happiness.

He positioned himself towards the front of the room, ready in case something happened, though he wasn't entirely sure what could happen. But he wanted to make sure Ava knew he was there for her. He hadn't been before, but he would be now.

He tried not to think about what that meant for his determination not to fall for her.

'Hello, ladies and gentlemen,' Ava said into the microphone they'd handed her. 'For those of you who don't know me, I'm Jaden's baby sister, Ava. And for those of you who *do* know me, you must be wondering why in the world Jaden would allow me to say something at his rehearsal dinner.'

The crowd laughed as Jaden pulled a face, his expression then relaxing into an easy smile. Noah turned his attention back to Ava. To anyone who didn't know her she'd look poised and relaxed. To those who did she looked tense and unhappy.

Noah clenched his jaw.

'But I managed to convince him so that I could tell you all how wonderful it is that he's finally found the love of his life in Leela.' She paused and smiled at them, and it seemed almost genuine. 'Actually, I'm going to *show* you, because I've come prepared with pictures!'

Noah was caught by her as she spoke, as she laughed, as she made the crowd laugh. She was perfect as she told stories of the different phases Jaden had gone through—goth phase included—and alluded to the women who'd been a part of those phases.

When she said that Leela had never been a part of any phase the crowd sighed. When she said she'd never seen her brother happier the crowd applauded. And when she wished them both well and toasted them the crowd drank to the couple and cheered as Ava kissed them both.

And still he was caught only by her. By the strength she'd shown in getting through it. By the love and affection she'd shown to her brother. Even though it had killed her.

When she left the room immediately afterwards Noah followed, finding her sitting at the top of the steps that led to Leela's parents' tennis court, her head in her hands.

'Hey,' he said quietly, sitting beside her, though all he wanted to do was take her into his arms and comfort her.

'Hey.' Her voice was raspy, but when she lifted her head, there were no tears on her face.

'That was pretty good,' he said after a moment.

'Funny and charmingly embarrassing?'

He chuckled. 'Exactly.'

'Great. So you'll support me as I get really, *really* drunk now?'

'You don't want to do that.'

'I don't.' She sighed. 'I just want to stop hurting.'

CHAPTER FOURTEEN

THE WORDS SAT between them and Noah didn't know what to do with them. He didn't want to push, but he also didn't want her to ruminate on it.

Just ask, dummy.

Nearly rolling his eyes at his inner voice, he said, 'Do you want to talk about it?'

'I don't think anyone's ever asked me that,' she replied after a long moment. 'Everyone just assumes I *don't* want to talk about it. Which is fair. I don't. But nor do they.' She paused. 'The Kellers have a talent for pretending things didn't happen. Or hiding their feelings about it.'

'Can't say I've noticed,' he commented dryly.

She laughed. 'You're practically part of the family and yet it hasn't affected *you*.'

'I'm not sure that's true.'

'Isn't it?' she asked, but didn't wait for an answer. 'You've always seemed pretty self-aware to me.'

'I'm not. I've only just realised I've been angry with my father for trying to protect himself from hurt. And that I've been blaming him for—' He broke off, knowing he couldn't say any more. Instead he picked up a stone and threw it across the court, wincing when it hit the net. 'I'm probably going to have to pick that up.'

'Probably.'

Silence lingered between them.

'I think…' He started to speak without realising, and when

his mind caught up to his mouth he almost stopped. But then he thought that the words were already there, and that if he wanted *her* to talk he needed to talk, too. 'Maybe you think I'm self-aware because something about you makes me feel like I can share things with you.'

'Or maybe you just need to talk.'

'No, it's you.'

'That's not true.'

'It's definitely true. Why else would I be sitting outside with you after your brother warned me not to? I could—'

'Wait—what?' She frowned. 'My brother told you *not* to come outside and sit with me?'

'Your brother told me that I needed to stay away from you.' He shrugged, but his emotion didn't feel as careless as the gesture.

'What a—' She stopped, shook her head. 'He had no right to do that.'

'He's looking out for you.' He paused. 'I don't know why he's decided to do that now. When it's too late to keep you from hurting like this.'

'He can't protect me from life,' she said after a moment. 'I fell in love. Got my heart broken. And he was there for me all through it.'

'He should have sussed the guy out. Clearly he wasn't right for you.'

'You don't know that.'

'I *do* know that,' he said. 'You're here, in pain, and not with this man. He wasn't right for you. And I bet you knew that long before he left you at the altar.'

She didn't reply, and suddenly something occurred to him.

'I'm sorry. I'm crossing the line.' His heart ached as he said it. 'I just assumed—'

'What?'

'That you're over him. I shouldn't have said—'

'No.' She interrupted him quietly. 'I *am* over him.'

She took a deep breath and lifted a hand to her face, before clasping it with her other hand and lowering them both between her knees.

'I'm not over what he did to me, but I'm over *him*.' She turned to look at him. 'You're right. He wasn't the right man.'

When unspoken words—unspoken emotions—stirred the air between them, hijacking the silence, highlighting the tension, Noah cleared his throat.

'So why didn't Jaden *do* something? Why didn't he warn the guy like he did me?'

'Maybe his warning abilities only came after his engagement.'

He laughed. 'Oh, no, those abilities have been alive and well since that time he caught us kissing. I still remember our discussion.' He winced. 'That's probably too civil a word, but you get the idea.'

He felt her surprise before he saw it. Before she angled her body; before her features twisted into an expression he'd have thought cute if he hadn't seen her eyes. If he hadn't seen the confusion, the anger, the hurt there.

The hurt bothered him the most.

'Exactly what kind of discussion, if not civil?'

'I…er…we just spoke about how inappropriate my actions were.'

'Your actions?' she repeated, tilting her head as she shifted even further away from him. 'You mean when you kissed yourself? Or when you kissed me and there was no reciprocation?'

'Ava, it's not—'

'Because *your* actions were inappropriate that day?' She stood now. 'Me wrapping my legs around you, pressing my body against yours, asking you—both verbally and non-verbally—to take me back to your place and—'

'Ava, please.' He stood now, too, his legs shaky. He couldn't hear her say those words again. Not when he'd been successfully running from them for most of the last seven years. 'You're upset about everything that's happened today—'

'How would *you* know?' She put her hands on her hips. '*What* do you know other than what I've told you?'

'Ava—'

'*No*, Noah. I can't be the bigger person right now. I can't pretend you blocking my emails doesn't bother me. Or ignore the fact that you've talked about me with my brother like I'm some kind of possession and not a woman with the ability to make my own decisions. Or,' she said with a frown, 'how that talking with my brother probably *led* to you blocking me.'

He gave a curt nod—he was helpless not to when she'd just confirmed everything he'd already known—and she rolled her eyes.

'Why the hell do I even bother?' she asked.

And walked away.

Men were ridiculous. They were annoying. They were the *worst*.

If she had her way she'd never have to deal with them again. Or at the very least she wouldn't have to stay at a dinner during which she was forced to look into the faces of two men who reminded her how ridiculous—annoying, the *worst*—they really were.

She'd detoured the moment she'd re-entered the room after her chat with Noah and had seen Jaden heading for her. Had gone so far as to wait in the bathroom for twenty minutes—not fun—so that she wouldn't have to speak with him.

By the time she came out the dinner was starting and Jaden was preoccupied. Noah, on the other hand, seemed to have been waiting for her. He nodded his head to the empty seat next to him and she nearly laughed. He thought she was going to sit next to *him*? Maybe she *should* have laughed, just to show him how ridiculous he was being.

Instead she ignored him and took a seat next to her parents.

How she got through the rest of the stupid evening, she had no idea. But as soon as dinner had ended and she knew people would no longer care whether she was there or not, she tried to leave the party.

Tried.

'Ava—wait.'

Ava clenched her jaw, then relaxed it and turned to face her aunt. She'd been avoiding the woman since she'd seen her glide in as if she was the queen of the party. Taking in her jewels and overly formal dress, Ava thought her aunt might actually believe that she was.

'I've been trying to speak with you all evening.'

'Really?' Ava arranged an easy smile on her face. 'I didn't realise.'

'I wanted to know how you've been.'

'Just peachy. I mean, as peachy as I *can* be after my fiancé—whom I loved—left me at the altar in front of my friends and family.'

Her aunt blinked, and satisfaction rippled through Ava. This was what her aunt wanted, wasn't it? To revel in Ava's misery. To take pleasure from the fact that her niece was struggling.

'Yes, well, that *was* what I wanted to know.' Her aunt smiled sympathetically. 'I can't imagine what it's like to re-build your life after something like that happens.'

'Hard. I've had days when I didn't want to get out of bed. Nights when I couldn't stop thinking about what was wrong with me. And then, of course, there are the people. Those who—for some strange reason—want to know about *what* happened without really caring *who* it happened to.' She let out a little sigh. 'Honestly, celebrating another wedding this soon has made *everything* better.'

There was a beat between Ava's last word and the feeling of utter dread as she realised she'd taken it too far. Damn it, why did she always take it too far?

'You told me you weren't going to keep on pulling people's legs like this, Ava!'

Ava's spine stiffened at Noah's voice, before her mind processed his words.

'I can't help it.' She gave him a smile she hoped was teasing, but she honestly couldn't be sure. 'It's so easy.'

'I know. But you make them panic.' Noah handed her a glass of champagne that he took from a waitress nearby and smiled at Ava's aunt. 'It was a running joke between us until I realised that she was freaking out her family.'

'This…this is a *joke*?'

'Afraid so.' Noah's smile was effortlessly charming. 'You know Ava's sense of humour.'

'I—I don't think I do.'

If Ava hadn't already embarrassed herself, she would have enjoyed her usually self-assured aunt's stammering.

'Of *course* you do,' Noah said, his smile widening. 'It's from her mother's side of the family.'

Ava stifled her laugh, and there was a long pause before her aunt gave a polite excuse and walked away.

It was just the two of them then, and she handed him back the champagne flute.

'Seventy points. It would be higher, but you used my embarrassment to get your points.'

'Which, in my humble opinion, should be the reason I get at least ninety points. I saw an opportunity and I went for it.'

'Eighty. That's my final offer.'

She didn't wait to see if he accepted, instead turning to the front door so that she could leave as she'd wanted to in the first place.

She got as far as the steps that led to the pathway a few metres from the door.

'You don't want to know how many points I gave you?'

She turned. 'For embarrassing myself?'

'For embarrassing your aunt. The point of this game.'

'Fine,' she said after a beat. 'How many?'

'Twenty.'

'*Twenty?*' She rolled her eyes. 'Keep your points.'

'Well, you started with fifty, by calling your aunt out for asking about you but not really caring. Then you lost thirty for lying about how you feel. Ten for each lie.'

'I didn't lie.'

'You said that you've struggled to get out of bed—' he

lifted a finger '—that you've wondered what was wrong with you—' another finger '—and that you *want* to be in this wedding.' He lifted a third.

Tired now, she sighed. 'You only have to deduct ten points. There was only one lie.'

She walked down the stairs and didn't bother to look back or stop when he called to her.

CHAPTER FIFTEEN

HE COULDN'T LET her leave like that. Not when he knew which one the lie was. Not when, after the second time she'd told him something was wrong with her, the truth made his stomach turn.

He ran until he was next to her, and when she sighed he ignored it.

'Just leave me alone.'

'Not when you're in this mood.'

She grunted, but again he ignored it. Instead he kept walking beside her, as if somehow his presence would manage to convince her that she could talk to him. That she could trust him.

But by the time they reached the car park, she still hadn't said anything.

He considered what he'd do if she got into her car and left the party. Would he get into his and follow her? He hadn't said goodbye to anyone—not Jaden, not his father—but he supposed he could make something up to satisfy them. But then he remembered the look Jaden had given him earlier—when he'd returned to the party shortly after Ava had—and he wondered whether anything he made up would be believable.

In the end he didn't have to make the decision. Ava stalked past her car and took a path just beyond the car park that he hadn't seen before. He hung back when the path became too narrow for him to walk next to her, and although he wanted to ask where they were going he just looked around him.

The path was enclosed by vines that created an archway the entire way down. Soft pink flowers clung to the vines and, without thinking, he picked one, then awkwardly stared at it in his hand. Before he could decide what to do with it his attention was drawn to the fact that the path had ended, opening up to a medium-sized dam hidden from the main property.

'Have you been here before?' he asked in a breathless voice, too amazed that something like this could actually be on someone's property to care.

'Once. A long time ago.'

She kicked off her shoes, tossed her bag to the side, then pulled her dress up to expose her legs to mid-thigh.

'It was during the day, at an extravagant party much like the one at the house now.' She breathed in deeply, and as she exhaled she looked at the sky. 'Personally, I prefer it like this. With the stars reflecting in the water from the sky. And a small ball of silver right over there for the moon.'

She nodded her head in its direction, and then walked to the edge of the dam, the water lapping over her feet.

'I don't know if that's a good idea, Ava,' he said carefully, as memories of the two of them in a similar situation taunted him.

'I don't care if it's a good idea.' She'd walked deeper into the water now, and it reached to her knees. 'It's cool and refreshing and it's making me feel better so I don't care.'

After a few more minutes he realised he wasn't going to convince her to sit on the grass with him. Sighing, he kicked off his own shoes, removed his socks and rolled up his black trousers.

He put his phone and wallet on top of the rest of their belongings and walked to the water. He hissed when the water touched his feet. But when she looked over lazily, and he was drawn by the seduction of it, he no longer cared that *cool and refreshing* wasn't quite how he'd describe the water.

'What are you doing, Noah?'

Even her words were seductive, he thought. But he didn't know if she'd intended them to be. Which made it even worse.

'You need someone to talk to,' he answered, instead of saying what he wanted to say. *I need to get you out of that dress and into my arms.* 'I'm here.'

She arched an eyebrow and his heart kicked.

'Something tells me that's not the only thing you're here for.'

Of *course* she'd be able to see through him.

'It's the only thing I'm asking for.'

Their eyes held for a moment, and then she shook her head. 'Why is it so important to you that I talk?'

'Because you've kept it all in for too long.' He paused. 'And you haven't told anyone what you're really feeling.'

'How do you know that?'

'I spoke with Jaden earlier. His reaction made me think that you haven't told *him* what you're feeling. The fact that your parents aren't rallying around makes me believe that you haven't told them either. And the way my father kept checking on you tonight tells me he suspects something, but doesn't know. And then, of course, there's the fact that you're standing here, almost waist-deep in a dam, which makes me think there are things you haven't figured out. Probably because you haven't said them out loud.'

She blew out a breath, and when her eyes met his they glistened slightly.

He took a step forward, but she shook her head, and he stopped. And then she sighed.

'Well, Noah, you're not wrong. Though I wish you were.'

Ava drew her dress up higher, so that the material of its skirt bunched just below her breasts. Then she moved deeper into the water.

'I wish it were as simple as this wedding reminding me of

the one I didn't have,' she continued. 'Or a Christmas wedding being a special reminder of my failure.'

'You didn't fail.'

'Of course I did.'

She spun, enjoying the way it sent ripples out across the rest of the water. Enjoying how it seemed so simple, uncomplicated. It inspired her to get through the rest of the conversation in the same way, even if what she was talking about *wasn't* simple and uncomplicated.

'I loved Christmas,' she said, just twisting gently now. It kept the ripples going, but didn't threaten her dress. 'You know how much I loved it.'

'Based on your opinion of my house, I thought you still did.'

Her lips curved at the dryness in his tone. 'I guess I still have some of that love inside me. But most of it's gone.' She sighed. 'The festivities I used to love just feel contrived now. The family time feels forced. Complicated and heavy. The things I used to love feel like they were a lifetime ago. Putting the tree up. Drinking and eating and laughing.'

'*We* just did that.'

'We did,' she said, surprise fluttering through her. 'But it was easier with you. You didn't keep looking at me to check if I was okay.'

'No,' he agreed. 'My reasons were different.'

She laughed softly. 'You're flirting with me even now?'

'Is it flirting if I'm being earnest?'

Not knowing how to answer him, she continued with the rest of her story. 'You weren't here. You didn't have to see how I looked when Milo left me in front of everyone I knew and loved. You didn't have to see me put on a brave smile as I followed him down the aisle, running after him as soon as I got out of that church.'

She tightened her grip on her dress.

'You didn't have to see him drive away and me sink to the floor. You didn't have to see me stay there, unable to cry because I knew people were watching me. You didn't have to help me up. You didn't have to help me into a car. And you didn't have to see me curl into a ball on my way home.'

'Ava…' he whispered.

She heard the horror in his tone. But all desire for simplicity had gone out of the window now. She'd been captured by her own tale. Ensnared by the emotions. The memories.

'I think the worst thing for them was that I was determined not to show anyone he'd hurt me. Halfway to my house I uncurled from the ball and demanded we go back to the church. And then I marched back in and told everyone we had food and alcohol and the party would go on.'

She laughed at her audacity now, and the sound was harsh.

'I made sure I spoke with every single person who attended that reception. I explained to them that Milo and I had made a mistake and decided to go our separate ways. That I was fine and he was fine, and I assured them they could enjoy themselves. Even though I hadn't spoken to Milo I already knew we wouldn't get back together. He'd humiliated me. And he didn't have the decency to tell me why. He didn't deserve me.'

'He didn't,' Noah said fiercely. 'He didn't deserve you.'

'Except,' she said softly, almost as if he hadn't spoken at all, 'I couldn't believe that. Not entirely. I could only think that there must be something wrong with *me*. That *I* didn't deserve *him*.'

'He told you that when he eventually spoke with you, didn't he?'

'Not in so many words.' She took a breath. 'He came to my house the next day. I'd sent my family away because I needed time. I wanted to stop pretending. I didn't want to be "on", and with them I felt like I had to be.'

She paused.

'He said I was too much work.' She blinked, and felt wetness fall down her cheeks. 'As if I were a project that needed tackling. As if I were a dilapidated house that needed to be rebuilt.' She looked at Noah now. Noted the fierce look in his eyes. Heard it echo in her tone. 'We were together for five years, and on our wedding day he discovered that he didn't want to work on this *project*. This *house*.'

'Please tell me he's somewhere in the world missing a digit.'

She gave him a look, though his words steadied her. 'If I'd removed something from his body, it wouldn't have been a finger or toe.'

He grimaced, and then laughed. 'Fair point.' He walked to her now, apparently not noticing he was soaking his trousers in the process. 'You're not too much work.'

'I might be.' She swallowed, and stilled when he brushed a thumb across her cheek, spreading the wetness of her tears over her skin.

'Not too much. Just…work. We're all work.'

'Not all of us are left at the altar because of it.'

'Because some of us are too scared to take that chance.'

He frowned, and she realised he was talking about himself. Perhaps he'd just discovered it about himself, and was reassuring her about something he didn't really believe was true.

'Taking chances is overrated,' she said under her breath.

He laughed, breaking the tension. 'I doubt most people in the world would agree with you.'

'Most people in the world haven't been left at the altar,' she said again. 'I have the moral high ground here, Noah. You don't want to mess with—'

She stopped as a huge wave of water washed over her. Partly because she was surprised—they were in a dam; there were no waves—and partly because all her efforts to keep her dress dry were now in vain.

'Did you—' She wiped the water from her face. 'Did you just *splash* me? When my hair and face are *perfectly* made up? When my dress—which is *very* expensive—is still—'

She was silenced by another wave of water. This time she didn't bother coming up. Instead, she sank under the water, knowing that inevitable panic would cause Noah to come closer.

Just as she'd thought, she felt his leg against her belly, and before he could do anything she'd come up in front of him and was pulling him down with her.

A part of her knew that he was letting her drag him down. He was much too strong for just the weight of her arms to pull him under. But, as if he'd accepted his punishment, he stayed under the water for as long as she held him down.

When they came up, he flicked his hair back and wiped his face.

'Fair.'

She stared, and then laughed. 'Of *course* that's all you're saying about this.'

He lifted a shoulder. 'It *is* fair. I started it.'

'Why?'

'It seemed like the perfect way to distract you.'

Softening, she rolled her eyes. 'Yeah, well, it's not only going to distract me, but also the entire party when we go back up there in soaked clothing.'

He winced. 'I didn't think about that.'

'No, I didn't think you did.' She sighed and pushed herself deeper into the water. 'But we're here now, and we're probably going to get into trouble anyway, so we might as well enjoy it.'

He hadn't thought his actions through, but now, watching Ava relax in the water, he couldn't make himself regret it.

'What is it with you and water?' he asked suddenly, surprising himself. 'You've always been at your happiest when you're swimming.'

'I don't know,' she said, straightening where she'd been floating on her back. 'I guess it was all the family holidays we spent in the water. Beaches, swimming pools, dams...' She sighed happily. 'Good memories.'

'I agree.'

Her eyes met his and immediately the energy around them snapped. He could have sworn he saw the water boiling. Because, as he'd intended, his words had made her think about the last time they'd been in the water together. About the memories they'd created then.

'No,' she breathed when he closed the distance between them.

Dutifully, he stopped. 'I'm sorry.'

'Don't be. I just… You mess with my head. And kissing you…' She shook her head.

And even though the curls on her head were misshapen with water—even though the make-up on her face was smudged—she was still the most beautiful woman he'd ever been drawn to.

'You don't think that's true for me, too? Because I guarantee what happened last week has kept me awake *every single night* since then. Fortunately, I'm only going back to the station after the wedding.'

'And you can take photos without having slept?'

'I can,' he confirmed, 'but I don't have to. I work freelance. According to my own terms. According to my own time. I've given myself some time off.'

She sucked her lip between her teeth and his body tightened.

'This isn't a good idea,' she said, but she swam closer and lifted her dress under the water, wrapping her legs around his waist.

'I know.' He put his hands under her butt and brought her tight against his body, so her mouth hovered just above his.

'Jaden could find us.'

'I don't care.'

'What about the warning?'

'I'm going to hell anyway, Ava. Might as well go down swinging.'

And with those words he kissed her.

No matter how many times he'd kissed her, it always felt new. Different. And yet somehow there was a familiarity that made every movement of their lips seductive.

The other times, he'd taken his time kissing her. Kissing was a leisure activity, after all. Created to be savoured, enjoyed. And kissing Ava had strengthened that belief for him. Her tongue moved in intuitive ways, and sent shimmers of pleasure through him. Her lips were soft, inviting, and pressed against his as if they belonged there.

Kissing her leisurely gave him the opportunity to feel the softness of her body under his hands. To feel its contrast with the hardness of his own. To enjoy the curves of her, the lines of her. To have desire travel lazily through him. To have awareness torture him.

Which was why it made no sense that he was kissing her now as if there would never be any more kisses.

He could sense her surprise as he deepened their kiss. But there was no resistance, and she tightened her arms around his neck, angling her mouth and inviting him to take more.

So he did.

He took and took, and wasn't surprised when she demanded more from him, too. Because that was who Ava was. Power. Fire. Strength. She matched him with every stroke; returned every caress with equal passion.

His fingers—his body—wanted more, and he suspected hers did, too. Just as he suspected that they would have both taken more—given more—if they hadn't been interrupted.

CHAPTER SIXTEEN

SHE NEEDED TO STOP. To stop kissing Noah. To stop kissing him in water. To stop enjoying the feel of his body under her fingers. But most of all she needed to stop kissing Noah in water, feeling his body under her fingers and *getting caught*.

As soon as she heard the giggling she pushed away from him. And then, for good measure, swam a short distance out. She rolled her eyes at herself, knowing that no one who stumbled upon them was going to believe that they were just there to talk. Even if that *had* been what they'd been doing initially.

But if she'd thought being caught kissing her brother's best friend was awkward, she wasn't prepared for the awkwardness of being caught by her brother's best friend's *father*... and the woman he was clearly sneaking off to make out with.

If the water around them had heated when they'd started kissing, it had iced over now. Noah's face had gone completely blank, though there was a twitch at his eye that betrayed his feelings.

'Noah,' Kirk said, his hand firm on the small of his guest's back.

Ava didn't recognise the woman, so she assumed it was one of Leela's friends. If she didn't hate being in this situation—seeing what it did to Noah—she would have been amused.

'I didn't realise anyone was here.'

Noah didn't reply. He just walked out of the water, and turned to Ava, his hand outstretched. She immediately started towards him—trying not to think about how her dress clung her body, or the fact that it was even more incriminating that she wasn't wearing a bra—and took his hand as soon as she could.

'We'll leave you two alone,' Noah said as they walked over and picked up their things.

'Noah—'

'It's fine,' Noah interrupted his father, giving him a smile that looked more like a grimace. 'I'll see you at lunch tomorrow.'

Her hand still caught in Noah's, she gave Kirk an apologetic look before following Noah to the car park. The journey was short, but the heaviness in the air around them made it feel endless, as if they were still moving through water.

She gave a sigh of relief once they got to the car park and saw that most of the cars were still there. Since she had her keys with her, she could leave without showing anyone what a mess she was. Or facing the inevitable questions when they saw who she'd got into a mess with.

'Are you okay?' she asked quietly, when Noah didn't take any steps towards his car.

'Fine.'

She winced. 'You don't have to pretend to be fine.'

'No?' When he turned to her, his eyes were cold. 'So you want to know what's going on inside my head after seeing my father sneaking off to—' He broke off on a curse.

'Yes. If it's going to make you feel better then, yes, tell me.'

'It won't make me feel better,' he said flatly. 'It's just going to annoy me even more.'

He walked towards his car then, but she hurried forward, blocking his path.

'Tell me.'

He didn't reply. Only moved to walk around her.

She shifted again. 'Tell me, Noah.'

'Nothing good will come out of it if I do, Ava,' he said in a warning tone. 'Just let me go.'

'I've confided in you—' she swallowed when the words caused her stomach to churn '—because I trust you. You can trust me, too.'

'And how is trusting you going to change the fact that seeing my father back there just reminded me that I can't run from my family's past?' he asked tightly. 'That no matter how much I want to, *I can't run*?'

The despair in his voice was the reason Ava didn't stop him when he walked past her this time. A few minutes later, he drove away. It happened so quickly that she was still staring at the dust his car had left behind long after it was gone.

And then, when she heard voices, she hurried to her own car and left, too.

It was late that night before she allowed herself to think about it. It was a coping mechanism she'd developed that was conducive to productivity but a nightmare for sleep. She could do everything she needed to do and ignore her thoughts, her emotions, but the minute she got into bed she'd think about it all.

It meant that she'd got a lot done after the end of her engagement. It also meant that she'd had too little sleep to be able to function in those first few months. She'd been on leave at first—had gone on her honeymoon alone, forced herself to enjoy it, or at least pretend to—and had returned more tired than when she'd gone an entire year without a single break.

She'd tried to keep doing her job, but the words had swum in front of her face, and the copy she'd turned in had been so riddled with errors her manager had suggested she take the rest of her leave days to try and pull herself together.

It had hurt her pride, that request. It had also caused her to realise the pride she'd thought she'd lost after being jilted was still there, alive and kicking. It had spurred her to the animal shelter the next day, and prompted her to ask for their least sought-after cat.

When they'd shown her Zorro—and told her how he'd been abused as a kitten—she'd fallen in love immediately.

He was the ugliest cat she'd ever seen, but when he'd rested his steady gaze on her she'd seen something there she didn't think anyone else had. Feeling a pull to that—feeling it resonate within herself—she'd adopted him.

And from the moment she'd brought Zorro home she'd felt better. She'd been able to go back to work the next week, and had worked her butt off to make sure her team knew she wouldn't be making the same mistakes.

It hadn't mattered that she'd still cried at night sometimes. It hadn't mattered that there had still been days when she'd felt as if she were a collection of puzzle pieces unable to fit together again. The only thing that had mattered was that the world saw her as whole. And if the world thought she was, maybe she'd believe it, too.

It had worked for the most part. Until this stupid wedding had come along—until it had brought Noah back and she had been forced to face just how incomplete she was. She didn't need the added complication of falling for Noah. Of being reminded of her feelings for him. Or that once upon a time she'd dreamt about a wedding for the two of them.

He'd hurt her when he'd left all those years ago. And, like most things in her life, she'd avoided thinking about it until she no longer could. Because she knew that if she acknowledged that Noah had hurt her she would have to acknowledge other things, too. That she'd put herself out there to *be* hurt. Because she'd had feelings for him.

And, as annoyed as she'd been at Noah for entertaining her brother's protectiveness back then, she knew that Jaden's feelings had affected the way she'd felt about the situation, too. She hadn't been able to imagine unsettling their relationship for something that would go nowhere. And, based on the way both she and Noah had responded to one another seven years ago, she hadn't seen it going anywhere.

But she could now. And the events of that night—his support, their arguments, the revelations, the kissing—told her she was right. Except that she wasn't sure she *wanted* it to go anywhere. Because if she did she'd have to face her very real fear: that she didn't deserve him.

Noah had known the lunch with his father was going to be awkward and long before he'd seen his father giggling with a woman half his age. But not that long before, he thought. In fact, the exact moment had been when his father had caught his eye as he'd been trying to get Ava's attention during the rehearsal dinner. Kirk had just raised a brow at him, but it had been enough.

So Noah wasn't too surprised at the silence that reigned during most of their lunch.

'Are you looking forward to the wedding?' his father asked, after their waiter had brought their starters and their conversation still hadn't consisted of much other than 'hello'.

'For Jaden's sake, yes.'

'But not for your own?'

He forked a crumbed mushroom with more force than necessary. 'Do people *ever* look forward to other people's weddings for their own sake?'

His father didn't reply, and Noah realised that was why silence was better. Everything was a minefield. An innocuous question about the wedding could lead down a very dark path. Noah had almost asked his father if *he* was looking forward to the wedding for his own sake. It *was* a decent place to pick up women, after all.

He popped another mushroom into his mouth and forced himself to chew. He didn't like the tone of the voice in his head. It sounded just like the part of him that still blamed his father, though he knew it wasn't fair.

'Ava tells me the two of you have struck up a friendship since I've been gone,' he said.

Oh, yes, because that *question won't explode in your face.*

'Yes.' Kirk's face softened. 'She's sweet. Didn't deserve the mess of last year.'

His father picked up his beer and took a long drag from it before shaking his head.

'I'll never forget the look on her face when that man walked out—'

'You were there?'

'Yes.' Kirk frowned. 'I thought you knew that?'

'I didn't realise your friendship had secured you an invitation to the wedding.'

'I was more her parents' guest than hers,' Kirk told him. 'We're friends, just like you and Jaden are. Though I think Ava was happy I was there.'

He chose not to reply to that, his mood too dark for him to trust what he might have said. Instead, he took a deep breath. And then he asked, 'Why didn't you tell me Ava was getting married?'

'Would you have wanted to know?'

'What kind of a question is *that*?'

'The kind a father asks when he knows that his son ignored his own invitation to said wedding.'

'That wasn't because I didn't want to know.' Noah clenched his jaw. 'I didn't get it.'

'Why not?'

'I—' He took a sip of water. 'I blocked her email address.'

'Why?'

'Because—' He shook his head. 'It's complicated.'

'Well, you'd better *un*complicate it, son. Ava's been through enough without you messing with her head.'

Noah stared at his father. 'You know *I'm* your son, right? You're not supposed to choose a random woman—' He broke off with a hiss. 'I'm sorry. I didn't mean that.'

'You probably did. And we'll get to that.' Kirk ate some of his salad before continuing. 'But in terms of Ava… You and I both know she's not "a random woman".'

Chastised—and more than a little jolted by his father's perceptiveness—he nodded.

'And I don't agree that my warning you against messing with her is choosing her over you. Especially since something tells me you're probably messed up about this, too.' He paused. 'So, if your plans don't involve you staying here long enough to clean up any mess you've made, you shouldn't be out swimming with her at midnight.'

He couldn't argue with that. Besides, Kirk had just given Noah the perfect segue into telling him why he'd arranged this lunch in the first place.

'I'll be here,' he said slowly. 'I'm moving back home.'

His father blinked. 'Back home?'

'Yeah.' He rubbed a hand over the back of his neck. 'I'm taking a break from photography for a while. At least, unofficially.'

'Are you moving back or are you taking a break?' His father's voice was stern. 'Those are two different things.'

They were, but he was trying to find a diplomatic way of telling his father about his plans. Now he thought being honest might be easier.

'I'm moving back, Dad. Permanently. And I'm taking a break from photography while I figure out what I want to do while I'm here.'

His father nodded slowly. 'Why?' he asked after a moment.

'I've missed you.'

Kirk reached out and squeezed Noah's hand. 'I've missed you, too. And you know I'd love to have you home again. But you left for a reason. What's changed?'

'Me.' He'd answered without thinking and now he realised it was the truth. 'And—I hope—us.'

Kirk stared at him for a moment, and then nodded. 'Let's start with us.' He paused. 'How about you tell me why seeing me with that woman last night upset you?'

CHAPTER SEVENTEEN

'TORTURE,' AVA SAID, unashamed of how miserable she sounded. 'It's bad enough that I have to do all this wedding stuff at Christmas, but now there are unexpected little meetings like this? To do what? Fold boxes for Christmas cookies? You're torturing me, Jaden.'

Jaden grimaced. 'If I had a choice, none of us would be folding any boxes.' He paused. 'I *am* sorry that this is at Christmas, though.'

She sighed. 'No, you're just sorry that it's *this* Christmas.'

She'd arrived at Jaden's house early, so that she could scold him privately for all the things Leela had been demanding in the last week. After all, she could hardly complain to the bride. But she knew that part of her motivation was also because she was still annoyed at him for his overprotectiveness of her with Noah.

Which she couldn't talk to him about directly. Because that was *not* a conversation she needed to have.

She walked to the fridge, looked longingly at the wine, but dismissed the thought instantly. She didn't need any more reason to loosen her tongue. Instead, she took out a soft drink can.

'Would it have been better at any other Christmas?'

Ava took a sip of her drink and turned to her brother. It was the first time they'd got anywhere close to discussing what had happened the year before. Or how his wedding might be affecting her.

'I think so. Time always makes things easier.'

Jaden nodded. 'You probably hate me for all this.'

'I don't hate you. I'm annoyed, yes. But not at you. At myself for…for the entire mess.'

She didn't pull away from him when he walked over and put an arm around her waist, resting her head on his shoulder instead.

'I didn't ever think it would go bad. Now, after everything, I'm annoyed that it was Christmas and that a holiday I used to love has been tainted in this way. And I… I blame myself for all of it.'

Jaden's face tightened, and he pulled her into a hug. She let herself be comforted by him—knowing it would be the only time she'd allow it—before she pulled away and took a step back.

'Now, let's just get through the box-folding and whatever other delights Leela has in store for us before the wedding, shall we?'

He smiled at her, but she thought she saw something on his face that looked almost reckless.

A moment later it was gone, and then the doorbell rang and Ava pushed it out of her head. It wouldn't benefit her, so what was the point in thinking about it? Besides, she had enough to think about now that she'd said something to Jaden about how she felt. And then there was Noah, whom she hadn't seen or spoken to since the rehearsal dinner the week before.

She greeted Leela and Tiff, who had arrived at the same time, but didn't move to hug her future sister-in-law as she should have because she had no desire to hug Tiff.

Not that she had anything against the woman. She just—

No, she did have something against the woman.

Tiff had had Noah's heart once. And she'd stomped on it. Ava was pretty sure that was part of what he'd alluded to last week. But she was a civil person—most days—and she could be an adult.

*An adult who won't hug a woman because of her past
with the man you—*

If Ava had ever experienced stopping her thoughts in
their tracks, it was in that moment, when that very annoying
voice in her head was taking liberties with the truth. *Liberties.* Because the actual truth was too terrifying to consider.

It tested her commitment to civility, so that when Noah
and Ken arrived she only nodded at them, and simmered in
her anger as she watched Tiff hug Noah.

'Well, everyone, thank you for coming on such short notice,' Leela said once everyone was settled with a drink. 'I
know we've been putting you through the wringer with this
wedding, but we really appreciate your help and support.
So tonight—'

'So tonight, as a thank-you,' Jaden interrupted, ignoring
the surprise on Leela's face, 'we're going to be taking you all
to the Christmas carnival at the high school down the road.'

Ava couldn't help the chuckle that left her lips at this announcement. Jaden shot her a look—*I'm doing this for you.
Please don't get me into any more trouble*—and she turned
it into a cough before gleefully clasping her hands together.

'This is the absolute *best* news you could have given us,
Jaden!' she said.

Again with the acting, Ava thought. But this time it was
for a much nobler cause than when she'd been lying for her
cat. Or teasing Noah.

She was saving her brother's future marriage.

'I can't believe you and Leela thought of thanking us in
such a considerate way. By taking us to the carnival you and
I used to go to every year at Christmas!'

Now she stood to hug both Leela and Jaden. When she got
to her brother, she whispered, 'Thank you,' and then stood
back and did a quick jump. 'This is *wonderful*!'

Leela gave her an uneasy smile. 'You're welcome.'

'Tricking us into believing we needed to fold boxes,' Noah
added, smirking when Ava looked at him and realised that

Jaden had given *him* a look, too. 'You're sneaky, future Mr and Mrs Jaden Keller. But we love you anyway.'

'Yes, well,' Leela said, her smile fading somewhat. 'We should probably get to it, then.'

'On a scale of one to ten, what are the chances Leela is going to castrate Jaden tonight?'

'One,' Ava said immediately. 'She wants a big family. She wouldn't risk it. However, I can't say the same for his limbs.'

Noah chuckled, more from relief that she'd answered than from what she'd said. He hadn't heard from her all week, though he knew that was because they'd been busy. She was still working, and he'd been helping Jaden with the wedding, and editing some pictures he'd taken before he'd come back home.

But he wasn't sure that that was it. He hadn't spoken to her since he'd acted like an ass—and revealed why in his little outburst—the night of the rehearsal dinner. He'd told himself to call her, but that had required a courage he hadn't conjured up yet. He'd also spent a lot of his energy trying to process the conversation he'd had with his father that day at lunch.

All of which were, of course, excuses.

'I think you deserve some points for your acting back there.'

'You know, I'm not even going to argue that that's against the rules. I accept.'

'Firstly, of course you do. Secondly, it's not against the rules. I'm fairly certain you orchestrated this in defence of yourself, somehow.'

She smirked. 'Not orchestrated. Just told my brother that this hasn't been the best time for me. His guilt did the rest.'

'Fifty points,' he said, pride surging inside him. Not only because she'd been honest with her brother, but because Jaden had actually done something about it. Their talk must have helped.

'You know this puts me ahead now, right?' she said.

'One-thirty for you, one-twenty for me?' When she lifted

her brows, he shrugged. 'I've been keeping track, same as you.'

They were walking behind the rest of the group. Jaden and Leela were far in the front—arguing, no doubt. When they all reached the line to enter the carnival, things went eerily silent. And then Tiff turned around and began asking Noah about his travels.

He could feel Ava stiffen next to him, and his annoyance at his ex trying to make conversation with him—*flirting* with him—was kidnapped by another emotion: satisfaction. Ava was *jealous*.

He immediately took a step back so that Ava was between him and Tiff, and deliberately included her in the conversation. Though it would have been worth it based solely on the fact that Ava relaxed as soon as he did so, it also managed to annoy Tiff. As soon as they got inside the carnival, she and Ken went their own way.

'Should I ask?' Jaden said, looking pointedly at Tiff's back.

'You could,' Noah replied, 'but I don't think it's going to get you any bonus points with your fiancée.'

Jaden glanced back to Leela with a grimace. She was at the bar, and when she turned they saw she'd ordered a large beer. Which she then downed.

'Yeah, she's not happy about this.'

'Why would she be?' Ava asked. 'You *knew* this wasn't going to go well for you. With her, I mean. You have no idea what it means to me.'

She stood on her tiptoes and kissed Jaden's cheek, and the affection and gratitude in her action did something to Noah's insides.

He and his father had never been overly affectionate with one another. They'd showed their love through spending time together. Doing things together. Which explained why, when Noah had told Kirk he was moving back home, his father's reaction hadn't been what he'd hoped for.

But he knew he couldn't have expected no consequences

for leaving. He'd found that out the hard way with Ava. And now he'd found it out with his father. But they were dealing with it. Just as they were dealing with the aftermath of their first real conversation about how his mother's actions had affected them. And how his father's subsequent relationships had affected Noah.

Lunch had been a real hoot.

'I know I should have warned her,' Jaden was saying, 'but it was a spontaneous decision.'

'Clearly,' Noah commented. 'Though not a bad one.'

'Tell that to my future wife.'

'What you *can* tell your future wife,' Ava said, 'is that you're going to fold all those boxes by yourself in apology. And then you can drop them at my house tomorrow and I'll fold them for you.'

Jaden brightened, but then frowned. 'You have work until Friday, Ava. You can't fold a hundred and thirty boxes by yourself.'

'The office is quiet this time of year,' Ava replied easily, though Noah could tell that wasn't true. 'Besides, I can sleep after the wedding. And unless you want to fold those boxes yourself, so that you can a) make sure there *is* a wedding, and b) get your wife to sleep in the same bed with you afterwards— or before—you'll take me up on the offer.'

'I won't argue with that.' He kissed Ava on the forehead. 'Now—damage control.'

'Don't let her get too drunk!' Ava called after him, and Jaden glared at her when Leela looked over.

'You're enjoying this, aren't you?' Noah asked.

'The fact that I'm no longer going to have to pretend to be happy while folding boxes or the fact that we're here?'

'I was talking about how you're treating Jade, but, yeah, I guess the other two reasons work.'

She angled her head. 'I'm not going to lie and say I'm not enjoying how this is turning out for Jaden. But I feel like he deserves some of it—and that it's about time.' She shrugged. 'I'm only human.'

Noah smirked. 'Aren't we all?'

They began walking together, and he couldn't help but think what a perfect date it would have been under other circumstances. The carnival rides lit up the entire rugby field of the high school, and the Christmas theme meant that there were assorted Christmas characters running around. There were a couple of elves, a couple of reindeer, and all the stalls had workers wearing red Christmas hats.

It was ideal for someone who loved Christmas. For someone like Ava. But he needed to remember it *wasn't* a date. And that the only reason Jaden wasn't walking with them was because he had his fight with Leela to worry about.

So he'd use this opportunity of being alone with Ava constructively, and take his father's advice: he'd face the consequences of what had happened.

'Listen, about the night of the rehearsal dinner—'

'No,' she interrupted him.

'What?'

'My brother has put his relationship on the line to give me tonight.'

'I think that might be an exaggeration.'

'I don't,' she said solemnly, but her eyes twinkled. 'I'm not going to waste his sacrifice by talking about *that*. In fact, I'm sorely tempted to go find Tiff, just so that we can play the game again and I can beat you.'

'Now, we *both* know that's an exaggeration,' he said with a smirk.

'Yeah, you're probably right.' She tilted her head. 'Doesn't mean we can't still earn points, though.'

'How are you thinking of cheating now?'

'Not cheating,' she said haughtily. 'A bonus round, if you will.'

'I will.'

'You don't even know the terms.'

'Doesn't matter. I'm still going to win.'

'Ha! Well, now I'm tempted to tell you that you have to

enter the carnival pageant.' Her eyes widened. 'Actually, that's been my plan all along.'

'Over my dead body.'

She sighed. 'I suppose you're right. There's no way you could enter and win it, thus winning the competition between us, too.'

He narrowed his eyes. 'The point of this competition is that we distract each other from the wedding.'

'And we can still do that.' She lifted her shoulders. 'Let's compromise, then, and say you'll win five hundred points if you enter the competition for at least one round.'

'What if I get through to the next round?'

'You'll get another hundred points. And so on. And so forth.'

After considering, he said, 'Fine. But you have to enter, too.'

She laughed. 'Oh, bring it *on*, Giles.'

CHAPTER EIGHTEEN

AVA WOULD READILY admit that entering a pageant because of a dare wasn't the smartest thing she'd ever done. But it wasn't the stupidest thing she'd done either. Not when her wedding, staying over at Noah's place and making out with Noah—numerous times—were all contenders for that title.

And certainly not when she added falling for Noah into the race.

Hell, entering the stupid pageant didn't even make the top ten.

As she went through the process of entering the competition it became clear which of those things *was* winning that title. Why else would she be challenging Noah to a competition? To enter the *pageant*? Why else would she be so determined to distract herself from that feeling in her stomach that told her how fast she was falling?

So she would enter the pageant. Even though she hated the thought of going up there and having people ogle her. Even though her simple white dress couldn't compare to the beautifully patterned and coloured dresses of the women around her.

When she learnt that the women's pageant took place before the men's pageant, she told herself there was no point in complaining about it. *She'd* done this. And, regardless of how unsteady all of this—the pageant, her feelings—made her, she'd put on a show for Noah *and* the entire carnival.

She might as well.

'Contestant number seventeen—Ava Keller!'

Ava blew out a breath and then walked the length of the catwalk—shoulders back, legs slanting over each other, channelling the seven-year-old Ava who'd practised for this moment all the time. She heard cheering as she posed—from more than one person—and looked into the crowd to find the entire wedding party waving at her.

When her eyes landed on Noah's he gave her a wink and she narrowed her eyes, determined to find some way to get him back.

The only way she could think of to do it was to win the stupid pageant.

'I'm not sure how you convinced her to do this, but I am happy to pay you for it.'

Noah smirked, but it was more an act than anything else. He'd had no intention of having Jaden witness his humiliation, let alone Tiff and the others. But Jaden had found him, and had asked about Ava, and he hadn't been able to lie.

But now, seeing the look on Ava's face, he wished he had.

'Has she ever done anything like this before?' Leela asked.

She seemed to be better now—presumably because Jaden had told her he'd take care of the boxes.

Jaden shook his head. 'She didn't even want to take part in her school concerts.' His smile widened. 'I'm going to record this for posterity.'

He took out his phone, took a few pictures of Ava posing, and then chuckled to himself. 'Gold!'

They watched as she walked down the runway—pretty professionally, Noah thought, though he wasn't sure he was qualified to make that evaluation—and then Jaden asked, 'How *did* you manage to convince her to do this?'

'A bet.'

'A bet?' Leela repeated. 'She's doing this because of a *bet*?'

'Yeah. I mean, you know how she is.'

He hoped they did. Because he wasn't quite sure what he was talking about.

'It must have been some bet, man,' Jaden said with a quirked brow, his eyes sharp.

'Yeah. She and I have actually both entered tonight. Whoever gets furthest in the competition has to…' He paused, and then said the first thing that came into his mind 'Has to do a solo dance at your wedding.'

There was a long pause before Leela said, 'You mean *after* the formalities, when the dance floor is actually being used?'

'Of course,' he said immediately. 'It won't affect your wedding at all.'

'Well…' Jaden said after a moment. 'You'd better hope she wins. I've seen you dance.'

He pulled a face at Jaden, but his insides loosened in relief.

'I'm actually supposed to go out there and *speak* now?' Ava asked the man who'd brought her the bad news. 'I thought the extent of this was walking around and letting people judge me?'

'That's not how pageants work, ma'am.' He frowned. 'Didn't they tell you you'd have to speak when you entered?'

I wasn't paying attention.

'I don't think so, no.'

'Well, we have a pageant every night at the carnival to choose a carnival king and queen for that day. It isn't anything too demanding. You just have a couple of pictures taken with the crown,' he said, sounding almost bored. 'But the actual competition is judged on how much you entertain the crowd. You just go out there and introduce yourself. If they like you, you make it into the next round. That's a group dance—we teach you when you're out there, and it's more about having fun than anything else—and then in the final round you answer some questions. Got it?'

'Got it,' she said, but she felt dazed. All she could think about was that her fate in the stupid pageant was based on people *liking* her. 'I'm also pulling out.'

'What?'

'I'm sorry. I can't entertain people.' She gave the microphone back to him and stepped away. 'Trust me, you don't want me out there.'

She didn't give him a chance to reply, and instead took a route back to her car where she knew no one would see her.

She sat there for a moment, breathing hard and fast, and then she drove the short distance back to Jaden's house. She used her spare key to get in, scribbled a note for him, and then transferred the unmade boxes to the car.

And then she went home, messaged Noah that she was okay—and Jaden, too, for good measure—and switched off her phone. And cuddled with her cat.

'She's pulled out.'

Everyone in their small group looked at Noah, but Jaden responded first. 'What do you mean, she's pulled out?'

'I mean she just sent me a message saying that I've won the bet and she's gone home because she isn't feeling well.'

Jaden took out his phone, blew out a breath. 'She sent me a message, too. But mine just says that she isn't feeling well so she's left. I'll call her.'

Noah let him do that, but he knew Ava wouldn't answer the phone. She wasn't the type to just run away. And she hadn't backed out because she wasn't feeling well. Something was wrong.

'Her phone's off. Maybe I should go see if she's okay?'

'She's fine,' Tiff said. 'I'm sure it's just stage fright. You don't have to spoil our evening because of her.'

'She's my sister,' Jaden said in a warning tone.

'Tiff's right, though.' Noah forced himself to say the words. 'I'm sure she's fine.'

'See?' Tiff said brightly, as if Noah's agreement somehow absolved her of any pettiness that had been in her answer. 'I told you.'

'I think I'll be off, too, though,' Noah said, trying hard not to clench his teeth. 'Early start tomorrow.'

'We literally just got here,' Tiff protested. 'Besides, we haven't had a chance to speak yet. We could—'

'No, thank you,' he interrupted. 'I'm happy to be in this wedding with you because of Jaden and Leela, but that is the only reason we're seeing each other now. If I had my way I would never have had to see you again after what happened. I'll see you all later.'

He'd almost reached the exit before Jaden caught up with him.

'That was...*intense*.'

'Yeah, sorry.' Noah exhaled. 'I just don't understand why she keeps trying to talk with me.'

'Because she's a human being who regrets what she did when she was just a kid.'

'She's told you that?'

'Yeah.' He grimaced. 'We've been friends for a while now. I didn't want to tell you—'

'Because you didn't want to upset me.' Jaden nodded. He blew out another breath. 'Look, I get that. And I'll apologise for embarrassing her, but I don't regret saying what I said.'

'You don't want to talk to her? You don't want closure?'

'I don't *need* closure. Not from her. Maybe after what she did—' He broke off, shook his head. 'I wasn't in love with her. Or I was, but it wasn't... I don't know. Complete.'

Jaden didn't reply for a moment. Then, 'Is it complete now?'

He didn't have to say that he was talking about Ava.

'I—' Noah cleared his throat. Stood taller. 'I think so.'

'You'd better know what you're doing.'

I have no idea. 'I do.'

'Be sure,' Jaden warned, his lips stiff, as though saying the words cost him something. 'She's been through enough.' He gritted his teeth. 'And I've made it worse.'

'She's already forgiven you,' Noah replied after a beat. 'She wouldn't be doing any of this if she hadn't.'

'Which makes me feel worse.' Jaden rubbed a hand over his face. 'Please, Noah, don't make me have to punch you. I have a lot of repressed anger that she didn't let me take out on her ex.'

'Understood.'

'And don't make me regret that you're back.'

His mouth curved. 'Can't guarantee that.'

Jaden's lips curved, too, though just a little. 'I guess it wouldn't be fair to ask. Not when I regretted your existence long before you even left.'

Noah laughed.

When the doorbell rang, Ava ignored it and snuggled closer to Zorro. Her cat was in one of his rare affectionate moods and was allowing her to put her arms around him. Not tightly enough to squeeze him, but enough to make the throbbing in her chest ease. She wasn't going to answer the door and mess that up.

But soon the ringing of the doorbell turned into a persistent knocking. And when the knocking became a pounding, Ava sighed and took a slow walk to the front door.

'What?' she said the moment she opened it.

Her heart swelled when she saw Noah, but then she remembered she could never be with him and it deflated almost as quickly.

'I could ask you the same thing,' he said, pushing past her into the house. 'Except I'd add "the hell" to the "what" to get my meaning across more clearly.'

She closed the door. 'Why don't you just say "what the hell?" then? It would sound a lot better than what you just said.'

'Fine. What the hell, Ava?'

'Actually, maybe it *was* better the other way,' she said, and lowered herself onto her couch. 'I could have just pretended I didn't know what you meant and sent you on your way.'

'Ava,' he said, his voice soft now. 'What's wrong?'

'Nothing. Fine,' she said when he gave her a look. 'Nothing that I have the energy to tell you about.'

'What happened at the carnival?'

'I told you, I don't have the energy to talk about—'

'Please.'

His tone had gone from soft to insistent, but it was the concern in that insistency that had her eyes filling.

She took a deep breath, and then stood up when it didn't make her feel any better. 'Tea?'

'No, thank you.' He paused. 'And you don't want tea either, Ava. You just want the distraction.'

'I *need* the distraction,' she said, and went to the kitchen before he had the chance to reply.

He didn't say anything as she made the tea, and the silence felt awkward. But he was there, she thought. And she took a moment to figure out how that made her feel.

It had been a long time since she'd had a rough night and someone had been there for her. She usually dealt with those nights alone, and once she was feeling stronger she'd visit Kirk. Or her brother, or her parents.

But having Noah there filled something inside her. And she'd forgotten what that felt like. Not to have to pretend. To want—despite how much she denied it—to talk. And not just to anyone—to *Noah*. It had always been Noah.

Damn it.

She hung her head as the kettle sounded, and could barely bring it up again so she could finish making her tea. She stirred the liquid for much longer than it required, and when she left the kitchen saw that Noah now sat on the seat she'd vacated, watching her.

Unwilling to think about whether he'd seen her have that moment in the kitchen, she set the tea down, sat and curled her feet under her body, and then waited for him to speak.

'I know what you're doing,' he said.

'Yeah? What?'

Please tell me because I have no idea.

'You're waiting for me to ask you what's wrong again.'

Her lips curved. 'You've always known me better than I've ever given you credit for.'

'Maybe not always,' he corrected her with a small smile.

'I think I've lost some of my ability since I left.' He paused. 'Help me to regain it.'

She looked down at her hands, watched as her fingers traced the lines of her palms as if she weren't the one controlling their movement.

'I don't know what went wrong. Or when.' Her fingers stilled, and then began to move again. 'I think I was too young when I met him. He was, too. We had ideas about who we wanted to marry and who we wanted to be, but when push came to shove neither of us were those people. Not for ourselves. Not for each other.'

'Ava,' he said slowly, on an exhalation of breath. 'Your life for the past seven years wasn't only tied to him. You've graduated since I last saw you. You have a successful career. Your family loves and supports you.'

'Those things aren't who I am. They're what I've achieved. And my family—' She exhaled sharply. 'They don't see the version of me who failed at my relationship. I mean, now they do, because I'm forcing them to. Because my quirky personality has turned surlier than usual and they have to tiptoe around me.'

'No one is tiptoeing around you.'

'*Everyone* is tiptoeing around me.' She threaded her fingers together. 'Jaden didn't speak to me about proposing to Leela until after he did it. And then, when they announced their engagement, they both glanced at me, checking to see how I would react. The pressure of that...' She shook her head. 'Trust me, I've been here this past year. I *know* how my family's behaviour towards me has changed.'

'And what about *your* behaviour?' he asked after a moment. 'I'm not talking about the surliness—we knew about that before, and we loved you for it. I'm talking about the fact that you've turned into this...this *unsure* person. That you don't trust yourself. That isn't you. You used to be the most self-assured person I knew.'

'Oh, no, that was just pretending. I was much too in love with you to show you I wasn't completely confident in myself.'

* * *

'You were…you were *in love* with me?'

Her mouth curved into a smile he'd never seen before. Shy, insecure, seductive. How could that even be a combination? he wondered. Or was that description just an indication that he was totally enthralled?

'Don't pretend you didn't know.'

'I *didn't* know. Trust me, if I'd known—'

'You would have what?' she interrupted. 'Kissed me? Freaked out? Moved away? Stayed away for the past seven years?'

'That's not fair.'

'But it's not untrue.'

'I didn't leave because of what happened between us.'

'Not entirely, no. But it was factored into your decision.'

She leaned forward, picked up her cup of tea. Gripped it between her hands. Why did it feel as if she was gripping his heart there, too?

'Though, of course, you won't give yourself the chance to think about the real reasons you left.'

'I *have* thought about them.'

'Have you, though?' She tilted her head. 'After everything that's happened over the last weeks?'

He narrowed his eyes, wondering what he'd done to put her in this mood. And then he remembered that she'd been in the mood before he'd got there, and because he'd been determined to check whether she was okay he'd put *himself* in this position now.

But that didn't mean he deserved this line of questioning. He didn't need to delve into his motivations for leaving— or his motivations for the other decisions he'd made in his life—any more than he already had.

Because for the past two weeks he'd done nothing *but* that. Because of her.

She'd reminded him that his father was human. Imperfect and human. Noah hadn't seen that before he'd left. Then, he'd wanted to leave because he hadn't wanted to see his father heartbroken any more. He hadn't wanted to witness the pattern of it. Especially after his relationship with Tiff had shocked him into realising he might repeat that pattern, too.

But now Ava's words made him consider something else. Something that fitted now that he saw how his mother's cheating had affected him. He'd gone from being heartbroken over a cheating girlfriend to kissing Ava and feeling something for her within weeks.

He'd seen the pattern take root. He'd seen himself becoming his father. Being cheated on and then quickly moving from one relationship to the next. It had screwed with him. He could see that now. And it had forced him into ignoring the fact that what had happened with Ava hadn't been the same as his father's relationships.

But he'd been scared. The cheating and his feelings for Ava and everything to do with his mother and father had somehow meshed and he'd been *terrified*. Terrified of what Ava had made him want.

A relationship. A future. Things he hadn't thought he could commit to. Things he'd been scared to face. And so he'd run.

'How did you know?' he asked her quietly.

'Because we're something,' she said simply. 'And you told me about how your father's choices made you feel.' She paused. 'And about your mother.'

Noah swallowed and wished he'd accepted the tea so that he'd have something to distract himself with. As he'd known she would, she let the silence extend. She was waiting for him to speak.

'The thing with Tiff... It shocked me.'

'Why?'

'Because I fell in love. Quickly. Stupidly. I ignored logic and I fell in love.'

'It happens to all of us.'

'But it shouldn't have happened to *me*. Not after what I'd seen with my father—' He cut himself off. Sighed. 'My father's relationships have bothered me my entire life. Because of their instability, yes, but also because I hated seeing my father hurt. That's one side of it.'

He lifted a hand, and then dropped it before he could do anything with it.

'The other side of it is I knew my mother had hurt him. And by doing that she hurt me with what she did, too—even though I only realised the truth of it after she died.'

He leaned forward, ran a hand through his hair.

'What happened with Tiff was like a perfect storm of... of *everything*.'

'The relationship moved fast, like your father's relationships. And then the cheating—'

'And you,' he interrupted, before he lost his nerve. 'Our kiss happened so quickly after Tiff—'

'And you thought you were turning into your father?'

He gave a curt nod. 'So I left.'

A long pause followed his words. 'You ran from it?' she asked softly.

He nodded again. 'And I called my *father* weak.'

'You're not weak. Neither of you are. You've both just had to deal with something tough.' She paused. 'But you can't run from it, Noah. It won't matter how far you go, or how hard you try to distract yourself. The fear, the pain... It stays with you.'

'Speaking from experience?'

'Yeah.' She lifted a shoulder. 'After I fell apart I tried to put myself back together again. But no matter how hard I tried, it didn't change the fact that some of the pieces had broken—had shattered—during the process. I'm still me—' she gave him a sad smile '—but there are some parts missing.'

'He stole them.'

She shook her head, and then she set the tea down and brought her knees up to her chest. Her position did something to him, and he was standing before he knew it, pushing her tea aside and sitting on the table opposite her.

'What is it? What are you not telling me?'

She shook her head again, and desperation—fear—made his tone insistent.

'Ava, I can't help you if I don't know.'

'You *do* know, Noah. I've told you—' She drew in a ragged breath. 'He didn't steal anything from me. He just saw what I couldn't—what I didn't before. That I'm...too much to be loved.'

CHAPTER NINETEEN

'YOU CAN'T BELIEVE THAT.'

His disbelieving tone soothed Ava's heart, but a louder, stronger voice soon sounded over it.

If you were lovable—if there wasn't anything wrong with you—why did Milo leave? And why didn't Noah stay?

'I'm not upset about it,' she said, lowering her legs and straightening her shoulders. She'd had enough of the self-pity. 'I'm glad I know. Now I don't have to set myself up for failure. I can adjust my expectations.'

She stood now, and tried to move away. When he did the same it brought their bodies close together. She didn't want to feel the spark being close to him always brought. She didn't want to be reminded of the expectations she'd once had for the two of them. The expectations she'd admitted to him and he'd brushed off.

'That's the worst thing I've ever heard.'

'It's the truth.' She forced herself to look him in the eyes. Accepted the quivering of her stomach as she did so.

'It's not the truth. You're not "too much". And, while we're at it, there's nothing wrong with you either. You're kind and sweet. I mean, it's under a couple of layers of other stuff,' he said when she opened her mouth. 'The surliness and the fire. But you wouldn't have agreed to be in Jaden's wedding if there wasn't something sweet and considerate inside you. You wouldn't have offered to fold these boxes—' he gestured to the cardboard she'd almost forgotten on the floor '—if you weren't a good sister.'

She didn't reply, lost in the longing for it to be as simple as he was making it out to be. But she wasn't the person he was describing. Or she *was*, but the balance was off. She was more surly than sweet. More blunt than kind.

She hated that those things came into her mind in the form of Milo's words. In the form of the expression on his face when he'd told her he didn't want to spend the rest of his life trying to avoid being snapped at. Or walking through it on eggshells because he was afraid of what she'd say.

'You don't believe me?' he asked.

'Because your perception is skewed. You…you care about me.'

'I do.' His voice was heavy with an emotion she didn't understand. 'Which is why you *should* believe me.'

'It's why I *don't* believe you. You're just like my parents. And, if I'm honest with myself, like Jaden, too. He gives me a hard time, but I know he loves me exactly as I am. And because of it he, my parents, and now you don't see me as someone who isn't perfect.'

He stared at her, and then laughed softly. 'You're not *perfect*, Ava.'

She frowned. 'Yeah, I know. I just said that.' But she hadn't expected him to agree.

'You *are* surly. And you're annoying. You needle me like no other woman I've met before. And your mouth is so sharp…' He lifted a hand, brushed his thumb over her lips as his other arm slid round her waist. 'And I wouldn't have wanted you so much if you were any different.'

And then he kissed her, and Ava's protests—her confusion— were engulfed by the emotions of that kiss.

His lips moved gently against hers, his tongue slipping between them. His hand moved from her waist up to her face, and it took her a moment to realise that he held her face in both his hands now. And that the embrace was as tender, as moving, as his kiss. She nearly wept.

Instead, she put her arms around his neck and told herself to fall into his light. She wished she'd put up her Christmas tree—wished she'd had the courage to celebrate the holiday she loved—so that the mental picture she'd always have of this moment would include Christmas. So that it would replace the broken picture she had of it now. Of Milo running from her. Of his face—ugly and twisted, and not the face of the man she knew—and his anger.

Determined to wipe it away, she pressed closer to Noah. And then she let her hands run over his body. The broad curves of his shoulders, the strength of his back. The slope between the bulge of his pecs, the valley between his abs. His body was the most extraordinary thing she'd ever touched, its lines and its curves a gift from heaven itself.

But the gift couldn't be for her. Even if he wanted to give it to her.

He felt the change in her and pulled back, hoping he hadn't crossed the line. But when he saw her face he realised that the line had been erased. No, that she was *about* to erase it. His heart jumped to his throat.

'You don't want this, Noah. Not really.'

Her breathless tone made the words all the more hurtful.

'You don't know what I want.'

'You don't either,' she said sadly. 'You think you want me because you want my body. But I can't—'

She broke off, shook her head. And then she cleared her throat and looked him dead in the eye.

Fire.

He was so in love with her.

'I can't give you my body without giving you more. And you don't want more.'

'Ava—'

'No, please, don't make this worse.' Despite the fire, her voice caught. But she didn't look away. 'Unless you're going to tell me that you're suddenly someone who wants to settle down. Who wants to stay in one place, buy a house—not as an investment, as a *home*—and raise kids, don't bother lying to me.'

'I didn't… I thought you didn't want that.'

'I was going to get married.'

He almost smiled at the roll of her eyes.

'Of *course* I want that.' She paused, and again her voice hitched slightly. 'Just because I think there's something wrong with me doesn't mean I believe I don't deserve that.'

'You do deserve it,' he said softly, urgently.

But he didn't say what he thought next.

Do I?

He'd spent all his life judging his father's choices. Blaming his father for his decisions. Ignoring the way Kirk had been affected by a cheating wife. Ignoring the way *he'd* been affected by it.

He'd used teenage heartbreak as an excuse to run away from it all. And now he was back. Older, and thoroughly chastised for being so unforgiving of his father's imperfections.

He'd make up for it now that he was back home. He and his father had already started at their lunch the other day. But he was less certain that he could move past the fear of relationships that seemed lodged inside him. And, though he wanted to with all his might, he was afraid to let go of the control. He was afraid to fall. To let himself be hurt.

If anyone could help him overcome the fear it would be Ava. He felt it in a deep part of himself that was only complete when he was with her. But she didn't deserve a man who was still figuring it out. And he didn't deserve the sweetness and the fire of her as he tried.

It wasn't that he didn't want more. It was that he couldn't give *her* more.

'I know I deserve it,' Ava said again after a moment. 'Which is why I'm going to ask you to leave.'

She shook her head when he opened his mouth and he stopped, unsure of what he would have said anyway.

So he left, and tried to figure out how he'd gone from avoiding relationships to wanting one so badly it hurt.

It was progress, she thought. Figuring out that she deserved to have the things she'd always wanted even though she wasn't perfect.

I wouldn't have wanted you so much if you were any different.

No, no, no. She was *not* going to spiral down that hole again. She'd spent days thinking about it. Nights. And it had had more of an effect on her than being jilted at the altar.

But now wasn't exactly the time to think about that. There must be some rule forbidding members of a wedding party from thinking about the possibility of the groom or bride being jilted. Especially on the day of the wedding.

Though there was no rule that said someone who *had* been jilted shouldn't be afraid of walking down an aisle again, even if they weren't getting married.

'Can you give me a moment alone?' Leela asked with a nervous smile, pressing a hand to her stomach.

Photographs had been taken, the groom and groomsmen were in place, and they were now only waiting for some of the guests to arrive before Leela and Jaden would make their vows.

'Yes, of course,' she said.

She and Tiff headed to the door, but Ava stopped as Leela called her back. She heard the door click behind her as she turned.

'This is probably not the best timing, but I wanted to tell you how sorry I am.'

Ava frowned. 'For what?'

'All of it. Forcing you to be a part of this.' She lifted a shoulder, offered a smile. 'You look gorgeous, though.'

Ava looked down at the navy blue lace dress and smiled back. 'Thank you. So do you. Though you don't need to hear that from me again.'

Leela's Cinderella-type wedding dress took up a significant amount of space in the room they'd got ready in, and Leela looked breathtaking in it.

'Thank you.'

'You're welcome.'

There was a pause.

'You didn't force me into this. I agreed. It was my choice.'

'I shouldn't have made you choose, though. I guess I got so swept up in wanting a Christmas wedding that I didn't give myself a chance to consider how much I could be hurting you. It wasn't until Jaden—' She broke off. 'I didn't tell him I was going to ask you to be a bridesmaid. I thought I'd surprise him because he loves you so much. He told me that I shouldn't have done it, and by then it was too late to take it back.'

'Thank you,' Ava said quietly. And felt the resentment she'd held for her brother—and for Leela—over the whole mess fade. 'I know I would have regretted letting Milo rob me of this moment if I hadn't agreed to it.' *Like he robbed me of so much else.* 'I'm glad you asked me. It's been hard, but it's been worth it.'

They smiled at each other, and then Leela let out a shaky breath. 'I'm so glad we're on the same page. I didn't want to enter my new family with the possibility of conflict lingering.'

Ava laughed. 'Oh, you're going to be a breath of fresh air for us. We don't talk about our issues,' she elaborated. 'In fact, I'm pretty sure if the roles were reversed Jaden would have carried this apology—and the admission—to the grave.'

'Oh, that'll change.' Leela winked at Ava. 'I have time.'

Ava left Leela alone then, joining Tiff outside.

'So,' Tiff said after a moment. 'You and Noah, huh?'

'No.' Ava frowned. Shook her head. 'No.'

'Yeah, you sound like you're telling the truth.' Tiff smirked when Ava looked over at her. 'Noah's father was… er…*entertaining* a friend of mine the night of the rehearsal dinner. At the dam, wasn't it?'

Hating that her skin was heating, Ava cleared her throat. 'Just a swim.'

'Sure.' There was a beat of silence. Then, 'I think part of the reason I did what I did was because I knew Noah didn't want me.'

'Oh, no. We don't have to talk about this.'

'I know.' Tiff smiled, and for the first time Ava thought it was genuine. 'But I guess I'm tired of being the bad guy. And of being jealous of you.'

'Bad guy—jealous? Of *me*?'

Tiff rolled her eyes. 'See, this is exactly what I'm talking about. The fact that you don't know how feisty and charming you are is *so* annoying. And then there's your face...' Tiff shook her head, but winked at her. 'Sickening.'

'I... I don't understand.'

'Noah never looked at me the way he looked at you, Ava. The way he *looks* at you.' Tiff's face tightened. 'I guess... I guess I was looking for someone to look at me that way. So I did something stupid—and I've done more, I promise you—and eventually I realised why. *Eventually*,' she said, tilting her head, 'meaning last week at the carnival.'

'I honestly don't know what to say.'

'So don't say anything.' Tiff shrugged. 'Or, no—do. Tell Noah I'm sorry. He'll believe it if it comes from you.'

And then they were being told the ceremony could start, and there was no more time to think about the bombshell Tiff had just dropped.

It was one of the worst things she'd ever done, walking down an aisle again. It didn't matter that it wasn't the aisle she'd walked down on her wedding day. It was just the *familiarity* of it. And the sympathy she felt coming from her side of the family.

It nearly caused her to stumble. But then she saw Kirk, and he nodded at her with a slight smile. And though her legs were still shaky she felt steadier.

And then her eyes met Noah's.

There was something on his face that made her want to

cry. But not because he was looking at her in pity. No, it was because he was looking at her as if he *saw* her. *Her.* The woman who'd grown up and taken chances. Who'd been bold enough to ask her brother's best friend to kiss her. Who'd eavesdropped on conversations. Who was fierce and honest and blunt.

He didn't look at her and see a failure. He didn't look at her and see what he needed to change.

I wouldn't have wanted you so much if you were any different.

And when her legs went wobbly this time, it had nothing to do with the fact that she'd walked down the aisle before. It was because she wanted to do it again. And this time she wanted to be walking towards Noah.

CHAPTER TWENTY

'I'M GOING TO regret this,' Noah said. 'I'm going to wake up every night for the rest of my life and regret this.'

'But hopefully this will mean you'll wake up every night next to Ava and you'll be able to entertain yourself!' Leela grinned when she saw Jaden's face. But mercifully—for all involved—she stopped talking.

'When did you become like this?' Jaden asked with a shake of his head. But he curved an arm around his wife's waist and nuzzled her neck.

'About four hours ago,' Leela said with a giggle. 'It came with the title of Mrs Keller.'

'Ooh, what else—'

'Please,' Noah begged. 'Don't make this worse than it already is.'

'Don't take your emotions over this stupid grand gesture out on us.'

'You need to talk me out of this.' He turned to Jaden. 'Tell me you don't want me to be with your sister. Tell me that I shouldn't do this and ruin your wedding.'

'I *don't* want you to be with my sister,' Jaden told him. 'But you can't ruin the wedding. Most of it's done, and I got what I wanted.'

He smiled at Leela, then turned back to Noah.

'Again, just so that it's clear: I don't want you to be with my sister. But…but you make her happy,' he said reluctantly. 'I've seen her smile more in the last two weeks than I have in the last year. Maybe even before that.' He paused. 'And since you've been back, I've also learnt more about how she's feeling than I have in the last year. So, you know...' Jaden shrugged.

It was as much approval as Noah was going to get, and it warmed his heart—before he remembered what he was planning on doing.

'That doesn't change the fact that Ava's going to hate it. I'm going to embarrass her. Just like at her own wedding.'

'You're right. There probably *is* a chance she's going to hate it. And that she'll be annoyed that she's being embarrassed in front of her family again.'

'Wow. Thanks.'

'There's also a chance that she might *not* be embarrassed,' Jaden continued. 'There's a chance that she might love it and accept that you're in love with her.'

He rolled his eyes and Noah laughed.

'Besides,' Leela said, 'maybe you need to balance the bad embarrassment with the good kind.'

'There's a *good* kind?'

'Well,' Jaden said as they got a signal from the band, 'you're about to find out.'

With unsteady legs Noah made his way towards the band. He was still pretty sure he was going to regret what he was about to do, but he wanted to show Ava that he was serious about what he was going to tell her.

He winced when the singer handed him the microphone and he remembered he wasn't going to *tell* her anything.

'Excuse me, everyone,' Noah said.

The entire crowd looked at him, but he soon found the face of the only person he really cared about.

'I have something to say, and I have the bride and groom's permission, so I'm not stealing anyone's thunder.'

He saw Ava glance at Jaden and Leela—Jaden nodded at his sister and Leela blew her a kiss—before she turned back to him with a frown.

What are you doing? she mouthed, but he only shook his head, and continued speaking into the microphone.

'You see, today's been a bit of a rough day for some of us here. Particularly for some of the people in the wedding party.' Ava's eyes widened, and she shook her head at him. 'And I'm not ashamed to admit that I'm one of them.'

He took a step off the platform where the band was playing and walked into the crowd. And then he took a deep breath, because he didn't think there would ever be anything more terrifying than confessing his feelings in front of over a hundred people.

'You see, for the longest time I was afraid of falling for anyone. I had commitment issues, and I had a lot of excuses as to why.'

He took his eyes off Ava for a moment to look for Tiff, and nodded at her. Then he found his father and gave him a small smile.

'The truth is, I was afraid of being hurt. And having feelings for someone—real, deep feelings—terrified me even more. So I ran.'

Now he looked back at Ava.

'But I'm tired of running. You make me want to stand still, Avalanche. You always have.'

With another breath he turned back to the band and nodded.

'And now I'm going to win *all* the points to prove it to you.'

The band began to play.

He was a terrible singer. He was a less terrible dancer. And all in all it made Noah's performance well worth the thousand points needed to win the game.

She bit her lip to keep from laughing as he belted out a note that had the whole room cringing, and then didn't bother when he did a little jiggle to accompany it. In that moment it didn't matter that she was fairly sure Noah had lost control.

It only mattered that she was laughing, and that for the first time in a year she didn't care that people were looking at her.

He walked towards her, taking her in his arms and giving her a twirl before bringing her up against him. The song ended, and his face crinkled into a smile, but she saw the nerves.

'A thousand points,' she told him breathlessly. 'You win fair and square.'

'Yeah?' His smile widened. 'That's great.'

'Oh, yes. *Especially* since the videographer got it for the wedding video.' She nodded over to the woman, who winked at them with a smile.

He groaned. 'I *knew* I was going to regret this.'

'You shouldn't,' she said, her heart hammering. 'It was—' She cut herself off, decision made. 'Why don't I show you?'

She pulled his head in for a kiss, and heard applause and cheers from her family. Having no desire to give them a show—other than the one they'd already had anyway—Ava pulled back almost immediately and angled her head in acknowledgment to the crowd.

Noah grinned at her, and then handed the microphone back to the singer of the band before taking her hand. 'Can we go somewhere to talk?'

'We probably should.'

And just like that she was brought out of the little bubble of joy she'd been in since he'd started speaking into that microphone.

It was still light outside, the sky soft with orange and yellow as the sun made its way to the horizon. It made the vineyard look soft, too—the vines, the abundance of grapes, the green hills and slopes in the background. Romantic. Beautiful. The perfect setting for a promise of for ever.

'Did you really like it?'

They were on the balcony overlooking the vineyard now, far enough away from the reception that they had privacy.

'I loved it.' She rested her forearms on the railing, let out a breath. 'Though I'm still trying to figure out why you'd do it.'

'You know why.' There was a pause. 'Hell, every single person in that venue knows why.'

'Yeah.'

She dipped her head and told herself that now wasn't the time to cry. But even the thought of crying made her want to cry. She hadn't trusted anyone enough to cry in front of them since she was a little girl. She didn't know how many times she'd cried in front of Noah since he'd been back.

Quick and fast. Tell him and then get out of here and cry in peace.

'Today's been interesting.'

'What makes you say that?'

She laughed quietly. 'No need for sarcasm.' She paused as he mirrored her position on the balcony. 'What I mean is that it was harder than I thought it would be. But then there were moments when it was easier, too.'

You're not making any sense.

She cleared her throat. 'It was hard going through a wedding again. Up until Jaden and Leela were pronounced husband and wife I held my breath. Because last year up until that moment things were going pretty well for me, too.'

'He did it just before you said your vows?'

'Yes.'

He swore.

Her lips curved. 'It gets easier thinking about it. Or maybe not thinking about it, but talking about it.' She angled her body towards him. 'Or maybe it's just easier with you.'

She reached out, took his hand.

'Which is why some of today was easy, too. You didn't look at me like I was broken. You saw *me*, and I can't... I can't tell you how much that means to me.' She cleared her throat when emotion clogged there. 'So when I felt over-whelmed—when I struggled to breathe and my throat closed, when the tightness in my chest made me feel like I was going to snap—I looked for you. And even when you weren't look-ing at me you made me feel better.'

His hand tightened on hers. 'What does that mean?'

'It means—' She let the air of her lungs slowly as she prepared to say the words. 'I think it means I love you. And not in the silly teenage way I used to, but—'

Her next words were stopped by his kiss, and selfishly she let herself have it. If only for a moment.

'I love you,' he said.

'I know.' She wrapped her arms around his waist, rested her head on his chest and squeezed her eyes shut. And then she pulled back and took a step away from him, lifting a hand when he moved to come closer. 'I know you *think* that.'

'I think—' He frowned. 'No, I *know* that. I embarrassed myself in front of an entire room full of people. I'm taking this risk even though—' he broke off. 'I haven't done any of this because I *think* I love you.'

'Okay,' she said slowly, 'maybe I didn't phrase that properly. I meant that…that what you feel for me is probably—'

'Love,' he interrupted flatly. 'I *love* you.'

'You *can't* love me, Noah. You can only love a whole person and I'm not… I'm not whole.'

'And yet here I am, offering you my love.'

'And your commitment?' she asked. 'Are you ready to commit to me, too?'

His expression tightened. 'Yes.'

She bit her lip. 'I don't want you to feel you have to say that.'

'No, that's not it.' The hand he had on the railing tightened. 'I'm…*scared*, Ava. I'm scared of being hurt. I didn't realise I could be until Tiff, after all the stuff with my parents—' He let out an unsteady breath. 'If you picked up hesitation it's because of that—not because I don't want to be committed to you. It's the same thing that happened the other night when you asked me about it.' He paused. 'I *want* to be in a relationship. I want to settle down, build a home, have a family. With *you*. Because you make me want it. Even though it still terrifies me, you make me want to risk it.'

A heady sensation passed through her, settling in her chest, and it took her a moment to realise it was hope.

'Why didn't you just tell me that the other night?'

'Because I thought you deserved more than me.'

His hands dropped to his sides and then he put them in his trouser pockets and stared out at the vineyard.

'I only realised my mom's cheating had affected me this deeply recently. I didn't—' He broke off, clenched his jaw. 'I want to give you everything you deserve, Ava. And I thought that because I'm still figuring things out I wouldn't be able to.'

'I think,' she said slowly, after a beat, 'that you've forgotten you told me I'm not perfect. And if I'm not perfect—and we both know I'm not—why would you think you had to be perfect for me?'

She could almost see him trying to formulate an answer, but he didn't respond and she bit back a smile.

'And since we're talking about it,' she continued, 'you said you had commitment issues earlier. I don't agree. I mean, you've had a relationship with the most difficult person I know—and I still question your taste for being friends with my brother—for most of your life. And you tried with your father, too. You didn't agree with him and yet you made sure to stay in touch. To see him every Christmas. You and I have had a pretty long relationship, too.' She let it linger. 'All of our relationships are forms of commitment. Not only the romantic ones.'

The features of his face relaxed slowly and the side of his mouth curved. 'I don't know how much of that is true. But I'd like to find out. With you. If you'll have me.'

'I want to. I want *you*.' She exhaled slowly. 'But I can barely look at myself in the mirror right now. All I see is... is a woman who was left at the altar.'

'So see yourself through my eyes.' He took a step closer, held her hands in his. 'See yourself through the eyes of a man who loves you.'

'I have.'

'He didn't love you, Ava. Not like I do.'

'I want—' She broke off and found herself struggling

against tears again. 'I want to believe you,' she said slowly, 'but it just feels like… *I* feel like… I can't,' she ended helplessly, when she couldn't formulate her thoughts, her emotions, coherently.

She wanted to say she didn't deserve him—but then he'd believe *he* didn't deserve *her*, and she knew that wasn't true.

So why was it so easy to believe it of herself?

'So all of this was for nothing, then?' he asked in a careful tone, letting go of her hands. 'Why try to convince me that I can be what you deserve—what you want—if you don't want me?'

'Of *course* I want you. I just—' Again she cut herself off. She couldn't explain it.

Silence stretched so far, so thinly between them that Ava wondered what would happen if it snapped. And then she watched as it did. When Noah ran a hand over his hair and walked back to the reception.

'I can't believe you agreed to this, Dad.' Noah's hand tightened on the steering wheel. 'You *know* how things ended between Ava and me and you still agreed to have Christmas with the Kellers. *And* you dragged me into your invitation.'

'You need to face it, Noah,' his father replied, just as he had before. 'You knew there was a chance this would happen, and you took that risk when you declared your love for your best friend's sister at his wedding.'

'Can you stop reminding me about that?'

'I've never been prouder,' his father said sombrely.

'So that's a no, then?'

Now Kirk grinned. 'Never.'

Noah grunted, and figured the only way he wouldn't rile himself up even more was if he kept quiet. He wasn't a glutton for punishment. He took no pleasure out of pain. And yet he'd agreed to attend the stupid Christmas party the Kellers were hosting, knowing it would be painful for him.

He'd returned to the reception at the wedding ready to put on the performance of his life. But when his feet had taken him directly to Jaden and Leela, and then to his father, and his mouth had told them that he was leaving, he'd realised he'd had his fill of performance for the day.

And so had Ava, it seemed, since Jaden had later told him—very sympathetically—she hadn't returned to the wedding either.

It had made things easier for them both, he'd realised when he'd thought about it. Because it would have seemed as if the two of them had escaped the wedding to be romantic. Which would have been his preferred ending to the day.

Instead he'd gone home feeling like a fool, and now he was being forced to see her again.

The Keller house was decorated as if the Wise Men themselves were coming to Christmas lunch. There was tinsel, stockings, Christmas elves, a giant, beautifully decorated Christmas tree, and a nativity scene. And outside on the porch—where he was informed they'd be eating—was a long table fully decked with red and green, along with the requisite Christmas crackers.

The lamb he and his father had brought had been taken out of his hands, a beer placed in them instead, and still he hadn't seen Ava. And of course he couldn't be the one to ask where she was.

'Surely it can't only be the four of us today?' Kirk asked, almost as if he'd heard Noah's thoughts.

'You're right,' Ruth Keller told him. 'Jaden and Leela are coming. They're picking up Ava on their way.'

'Why isn't she coming in her own car?' he heard himself ask, kicking himself as he did.

'Oh, I don't think she wanted to drive alone today,' Ruth told him kindly. 'This is difficult for her after last year. We've had to force her out of the house.'

'Oh.'

'You're surprised?' Ruth said after a moment. 'I'm sure that's because Ava's given you the impression that she's fine.'

'No, ma'am,' he said truthfully. 'She's never quite been able to do that with me.' He cleared his throat. 'I'm surprised because she's given me the impression that you and Uncle Sam aren't aware she's struggling.'

Ava's parents exchanged a look, and then Ruth said, 'Of course she has. That girl would eat her own limbs to make sure we're not in pain.' She sighed. 'I wish she would just be honest with us.'

'I think she thinks—' Noah hesitated, wondering if he was betraying Ava's confidence by telling them this. But then he saw the expression on Ruth's face and continued. 'She thinks it's *her* fault that the wedding was called off. And she doesn't want to tell you the truth about how it's been affecting her because she's afraid you'll think poorly of her.'

Ruth's face blanched; Sam's tightened. For a moment an awkward silence thrummed in the room. Then the doorbell rang—of course Ava would arrive *now*—which broke the tension.

'Thank you for telling us, Noah,' Ruth said quietly, nodding at Sam to get the door. 'And, for what it's worth, we think you and Ava would make a lovely couple.'

She got up then as well, and followed her husband inside.

'That's a hell of a thing you just did,' Kirk commented.

'Yeah. I just hope I didn't make things worse.'

'I don't think so.' There was a beat before Kirk continued, 'You know her better than anyone else does.'

Noah looked at his father with a frown, but there was no time to discuss it further. Jaden and Leela walked in first—looking appropriately loved up—followed by Ava.

Concern immediately flared inside of him at the sight of her pale face. At her strained expression. When she saw him her eyes lit, before going dim again. And when she gave him a slight nod and kissed his father on the cheek, Noah thought he heard his heart shatter in his chest.

One day Christmas would feel like it used to.

At least that was what she told herself.

There wouldn't be tension as everyone avoided talking about the elephant in the room. Last year it had been her wedding; this year it was her and Noah. There wouldn't be furtive glances at her. Those expressions of concern, of curiosity. And, in Noah's case, the complete avoidance of her.

She deserved it. But for a moment when she'd walked into the room she'd forgotten that she'd spoilt it all. She'd only remembered that they were in love and she'd felt that heady hope again. And then the memories had flooded back and she'd realised she'd only been fooling herself.

But some day Christmas would go back to being wonderful. She'd be happy again, and she'd feel festive. Her family's laughter wouldn't grate on her emotions; their happiness wouldn't make her ill with longing. It would just be a holiday she could spend with the people she loved and enjoy the festivity of it.

For now, she had alcohol.

'Maybe you should go easy on the champagne,' Jaden said as he joined her on the porch steps.

'I'm offended. This is only my third glass.'

'But you barely ate.' Jaden took the champagne from her and downed it, then handed her the empty glass. 'You're welcome.'

She grunted, and set the glass on the step next to her. He was right. And the whole alcohol thing had been more of a distraction than anything else.

'Why are you sitting out here alone with champagne anyway? Noah left an hour ago.'

'It's not about him.'

But it was. Partly.

'Ava,' Jaden said, in his *I'm your big brother* voice, 'I say this with the utmost love, but you have to stop feeling sorry for yourself.'

'Excuse me?'

He winced, but said, 'You heard me.' He waited a beat before he continued. 'It's been a year. Long enough for you to snap out of your self-pity.'

'I'm *not* feeling sorry for myself. And even if I were, who the hell are you to tell me I can't? You, with your perfect wedding and your brand-new wife?'

'I'm your brother.' He put an arm around her shoulders. 'And I love you. Which is why I can be honest with you.' He squeezed her shoulder, then pulled his hand back. 'Look, no one is saying that what happened last year didn't suck. It did. But you're using it as an excuse not to move on.'

'Because of Noah?'

'Yes.' He was unperturbed by her surly tone. 'And because after last year, you think there's something wrong with you.'

'Who told you that?' she asked sharply.

'Heard it through the grapevine.'

'Noah.'

'Actually, from Mom and Dad—the moment you were out of earshot.' He tilted his head. 'But they heard it from Noah.'

'I should never have told him.'

'I'm glad you did. We all are. Or we wouldn't have the chance to tell you that you're absolutely wrong if you think it's true.' He paused. '*And* that you're feeling sorry for yourself.'

She sucked in her lip as it wobbled. 'It *is* true.'

'Ava—'

'No, Jaden, it *is*. Milo told me—'

'Milo was selfish. He always knew you were too good for him and yet somehow he managed to make you believe it was the other way around.'

She blinked. And then took a very deliberate breath when the air simply vanished from her lungs.

'I don't know… I don't know what to say.'

'Don't say anything. Just believe it.'

There was a long pause while she tried to figure out how she *could* believe it. No, first she was trying to figure out whether her brother had always felt that way about her ex-fiancé. Had her parents felt the same? And, if so, why had none of them told her?

'You wouldn't have believed us if we'd told you.' Jaden's eyes crinkled when her head turned sharply, and he gave her a wry grin. 'I've known you for all of your twenty-five years, Ava. I know how your mind works.'

'Okay, as disturbing as that is, it isn't the most disturbing thing you've said to me today.' She paused. Exhaled. 'I wish you'd told me. It could have saved me a lot of heartache.'

'And then I'd have had to tell you "I told you so", and while I would have enjoyed it, I don't think you would have.' His lips curved, then his smile faded. 'It's something I'll regret all my life. I know what it's like to fall in love when you're young.' He paused. 'I think it was worse for you, because you were so determined to prove that that kiss I'd walked in on—' he shuddered '—between you and Noah didn't mean anything.'

'What is *happening*?' Ava asked, her eyes wide. 'Are you revealing every single thought you've ever had?'

'No. I'm just lifting the carpet we sweep all our opinions under.' He let out a breath. 'If anything I've said today isn't true, then by all means forget it. But I always thought you'd come to these realisations yourself. The fact that you haven't points to the whole feeling sorry for yourself thing.'

She sighed with a shake of her head. Paused to consider it. 'Maybe you're right and I *do* feel sorry for myself. But, freaking hell, my fiancé walked out on me at the altar. *Can't* I feel sorry for myself?'

'Of course you can. And you have,' he added. 'But if you let it interfere with this thing with Noah—' he rolled his eyes '—then maybe there *is* something wrong with you.'

Now she rolled *her* eyes. 'Ah, my ever-sensitive brother.'

'And my dorky—but perfect—little sister.' He kissed her on the cheek and then stood up. 'Now, take some time to think about your sins and then come inside and let Mom and Dad tell you exactly what I just did but in a nicer way.'

He took one step away, and then paused. 'And if you ever, *ever* make me advocate for a relationship between you and Noah again, please know that I will strangle you in the process.'

She laughed softly as he walked away, and then took a

deep breath and watched as the sun began to lower behind the mountains she could see from her parents' house. Her eyes stayed there as her mind whirled. As she realised that Jaden had been right about her relationship with Milo.

She'd known they weren't right for one another, though she hadn't quite thought that she was better than him. But there had been signs that had pointed to how mismatched they were long before she'd realised it. Signs she hadn't given herself permission to see even after he'd left.

She was too strong-minded for someone like him. And maybe that was why she hadn't listened when her gut had told her they didn't fit.

She hadn't listened to it for five years. *Five years*. Even when there had been an extra flutter of panic in her chest as they'd approached the wedding she'd ignored it. She could see now that the fluttering had been warning her. And it had stayed with her after, saying the *I told you so* Jaden hadn't wanted to.

How, then, had she managed to turn it into a critique of who she was?

Because it had been easier, she realised. Easier to believe that Milo was right, that she needed to be fixed. That way she'd been able to nurture the hurt inside her. She'd been able to hold it close and use it as an excuse not to move on. Because if she didn't move on she wouldn't get hurt again.

It took some time for the realisation to settle inside her. And for her to figure out what it meant that she and Noah had the same fears about being in a relationship.

They each thought they didn't deserve the other. They were both scared of getting hurt. But he'd taken a chance and proclaimed his love for her nevertheless. He'd been brave and she hadn't.

But she wanted to be brave. Because now she understood that she couldn't wait for her fears to disappear. She'd be putting her life on pause again if she did wait. She'd figure it all out, just as Noah would. And she was determined that they'd figure it out together.

But first she had to go inside the house and face her parents. And then she had to convince her brother to get involved with her and Noah one more time...

CHAPTER TWENTY-ONE

WHAT *WAS* IT with the Keller family and trying to get him to celebrate with them? It was enough to make him consider leaving again.

But when his father's face popped into his mind—and he thought of the ease their relationship had slid into since they'd had that talk—he knew that it was an exaggeration. He was just miserable because he was in love. And the woman he loved didn't want to be with him.

His only consolation was that Ava wasn't going to be attending Jaden's New Year's Eve party. After the Christmas tension he didn't think they'd survive another occasion together. His stomach still felt jittery because of it, and it had almost nothing to do with how unhappy Ava had been.

Almost.

Was she unhappy because she wanted to be with me?

He pushed the thought to the back of his mind. Thinking about that would do him no good now. Nor would remembering that light in her eyes when she'd first seen him.

No good. No good at all.

He pulled into the driveway at Jaden's house, and was surprised to see only three cars there. He recognised one as belonging to Jaden's parents, but the other two he wasn't sure about. Until he realised he'd seen them there before and groaned.

The rest of the wedding party. *Great.* Now Tiff would be able to see his unhappiness.

Not that it mattered, he told himself, getting out the car. He'd come to accept that his relationship with Tiff had been a teaching moment in his life. And he'd resented her more for his own reasons than for anything *she'd* ever done to him.

He needed to move on.

He thought he had.

He grunted at the unwelcome thought, and then rang the doorbell. He was surprised to see Tiff open it.

'Hi,' she said.

'Hi.' He waited as she stepped back, and then he moved past her. 'It's good to see you again.'

'It is?'

Her surprise made him feel guilty. Until it was replaced with confusion.

'Ah, she told you,' she said.

'I'm sorry?'

'Ava. She told you I was sorry.' She smiled at him. 'I told her you'd listen to her. But I'm still glad I have the opportunity to tell you in person. I'm sorry…about everything.'

It took him a moment to process all the information, but then he nodded. 'I'm sorry, too. For how I've handled things…since.'

'Great.'

'Great.'

There was a pause. Then, 'Well, you can just go through. Everyone is on the deck.'

After that surprising exchange, the rest of the night was uneventful. The conversation was easy for the most part, except for the unexpected mentions of Ava's name and the uncomfortable glances at him, which he ignored.

Half an hour before midnight his father strolled in.

'Dad?' He stood. 'What are you doing here?'

'I couldn't let the first New Year's Eve my son spends at home in seven years pass without us being together.' He slapped Noah on the back.

'So, what? You pitch up half an hour before midnight?' he teased, but he was pleased.

'Yeah, well… I had some things to take care of.'

He winked at Noah, and then the lights went out and a familiar song began to play.

Noah's jaw dropped when he saw Ava walk onto the deck.

She felt a new appreciation for the embarrassment Noah had put himself through at Jaden's wedding. Here, she was only performing in front of her family—and Tiff and Ken, though they didn't really count. But then, none of them did when she made eye contact with Noah.

Her cue came and she lifted the microphone Jaden had plugged into his sound system and began to sing the song Noah had sung to her at the wedding. It was a silly Christmas song, about Father Christmas and his elves, and when she'd been practising she'd realised that Noah had chosen the song because of the jokes they'd made with one another when she'd been staying at his place.

The singing had been easier to perfect than the dancing. She'd watched the video of Noah's performance that Kirk had recorded on his phone and graciously sent her over and over again, but some of the moves were Noah originals and hard to imitate. Not to mention the fact that she was wearing his firefighter uniform.

No one could accuse her of not going all out for love. She only hoped it would work.

She beguiled him—and heaven only knew why. Though he knew she was a good dancer, she couldn't move very well in his uniform, and his helmet kept falling over her face during the song.

But still she was beguiling. So much so that he only realised they were alone when the music stopped and she stood in front of him.

'Pretty decent show,' he commented. 'Not as good as mine, though. I'd give you nine hundred points.'

'I'm pretty sure that still makes me the—' She cut herself off as the helmet slipped over her face again.

Grinning, he took it off her head. 'You were going to say winner, and even my helmet knew you'd be lying.'

'Fair enough.' She paused. 'It wouldn't be the first time, I guess.'

'That my helmet knew you were going to lie?'

'That I lied,' she said, with a smile that turned his heart over.

'What do you mean?'

'I mean— What do you *think* I mean?' she asked. 'What do you *think* me getting your father to get me your fire-fighter's uniform and send me the video of you performing that ridiculous song so that I could perform it and also getting my brother to invite you to this party means?'

She was out of breath when her speech was over, and while she caught it his mind played catch-up.

'You're saying you planned this?'

She rolled her eyes. 'Duh.'

'Why?'

'Why do you *think*?'

He opened his mouth, then shook his head. 'That's not fair.'

'Really?' Her brow furrowed. 'Okay, fine. I love you, Noah, and I want to be with you.'

His stunned silence slithered into her chest and gripped her heart.

'What…what changed?'

She was prepared for this. She exhaled. 'I realised I was scared, too. Of not being what you deserve. Of being hurt. I couldn't bring myself to move on because of it.'

He didn't reply immediately. 'You know what I think?' His voice was quiet. 'We should stop getting in our own heads about this and just admit we deserve each other.'

She smiled, the pressure in her chest easing. 'I agree.'

He smiled back. 'I won't hurt you, Avalanche.'

'I know.' She lifted a hand to his cheek, and then dropped it. 'It's still terrifying. All of this is.' She slid her fingers into her hair, puffing out her curls where they'd been flattened by his helmet. 'Milo and I weren't right for one another. But… but I can't deny he made some good points.'

'Ava—'

'It's not just going to go away,' she said softly. 'These insecurities are here. The fears are, too. I have to work through them. But I won't let them keep me from being with you, if that's still what you want. Especially since my dear brother has reminded me of how getting into a relationship with the first man who was interested in me after you left might have been a sign of how much I was running away from my feelings for you.'

'I…' He dragged the sound out. 'I did *not* see that coming.'

She laughed. 'Neither did I. *Jaden* had to point it out.' She did a mock shudder. 'He wasn't happy about it.'

'I can imagine.' He let out a breath.

'It was easier for me to stop living,' she said after a moment. 'It meant I didn't have to get hurt again or do anything about the brokenness inside me.' She took a step forward, her heart hammering. 'But if you're willing to be patient as I put myself together again—properly this time—'

He cut her off with a kiss.

It was relief more than anything else, but he sank into the passion, the fire, the *home* of kissing her. And then he pulled back, told himself he needed to be sure.

'I don't want you to do this because when we're together things are awkward. We can go back to…to being friends.'

'I thought you said we weren't ever really friends?'

He acknowledged the hit with a nod. 'You know what I mean.'

'I do.' Her smile faded. 'I do miss you. And I don't want things to be awkward. But, more importantly, I love you and I want to be with you. It's that simple.' She drew in a breath. 'If that's still what you want.'

'It is.' He paused. 'If you're willing to be patient with me as I work through my own stuff.'

'For as long as it takes.' She smiled. 'Thank you for not drawing that out.'

'I wanted to.'

Her smiled widened, heating his insides. 'Can't blame you for it. I wanted to, too.'

'Except you didn't want to do it to someone you love.'

'I guess.' She lifted a hand, brushed his lips with her thumb. 'I wouldn't know.'

'Because you've never really been in love before?'

'Not like this, no.'

He slid his arms around her body, drew her closer. 'Me neither.'

They stood like that for a moment, and then she said, 'My brother must be hating having to watch this.'

'They're watching?'

'Every single one of them.' Her eyes shifted to behind him, and then moved back to his face. 'Should we give them something to look at?'

'You mean besides the fireworks?'

As he said it, the first set of fireworks went off.

He smiled. 'Happy New Year, baby.'

'Happy New Year,' she replied, and pressed her lips to hers.

EPILOGUE

Two years later, Christmas Day

'LOOK, YOU OWE me this. I saved your life. It's the least you can do.'

Zorro stared at Noah, only one message clear in his eyes. *I hate you for doing this to me.*

Which was a fair point, Noah thought, amusing himself by playing with the bow around Zorro's neck. But then his phone beeped and his heart jumped into his throat.

Showtime.

He picked Zorro up, and thanked the cat for not resisting. Then he tentatively put the cat on the kitchen counter, which had now been cleared of the Christmas spread that had been there only a few hours ago.

He and Ava had hosted their families at his house this year. His father had come with his girlfriend—a woman he'd been dating for over a year now and was 'taking it slowly' with, as he'd told Noah—as well as Ava's parents, Leela and Jaden and their new bundle of joy.

Throughout the day Noah had watched Ava. Watched as she'd laughed, as she'd joked. He'd watched as she'd teased her brother, as she'd played with her niece. And all he'd been able to think about was how far she'd come. About how a short two years ago she'd been in so much pain that she hadn't even managed to smile at her family.

That Ava was gone.

And because he could see the version of himself from two years ago had disappeared, too—how he no longer feared being hurt, or shied away from his mother's memory—he knew it was time for the next step in their relationship.

He heard her car pull into the driveway and silently thanked his father for giving him the heads-up that she'd left his house. They'd made up some reason for her to take a quick trip to Kirk's after everyone had left. He didn't remember what that reason was now, though that was probably nerves. But because of that made-up reason, he was now ready.

'Honestly, I love your father, but he needs to figure out what's important in life. Particularly at Christmas.'

Noah smiled when she walked in, but his eyes were on Zorro, who'd leapt off the counter and was now searching the kitchen floor for food morsels.

'He asked me all the way back to his house to give me a box of chocolates. *Chocolates*.'

So *that* was what it had been, Noah thought.

'He could have just brought them with him.' She frowned at him. 'What are you doing?'

'I have drinks, popcorn and dessert for a night in.' He walked to her and gently pushed her towards the living room, away from the cat. 'I thought you might want a quiet evening after the busyness of today.'

'Sounds amazing.'

But she didn't sit when she got to the couch—just turned and put her hands on her hips.

'You're acting weird.'

'No.'

He walked back to the kitchen and blocked the cat from darting into the living room. There was a beat when Noah thought Zorro would try again, but then the cat sat down and started licking his leg.

'Something to drink?'

'Noah, you *are* acting weird. Either you tell me why, or I start the Christmas karaoke up again.'

'Oh, please, *no*.'

Deciding that all he needed for it to be perfect was her, him and the damn cat, he sighed.

'Fine. But I *had* hoped it would go better than this. You and I would be watching our movie. You'd sigh, tell me how I've helped you to love Christmas again, and in would trot Zorro...'

She narrowed her eyes. 'Some of that might happen. But I don't understand—'

She stopped when Noah picked up the cat, her eyes widening as she took in the bow around his neck.

'Oh, he's *festive*.' She walked over to him and took the cat from his hands, just as he'd anticipated she would. 'How did you manage to get him to sit still?'

'I asked very nicely. Told him that if he did I'd legally adopt him.'

'Adopt—'

She broke off as Noah lowered to his knee and her eyes filled. True to who she was, she tried to blink the tears away, but she drew the cat in closer. When Zorro protested, she moved to put him down.

And then she saw the ring.

'Noah.'

It was both a gasp and an exhalation of air, and he didn't think he'd ever hear as beautiful a sound again. He took Zorro from her, untied the ring from his neck and gave him a little scratch on the head before letting him go.

True to who *he* was, he ran and hid under the closest table, unimpressed with the past few minutes.

'Ava, you know how much—'

'Noah,' she said again, and her voice was impatient this time. 'I love you, and I'm sure whatever you've planned to say is going to be beautiful, but you can say it to me later, okay? There's only one thing I want to hear right now.'

When he grinned, she shook her head, took the ring from his hand and slid it onto her finger.

'Never mind. I don't even have to hear it. *Yes*. Yes, I will.'

He straightened with a chuckle, but it was cut off when she kissed him. When they pulled apart, she grinned.

'So, how do you feel about wedding planning? Because I vote we get a wedding planner...'

* * * * *

AN UNEXPECTED CHRISTMAS BABY

TARA TAYLOR QUINN

For my mom, Penny Gumser, who is
still showing me the meaning of the word *mother*.
And who still reads every word I publish. I love you!

Chapter One

"Dearly Beloved, we are gathered here today—"

The ceremony had been a dumb idea.

"—Alana Gold Collins to rest. The Father tells us—"

Hands together at his belt buckle, Flint Collins stared down past the crease in his black pants to the tips of his shiny black shoes. *Alana Gold.* Such a lofty name. Like a movie star or something.

Alana Gold. Not much about his mother's life had been golden. Except her hair, he supposed. Back when she'd been young and pretty. Before the hard life, the drugs and prison had had their way with her.

"—all will be changed at the last sounding of the bell…"

The Father might have imparted that message. The Bible surely did, according to the preacher he'd hired to give his mother a funeral. *Dearly Beloved*, he'd said. That would be Flint. The dearly beloved. All one of him.

He'd never known any other family. Didn't even know who his father was.

Footsteps sounded behind him and he stiffened. He'd asked her to come—the caseworker he'd only met two days before. To do the...exchange.

Dearly Beloved. In her own way Alana had loved Flint deeply. Just as, he was absolutely certain, she'd loved the "inheritance" she'd left him. One he hadn't known about. One he hadn't yet seen. One that had arrived behind him.

"So take comfort..." That was the preacher again. For the life of him, Flint drew a blank on his name as he glanced up and met the older man's compassionate gaze.

He almost burst out with a humorless chuckle. *Comfort?* Was the man serious? Flint's whole life had imploded in the space of a week. Would never, ever, be the same or be what he'd planned it to be. Comfort was a pipe dream at best.

As the footsteps in the grass behind him slowed, as he felt the warmth of a body close to him, Flint stood still. Respectful.

He'd lost his business before it had even opened. He'd lost the woman he'd expected to marry, to grow old beside.

Alana Gold had lost her life.

And in her death had taken part of his.

The preacher spoke about angels of mercy. The woman half a step behind him rocked slightly, not announcing herself in any way other than her quiet presence. Flint fought to contain his grief. And his anger.

His entire life he'd had to work longer, fight harder. At first to avoid getting beaten up. And then to make a place for himself in the various families with whom he'd been temporarily settled. He'd had a paper route at twelve and delivered weekly grocery ads to neighborhoods for pennies, just to keep food on the table during the times he'd been with Alana.

The preacher spoke of heaven.

Flint remembered when he'd been a junior in high school, studying for finals, and had had to spend the night before his test getting his mother out of jail. She'd been prostituting that time. Those were the charges. She'd claimed differently.

But then, Alana's troubles had always been someone else's fault.

In the beginning they probably had been. She'd once claimed that she'd gotten on the wrong track because she'd been looking for a way to escape an abusive father. That was the one part of her story Flint fully believed. He'd met the guy once. Had opted, when given the chance in court, to never have to see him again. Sometimes it worked in a guy's favor to have a caseworker.

After Alana's prostitution arrest during his finals week, he'd expected to be seeing his caseworker again, to have her come to pick him up and take him back to foster care. Instead his mother had been sitting in the living room when he'd gotten home from school the next day, completely sober, her fingernails bitten to the quick, with a plate of homemade chocolate-chip cookies on her lap, worried sick that she'd made him fail his exam.

Tears had dripped down her face as he'd told her of course not, he'd aced it. Because he'd skipped lunch to cram. She'd apologized. Again and again. She'd always said he was the only good thing about her. That he was going to grow up to be something great, for both of them. She'd waited on him hand and foot for a few weeks. Had stayed sober and made it to work at the hair salon—where she'd qualified for men's basic cuts only—for most of that summer.

Until one of her clients had talked her into going out for a good time…

"Let us pray."

Flint's head was already bowed. The brief ceremony was almost over. The closed casket holding his mother's body would remain on the stand, waiting over the hole in the ground until after Flint was gone and the groundskeeper came to lower her to her final rest.

Moisture pricked the backs of his eyelids. For a second, he started to panic like he had the first day he'd gone out to catch the bus for school—a puny five-year-old in a trailer park filled with older kids—and been shoved to the back of the line by every one of them. He could have turned and run home. No one would have stopped him. Alana hadn't been sober enough to know, or care, whether he'd made it to his first day of school. But he hadn't run. He'd faced that open bus door, climbed those steps that had seemed like mountains to him and walked halfway to the back of the bus before sitting.

He was Alana Gold's precious baby boy and he was going to *be* someone.

"Amen." The preacher laid a Bible on top of the coffin.

Amen to that. He was Alana's son and he was going to be someone all right.

"Mr. Collins?"

The voice, a woman's voice, was close to him.

"Mr. Collins? I've got her things in the car, as you asked."

Her things. Things for the inheritance Alana had left him. More scared than he could ever remember being, Flint raised his head and turned it to see the brunette standing behind him, a concerned look on her face. A pink bundle in her arms.

Staring at that bundle, he swallowed the lump in his throat. He wasn't prepared. No way could he pass *this* test. In her death, Alana had finally set him up for failure.

She'd unintentionally done it in the past but had never succeeded. This time, though...

He reminded himself that he had to *be* someone.

Brother? Father? Neither fit. He'd never had either.

A breeze blew across the San Diego cemetery. The cemetery close to where he'd grown up, where he'd once seen his mother score dope. And now he was putting her here permanently. Nothing about this day was right.

"Prison records show that your mother had already chosen a name for her. But as I told you, since she died giving birth, no official name has been given. You're free to name her whatever you'd like..."

Prison records and legal documents showed that his forty-five-year-old mother had appointed him, her thirty-year-old son, as guardian of her unborn child. A child Alana had conceived while serving year eight of her ten-year sentence for cooking and dealing methamphetamine in the trailer Flint had purchased for her.

The child's father was listed as "unknown."

He and the inherited baby had that in common. And the fact that their mother had stayed clean the entire time she'd carried them. Birthing them without addiction.

"What did she call her?" he asked, unable to lift his gaze from the pink bundle or to peer further, to seek out the little human inside it.

He'd been bequeathed a little human.

After thirty years of having his mother as his only family, he had a sister.

"Diamond Rose," the caseworker said.

Flint didn't hear any derogatory tone in the voice.

Alana had been gold. A softer metal. He was Flint, a hard rock. And this new member of the family was diamond. Strong enough to cut glass. Valuable and cherished. And Rose... Expensive, beautiful, sweet.

He got Alana's message, even if the world wouldn't. "Then Diamond Rose it is," he said, turning more fully to face the caseworker.

The woman was on the job, had other duties to tend to. She'd already done a preliminary background check but, as family, he had a right to the child even if the woman didn't want to give her to him. Unless the caseworker had found some reason that suggested the baby might be unsafe with him.

Like the fact that he knew nothing whatsoever about infants? Had never changed a diaper in his life? At least not on a real baby. He'd put about thirty of them on a doll he'd purchased the day before—immediately after watching a load of new parenting videos.

He reached for the bundle. Diamond Rose. She'd weighed six pounds, one ounce at birth, he'd been told. He'd put a pound of butter on a five-pound bag of flour the night before, wrapped it in one of the new blankets he'd purchased and walked around the house with it while going about his routine. Figured he could do pretty much anything he might want or need to do while holding it.

Or wearing it. The body-pack sling thing had been a real find. Not that different from the backpacks he'd used all through school, although this one was meant to be worn in front. Put the baby in that, he'd be hands free.

The caseworker, Ms. Bailey, rather than handing him Diamond Rose, took a step back. "Do you have the car seat?"

"I have two," he told her. "In case she has a babysitter and there's an emergency and she needs to be transported when I'm not there." He also had a crib set up in a room that used to be designated as a spare bedroom. Stella, his ex-fiancée, had eyed the unfurnished room as her temporary office until they purchased a home more in line with her wants and needs.

In an even more upscale neighborhood, in other words.

Ms. Bailey held the bundle against her. Flint didn't take offense. Didn't really blame the woman at all. If he were her, he wouldn't want to hand a two-day-old baby over to him, either. But during her two days in the hospital the baby had been fully tested, examined and then released that morning. Released to him. Her family. Via Ms. Bailey. At his request, because he had a funeral to attend. And had wanted Alana's daughter there, too.

"As I said earlier, I strongly recommend a Pack 'n Play. They're less expensive than cribs, double as playpens with a changing table attachment and are easily portable."

Already had that, too. Although he hadn't set it up in his bedroom as the videos he'd watched had recommended. No way was he having a baby sleep with him. Didn't seem... He didn't know what.

He had the monitors. If she woke, he'd have to get up anyway. Walking across the hall only took a few more steps.

"And the bottles and formula?"

"Three scoops of the powder per six ounces of water, slightly warm." He'd done a dozen run-throughs on that. And was opting for boiling all nipples in water just to be safe in his method of cleansing.

He noticed the preacher hovering in the distance. The man of God probably needed to get on to other matters, as well. Flint nodded his thanks and received the older man's nod in return. As he watched him walk away, he couldn't help wondering if Alana Gold would be more than a momentary blip in his memory.

She would be far more than that to her daughter.

Ms. Bailey interrupted his thoughts. "What about child

care? Have you made arrangements for when you go back to work?"

Go back to work? As in, an hour from now? Taking Monday morning off had been difficult enough. With the market closed over the weekend, Mondays were always busy.

And he had some serious backtracking to do at the firm.

In the financial world, things had to be done discreetly and he'd been taking action—confidentially until he knew for sure it was a go—to move out on his own. Somehow his plans had become known and rumors had begun to spread with a bad spin. In the past week there'd been talk that he'd contacted his clients, trying to steal their business away from the firm. A person he trusted had heard something and confided that to him. And then he'd had an oddly formal exchange about the weather with Howard Owens, CEO and, prior to the past week, a man who'd seemed proud to have him around. A man who'd never wasted weather words on Flint. They talked business. All the time. Until the past week.

There was no way he could afford to take time off work now.

"I'm taking her with me." He faced Ms. Bailey, feet apart and firmly grounded. He had to work. Period. "I have a Pack 'n Play already set up in the office."

The woman frowned. "They'll let you have a baby with you at work?"

"My office is private. I'll keep the door closed if it's a problem." The plan was short-term. Eventually he'd have to make other arrangements. He'd only had a weekend to prepare. Had gotten himself trained and the house set up. He figured he'd done a damned impressive job.

Besides, that time Campbell's dog had had surgery, the guy had brought it to the office every day for a week. Kept it in his office. As long as you were a money-maker and didn't get in the way of others making money, you were pretty much untouched at Owens Investments. They were like independent businesses under one roof.

Or so he'd been telling himself repeatedly in the couple of days since he'd realized he couldn't open his own business as planned. Not and have sole responsibility for a newborn. Running a business took a lot more than simply making smart investments. Especially when it was just getting off the ground.

He'd already shut down the entire process. Withdrawn his applications for the licenses required to be an investment adviser to more than five clients and regulated by the SEC in the State of California. Lost his deposit for a proposed suite in a new office building.

If she thought she was going to keep his sister from him now...

Another breeze blew across his face, riffling the edge of the blanket long enough that he caught a flash of skin. A tiny cheek? A forehead?

Panic flared. And then dissipated. That bundle was his sister. His family. Only he could give her that. Only he could tell her about her mother. The good stuff.

Like the times she'd look in on him late at night, thinking he was asleep. Whisper her apologies. And tell him how very, very much she loved him. How much he mattered. How he was the one thing she'd done right. How he was going to make his mark on the world for both of them.

The way she'd throw herself a thousand percent into his school projects, encouraging him, making suggestions, applauding him. How talented she was at crafty things. How she loved to watch sappy movies and made the best popcorn. How she'd want to watch scary movies with him and he'd catch her looking away during the best parts. How she'd never made a big deal out of his mistakes. From spills to a broken window, she'd let him know it was okay. How she'd played cards with him, taught him to cook. How she'd laugh until tears ran down her face. How pretty she used to be when she smiled.

The images flying swiftly through his mind halted abruptly as Ms. Bailey began to close in on him, her arms outstretched.

Hoping to God she didn't notice his sudden trembling, he moved instinctively, settled the weight at the tip of the blanket in the crook of his elbow and took the rest of it on his arm, just as he'd practiced with the flour-and-butter wrap the night before. She was warm. And she squirmed. Shock rippled through him. Ms. Bailey adjusted the blanket, fully exposing the tiniest face he'd ever seen up close. Doll-like nose and chin. Eyelids tightly closed. Puckered little lips. A hint of a frown on a forehead that was smaller than the palm of his hand.

"From what I've seen in pictures, she has your mother's eyes," Ms. Bailey said, a catch in her voice. Because she could hear the tears threatening in his? A grown man who hadn't cried since the first time they'd carted his mother off to prison. He'd been six then.

She has your mother's eyes.

He had his mother's eyes. Deep, dark brown. It was fitting that this baby did, too. "We'll be getting on with it, then," he said, holding his inheritance securely against him as he moved toward his SUV, all but dismissing Ms. Bailey from their lives.

Having a caseworker was a part of his legacy that he wasn't going to pass on to his sister.

Reaching the new blue Lincoln Navigator he'd purchased five months before and hadn't visited the prison in even once, he felt a sharp pang of guilt as he realized once again that he'd let almost half a year pass since seeing his mother.

Before he'd met Stella Wainwright—a lawyer in her father's high-powered firm, whose advice he'd come to rely on as he'd made preparations to open his own investment firm—he'd seen Alana at least twice a month. But once he and Stella had hooked up on a personal level, he'd been distracted. Incredibly busy. And…

He'd been loath to lie to Stella about where he'd been—in the event he'd visited the prison—but had been equally unsure about telling her about his convict mother.

As it turned out, his reticence hadn't been off the mark. As soon as he'd told Stella about his mother's death, and the child who'd been bequeathed to him, she'd balked. She'd assumed he'd give the baby up for adoption. And had made it clear that if he didn't, she was moving on. She'd said from the beginning that she didn't want children, at least not for a while, but he'd also seen the extreme distaste in her expression when he'd mentioned where his mother had been when she died, and why he'd never introduced them.

Her reaction hadn't surprised him.

Eight years had passed since he'd been under investigation and nearly lost his career, but the effects were long-lasting. He'd done nothing more than provide his destitute mother with a place to live, but when his name came up as owner of a drug factory, the truth hadn't mattered.

Stella had done a little research and he'd been cooked.

Opening the back passenger door of the vehicle, he gently laid his sleeping bundle in the car seat, unprepared when the bundle slumped forward. Repositioning her, he pulled her slightly forward, allowing her body weight to lean back—and slouch over to the side of the seat.

Who the hell had thought the design of that seat appropriate?

"This might help."

Straightening, he saw the caseworker holding out a brightly covered, U-shaped piece of foam. He took it from her and arranged it at the top of the car seat as instructed. He was pleased with the result. Until he realized he'd placed the sleeping bundle on top of the straps that were supposed to hold the baby in place.

Expecting Ms. Bailey to interrupt, to push him aside to show him how it was done—half hoping she would so she wasn't standing there watching his big fumbling fingers—he set to righting his mistake. The caseworker must be thinking he was incapable of handling the responsibility. However, she didn't butt in and he managed, after a long minute, to get the baby harnessed. He'd practiced that, too. The hooking and unhooking of those straps. Plastic pieces that slid over metal for the shoulder part, metal into metal over the bottom half.

He stood. Waited for a critique of his first task as a... guardian.

Handing him her card, reminding him of legalities he'd have to complete, Ms. Bailey took one last look at the baby and told him to call her if he had any questions or problems.

He took the card, assuring her he'd call if the need arose. Pretty certain he wouldn't. He'd be like any normal...guardian; he'd call the pediatrician. As soon as he had one. Another item he had to add to the list of immediate things to do.

"And for what it's worth..." Ms. Bailey stood there, looking between him and the little sister he was suddenly starting to feel quite proprietary about. "I think she's a very lucky little girl."

Wow. He hadn't seen that coming. Wasn't sure the words were true. But they rang loudly in his ears as the woman walked away.

Standing in the open space of the back passenger door, he glanced down at the sleeping baby, only her face visible to him, and didn't want to shut the door. Didn't want to leave her in the big back seat all alone.

Which was ridiculous.

He had to get to work. And hope to God he could mend whatever damage had been done by his previous plans to leave. He had some ideas there—a way to redeem himself, to rebuild trust. But he had to be at the office to present them.

Closing the door as softly as he could, he hurried to the driver's seat, adjusted the rearview mirror so he could see enough of the baby to know she was there and started the engine. Not ready to go anywhere. To begin this new life.

He glanced in the mirror again. Sitting forward so he could see the child more clearly. Other than the little chest rising and falling with each breath, she hadn't moved.

But was moving him to the point of panic. And tears, too. He wasn't alone anymore.

"Welcome home, Diamond Rose," he whispered.

And put the car in Drive.

Chapter Two

"Dad, seriously, tell me what's going on." Tamara Owens faced her father, not the least bit intimidated by the massive cherry desk separating him from her. Or the elegantly imposing décor throughout her father's office.

She'd seen him at home, unshaved, walking around their equally elegant five-thousand-square-foot home in boxers and a T-shirt. In a bathrobe, sick with the flu. And, also in a bathrobe, holding her hair while she'd thrown up, sick with the same flu. Her mom, the doctor in the family, had been at the hospital that night.

"You didn't put pressure on me to move home just because you and Mom are getting older and I'm your only child." It was the story they'd given her when they'd bombarded her with their "do what you need to do, but at least think about it" requests. Then her father, in a conversation alone with her, had given Tamara a second choice, an "at least take a month off and stay for a real visit" that had made the final decision for her. She'd gotten the feeling that he needed her home. She'd already been contemplating leaving the East Coast, where she'd fled two years earlier after having lived in San Diego her entire life. Her reputation as an efficiency consultant was solid enough to allow her to branch out independently, rather than work through a firm without fear of going backward. Truth be told, in those two years, she'd missed her folks as much as they'd missed her, in spite of their frequent trips across the country to see each other.

She'd lived by the ocean in Boston, but she missed Southern California. The sunshine and year-round warmth. The two-year lease renting out her place by the beach, not far from the home she'd grown up in, had ended and the time seemed right to make the move back home.

"And you didn't ask me down here to have lunch with you just to catch up, either," she told him. Though his thick hair was mostly gray, her father, at six-two, with football shoulders that had absolutely no slump to them, was a commanding figure. She respected him. But he'd never, ever, made her feel afraid of him.

Or afraid to speak up to him, either.

Her parents, both remarkably successful, independent career people, had raised her to be just as independent.

"I wanted to check in—you know, just the two of us— to see how you're really doing."

Watching him, she tried to decide whether she could take him at face value. There'd been times, during her growing-up years, when she'd asked him for private conversations because her mother's ability to jump too completely into her skin had bothered her. And times when he'd wanted the same. This didn't feel like one of those times.

But...

"I'm totally over Steve, if that's what you want to know,"

she told him. "We've been talking for about six months now. Ever since he called to tell me he was getting married. I spoke with him a couple of weeks ago to tell him I was moving home. I care about him as a friend, but there are truly no regrets about our decision to divorce."

The passion between them had died long before the marriage had.

"I was wondering more about the…other areas of your life."

Some of those were permanently broken. She had an "inhospitable" uterus. Nothing anyone could do about that.

"I've come to terms with never having a baby, if that's what you mean." After she'd lost the fourth one, she'd known she couldn't let herself try again. What she'd felt for those babies, even when they'd been little more than blips in an ultrasound, had been the most incredible thing ever. But the devastation when she'd lost them…that had almost killed her. Every single time.

She couldn't do that again.

"There are other ways, Tam."

She shook her head.

"Adoption, for instance."

Another vigorous shake of her head was meant to stop his words.

"Down the road, I mean. When you meet someone, want to have a family…"

She was still shaking her head.

"Just give it some time."

She'd given it two years. Her feelings hadn't changed. Not in the slightest. "Knowing how badly it hurts to lose a child… It's not something I'm going to risk again. Not just because I'm afraid I'd miscarry if I got pregnant again, although it's pretty much assured that I would. But even without that, I can't have children. Whether I lost a child through miscarriage or some other way, just knowing it could happen… I can't take that chance. The last time, I hit a wall. I just don't— I've made my peace with life and I'm happy."

A lot of days she was getting there. Had moments when she *was* there. And felt fully confident she'd be completely there. Soon.

"But you aren't dating."

Leaning forward, she said, "I just got back to town a week ago! Give me time!"

He didn't even blink. "What about Boston? Didn't you meet anyone there?"

"I was hardly ever home long enough to meet anyone," she reminded him. "Traveling all over the country, making a name for myself, took practically every second I had."

The move to Boston had been prompted by an offer she'd had to join a nationally reputed efficiency company. She'd been given the opportunity to build a reputation for herself. To collect an impressive database of statistical proof from more than two dozen assignments that showed she could save a company far more money per year, in many departments, than they'd pay for her one-time services. Her father had seen the results. He'd been keeping his own running tally of her successes.

"You did an incredible job, Tam, I'm not disputing that. I'm impressed. And proud of you, too."

The warmth in those blue eyes comforted her as much now as when she'd been a little kid and fallen off her bike the first time he'd taken off the training wheels. She hadn't even skinned her knee, but she'd been scared and he'd scooped her up, made her look him in the eye and see that she was just fine.

"I guess it's a little hard for me to believe that emotionally you're really doing as well as you say, because I don't see *how* you do it. I can't imagine ever losing you… I don't know how I'd have survived losing four."

"But you *did* lose four, Daddy. You were as excited as anyone when you found out I was pregnant. Heck, you'd already bought Ryan his first fishing rod…"

She still had it, in the back of the shed on her small property. She'd carried Ryan the longest. Almost five months. They'd just found out he was a boy. Everything had looked good. And then…

Through sheer force of will, she stopped the shudder before it rippled through her. Remembering the sharp stabs of debilitating physical pain was nothing compared to the morose emptiness she'd been left with afterward.

"I'm not as strong as you are." Howard Owens's voice sounded…different. She hardly recognized it. Tamara stared at him, truly frightened. Was her father sick? Did her mother know? Was that why they'd needed her home?

Frustrated, she wanted to demand that he tell her what was going on, but knew better. The Owens and their damned independence. Asking for help was like an admission of defeat.

"Of course you are," she told him, ready to hold him up, support him, for whatever length of time it took to get him healthy again. If, indeed, he was sick. She slowed herself down. She'd just been thinking how healthy, robust, strong he looked. His skin as tanned as always, that tiny hint of a belly at his waist… Everything was as it should be. He'd been talking about his golf scores at dinner the night before—until her mother had changed the subject in the charming manner she had that let him know he was going on and on.

Tamara had been warmed by the way her mother had smiled at her father as the words left her mouth—and the way, as usual, he'd smiled back at her.

She and Steve had never had that; they'd never been able to communicate as much or more with a look as they had with words. In the final couple of years, not even words had worked for them…

"Anyway," she continued, pulling her mind out of the abyss, "you're the one who taught me *how* to do it," she said, mimicking him. "It's all about focus, exactly like you taught me. If I wanted to get good grades, I had to focus and study. If I wanted to have a good life, I had to focus on what I wanted. If I wanted to overcome the fear, I had to keep my thoughts on things other than being afraid. And if I want to be a success, I just have to focus on doing the best job I can do. Focus, Dad. That's what you've always taught me and what I've always done. In everything I do."

It was almost like she was telling him how to make it through whatever was bothering him.

He'd always been her greatest example.

Howard's eyes closed for longer than a blink. When he opened them again, he didn't meet her gaze. And for the second time fear struck a cold blow inside her. *Focus on the problem*, she told herself. Not on how she was feeling.

To do that, she had to know the problem.

"What's going on, Dad?" There was no doubt that his call to her asking her to come home had to do with more than missing her. How much more, she had to find out.

"Owens Investments was audited this past spring."

Her relief was so heady she almost saw stars. It was business. Not health. "You've got some misplaced files?" she asked him. "You need me to do a paper trail to satisfy them?" Her Master's in Business Administration had been a formal acknowledgment of her ability, but Tamara's true skills, organization and thoroughness, were what had catapulted her to success in her field. If a paper trail existed, she'd find it. And then know how to better organize the process by which documents were collated so nothing got lost again.

Her father's chin jutted out as he shook his head. "I wish it was missing files. Turns out that someone's been siphoning money from the company for over a year. And I'm not sure it's stopped. If it continues, I could lose everything."

Okay. So, not good news. Also not imminent death. Anything that wasn't death was fixable.

"I need your help, Tam," Howard said, folding his hands on the desk as he faced her. "Money is a vulnerable business. A lucrative one, but vulnerable. If our investors hear there's money missing, they'll get nervous. There could be a massive move out…"

She could see that. Was more or less a novice about the ins and outs of what he did, but she knew how companies worked. And the importance of consumer trust.

"I was hoping I'd be able to figure out what's going on myself, no need to alarm you or bring you home, but I haven't been able to find the leak. I need you to come in and do what you do. To give us a once-over, presumably to see if you can save us money. In reality, I'm hoping that you can give everything more of a thorough study without raising suspicions the way it would if I was taking a deeper look."

She nodded, recognizing how hard it was for her father to have to ask for help. Thinking ahead. Focusing on the job.

"People are going to know I'm your daughter. They might be less comfortable speaking with me."

He shook his head again. "I've thought of that. A few will know, of course. Roger. Emily. And Bill. For the rest, it works in our favor that you kept your married name because it was the name you became known under in the business world. People will have no reason to suspect."

Roger Standish, Emily Porter and Bill Coniff. CFO, VP and Director of Operations, respectively. Her father's very first employees when he'd first started out. She'd met them all but it wasn't as if he'd been close friends with his business associates. He was closer to his clients. Many of those she knew better than her own aunts and uncle. Still, none of his top three people would rat her out to the employees. Unless…

"What if the problem rests with one of those three?"

"I guess we'll find that out," he said, raising a hand and then running it over his face. Clearly he'd been dealing with the problem for a while. Longer than he should have without saying anything. She was thirty-two, not thirteen.

"Does Mom know?"

"Of course. She wanted me to call you home immediately."

"You should have."

"Your happiness and emotional health mean more to me than going bankrupt."

Feeling her skin go cold again, she stared at him. Was it that bad?

"Your well-being is one of the top factors that affects my emotional health," she couldn't help pointing out to him.

With a nod, he conceded that.

He was asking for her help. Nothing else mattered.

"How soon can I start?" she asked.

"That was going to be my question."

"When you finally got around to telling me you needed something…" The slight dig didn't escape him.

"I was going to tell you today. I was just having a bit of trouble getting to it. You've been through so much and I don't like putting more on you…"

"I make my living by having companies put more on

me. It's what I do, what I strive for." She grinned at him.
He grinned back.

Her world felt right again.

"So…is now too soon?"

"Now would be great. But…there's one other thing."

The knot was back in her stomach. *Please, not his health.* Had he waited until the stress had taken a physical toll before calling her? "What?"

"I don't want to prejudice or influence your findings, but there's one employee in particular who I think could be the one we're after. Although I wasn't able to find anything concrete that says it's him."

Pulling the tablet she always kept in her bag onto her lap, she turned it on. Opened a new file. "Who is he? And why do you suspect him?"

"His name's Flint Collins. I took him on eight years ago when he was let go by his firm and no one else would hire him. He'd only been in the business a year, but had good instincts. He was up-front about the issues facing him and looked me straight in the eye as we talked. He was… He kind of reminded me of myself. I liked him."

Enough to have been blinded by him? "Have I ever met him? Flint Collins?"

"No." Her father didn't have office parties at home. And rarely ever attended the ones he financed at the office.

"So what were his issues eight years ago?"

Not really an efficiency matter, she knew, unless, of course, he was wasteful to the point of being a detriment to the company. But then, this wasn't just an efficiency case.

This was her father. And she was out for more than saving his firm a few dollars.

"His mother was indicted on multiple drug charges. She'd been running a fairly sophisticated meth lab from her home and was dealing on a large enough scale to get her ten years in prison."

Had to be tough. But… "What did that have to do with him, specifically?"

"The trailer she lived in was in his name. As were all the utilities. Paid by him every month. He had regular contact with his mother. He'd already begun to make decent money and was investing it, so he was worth far more than average for a twenty-two-year-old just out of college. Investigators assumed that part of his wealth came from his cut of his mother's business and named him as a suspect. They froze his assets. Any investors he had at the firm where he worked got scared and moved their accounts. It was a bad deal all the way around."

"Was he ever formally charged?" She figured she knew the answer to that. He wouldn't be working for her father as an investment broker if he had been. But she had to ask.

"No. He says he had no idea what his mother had been doing. Seemed to be in shock about the whole thing, to tell you the truth. A warrant for all his accounts and assets turned up no proof at all that he'd ever taken a dime from anyone for anything. All deposits were easily corroborated with legitimate earnings."

"How'd he do for you?"

"Phenomenal. As well as I thought he might. He's one of our top producers. Until recently, I never suspected him of anything but being one of the best business decisions I'd ever made."

"What happened recently?"

"He hooked up with a fancy lawyer. His spending habits changed. He bought a luxury SUV, started taking exotic vacations, generally living high. I'm not saying he couldn't afford it, just that a guy who's always appeared to be conservative with his own spending was suddenly flashing his wealth."

As in…he'd come into new wealth? Or felt like he'd tapped into a bottomless well? Or was running with a faster crowd and needed more than he was making?

"There's more," her father said. "Last week Bill told me he'd heard from Jane in Accounting that she'd heard from a friend of hers in the office of the Commissioner of Business Oversight that Collins was planning to leave. That he was filing paperwork to open his own firm. Bill says he heard that Collins was planning to take his book of business with him."

She disliked the guy. Thoroughly.

"He can't do that, can he? Solicit his clients away from you?"

"No, but that doesn't mean he won't drop a word in an ear here and there." Howard slowly tapped a finger on the edge of his desk, seeming to concentrate on the movement. "As I said, money is a vulnerable business. His clients trust him. They'll follow him of their own accord."

"So he's going to be direct competition to the man who took a chance on him?" *Hate* was such a strong word. She didn't want it in her vocabulary. Anger, on the other hand…

"I left another firm to start Owens Investments." Her father's words calmed her for the immediate moment. "He was doing what I did. Following in my footsteps, so to speak. I just didn't see it coming from him. I thought he was happy here."

"Unless he's leaving because he knows someone is on to the fact that money is being misplaced."

"That's occurred to me, too. About a hundred times over the past week. A guy who's opening his own business doesn't usually start spending lavishly. And if he was the decent guy I thought he was, he would at least have let me know his plans to leave. Which is what I did when I was branching out.

"And, like I said, he's the only one here who's made any obvious changes in routine or lifestyle over the past year. I did some checking into health-care claims and asked around as much as I could, and no one seems to be going through any medical crisis that would require extra funding. I'm not aware of any rancorous divorces, either."

"So... I start now and my first visit is to Mr. Flint Collins."

Howard nodded. "We need to get a look at every file he has while everything is still here."

Which might take some time. "Do you know how soon he's planning to leave?"

"Technically, I don't actually know that he's going. Like I said, this is all still rumor. He's given me no indication or made any official announcement about his plans."

"But it could be soon?"

Howard shrugged. "Could be any day. I just hope to God it's not. Even if he's not the one who's been stealing from me, he's going to do it indirectly unless I can get to his clients first. I've already started reaching out—making sure everyone's happy, letting them know that if there's any question or discomfort at all, to contact me. I'll take on more accounts myself rather than lose them."

Even then, her dad would have to be careful. He couldn't appear to be stabbing a fellow broker in the back just to keep more profits for himself. She did know *some* things about his business. She also remembered a time when she'd been in high school and another broker had left the firm. Her dad had talked to her mother about a party for the investors who'd be affected, which they'd had and then he'd acted on her advice as to how to deliver his news. She just couldn't remember what that advice had been. What stuck in her mind was that her father had taken it.

Which had given a teenage Tamara respect for, and faith in, both of them.

Standing, she asked her dad for a private space with a locking door that she could use as an office. Told him she'd need passwords and security clearance to access all files. And suggested he send out a memo, or however they normally did such things within the company, to let everyone know, from janitorial on up, that she'd be around and why, giving him wording suggestions. Everything that came with her introductory speech on every new job she took. She had a lot of work to do.

But first she was going to introduce herself to Flint Collins.

While her heart hurt for the young man who, from the sound of things, had a much more difficult upbringing than many—certainly far more difficult than she'd had—that didn't give him the right to screw over her family. Karma didn't work that way.

Chapter Three

Flint took the back way into his office. Leaving the base of the car seat strapped into the back of his SUV, he unlatched the baby carrier, carefully laid a blanket over the top and hightailed it to his private space.

Lunchtime at Owens Investments meant that almost everyone in Flint's wing would be out wining and dining clients, or holed up in his or her office getting work done. His door was the second from the end by the private entrance—because he'd requested the space when it became available. He wasn't big on socializing at work and hadn't liked being close to the door on the opposite end of the hall, which led to reception.

He'd never expected to be thankful that he could sneak something inside without being seen. That Monday he was.

Everyone was going to know. He just needed time to see Bill. His boss, Bill Coniff, was Director of Operations and, he was pretty sure, the person who'd ratted him out before he was ready to go to Howard Owens with his plan to open his own firm. Jane in Accounting had told him about the rumor going around, and said she'd interrupted Bill telling Howard. According to Jane, Bill had twisted the news to make it sound like Flint had been soliciting his current clients to jump ship with him.

Flint would get out of the business altogether before he'd do that.

Business was business. Howard had taught him that. Flint was good at what he did and could earn a lot more money over the course of his career by having his own firm. Could make choices he wasn't currently permitted to make regarding certain investments because Howard wasn't willing to take the same risks.

He felt that to live up to his full potential, he had to go, but he'd been planning to do it ethically. With Howard fully involved in the process—once there was a solid process in which to involve him.

But in less than a week his life had irrevocably changed. Forever. His focus now had to be on making enough money to support a child, not taking risks. To provide a safe, loving home. And to have time to be in that home with the child as much as possible.

How the hell he was supposed to go about that, he had no real idea. First step had been watching all the videos. Buying out the baby store.

And the next was to humble himself, visit Bill Coniff and ensure his current job security. To beg if it came to that.

He spent a few minutes setting up the monitor system he'd purchased for his office, putting the remote receiver in his pocket and taking one last glance at the baby carrier he'd placed on the work table opposite his desk. The floor was too drafty, the couch too narrow. What if she cried and moved her arms and legs a lot and the carrier fell off?

Ms. Bailey had said that the infant had been fed before she'd brought her to the gravesite. Apparently she ate every two hours and slept most of the rest of the time. By his math, that gave him half an hour to get his situation resolved before she'd need him.

Testing the monitor by talking into it and making sure he heard his own voice coming out of his pocket, he left the room, closing the door behind him. Should he lock it? Somehow, locking a baby in a place alone seemed dangerous. Neglectful. But he couldn't leave the door unlocked. Anyone could walk down that hallway and steal her away.

Was he wrong to vacate the room at all?

People left babies in nurseries at home and even went downstairs. Bill's office was two doors away from his. He'd see anyone who walked by. Unless whoever it was came in through the private door. Only employees had access to that hall.

There were security cameras at either end.

If there was a fire and he was hurt, a locked door would prevent firefighters from getting to Diamond Rose.

Decision made, he left the door unlocked.

"Please, Bill, I'm asking you to support me here. I'm prepared to plead my case to Howard. Just back me up on it. I don't know who started spreading the rumors or how far they've reached, but I'm fairly certain they made it to Howard's office..."

On her way to knock on the door of one Flint Collins, Tamara stopped in her tracks. Standing in a deserted private hallway in two-and-a-half-inch heels and her short black skirt with its matching short jacket, plus the lacy camisole her mother had bought to go with the ensemble, she felt conspicuous. But something told her not to move. She'd dressed for a "professional" lunch with her father, not for real business. But business was at hand.

"You're telling me you didn't file paperwork to open your own investment firm?"

She recognized Bill's voice coming from the office with his name on the door. Based on what her father had told her, she figured Bill had to be speaking with Flint Collins. Did her father know Bill was intending to handle the matter?

"No. I'm not saying that. I'm telling you I no longer have plans to do that and would like to do whatever I need to, to ensure my job security here."

"Your plans to hurt this company by soliciting our customers didn't work out, so now I should trust that you're here to stay?"

Bill was in the process of firing the guy? He couldn't! Not yet! She needed time to investigate him while his files were all still in his office at the company. While he didn't know he was being watched.

"I did not, nor did I intend, to solicit anyone. I intended to have a meeting with Howard and do things the right way."

"And now you don't plan to leave anymore."

"Now, in light of the rumors that went around last week, I'd like to guarantee that I have job security here and I was hoping for your cooperation. You know the money I make for this firm, Bill."

"*You* know how important trust is to this firm."

Tamara took a step forward. She couldn't let Bill fire the man, but wasn't sure how to prevent that from happening without exposing more than she could if she was going to be effective in her task.

"I'm willing to sign a noncompete clause to prove my trustworthiness."

"Wow, I like the sound of that!" Tamara burst into the room with a smile that she hoped Bill would accept at face value. She and her father had decided that even his top people shouldn't be told her true reason for being there. At the moment, they could only trust each other.

But he'd called all three of them before she'd left his office, telling them she was going to be doing an efficiency study and that he'd like their cooperation in keeping her relationship to him quiet. Howard wanted to make sure that as she moved about the company, she'd have their full support. She was working under her married name of Frost. Howard had explained that he'd thought people would be less nervous around her if they didn't know she was his daughter.

"Tamara? So good to see you!" Bill turned to her, an odd combination of welcoming smile and bewildered frown warring on his face.

"As you know, Bill, I'm here to study operations on all levels and find ways for Owens Investments to show a higher profit by running more efficiently," she said, holding out her hand to shake his.

Luckily she had her professional spiel down pat. Normally, though, the words weren't accompanied by a pounding heart. Or the sudden flash of heat that had surfaced as she'd looked from Bill to his conversation mate and met the brown-eyed gaze of the compelling blond man she'd been predisposed to dislike on sight.

At first Flint had absolutely no idea who the beautiful, auburn-haired woman with the gold-rimmed green eyes was as she interrupted the meeting upon which his future security could very well rest.

Bill quickly filled him in as he introduced the efficiency expert Howard Owens had hired. Apparently a memo had been sent to Flint and all Owens employees in the past hour. He, of course, had been busy burying his mother and becoming a guardian/father/brother and hadn't gotten to the morning's email yet.

Thinking of the baby girl he'd left sleeping in his office, he reached for the monitor in his pocket, thumb moving along the side to check that the volume was all the way up. He'd been gone almost five minutes. Didn't feel good about that.

"It seems to me, Bill, that if we have a broker on staff who's willing to sign a noncompete clause, then we should give him that opportunity. If he doesn't produce, we can still let him go. If he does, our bottom line has more security. We don't lose either way. Efficient. I like it."

Flint wasn't sure he liked *her*. But he liked what she was saying, since it meant Diamond Rose would have security.

"Unless you know of some reason we shouldn't keep him on?" she asked. "Other than what I just overheard, that he'd been thinking about opening his own firm?"

She looked at him. He didn't deny the charge. But he wasn't going to elaborate. Other than Bill, Howard Owens was the only one to whom Flint would report.

It seemed odd that this outside expert happened to be in the hall just as he'd been speaking with Bill. As though some kind of fate had put her there.

Or a mother in heaven looking out for her children?

The idea was so fanciful, Flint had a second's very serious concern regarding his state of mind. But another completely real concern cut that one short. His pocket made a tiny coughing sound.

All three adults in the room froze. Staring at each other.

And Flint's brand-new little girl made another, half-crying sound. In a pitch without weight. Or strength.

The woman—Tamara Frost, as Bill had introduced her—stared at his pocket. For a second there she looked... horrified. Or maybe sick.

"Not that it's any of my business but...do you have a newborn baby cry as your ringtone?" Her voice, as she looked up at him, sounded professionally nonjudgmental—although definitely taken aback.

Probably didn't happen often... Guys with the sound of crying babies in their pockets during business meetings.

Diamond Rose released another small outburst. Twenty minutes ahead of schedule. He had to get back to her. His first real duty and he was already letting her down. He'd had no time to prepare the bottle, as he'd expected to.

"I'm sorry," he said, looking from Bill to their expert and then heading to the door. "I have to get this."

Let them think it was his phone. And that the call was more important at that moment than they were.

Just until he had things under control.

Chapter Four

She was coming down with something. Wouldn't you know it? First day of the most important job of her life to date—because it was for her father, her family—and she was experiencing hot flashes followed by cold shivers.

That could only mean the flu.

Crap.

"So…you're good with keeping him on?" She looked at Bill and then back to the doorway they'd both been staring at. She'd been listening for Mr. Collins's "hello" as he took the call that was important enough for him to leave a meeting during which he'd been begging for his job. She'd wanted to hear his tone of his voice as he addressed such an important caller.

Business or pleasure?

"Your father said you're the boss." Bill's words didn't seem to have any edge to them.

"Well, he's wrong, of course." She was smiling, glad

to know she didn't have to worry about stepping on at least one director's toes. "But it makes sense, from an efficiency standpoint, to keep on a broker who's willing to sign a noncompete clause. Unless you know of some reason he should go? I heard him say he makes the company money. Is that true?"

"He's one of our top producers."

She knew that already, but there was no reason, as an efficiency expert who hadn't yet seen her first file, that she should.

"You have some hesitation about him?"

She'd asked Bill twice if there was a reason Flint Collins shouldn't stay on. Bill hadn't replied.

He gave a half shrug as he looked at her and crossed to his desk, straightening his tie. "None tops the offer he made a few minutes ago. Still, I don't like having guys around that I can't trust."

He had her total focus. "He's given you reason to mistrust him?"

Bill shook his head. "Just the whole 'opening his own shop' thing."

"It's what my dad did—left a firm to start Owens Investments. And you helped him do it."

"We did it the right way," Bill said. "The first person your father told, before taking any action, was his boss. None of this finding out from a friend in the recorder's office. Makes me wonder what else he isn't telling us…"

Made her wonder, too.

"I'm going over all the company files. He'll know that as soon as he reads his email. Seems like if he's untrustworthy, he'll have a problem with that."

"If he's got anything to hide, you aren't going to find it."

Maybe not.

Ostensibly her job was to come up with ways for Owens

to make more money. "He's a top producer and wants to sign a noncompete agreement."

"Right when he was getting ready to go into business for himself," Bill said, frowning. "Like I said, kind of makes you wonder why, doesn't it?"

"Is it possible that any of his applications for the various licenses were turned down for some reason?"

"From what I heard, he'd been fully approved."

"Could you have heard wrong?"

Bill shrugged again. "Anything's possible."

She nodded. She needed to get hold of Flint Collins's files.

"He came to you knowing he had to contend with trust issues and was armed with a plan that benefits Owens Investments," she said. She wasn't sure how to interpret that yet. Had he seen that he could make more siphoning off money from her father than he would on his own?

"He's a smart businessman."

"So, are you okay with keeping him on or will you be letting him go?" She couldn't allow him to think it really mattered to her. Or that she intended to push her weight around, beyond efficiency expertise.

If Bill planned to fire Collins right away, she'd go to her father, have him handle the situation. She hoped it didn't come to that.

"Of course I'm keeping him on," Bill said. "He's making us a boatload of money. But I don't trust him and I'll be watching him closely."

Her father had a good man in his Director of Operations. Smiling, Tamara told him so, thanked him and promised to do all she could to stay out of his way.

Shouldn't be hard. She had a feeling Flint Collins would be taking up most of her time.

Maybe an efficiency expert wouldn't be able to find

whatever he might be hiding, or anything he might be doing to rip off her family, but a daughter out to protect her father would.

By whatever means it took.

Tamara was certain of that.

For a man who liked to plan his life down to the number of squeezes left in his toothpaste tube, Flint figured he was doing pretty well to be at his desk, with his computer on, twenty minutes after leaving Bill Coniff's office.

His "inheritance," the tiny being who was now his responsibility for life, lay fed, dry and fast asleep in the car seat–carrier combination, her head securely cushioned by that last little gift from the caseworker. He'd placed her on the table across the room, but sitting at his desk, he wasn't satisfied. The carrier was turned sideways. He couldn't see her full face to know at a glance that her blanket hadn't somehow interfered with her breathing, say if she happened to move in her sleep.

Clicking to open his client list, he crossed the room and adjusted the carrier, turning it to face his desk. Looked at the baby. Noticed her steady breathing.

She had the tiniest little nose. Probably the cutest thing he'd ever seen.

She was going to be a beauty.

Like their mother…

He planned to keep her under lock and key. Away from anyone who could attempt to hurt her…

Taken aback by the intensity of that thought, telling himself he wasn't really losing his mind, he returned to work. Found the client file he wanted. Opened it.

On Friday, before his world had completely crumbled, he'd made an investment that was meant to be short-term. A weekend news announcement had caused the stock to plummet, but it would rise again, for a few days at least, before it either plummeted long-term or—as he hoped—held steady. He figured he'd have five days max. Preferably three. The risk was greater than Howard would want, but the potential return should be remarkable enough to secure his job, at least for now.

As long as the risk paid off.

Flint clicked on certain files, clicked some more. Looked at numbers. Studied market movement. It occurred to him that he should be nervous. If he'd invested at a loss, it could potentially mean his job. He knew Bill had been about to fire him when fate had sent in the consultant Howard had hired.

He wasn't nervous. Flint took risks with the market. But only when his gut was at peace with them. His financial gift was about the only thing he trusted.

Glancing up, he checked his new responsibility. He could see movement as she breathed. Stared as a fist pushed its way out of the blanket. Who'd have thought hands came that small? Or that people did?

She looked far too insecure on that big table made for powerful business deals between grown men and women.

Market numbers scrolled on his screen. They were still going up. But they could take a second rapid dive; his guess was they would. And soon. They'd already climbed higher than he'd conservatively predicted, but not as high as he'd optimistically hoped.

Pushing back from his desk, he crossed the room again, lifted the carrier gently, loath to risk waking his charge. With his free hand, he pulled a chair back to his desk, positioning it next to his seat, along the wall to his left. Away from the door and any unseen drafts. Satisfied, he settled the carrier there, glanced at his computer screen and pushed the button to sell.

At a price higher than he'd hoped.

Five minutes later, the stock started to drop.

He still had his touch. And a fairly good chance of securing his job. Even Bill couldn't argue with the kind of money he'd just made.

As was her way, Tamara studied before she went into action. She didn't take the time she would later spend going over individual accounts, one by one, account by account, figure by figure. But when she approached Flint Collins's office late Monday afternoon, she not only knew every piece of information in his employee file, but she was familiar with every account he'd handled in the nearly eight years he'd been working for her father.

Aside from the part about suspecting that he was stealing from them, she was impressed. And more convinced than ever that if anyone could succeed in taking money from Howard without his knowing, it could be Collins. The man was clearly brilliant.

He'd been a suspect in the drug production and distribution that had put his mother in prison; he'd also grown up with her criminal history. According to a pretty thorough background check, the only consistent influence in his life had been his mother—in between her various stints in jail.

The first of which had come when he was only six. She'd been sentenced to three months. Tamara had seen a list of his mother's public criminal record in his file. Probably there because of Flint's ties to her latest arrest. She'd also seen that the woman was only fifteen years older than her son. A child raising a child.

Funny how life worked. A young girl who, judging by the facts, had been ill-equipped to have the responsibility of a child and yet she'd had one. While Tamara...

No. She wasn't going backward.

Passing Bill's open door, she waved at the director who was on the phone but waved back. Smiled at her. And her heart lifted a notch. She'd managed to get her way and not make an enemy. It was always good to have a "friend" among the people she was studying.

A couple of steps from Flint Collins's closed door, she stopped. That damned baby cry was going off again. She didn't want to interrupt his call. Nor did she want to wait around while he talked on the phone.

And really, what kind of guy had a crying newborn as his ringtone?

Not one she'd ever want to associate with, that was for sure.

However she didn't want to get on the guy's bad side. Not yet, anyway. She needed him to like her. To trust her.

She might even need to learn about his life if she hoped to help her father. According to Bill, anyway. The director was pretty certain that Collins wouldn't have hidden anything he was doing in files to which she'd have access.

The crying had stopped. She didn't hear any voices. Had whoever was calling hung up?

Deciding to wait a couple of seconds, just in case he was listening to a caller on the other end, Tamara cringed as the baby cry started back up. Sounding painfully realistic. How could he stand that?

Apparently he'd let the call go to voice mail. And whoever had been at the other end was phoning back. Was Collins ignoring the call? Unless he wasn't there? Had he left his cell in his office?

A man like Flint Collins didn't leave his cell phone behind.

Tamara knocked. And when there was no answer, tried the door. Surprisingly the knob turned. The office was impressive. Neat. Classy. Elegant.

And had nothing on the spread of male shoulders she saw bending over something to the side of his desk. Or the backside beneath them.

"Why aren't you answering your phone?" she blurted. The crying had to stop. It was making her crazy. She had business to do with him and—

The way those shoulders jerked and his glance swung in her direction clearly indicated that he hadn't heard her enter. Making her uncomfortably aware that she should probably have knocked a second time.

How hadn't he heard her first knock?

The thought fled as soon as she realized that the crying was coming from closer to him. There by the window. Not from the cell phone she noticed on his desk as she approached.

And then she saw it…the carrier…on the chair next to him. He'd been rocking it.

"What on earth are you doing to that baby?" she exclaimed, nothing in mind but to rescue the child in obvious distress. To stop the noise that was going to send her spiraling if she wasn't careful.

"Damned if I know," he said loudly enough to be heard over the noise. "I fed her, burped her, changed her. I've done everything they said to do, but she won't stop crying."

Tamara was already unbuckling the strap that held the crying infant in her seat. She was so tiny! Couldn't have been more than a few days old. Her skin was still wrinkled and so, so red. There were no tears on her cheeks.

"There's nothing poking her. I checked," Collins said, not interfering as she lifted the baby from the seat, careful to support the little head.

It wasn't until that warm weight settled against her that Tamara realized what she'd done. She was holding a baby. Something she couldn't do.

She was going to pay. With a hellacious nightmare at the very least.

The baby's cries had stopped as soon as Tamara picked her up.

"What did you do?" Collins was there, practically touching her, he was standing so close.

"Nothing. I picked her up."

"There must've been some problem with the seat, after all…" He'd tossed the infant head support on the desk and was removing the washable cover.

"I'm guessing she just wanted to be held," Tamara said. What the hell was she doing?

Tearless crying generally meant anger, not physical distress.

And why did Flint Collins have a baby in his office?

She had to put the child down. But couldn't until he put the seat back together. The newborn's eyes were closed and she hiccuped and then sighed.

Clenching her lips for a second, Tamara looked away. "Babies need to be held almost as much as they need to be fed," she told him while she tried to understand what was going on. "The skin-to-skin contact, the cuddling, is vitally important not only to their current emotional well-being but to future emotional, developmental and social behavior."

She was quoting books she'd memorized—long ago—in another life. He was checking the foam beneath the seat cover and the straps, too. Her initial analysis indicated that he was fairly distraught himself.

Not what she would've predicted from a hard-core businessman possibly stealing from her father.

"Who is she?" she asked, figuring it was best to start at the bottom and work her way up to exposing him for the thief he probably was.

He straightened. Stared at the baby in her arms, his brown eyes softening and yet giving away a hint of what looked like fear at the same time. In that second she wished like hell that her father was wrong and Collins wouldn't turn out to be the one who was stealing from Owens Investments.

She didn't move. Just stood frozen with her arms holding a baby against her.

"Her name's Diamond Rose." His tone soft, he continued to watch the baby, as though he couldn't look away. But he had to get that seat dealt with. Fast. The lump in her throat grew.

"Whose is she?" She was going to have to put the baby down. Sooner rather than later. Her permanently broken heart couldn't take much more. The tears were already starting to build. Dammit! She'd gone almost two months without them.

"Mine...sort of."

Her head shot up. "Yours?" She glanced at the cell phone on his desk and then noticed the portable baby monitor. "You don't have a baby crying ringtone?"

"No."

"You have a baby?"

There'd been nothing in his file. According to her father, he'd only been dating his current girlfriend—some high-powered attorney—for the past six months. He'd brought her to a dinner Howard had hosted for top producers and their significant others. And had explained where and how they'd met. Which was pertinent because soon after he'd taken the first full vacation he'd had in eight years.

"She's not mine," he said then frowned, glancing at Tamara hesitantly before holding her gaze. "Legally, she is. But I'm not her father."

"Who is?" His personnel records hadn't listed any next of kin other than an incarcerated mother.

He shrugged. "That's the six-million-dollar question. No idea. Biologically she's my sister."

Tamara flooded with emotion. She couldn't swallow. Standing completely still, concentrating on distancing herself from the deluge, focusing on him, she waited for her skin to cool. With a warm baby snuggled against her chest.

She had to get rid of that warmth.

Get away from the baby.

"Your mother had a baby?" she heard herself ask, sounding only a little squeaky.

He nodded.

"I thought she was in prison…" She suddenly realized she might have revealed too much. She was being too invasive for a first business meeting. "Um, Bill told me. He said you'd overcome a…difficult past."

He nodded. "She was. And the fact that she was a convict makes the question about Diamond's father that much harder to answer. Who's going to admit to fathering a child illegally?"

Her nerves were quaking. "She gave birth in prison?"

"Three days ago."

She'd been right. The child was only days old…

Days older than any of hers had lived to be.

"And she gave her to you?" She wasn't going to be able to keep it together much longer.

He'd agreed to take a baby. That said something about him. He needed to take her from Tamara.

He'd taken on a child. But then, his mother, a criminal, had agreed to take him on, too. By birthing him. Keeping him.

"My mother died in childbirth."

Flint's shocking words hit her harder than they would

have if she'd been on the other side of the room. Or in another room. Speaking to him on the phone.

Knees starting to feel weak, she knew she was out of time. "And just like that, you become a father?"

"Just like that."

There were things she should say. More questions to ask. But Tamara simply stood there, staring at him.

Unable to move.

To speak.

She was shaking visibly.

And had to get rid of the bundle she held.

Pronto.

Chapter Five

"Here, you need to take her."

As the pink-wrapped bundle came toward him with more speed than he would've expected, Flint reached out automatically, allowing the baby's head to glide up to his elbow, her body settling on his lower arm. While holding a baby was still foreign to him, he was beginning to notice a rhythm, a sense of having done it before.

"She needs to bond with you." The woman was a stranger to him and yet she was sharing one of the most intimate experiences in his life. His coming to grips with a reality he had little idea how to deal with and a role he was unsure of. Burying his mother. Meeting his sister. Becoming for all intents and purposes, a father. All happening in one day. He'd been about to lose it—and she'd saved him.

Just like she'd saved him from almost certain job loss earlier.

Could she really be, somehow, heaven-sent? By his

mother, not any divine source watching out for him. He'd long ago ceased hoping for that one.

Did he dare even think of his mother making it to an afterlife that would allow her to help her baby girl?

Was he losing his damned mind?

"Until two days ago, I didn't know the first thing about children." He hardly remembered being one. It seemed to him he'd grown up as an adult. "Babies in particular."

"You've had her for two days?" The woman had backed up to the other side of the desk and was halfway to the door. A couple of times she'd rubbed her hands along shapely thighs covered by a deliciously short skirt and was now clasping them together as though, at any second, they might fly apart.

"I just got her today," he said, calming a bit now as the baby settled against him as easily as she had with the efficiency expert. It was the first time he'd actually held the infant.

All he'd done so far was pick her up to lay her on a pad on the table. And to put her back in her carrier to feed her. That was it.

"So, how often does the holding thing need to happen?" How far behind was he?

"All the time." She was nodding, as though following the beat of some song in her head. Rubbed her thighs again, then was wringing her hands. Then reached for the doorknob. "When you're feeding her, certainly, and other times, too. Whenever you can. There are, um, books, classes and, you know, places you can go to learn everything..."

"I spent the weekend crash coursing. I guess I zoned out on the holding part."

"Parents holding their babies is a...biological imperative. They can't get enough of it. The babies, I mean. And..."

She turned away as though she couldn't wait to escape. Which made no sense to him, considering how naturally she'd rescued Diamond Rose from his inept attempts to "parent" her.

"What did you want?" His question was blunt but he wasn't ready for her to go. Not until his baby sister had a few more minutes with him—while he still had the efficiency expert's child-care guidance. To make sure Diamond was satisfied, for now, with what he could do for her.

"Um…oh, it can wait."

She glanced at the baby again, her eyes lingering this time. And then she seemed unusually interested in the wall on the opposite side of the room.

"Seriously. You needed something from me. I'm here to work." He couldn't afford to be a problem, considering how badly he needed this job.

The expert took a step away from the door and he waited for the business discussion to start. Tried not to pay attention to how beautiful she was. Like no woman he'd ever encountered before. A compelling combination of business savvy, sexy, glamorous and natural, too.

He thought her name was Tamara, but wasn't positive he was remembering correctly. He'd been a bit distracted when they'd met earlier.

But if he could get her to put in a good word with Howard on his behalf…

"I'm sorry about your mother." She sounded a little less harassed.

He nodded. Settled his bundle a little more securely against him.

She stared at the crook of his arm, then looked around the office. Seemed to spy the Pack 'n Play still in its box tucked away by the long curtain on the far window. "I guess you haven't had time to make child-care arrangements."

Efficiency expert. Finding a problem with his efficiency?

"I sold three thousand shares at 475 percent of their purchased value today." He'd made an outrageous amount of money for a client who liked to take risks. And a hefty sum for the brokerage, though it wasn't an investment Howard would have approved of because of the risk. He could just as easily have lost the entire sum.

The efficiency expert blinked. Gave her head a little shake. Drawing his attention to the auburn curls falling around her shoulders.

"I...asked about child care?" She sounded as though she was doubting his mental faculties now. She could join the club. If ever a man had lost it, that was him.

"Because if you need help, I know someone…"

Oh.

"I need to find out if I have a job first," he told her. Bill hadn't fired him. But he hadn't said his job was secure, either. Flint hadn't heard from him all afternoon. Or from Howard.

Either of them could have seen the sale he'd made, with their access to the company's portfolios. He assumed they both had. They were that kind of businessmen. Always on top of what mattered.

Which was why he was working there.

"Were you intending to open your own business? I heard Mr. Coniff ask about that as I approached his officer earlier."

Not an efficiency-related question. But it was a human one. He was standing there, holding a baby, and had just told her, before he'd made anyone else in the company aware, that the child was suddenly his.

And that he'd lost his mother.

He'd also told her that he wasn't sure he still had a job.

"Yes, I was in the process of opening my own business." No point in denying the truth. Lying wasn't his way. "I intended to tell Howard as soon as the final paperwork was in order."

"And now you aren't?"

Diamond Rose sighed. He felt that breath as if he'd taken it himself. "Starting a new business, especially in this field, takes an eighteen-hour-a-day commitment and comes with more than average financial risk. I can no longer afford the time or the risk."

"Because of the baby."

Because he had no idea how to be a father. He had to learn. "I'm her only family."

She nodded, looking at him, meeting his gaze. Not glancing, even occasionally, at his baby sister. She wasn't wringing her hands anymore, either, which he considered to be a good thing.

Still…

"Howard doesn't know about her yet. I didn't actually see her myself until this morning. I'd appreciate it if you'd give me a little time to get my act together before you say anything."

"I work for him," she said. And then, "How much time?"

He calculated…between the month he'd probably need and the minute or two she seemed willing to give him. "Twenty-four hours, max."

She watched him.

"I've got sixty times that in vacation days coming to me." From an efficiency standpoint, she wouldn't be risking anything. He could certainly ask for twenty-four hours.

"But you…didn't take today off."

"I rarely take time off. And I had stocks I had to sell or risk a big loss."

He'd had all the losses he could handle. His mother. His fiancée. His business. All at once. In the past couple of days. Astonishing that he was still standing there.

Except that he'd had no choice. Someone had to take care of his mother's brand-new baby.

Tamara—yes, that was definitely her name, Tamara Frost—was silent. A few long seconds later she said, "I see no harm in allowing you the time to go to your boss yourself."

He could have kissed her. He shook off the feeling. He'd just met the woman! Whether or not she was his mother's way of helping him from the great beyond, he had no time— and no mental or emotional capacity—to engage in any kind of liaison.

Yet he clung to the idea of having her on his side.

"Thank you."

"So…you just got her this morning? And came straight here?" She sounded a bit incredulous.

"I had stocks I had to sell," he repeated. A job to save. He couldn't afford a big loss on top of everything else. That much he knew. He needed Howard Owens to need him around; he certainly didn't want to give the older man more reason to fire him.

Her expression changed. Softened, although she hadn't looked at the baby again. Not in a while. "I'd like to give you the name of a friend of mine. She runs a day care not far from here. Most places don't take infants younger than six weeks, but considering your circumstances, I'm pretty sure she'd make an exception. I promise you, you won't be sorry. She treats the children in her care like they're her own. Gets to know them. Loves them. Babies get dedicated holding time. She takes everything that happens to her kids personally."

He wasn't ready to pass off his bundle to a stranger. Not out of his sight, at least.

Ms. Frost had given him twenty-four hours to report to Howard with some kind of baby management plan—well, to report to Howard that he had a child. Having the plan was his own stipulation.

"Does she watch your children?" Tamara wasn't wearing a ring, but she'd been such a natural with Diamond Rose… Seemed to know everything about babies…

A shadow passed over Tamara's face. He pretended not to notice. But when you knew the depth of sorrow yourself, you noticed.

"I don't have children. My work is my life. My job requires a lot of travel. It's not as if companies can come to me! And I don't think it's right to have children and then not be there to raise them. I love what I do, so I made a conscious choice."

Then why the shadow in her eyes?

And what business was that of his?

Particularly since he already owed her so much. She'd interrupted at exactly the right time that morning, preventing him from losing his job, at least temporarily.

Giving him time to close the deal he'd opened at the end of the prior week. To make his company so much money, it would be harder to fire him.

She'd agreed he could have time to come up with a plan to present to Howard regarding his changed life status. A way to convince him that in spite of everything that had happened, he was still a smart business risk.

And she was the expert Howard had just hired— meaning Howard most likely trusted her implicitly. If Flint could stay on her good side…

"I'd appreciate your friend's information," he said. He nodded to a pad and pen on his desk that she could use to write down the woman's name and phone number. All the while, he held the sleeping newborn between his left arm and body.

He could do this. Work. Take care of business. And a baby.

As long as his baby sister didn't cry again. He'd hold her. Feed her. Burp her. Change her. And hold her again. How hard could it be?

"I'll leave you to it, then..."

Momentary panic flared as Tamara Frost walked back to the door of his office. "Wait!"

She turned.

"You... What did you want? Initially?" She couldn't have come to give him her friend's number. She hadn't known he had a baby. "When you knocked at my door?"

"I'm going to be conducting interviews with all department heads, with all top producers and with some randomly chosen office staff throughout the next week or so. I stopped by to set up an appointment to meet with you. But clearly you need to get your ship in order before I climb aboard."

She was smooth. All business. If he hadn't already been attracted to her, he'd have fallen right then. He wasn't going to start anything—or even think about it. But he couldn't help his reaction and was smart enough to acknowledge it to himself. Rather that than have it club him over the head at some point. Now *that*, he couldn't afford.

Reminding himself he'd decided to stay on her good side, to shield his position with Howard, he sent her a smile reserved for his best clients. "Whatever works for you," he told her. "I'll make myself available." Career came first with him.

The bundle in his arms blew a loud fart.

He'd forgotten, for a brief second, that he was no longer the man he'd been.

"Talk to Mallory," Tamara said, referring to the friend whose number she'd written down. "Talk to Howard. And then give me a call."

"I don't have your number."

"It's in the email sent to everyone this morning."

It was late afternoon and he'd yet to read any company-related mail. He'd handled his clients' correspondence, though. Made all his phone calls. Set up a couple of important lunches for later in the week.

Flint would have come up with some charming, pithy response if the expert had waited a little longer. Apparently she was too efficient for that.

Watching the door close behind her, he glanced at the baby in his arms and felt...weak.

The boy who'd been resilient enough to get on a school bus as a runt kindergartener and sit among the bullies wasn't sure how he was going to proceed through the next hour.

Chapter Six

Tamara canceled dinner with her parents two hours after she'd accepted her mother's invitation. Dr. Sheila Owens had reached her after rounds that afternoon, thrilled that Howard had finally spoken with Tamara about his business problems and that she was already at work, trying to find the thief who was stealing from them. Sheila had wanted them to meet as a family and talk about the issue.

Tamara decided her best efforts would be spent poring over files instead. To begin with, eight years' worth of Flint Collins's investments transactions.

First, though, she'd suggested to her father that someone get Collins to sign that noncompete clause and let him know he wasn't on the brink of being fired. Half an hour later she received a call from him, saying that Collins had just come out of Bill Coniff's office and that Coniff had the signed form in his possession. Smiling as she hung up, she was satisfied with her day's work.

And happier than she should be to know that the man she'd so recently met was no longer worrying about being gainfully employed. Flint Collins had enough to deal with at the moment.

She couldn't go soft on him, though. That was how a lot of white-collar criminals succeeded in their fraudulent efforts. By charming those around them, winning the trust of those they were cheating.

At the same time, the guy was human, not yet proved guilty of anything other than wanting to branch out on his own, and deserving of some compassion on the day he'd buried his mother.

She looked away from the computer screen in her compact new office on the third floor of the building her father owned. She had a feeling it had been a big storage closet of some kind prior to being hastily converted for her. Howard knew better than to lay down the red carpet for a paid consultant he supposedly didn't know other than by reputation.

At least the room was private.

She'd had worse in the two years she'd been on the road.

A window would have been nice.

Oh, God… That baby…

Glancing at the time in the corner of her computer screen, she picked up the phone. She'd left one message for Mallory. But it was five o'clock now. Most of the children would have been picked up. And Flint Collins would be calling, if he hadn't already.

She needed to speak with her friend.

"I was about to call you," Mallory said when she answered. "I got your message, and I have one from Mr. Collins, too. He needs to speak with me by tomorrow afternoon, he said."

She'd given him a deadline to talk to her father. Not that

he had to have day care arranged before letting his bosses know that he'd just become a father. Of sorts.

"So you haven't spoken with him?"

"No, your message said I should talk to you first."

Tamara nodded. She thought she'd asked that but couldn't be sure. She'd been a bit off her mark when she'd made the call, having come directly from Flint Collins's office.

Where she'd had a newborn baby snuggled against her chest.

A chill swept through her and her insides started to quake again. Until she focused on the computer screen. The rows of numbers she'd been studying.

It was all about focus.

When she could feel the bands around her chest loosening, she told Mallory about Flint Collins suddenly finding himself the sole caregiver of a newborn baby. She didn't include the personal details. That was for him to share, or not, as he chose. His personal situation wasn't why she was calling.

"I held the baby, Mal," she said in the very next breath. "I was in his office and I didn't know she was there. I heard her cry and saw that he was just standing there, in front of her carrier. Maybe he was rocking it or something, I don't know. But without thinking I went right up and unstrapped her and picked her up."

The silence on the other end of the line wasn't a surprise. Mallory's calm tone when she said, "What happened next?" was different than Tamara had expected.

Only a handful of people knew the true extent of her struggles, how close she'd come to thinking she'd never have another happy moment. Mallory was one of them.

Because Mallory had been there, too, a few years before. They'd met in a small counseling group designed solely for young mothers who'd lost a baby.

"I started to unravel," she admitted. "Not as quickly as I would've expected, but I was working and it took a while for that barrier to break down."

She could feel the bands tightening around her lungs again. Her entire chest. Her ribs. Physical manifestations of the panic she fought, less often now, but still regularly enough that she'd stayed in touch with her support group.

"So, basically, you held it together."

"On the surface."

Their psychiatrist had offered them all medications, individually, of course. She and Mallory had preferred not to depend on drugs and opted to fight the battle on their own. And because neither one of them had ever remotely considered actually taking her own life—on the contrary, they'd both been in possession of enough equilibrium to maintain careers—they'd been left to their decisions without undue pressure.

"And what about now? How do you feel?"

They were supposed to be talking about Flint. And that...needy little child.

"Like I want a glass of wine and a jet to someplace far, far away." She had to be honest. It was the only way to succeed on her personal survival mission. "I've got the jitters, my hands are sweaty on and off."

She'd had hot and cold flashes, too, but didn't mention them. They didn't have anything to do with the infant. Although, come to think of it, both had happened in the presence of Flint Collins. During the first, though, they'd been in Bill Coniff's office and she hadn't known Flint was a new dad. She'd thought she had the flu, but no other symptoms had developed.

She was so busy convincing herself that the hot and

cold flashes, something new in her panic world, had nothing to do with the baby, that she'd walked herself right into another mental trap. Were the flashes because of *Flint*? Because of how incredibly attractive he was? Like, Hollywood ad attractive?

Was she *physically* reacting to him? As in being inordinately turned on?

No. Tamara shook her head. *Don't borrow trouble*, she told herself.

"What's wrong?" she asked when she realized Mallory hadn't responded to her list of symptoms.

"I was hoping…"

She knew what Mallory would've been hoping. They'd had the discussion. Many times.

Now they'd had the experiment Mallory had begged for and Tamara had always point-blank refused.

She'd held a baby. It had been horrible.

"Absolutely not." She made her point quite clear. "Never again."

"Maybe because you were so convinced it was a bad thing…" Mallory, bless her heart, refused to give up.

Tamara had nothing more to say on the subject.

"It works, Tamara, I swear to you. If you'd just try. Give it a chance. I'm living proof, every single day. If you knew how much healthier I am… How much happier… How much stronger…"

She'd only met Mallory after the other woman's infant son had died, yet Tamara knew her well enough now to be certain that Mallory had always had a core of strength.

"I get comfort from them—real, lasting comfort— knowing that little ones are on this earth, healthy and robust and happy and full of love."

"I know you do." And it wasn't that Tamara didn't want

a world filled with healthy, robust, loving babies. She did. Very much. She just couldn't have them in *her* world.

Because her heart knew the pain of four babies who hadn't been healthy enough to make it into the world alive. She knew the pain of losing a baby that everyone had thought was healthy. It happened. Babies died. In the womb and out of it, too. She'd survived losing Ryan. Barely. She couldn't afford the risk of another bout of that kind of pain and the residual depression.

"I'm not you," she said now, aware that it wasn't what Mallory wanted to hear.

Silence hung on the line again. But not as long this time.

"So tell me about this guy you referred. Flint Collins? You said I should speak with you first…" Her voice trailed off in midsentence and then Mallory continued. "Or was that it? It was about how you felt when you held his baby?"

"No." She'd had hot flashes both times she'd been with Flint. Not just because of his looks. He was confident, capable, successful—and had chosen to give up his business dream to care for a sister he hadn't even known he had. He had a baby who desperately needed a mother. He'd be a great match for Mallory.

She shook her head. No, he had a girlfriend. And besides…

"I need your word that what I'm about to tell you stays between you and me. Period. No one else."

"Of course. I assumed everything we told each other was that way. The two of us—our conversations are like an extension of being in session, right?"

The tone of voice… Tamara could picture the vulnerable look that would be shining from Mallory's soft blue eyes.

"Right," she said. "I just… This isn't about us and I needed to make certain…"

"You and me, our friendship—we're sacred," Mallory said, her voice gaining strength.

"Okay, good." Tamara took the first easy breath she'd had since she'd stepped into Flint's office. "I found out today why my mom and dad wanted me home so badly. Dad needs my help at Owens Investments. Someone's stealing from him and he suspects it might be Flint Collins. I'm working as an efficiency expert for him as a cover so I can have access to all the company files and employees, to stick my nose anywhere I want, to see if I can find some kind of proof for Dad to take to the police."

"Why doesn't he hire a detective?"

"Because right now only his accountant knows. If word gets out that there's something untrustworthy going on in the company, his investors will take off like birds flying south for the winter."

"How sure is he that Collins is his guy?"

"The evidence is stacked against him at the moment. But it's all hearsay and circumstantial."

"And he's a new dad?"

"I'll let him fill you in on the details. But, Mal? Whatever he's doing in his business life, this baby… She's only three days old. If ever a baby needed you, it's her. Even more so if it turns out her dad's involved in criminal activity. I felt you had to know, in case something comes down and there's some reflection on your business."

Not too long ago, a woman had showed up at Mallory's day care claiming that one of the kids was the woman's two-year-old son, who'd been kidnapped. Things had been rough going there for several weeks. And then the woman's story turned out to be true. That had all taken place before Tamara had returned from Boston, but she'd heard about it over the phone.

"No one can blame a newborn baby for anything. But I'll be careful not to let him see the books," she said with a chuckle.

Tamara smiled, too. An easy smile. One that felt natural. Her breath came more easily, too. She'd known she could count on Mallory.

And maybe, if Flint wasn't the thief, he and Mallory could make a family for that precious baby—

No, he had a girlfriend. Some powerful lawyer.

Because he was hedging all his bets as a smart investor would? In case he needed a top-notch lawyer?

She couldn't help wondering, as she ended her call with Mallory, what that rich girlfriend, who'd apparently been responsible for a change in Flint's spending habits, or at least his driving and vacation habits, thought of having a convict's baby to raise?

And then berated herself for being so catty.

The other woman was probably perfectly wonderful. She might already be making plans for the baby's care and Flint had just taken Mallory's contact information to give them options.

In any case, it was none of her business.

Yes, she thought again. Flint Collins and his new life were absolutely none of her business. She'd simply been the one to walk in on his intense day.

She looked back at her computer screen.

Focus. That was all it took. Focus.

Chapter Seven

"Bathing your newborn baby with the umbilical cord stump still attached is fine," the pediatrician in the video confirmed. *"There is no great risk that the stump will get infected. Take care to make sure that the area is thoroughly dried."*

Holding his sleeping sister in the crook of one arm, Flint paused his continued scouring of articles and videos on the internet—all from verified, legitimate pediatric sources and nationally recognized clinics and associations. He found this video particularly informative, considering his current dilemma.

"It is not necessary to bathe your baby every day," she continued. *"Up to three times a week, for the first year, is fine. As long as you're quick and thorough with diaper changes and burp cloths, you're cleaning the critical areas often enough. Daily bathing is not recommended, since it can dry out the baby's skin."*

Okay. Good. He didn't have to deal with a bath his first night. Her first night with him.

He could have hired a nurse to help out with this transition stage, but hadn't really even considered doing so. He'd always taken care of himself—and his mother when he could. He'd take care of Diamond, too. The baby wasn't going to be shoved off on strangers anytime that he was available to care for her. As he'd been so many times.

"Dodged a bullet on that one, Diamond Rose," he said, glancing at the sleeping baby. He'd been doing that a lot, all day. Glancing at her. He'd even caught himself staring at her a time or two.

It was just so hard to believe she was there. His flesh and blood.

A rush of love he couldn't have imagined swamped him. He acknowledged it. And moved on. He'd learned a long time ago to move on when it came to those kinds of emotions.

A guy had to cope, to push forward. To accomplish.

"It's best to use a small plastic tub, or a kitchen sink, when bathing a newborn..."

Clicking to open an additional browser window, he shopped for plastic tubs. Found one at the local children's store he'd spent bundles in that weekend. How had he missed the tub aisle? He added it to the shopping list he'd made for the following day.

And thought about Tamara Frost. Wondering what she was doing. If she had a significant other and was with him. She hadn't been wearing a wedding ring, but that didn't necessarily mean anything these days.

He wondered how she'd react if he gave in to the urge that had been nagging at him most of the evening and called her.

Before he'd figured out his immediate plans. Before speaking with Howard as she'd instructed.

He'd spoken with Mallory Harris and had an arrangement to meet with her the following day, time to be determined.

First priority was Howard Owens. He'd sent off an email that afternoon, requesting an in-person meeting as soon as possible. Once he heard back, he'd schedule—or reschedule—everything else.

He checked his email again. No response yet.

Nothing from Stella, either, not that he'd expected anything. She'd made her feelings perfectly clear. The baby or her. His choice was in his arms, breathing against him.

Maybe he should be missing Stella more than he was, or at least be hurting… Maybe he would at some point. There just wasn't room enough right now. His capacity for grief was taken up with Alana Gold.

The woman who'd taught him a long time ago that no matter how much he loved her, it wouldn't be enough to keep her home with him. Not forever.

Having Stella in his life had been wonderful. And yet part of him had always believed it wouldn't last.

Glancing at the clock, Flint figured he had another hour and fifteen minutes before he'd need to measure formula, heat, change, feed and burp again. Adjusting the baby so she was lying against him, propped in the curve of his body, and freeing enough of his left arm to allow him to type, he clicked on the most used site on his browser's favorite bar—the stock exchange.

Twelve-eleven a.m.
One-oh-six a.m.
One fifty-two a.m.
Wiping the tears from her cheeks, Tamara sat up in

bed. Turning on the bedside lamp she'd purchased from an antiques mall before she'd moved east, she pulled her laptop off the nightstand and flipped it open—the third time since she'd gone to bed that she'd done it.

She'd focus. Work until she couldn't keep her eyes open. And then she'd sleep. Until she woke up shaking again.

The nightmares weren't the same. But they all *felt* identical. Sometimes she'd be holding Ryan, feeling so incredibly happy. Complete. And then she'd wake and the devastating loss would be as fresh now as though she was feeling it for the first time.

She didn't completely hate that dream. Those moments holding her baby—they were almost worth waking up for.

That night they were the other kind. The ones where she wasn't even around children at all. She'd be someplace—sometimes she recognized it, sometimes she didn't—and she couldn't get out. It could be a maze. A building. A hole in the ground.

Sometimes she'd be on a path in the dark with so many obstacles she couldn't move.

She'd hear a cry. Someone needing her. And she could never get to whoever it was.

Or she'd reach the end of the path and there'd be a dead baby. Wrapped in a beautiful blanket. Always wrapped in that blanket.

Once there'd been an empty casket.

In the beginning she'd been inside her own womb multiple times. Trapped. Unable to get out.

She'd had that dream again tonight. Before the 1:52 a.m. wakening. Which was why she was sitting up.

She could take a sleeping pill. Knock herself out.

The thought gave her comfort. Knowing she wasn't going to do it gave her determination.

Focus gave her peace.

Damn Flint Collins. Bringing his newborn baby sister to work. She wasn't going to think about him, other than to dissect his dealings with Owens Investments down to the last cent. Every investment. Every sale. Every client. Every expense report. Every report he ever wrote, period.

How his first night with a brand-new baby was going was not her concern.

The vulnerable look in those dark brown eyes didn't mean he wasn't guilty of theft.

The baby resting against that gorgeous, suited torso had no bearing on his business dealings.

Tamara was not going to have a relapse.

She was going to focus.

Setting his phone to wake him every two hours, knowing he was going to be up several times during the night, Flint had considered himself fully prepared for his first night as a brother/father. Or at least his first night as the sole responsible person for his "inheritance."

When at 1:52 a.m. he was up for the fourth time, holding a bottle to a sleeping baby's mouth, he didn't feel capable of anything more. She'd cry. He'd feed her. She'd fall asleep sucking on the nipple. He'd put her back to bed and within half an hour her cry would sound on the monitor again, waking him.

At a little after one, he'd let her cry. She wasn't due for another feeding until two thirty. She was dry. Surely she'd fall back asleep.

She hadn't.

He'd changed her Pack 'n Play sheet.

He'd changed her diaper, even though she'd been completely dry.

He'd checked the stump of her umbilical cord.

And used the axillary thermometer under her arm. It had registered perfectly normal.

So he'd put the bottle back in her mouth and she'd sucked and swallowed for a few minutes before going back to sleep.

He hadn't heard from Howard Owens. Had Tamara put in a good word for him? Or broken her promise and told his CEO that Flint had a crying baby in his office?

Even if he heard from Howard first thing, inviting him up, how sharp was he going to be in the morning on less than two hours' sleep?

He had to get some rest. Parents didn't stop requiring sleep the second they had a kid. His mom had slept.

Not that his mother was the greatest role model but, in this case, the thought made sense.

Settling the baby in her Pack 'n Play, double-checking the monitor, he quietly crossed the hall to his room, slid between the sheets and closed his eyes.

A vision of Tamara Frost was there. Her fiery hair, a cross between brown and red, curling and long, framing the gold-rimmed green eyes...

His eyes open, he stared at the ceiling for a couple of seconds before closing them again. He was supposed to be resting, not getting turned on.

Memories of the gravesite that morning assailed him. And then Bill Coniff's distrusting face when Flint had asked for job security.

The sale he'd made had been a success. He had a client for life on that one. And earned his job security, as it had turned out.

He'd signed the noncompete. Financially he was sound. Careerwise, he'd still be doing what he was good at.

Tamara Frost wanted a sit-down with him—

The monitor beside him blew that thought away.

Diamond Rose was awake again. Desperate now, he picked her up, wasn't even surprised when she quit crying the second he was holding her. With his free hand, he hauled her portable playpen into his room. It wasn't what he'd planned, but it now seemed the only sensible choice.

The playpen went right next to the bed, He placed the baby inside while she was still awake, talking to her the whole time, then lay down beside her, keeping his hand on the netted side of the crib.

"I'm right here, Little One," he said. "Right here. I'm always going to be right here. For as long as I live. That's the one thing you can count on. And I'm going to give it to you straight, too. That's what I do. Mom always said I was going to *be* someone."

He paused, thinking that last statement highly inappropriate. Stupid, even. Diamond Rose's eyes half blinked open.

"We'll get better at this." He started talking again immediately. "We'll figure it out together. No—scratch that. *You're* great. I'll get better. *I'll* figure it out. You go ahead and be a newborn. And then someday you'll be a kid, and I'll still be here, still figuring things out. You won't need to start doing that until you're at least ten. Maybe twenty. Yeah, twenty works. We'll revisit it when you're twenty and see where we're at…"

The baby was zonked. But just for good measure, Flint kept right on telling her how it was going to be until he'd talked himself to sleep.

How could a woman accomplish the tasks before her if the people in her life insisted on pulling her into distractions she could ill afford?

Hating the thought, retracting it immediately, Tamara

picked up the phone when she saw Flint Collins's name pop up.

Yeah, she'd added him to her contacts. Because she'd given him her number and if he was calling, she wanted a warning before she picked up.

"Hello, this is Tamara," she said in her most professional voice.

"I'm available to meet with you at your earliest convenience."

"I'm sorry, who is this?"

"Flint. Collins. You asked me to phone to set up a meeting after I met with Howard Owens. I'm calling to let you know I've done that."

His voice, all masculine confidence, didn't sound like he was reporting anything—and shouldn't be sending chills all the way through her.

"Yes, Mr. Collins. I've got meetings scheduled all day today. Let me see where I can fit you in."

She hadn't scheduled even one yet. She had people waiting to hear on times. She'd been waiting on him. Because, at the moment, her father didn't give a damn about the efficiency of his staff.

"You've met with Mr. Owens already today?" she asked inanely, buying herself a moment to cool down. She knew he had, and not just because he'd told her so. She'd had a call from her father the minute Flint Collins had left his office.

Just as she'd had a call from Mallory earlier that morning, the second she'd had Diamond Rose in her care. For the first time ever Tamara had almost had to ask her friend to stop talking. The way Mallory had gushed over the baby, thanking her for the chance to help care for the motherless infant. And then stating again that she couldn't believe the baby hadn't worked her magic on Tamara.

That had been right about the time Tamara had begun second-guessing the wisdom of her decision in sending Flint to Mallory.

But she'd quickly recovered. She'd made the right choice for Diamond Rose, first. And for Mallory, too.

Flint Collins was still on the line, having told her that not only had he met with her father, but that Howard Owens had been completely decent about everything— about keeping him on and the fact that he suddenly had sole care of an infant.

There it was again. *Sole care.* Her father had told her the same thing, adding that he'd suggested Flint take a few weeks off to get acclimated to this major change in his life. Flint had demurred, saying he already had care plans in effect for the infant. Tamara had wanted to ask about the lawyer girlfriend her father had mentioned the day before—clarifying that "sole care" meant that Flint was the child's only guardian, for now. But she hadn't actually voiced the question.

She still didn't know why she'd hesitated. Just that bringing up Collins's girlfriend to her father had seemed... uncomfortable.

Which made no sense at all.

She looked around her small office. And pictured his, which would undoubtedly still have the baby smell. Or at least her memory of it. "Can you do lunch?" she finished.

Yes, a nice public meeting. Over food. Something to do while she questioned him about...she wasn't sure what. So far, the figures that had put her to sleep the night before were all adding up, and all looked legitimate.

What she needed to see was his personal bank account.

His personal tax records.

She had no access to either.

"Lunch would be fine," Flint said, suggesting a place

that she recognized. Close to the office but more upscale than they needed. A third-floor place down by the pier, overlooking the ocean.

She needed him fully cooperative—willing to give her the goods on himself when she didn't even know where to look—so she graciously accepted. Agreed to meet him in the lobby to walk the short distance between her father's building and the restaurant.

Although it was the first of November, San Diego was San Diego, no matter what season it was. She wouldn't be cold in her navy formfitting dress pants and short navy jacket. And the wedged shoes... Having worn five-inch heels more times than she could count, she figured she could walk in pretty much anything.

She just hoped she wasn't walking *into* something that would turn out to be more than she could handle.

Her father was counting on her.

Chapter Eight

She never should have agreed to walk over to the restaurant with him. While the day was pleasant, and being out in the sun with the blue skies overhead was even better—especially considering the windowless room where she'd spent her morning—Tamara still regretted her choice. The people milling around them, tourists lollygagging and business people bustling, left her and Flint Collins in a world of their own.

At least that was how it felt to her.

While people could probably hear what they said, with everyone moving at a different pace, no one could follow their conversation.

Making their togetherness seem too personal. Too intimate.

To begin with, they just talked about being hungry. About the restaurant. They'd both been there many times.

She liked their grilled chicken salad. He was planning on the grilled chicken and jalapeño ciabatta.

It didn't surprise her that he was a daring eater. Preferred his food hot.

The crowds forced them closer together than she would've liked. At one point he put a hand at her back to lead her ahead of him as they crossed the street.

He didn't touch her, exactly, but she could feel the heat of his presence.

Looking down, she could see the tips of his shining black shoes and the hem of the dark gray business pants he was wearing with a white shirt and red power tie.

New baby or not, he'd been perfectly and professionally put together when he'd greeted her in the lobby earlier. She hadn't asked about Diamond Rose. If she wanted to get closer to him for the sake of her father's investigation, she probably should ask—

"You mentioned that you travel all over the country to the companies you work for, like Owens Investments, yet you seem so familiar with the area. Are you staying nearby?"

"I was born and raised in San Diego." She didn't see any harm in telling him that. "I work locally as much as I can, but I need to be free to go where the jobs take me."

At least that was the plan—to work locally as often as possible. She'd only started to send out her portfolio to companies in the area. She'd always gone where she'd been sent, but she wasn't with a big firm anymore. She was on her own and would be responsible for finding her own work.

As soon as she finished the job she was on.

She'd spoken with her father again, just before leaving for lunch. She'd been through every line item she had on Flint Collins, she'd told him, and had found absolutely nothing that raised a single question mark. Other than that the man pushed the boundaries on risk-taking.

A few of his investments had seemed questionable because of the amounts and the commodities those amounts were spent on—until she'd followed them through to the sale that had grossed impressive amounts.

He'd had a few losses, too, but they were minimal in comparison.

Her father still suspected Collins was behind the thefts. However, he agreed that she should spend equal time on others in the company. She'd already started to do that.

And in the meantime, people who spent time with someone noticed things.

So maybe that was her "in" with Flint. Maybe she had to spend time with him, eyes wide open, and look for whatever could help her father.

While she simultaneously scoured the files of everyone else in the company.

If she failed, her father was going to have to go to the police. Investors would learn that Owens Investments had trouble in the ranks and the client list would dwindle.

Not only would her father's company be at risk of going under, but Flint Collins's job security would be at risk, as well—if he wasn't the thief.

So, in a way, she could be helping him by spying on him.

The thought was a stretch.

Tamara went with it anyway. She was going to help her father. She'd been her parents' only shot at being grandparents and she'd failed them there. She knew it wasn't her fault but...

She wasn't going to fail them here.

Flint had called ahead to make certain they wouldn't have to wait for a table. He'd requested a booth—strictly for the privacy. The fact that they got one by the window facing the ocean was a gift, but one he wasn't surprised to receive. He frequented the restaurant. Almost always with clients who had a lot of money to spend.

"Excuse me a second," he said, pulling out his phone as soon as they'd ordered drinks. Raspberry iced tea for both of them, something the restaurant was known for. Touching the icon for the new app he'd downloaded that morning at the Bouncing Ball Daycare, Flint waited for the portal to open. Mallory Harris had cameras installed in the nursery and with the app he could check in on Diamond Rose whenever he wanted.

Mallory was also keeping a detailed feeding spreadsheet for him—at his request—but, as it turned out, something she normally did anyway.

He'd checked in on his new family member before heading down to the lobby and his meeting with Tamara. But half an hour had passed since then.

That was the longest he'd gone without seeing his baby sister since she'd been placed in his arms the day before. In the office, he'd had his phone propped up on his desk where he could see the screen app at all times.

She'd cried twice to be fed, an hour after he'd dropped her off and then an hour and a half later. He hoped he hadn't missed the next one...

Almost as though on cue, the sound came—a little warning first, more of a cough than a cry. But if they didn't get to her soon, she'd be wailing so hard it would sound like she was going to suffocate or something.

As the second cry followed the warning, a foot hit his shin under the table.

"I'm sorry." Tamara moved in the booth, placing herself more to his left rather than directly across from him.

The accidental touching of their bodies under the table

wasn't attention-worthy. But her hands were clasped so tightly together he could see her knuckles were white.

She was tense.

Because he'd been looking at his phone rather than listening to her questions? He couldn't blame her, really; this was a business lunch. But their food hadn't even been delivered yet.

Still, he set the phone on its stand, pushing it off to his right. He could keep an eye on it and still give her his attention.

"I'm the one who should apologize," he told her in his most affable tone. "Being on my cell—that was rude of me." He couldn't afford to have her thinking that he was wasting business time on personal pursuits. He needed her to know he was in no way a threat to the company's efficiency.

On a hunch, and feeling friendly toward her due to her help the day before—the godsend her friend Mallory was turning out to be—he moved the phone so she could see.

"Mallory has cameras installed, and that means I can keep an eye on Diamond Rose," he explained. And then hastened to add, "This allows me to set my mind at ease where she's concerned so I can focus fully and completely on the job at hand. I'm all yours."

She was staring at his phone, her lips tense now, too.

"I'm glad things worked out with Mallory," she said, her delivery giving no indication that she was upset with him or his activity. On the contrary, she sounded genuine.

Diamond Rose's cries were growing more intense. Tamara looked around them and although his phone's volume was already on its lowest setting, he muted it completely. Mary Beth, the grandmotherly woman Mallory had introduced to him this morning as one of the Bouncing Ball's full-time nursery personnel, appeared on screen, scooping up the baby and holding her close.

Flint relaxed as Diamond Rose snuggled against Mary Beth. He'd made it in time for feeding.

"How'd it go last night?" Tamara was smiling at him now.

He'd thought her heaven-sent before, but that smile... Yeah, she was something.

"With the baby, I mean," she added when he failed to respond in a timely fashion. She was watching him, not his phone. And seeming to care about more than just the business reason for their lunch.

Her look felt...personal.

Of course, he *was* a bit sleep deprived.

"It was rough." He told her the truth, but he grinned, too. "Still, we made it through." He told her about the number of times the baby had cried, shortly after being fed and changed. About going back and forth between his room and hers, and his eventual desperate fix—the Pack 'n Play on the floor right next to his bed.

He was honest with her because he was done living a double life: the convict's kid and the successful businessman. Done lying to himself about who he was.

If he was going to be worthy of that completely innocent little girl taking that bottle on his screen, if he was going to teach her how to come from what they'd come from and still be a success, then he'd have to quit denying to himself that he was different from most of the people in the world he inhabited.

Not that any of this had to do with his first night with a newborn, or was in any way related to the question he'd just been asked. It was simply a reminder of the mode of thinking he was bringing into the meeting ahead. The life ahead.

Emotionally, Stella's leaving hadn't hit him as hard yet as it was bound to, but he knew he wasn't going through that again—a rejection after he was fully committed. A rejection based on something over which he had no control and couldn't change. He was the son of a convict. He'd grown up with her as the constant in his life. Loved her. And the child she'd borne on her prison deathbed. If someone was going to have a problem with the baggage he carried, at least he'd know up front. No more hiding.

He'd had enough disappointment for one lifetime.

"Obviously she didn't like being in a room alone," Tamara was saying while thoughts flew through Flint's brain at Mach speed. "She needed to be close to you, but probably not right up to the bed. I'll bet if you keep her playpen in your room, but along the wall, and put her to bed there, where she can be aware of your presence, you'll both sleep better."

He nodded, finding the concept of a baby in his room with him every night a bit...alarming, but was not completely unfond of the idea. "You seem to know a lot about children."

Her lips tensed again. But then he wasn't sure as she almost immediately smirked and said, "Mallory's my closest friend," as though that explained everything.

And he supposed it did. If Mallory shared the details of her work life on a regular basis.

"How did you two meet?" High school? Grade school, maybe? He knew plenty of people whose friendships went that far back. Whereas he didn't have any from a year ago. Or the year before that.

Other than Stella and Alana Gold, Flint had avoided personal relationships outside one-night stands.

He had clients who went almost as far back as high school, though.

"We were in a women's group together," Tamara said, glancing at his phone and then quickly away. She turned, facing the room, as though looking for their lunch.

"Businesswomen?" He wasn't going to try to explain his curiosity, but Tamara had arrived in his life at a critical time and, as a result, he felt drawn to her.

That was what he believed, anyway. "We were all women who worked, yes," she said. Then added, "Mal's one of the brightest, most successful women I know, on all levels. She's savvy and makes good money. Her day care is always close to maximum capacity, and yet she hasn't become hardened by the shadow sides of business ownership. Like the people who don't pay on time, or at all. The ones who find fault with everything. The hours. Nothing gets to her. She's a nurturer to her core."

He nodded again, not sure why she was selling her friend so hard when he'd already signed a contract with her. The deal was closed. But he liked listening to her talk. Liked how the gold rim around the green of her eyes glistened as she spoke about her friend.

Hell, he liked just sitting across the table from her.

She was there on business.

"You said you had some things to discuss with me?" He'd answer whatever questions she had and was fully confident she'd find nothing wasteful in the way he worked. Then he'd see if maybe she'd have dinner with him sometime. Just dinner. Nothing to do with business.

"Only some clarifications," she explained, taking a sip of her iced tea. Over the next twenty minutes, through the delivery of lunch and eating of same, she talked about several of his dealings during the years. Her questions were strictly from memory, no notes. She asked for justification of certain expenses, mostly making sure that she understood things as the way she thought she did.

He enjoyed talking to her about work even more than talking about her friend. He was good at what he did. One of the best around. And she was a quick and avid learner.

She also seemed genuinely interested. More than Stella had ever been.

He talked about the money saved in throwing one lavish, weekend-long yacht party for a number of investors, rather than many expensive dinners with individuals, mentioning not only the obvious savings on the event costs, but other advantages—like the adrenaline that kicked up when investors talked together about investments.

"Everyone wants to get in on the best deal," he reiterated as the waitress cleared away their plates.

"You drive the market, affect stock prices, by persuading everyone to invest in one thing," she said.

He shook his head. "We discuss the market, in small groups and as a whole, and where we think the trends are headed. Not everyone invests in the same way. They all get excited about investing in whatever they think is the best bet after all conversations are through."

She smiled as she studied him. "In other words, you drive their desire to invest," she summed up.

"Maybe. They have to *want* to invest to get involved in the conversation."

The bill was delivered and he reached for it. He'd suggested the place, but when she took it from him, he didn't try to stop her. This was her lunch, he knew it would be expensed, and he didn't want to insult her. But he hoped there'd be a next time, and that it would be his treat.

As he'd observed earlier, she'd been put in his path at a critical time. And she already knew all about his mother. She'd seen his employee file, so she'd know about his own troubles eight years before. And she'd met Diamond Rose.

She was only with him because she had to be. He didn't miss that point. But if she accepted a personal invitation...

He waited until they were almost back at the office, until they were talking about the weather, clearly not a business discussion, before he asked, "Would you be interested in doing this again sometime? Not as a date, but just having lunch together? If you come up with any more questions about what we do at Owens, I'd be happy to answer them, and you've given me so much insight on raising newborns, I'd just like to say thank you."

Anything later than lunch involved Diamond Rose, and he wasn't ready for that.

"I..." Shaking her head, she let her words trail off.

She was going to turn him down. He was more disappointed than he'd expected to be, but waited for what would no doubt be a polite brush-off.

Or, God help him, was she going to report him to Howard for sexual harassment? He hadn't touched her. Or indicated that he wanted to. He'd just invited her to lunch.

He started to sweat anyway. In his experience, based on who he was, his background, people were more apt to assume he was guilty than the guy next door. Even if he *was* the guy next door.

That mess eight years ago had nearly stolen any hope he'd had of making a decent life for himself.

His mother's death three days ago had stolen even more...

"I'd actually like that, thank you. I'm pretty sure that between now and then I'll come up with more questions and the way you explain things, enough but not too much..." Tamara said after a noticeable time had passed.

Flint had no idea why she'd changed her mind, but he was certain she had. And he was glad of it, too—enough so that he wasn't going to question his luck.

He'd press it, though. "Sometime this week?" he asked. He had a business lunch scheduled for the next day. "Thursday?"

"Thursday would be good."

Okay, then. That was set. He'd been off-line from Diamond Rose for at least twenty minutes and from commodities reports for almost two hours. Holding the door open for Tamara, he thanked her for lunch, told her to contact him if she had any other questions, then wished her a good rest of the day and hightailed it to his office.

Keeping to his priorities was paramount. That was a promise to Alana. And to Diamond Rose.

Chapter Nine

Tamara was too busy Tuesday afternoon to think about the complexities of her lunch meeting. But they were there, a steady presence in the background of her day. She'd visited the head of every department. Had looked at their bottom lines.

Finding very little, even as an efficiency expert, to offer her father, she started to feel overwhelmed. She had some ideas on making the mail room run more smoothly. Thought maybe a delivery service would work better than the current system of having a driver on-site, ready to go if the need arose. Yes, the driver handled other menial tasks when he wasn't driving, but they were tasks that could easily be incorporated into the daily routines of several different employees.

None of which was going to make a damn bit of difference if she couldn't find something really out of place.

Granted, she'd only gone over one broker's files in

depth—Flint's. There was at least a week's worth of information to weed through, already downloaded on her computer that morning, pertaining to all accounts and monies. Everything from commissioned earnings to an annual fund-raiser to benefit underprivileged children that her father had been running around Christmastime every year since Tamara's first miscarriage.

Next, she'd be looking at supply purchases and expense reports.

And figured she could study numbers, tally up columns, run down bids and purchase orders for months and still not find what she needed.

At the end of the day, she went to her father. She needed to know more about the specifics of what his accountant had found.

"I don't think it's Flint Collins," she said the second she sat with him on the solid leather couch at the far end of his office. He'd poured her a glass of tea with ice. And had a shot of whiskey for himself.

One shot. That was what he had every day before leaving the office. His way of unwinding, he'd always said, of leaving the stresses of his business day right where they belonged.

"He's worked too hard to get where he is to jeopardize it over money," she said. That was her gut instinct. At least, that was what she called whatever it was that was driving her to want to help him.

"I went through every single client transaction, Dad. Every expense report. Granted, I didn't study every line item, or look up every purchase order, or check actual filed expense reports against his reimbursements. But I did look at a lot of them, and at overall figures. I couldn't find ten cents that had been misappropriated. Now, if he's claiming expenses he shouldn't be, that's something I can check, but I need more concrete information or I'm wasting valuable time spinning my wheels."

Naïve of her to think she'd just open up a ton of files and come across some glaring discrepancy. Or even a slightly buried one. She was used to comparing figures others didn't look at—like expenses and supplies for each person compared to others working the same or similar job. Looking for waste.

Not looking for a crime.

"I found a couple of people 'stealing' from the company I was at a couple of months ago," she continued, half afraid he was going to be disappointed in her. Which made no sense, considering her parents had been her biggest champions her entire life.

So why the feelings of guilt? As if there was something going on she didn't want him to know about?

"They worked different shifts and were taking turns clocking out for each other so they'd both get overtime pay when they weren't even working their forty-hour shifts."

"And, of course, expense reports not gelling with actual receipts and time stamps has come up more than once, since clamping down on misuse of those perks, or cutting back on some of the more extravagant ones, are the easiest ways to save a company money."

Howard sipped his whiskey. He was frowning as he studied her.

"I didn't want to prejudice you," he said when she fell silent. "And I don't want to hang Collins without giving him a fair shake," he added. "I like the guy. He's always done what he said he'd do. Every single time. Truthfully, I'm not even sure I'll press charges if it turns out to be him, as long as he makes full restitution and agrees to get out of the business permanently. Only a couple of people know about the fraud at this point. My accountant, and you. For the overall health of the business, I'd like to keep it that way."

Sitting forward, he put his glass on the table, elbows on his knees, and faced her. "Who knows? You could've found something as simple as two expense account reports coming out of one business lunch."

"Two different people claiming the same lunch?" If it was done all the time, the money would add up. She got that her father didn't want anyone in the company to know he was checking up on them, but something like that would've been easy for him to discover without her help and without raising too many alarms in his ranks.

"More like two expense reports, each claiming half of one lunch when only one employee was there."

She frowned. She could see duplicity in that but… "If they each claimed only part, then the company wouldn't be out any money."

Unless…

"You think someone, say Flint Collins, has somehow managed to secure *two* expense accounts—both in his name? And is using one to reimburse himself and the other to treat himself to a more expensive lifestyle at the company's expense?"

He supposedly had that rich girlfriend he was keeping up with, although, to date, she'd seen no indication of another woman in his life.

He'd asked her to have lunch with him. Partially, as a thank-you for helping him out with his sister. Not that she'd done anything. But would a man who was in a relationship do that?

Immediate reasons came to mind why he might. Not least of which might be that he was unethical.

"How much do you know about trading?" her father asked.

She knew there were a lot of legal guidelines; that a lot of people had used a lot of different ways to cheat while doing it. And she knew that the world's economic security revolved around the stock market.

"Not enough."

"I thought not knowing too much would make it easier for you to find what we're looking for, because obviously it's designed to be missed by those of us closely involved. I also wanted to find out if it appeared that I was doing anything shady. If you were able to discover records that put you in doubt as to my culpability. I needed to know what someone looking from the outside would find, where a trail might lead, in case it led back to me. I'm not completely sure I'm not being framed. Luckily you haven't found anything." He stood, went across the room to a row of built-in file drawers and started thumbing through folders.

She hoped that was true—that her father wasn't being framed. Because she'd held that baby and it was messing her up. She was off her game, going to fail her father, if she didn't get some help with this assignment. Maybe whatever he was looking for over there in the cabinet would make the difference, would give her a chance to deal with the way she felt and the effect it was having on her ability to do what she needed to do.

This was why Tamara didn't hold babies. Couldn't hold them.

Unlike Mallory, who'd held her son every day for almost five months before he'd died and took comfort from the feeling of a baby in her arms, Tamara had never been able to hold her own child. Not even Ryan, who'd been fully viable when he'd been born four months early.

And while, for the most part, Tamara had recovered, the one thing she could not do was hold a child. It wasn't as if a woman couldn't live a full, productive, happy life without ever holding a baby. Particularly a woman who knew she was never going to have children of her own.

Howard was back, handing her some files. "These are the basic rules of trading," he told her. "You can find the same kind of thing on the internet, but this is something I put together for a college career day I was doing a few months ago. You won't need to know any more than that."

She took the files.

He emptied his glass. "You ready to go meet your mother for dinner?" he asked. She'd taken a rain check the night before. Her mother had already cashed it in.

They stopped by her place to drop off her car and then, in the front seat of her father's Lincoln, she leafed through the material he'd given her—thinking of Flint Collins as she did.

Getting glimpses of him in his world.

Which was also her father's world, she reminded herself.

"Basically, what we're looking at here is a pattern day trader. Someone who makes a certain number of day trades over a set period of time. Four or more in five days, for example. Day traders can trade with a large enough margin to buy and sell with less in the account than is actually being spent. But a pattern day trader has real advantages in that, for him, the margin is larger. He can trade for up to four times the cash value in the account, which about doubles the normal margin. That gives him what's called 'day trader buying power' and is a measurable leverage."

She got enough of what he was saying to nod with some confidence.

"Someone in Owens Investments is using my broker license, basically signing in as me, to make trades that rose to pattern day trader status. The log-ins were from various computers in the building—any of which I could have accessed, and all in secure areas out of view of surveillance cameras. They were made at various times throughout the day.

"The trader was using monies from an account I set up for charitable donations," he explained, "without ever really withdrawing money.

"Whoever it was would make four day trades in a four-day period, meaning they bought and sold in one day, all small trades that lost nothing, but gained little, so no withdrawals were made. Then, on the fifth day, he'd use the day trader buying power to buy and sell for enormous profit."

Howard paused to take a breath as they approached the turn into the upscale neighborhood where she'd grown up.

"At the beginning and the end of every day, the account looked just as it always did, with no visible withdrawals or deposits. One of the things about pattern day trading is that accounts can't be held overnight, so there was a guarantee of ending the day the same way it began." He took another deep breath before adding, "We presume the daily profits went into an offshore account. But we've been unable to trace it due to a complicated computer trail and legalities being different from country to country."

"What happened when he—or she—made a losing trade? Was the money put back?"

"That didn't happen."

"This person traded every day without a single loss?" It meant this trader—or traitor, she thought wryly—had to be damned good.

Signaling the turn, Howard shook his head. "There were only a handful of weeks this was done. Money was made with the use of Owens Investments' funds, but there's no accounting for that cash. It looks like I made a considerable amount of money I didn't report."

Her heart was thudding in her chest. "Can you go to jail for that?"

When he shook his head a second time, Tamara almost cried with relief. "We've already submitted corrected tax returns," he said, "claiming an oversight and paying all appropriate taxes and fees."

"On money you never had."

"That's right. There's a lot more to it, of course. I'm giving you a vastly simplified version. But you've got the gist. The only other thing we found were those expense reports, splitting bills. They were always split between various brokers and me. Basically, someone was tagging me onto various expense reports, from every broker in the house, over the past year."

"Someone was turning in expense reports in your name?" she asked, incredulous.

"That's right."

"What happened with the money?"

"I have all my expense-report checks deposited directly into the charitable donation account."

They'd turned into the long circular drive, pulling up to the fountain in front of her parents' home. That fountain had been the site of family photos commemorating just about every meaningful event in her life—including each time she'd come home to tell her parents she was pregnant.

They'd taken one when she'd left to move to Boston, too. She'd been sick to her stomach that day. And felt like throwing up now, too.

"Who in the company knows you don't keep expense monies reimbursed to you? Who knows you deposit them?"

"Any number of people. My top management, of course. It's a tax write-off. I offer the option to all my managers. But others know, too."

"Which traders know?"

He shrugged but his glance was filled with sadness as he said, "Any of them could, depending on whether or not the people I've told have talked about it."

"Have you ever told any of your traders directly?"

Her stomach in knots, she knew what was coming. She knew why her father suspected Flint Collins.

"One," he said. "Because he mentioned at the Christmas Charity Fund Auction a couple of years ago that he wanted to give back to the company by way of charitable donation. So I told Flint Collins and offered to have his monies deposited into the account."

And Flint Collins, she knew, as a top producer, was inarguably good enough to have made the trades in question without a loss.

He was also a risk-taker. The day she'd met him, he'd made the company an incredible amount of money on a deal that could easily have lost a bundle.

Her heart felt as though it had been pumped full of lead.

"Did he take you up on the offer?"

"Yeah. Until he started dating Stella Wainwright. That was when he bought the Lincoln SUV. I heard of at least two weekend trips he took to exotic locations using a private jet. And he quit donating to the charitable account."

The rich girlfriend had a name.

Tamara didn't want to care anymore whether she existed or not.

She cared about her lunch date on Thursday, though. She might not be making any real progress within the company, but she had an in, just the same. A way to help her father.

She was going to get to know Flint Collins. To infiltrate his life as much as he'd let her and find out everything she could about him.

Just as a supposed friend, of course. She wasn't going

to prostitute herself. Besides, she'd already made up her mind that if by some chance the man turned out to be innocent, she still wouldn't pursue any attraction she might feel for him. But maybe she'd try to set him up with Mallory. If he was half as good a guy as he led one to believe, they'd be perfect for each other.

If he wasn't a crook.

Mallory and Diamond Rose would be perfect for each other. That was what she was really thinking.

As she followed her father into the house, she thought about Stella Wainwright. Wondered about her. Planned to look up her father's firm when she got home. Only for Mallory's sake. Or Diamond's.

In the event that Flint Collins was on the up-and-up.

Yeah, she was bothered about the woman—for Mallory's sake. Which meant she was getting ahead of herself.

Wait until the man's name was cleared first.

Or not cleared.

Then try to find out more about his girlfriend.

Like, why the woman wasn't helping the poor guy, leaving him to sleep with a Pack 'n Play next to his bed so he could get a few minutes' rest.

Again, not her problem.

Or concern.

So why, as she put on a bright face for her parents and focused on giving them no cause for worry on her behalf, was she still thinking about Flint Collins and how he seemed to deserve more than he was getting from Stella Wainwright?

Chapter Ten

Flint had slept better on Tuesday night. Taking Mallory's advice, he'd laid down as soon as Diamond Rose did after dinner and then alternated dozing and lounging for the rest of the night whenever she slept. He hadn't gotten anything else done, but he'd woken on Wednesday morning feeling a hell of a lot better than he had since the call from the prison warden telling him his mother had passed away.

Wednesday evening wasn't as good. He'd set it up to be—had had a great lunch with one of his most lucrative clients and a successful afternoon of trading because of it.

And Diamond Rose seemed to be getting into a schedule of eating every two hours and sleeping well in between. He'd watched her on and off all day, and Mallory's report had been positive.

He'd even dared a stop at the grocery story on the way home from the day care, disconnecting the carrier from the car seat as if he'd been doing it all his life, looping the handle over his forearm and setting it into the grocery cart as soon as he got inside.

If he'd been on the lookout for a woman, he would've been amused by the attention he was getting from the few after-work shoppers—obviously so based on their business attire—who were, like him, he imagined, buying something for a quick dinner.

Two of them met his gaze and smiled. A third stopped and reached down, as though to pull back the blanket looped over the handle of the carrier, effectively building a tent around Diamond Rose. But his quick turn forestalled that move. The woman apologized, said she was a single mom of two little ones, then handed him her card and said to give her a call if he had any questions or needed help or advice.

How she'd known he wasn't married, he had no idea. And then, upon further reflection as he walked the aisles, he wondered if she hadn't cared one way or the other.

Which led him back to the place he'd landed, on and off, all day. Tamara Frost. She'd accepted his invitation to lunch. He'd casually mentioned her to Mallory when he'd received his personal report on Diamond Rose's day, but had gleaned nothing, other than that she worked hard and excelled at her job.

Things he already knew.

He paused at the deli, considering premade pork barbecue and coleslaw. Both looked one step away from congealed.

In his other life he'd have treated himself—and Stella—to an expensive dinner. As it was, he settled for frozen lasagna that could do what it needed to do in the oven without his supervision.

He made it home without mishap. He'd timed it so that Diamond Rose slept through the entire outing. He put his food in the oven and, when she woke up, was ready with a diaper and a warm bottle. He had her back to sleep in record time and was considering a beer—the hardest he liked his alcohol most days—when there was a knock on his door.

He wasn't expecting anyone and didn't ever have drop-in visitors. His thoughts immediately flew to the police, coming to bring yet another bout of bad news about his mother. He was halfway to the door before he realized it wouldn't be the police. At least not about his mother.

He was never going to have another of those visits. The awareness settled on him—with relief, since he was free from that dread now, and with sadness, too. His mother was gone. Any hope he'd held of her ever turning herself around was gone with her.

To his shock, a uniformed officer stood outside his door.

"Are you Flint Collins?" the woman asked.

"Yes."

"You've been served, sir," she said, handing him an envelope.

By the time he glanced from it to her, all he could see was her back.

Tense from the inside out, Flint glanced at the baby sleeping in her carrier on his kitchen table, with the idiotic idea that he didn't want to open the envelope in front of her. Whatever it was, he was going to shield her from it.

Shield her from a life in which officers appeared at your door—for any reason at all.

Was he being sued?

Or, God forbid, was someone after Diamond Rose? Challenging his right to her?

Turning around, he tore open the envelope. No one was taking the baby from him. He had money. He'd fight...

What the hell?

He'd been issued a restraining order. By Stella. Reading it, he could hardly believe what he was seeing. Stella was afraid he was going to hurt her. That he was going to retaliate for her breaking up with him. He was not to distribute any pictures of her that might be in his possession. He was to gather up any of her belongings still in his home—she'd provided a list—and leave them outside his front door, at which point the woman who'd delivered the order would take them and would leave a box of his things in return.

The next sheet was a legal agreement whereby he agreed not to attach to any Wainwright holdings, not to mention them, or say he'd ever been associated with them, not to claim anything of theirs as his, for any reason. Stella agreed to the same, regarding him and his family. It was further understood that any child he had in his custody had no relation to, or bearing on, her.

When he got through the last sheet, he started back at the first. She'd gone to court and requested a restraining order. There was a legal document filed with his name on it. A court date would be set within the next three weeks to allow him to dispute the claims therein, and the order would either be dropped for lack of cause or put into effect for up to three years.

It was the paragraph on the second page that got to him. *Defendant.* Him. He was a defendant. His whole life, even eight years before, he'd managed to keep himself clean, no charges filed against him ever. And now…he was a defendant?

Flint's entire being slumped with fatigue. The weight on his shoulders seemed about to push him to the floor as he read the claim.

> *Defendant has a history of criminal influence and, upon victim asking to end relationship, wouldn't take*

*no for an answer to the point of victim being fright-
ened for her and her family's safety and well-being.*

When Stella had said she was breaking up with him,
he'd given her a chance to calm down, to get used to the
idea of the secret he'd kept about his mother's identity. Because Stella had known the man he'd become. Collins was
a common enough name. There'd been no reason for her
to remember a court case from eight years before when
it had had nothing whatsoever to do with her area of law.
Small-time drug dealers didn't touch corporate lawyers.

But she'd looked up the case. And when, after a few
hours, he'd stopped by her office to see her, thinking they
could talk, she'd been pissed off. He'd waited outside and
she'd warned him not to stalk her.

Stalk her?

That had been that. He'd left. And hadn't tried to contact her since.

He was no threat. Had never been a threat.

But the Wainwright name was apparently too pristine
to be linked, in any way, with his.

Or Diamond Rose's.

In the end, that was what stuck in his throat. The fact
that she'd mentioned his newborn baby in her dirty court
papers.

Glancing at the sleeping baby, he grabbed a garbage bag,
collected the things on Stella's list, down to the toothbrush
he'd meant to throw away, thankful he'd been too distracted
to do that yet—could he be sued for a toothbrush?—and
left the bag out on the porch, looking over at the waiting
unmarked car at his curb. He'd sign her document in the
morning, with a notary present.

And he'd call an attorney, too. One who was good
enough at his or her job to go head-to-head with the Wainwrights. He wanted the whole mess gone before anyone

was the wiser. Wanted no evidence it had ever existed. There was no way in hell he was going to live under the threat of a restraining order for the next three years. Anytime Stella wanted to, she could "run into" him somewhere and claim he'd violated the order. He could end up in jail.

The idea gave him the cold sweats. His whole life, everything he'd worked for…

He was going to "be someone," his mother had told him so many times. What he'd taken her words to mean was that he'd never see the inside of a jail cell.

He'd barely escaped the nightmare eight years before. And had been hell-bent ever since on making sure he never came remotely close again.

He wasn't a defendant. Wasn't ever going to be a defendant. That order had to go away.

When the baby awoke, he was bothered enough by Stella's bombshell that he forgot to be nervous about giving his little one her first bath. Mallory had offered him some pointers and he'd watched several internet videos, too.

He talked to Diamond Rose the whole time, taking care to keep his voice soft, reassuring. He'd turned up the heat in the house first, kept the water tepid and a towel close so she wouldn't get cold, and he worked as rapidly as he could with big hands on such a small, slippery body. In the end, the two of them got through the process without any major upsets.

Something else came out of the evening. Any feelings he might still have had for Stella were washed down the drain with the dirty bathwater.

Too bad about his frozen dinner, though. It dried out in the oven.

Tamara had expected Flint to take her to an establishment not unlike the one they'd visited for lunch on Tuesday.

Instead they'd gone to Balboa Park, sitting in the sun on a cement bench, having a wrap from a nearby food truck—possibly one of the best-tasting meals she'd ever had.

With a man she found more attractive than any other man she'd ever shared lunch with. Business or otherwise.

What was it about Flint Collins that did this to her? It wasn't like he was drop-dead model material, not that she went for that type. Yeah, he was fine-looking—enough that she'd noticed several other women checking him out during the time they'd been in the park. But the blond hair and brown eyes, the more than six-foot-tall lean frame, even the expensive clothes, could've been matched by any number of other "California blond" men. The state was flooded with them.

"I saw a brochure at the Bouncing Ball this morning," he told her. "The founder of this food truck is a lawyer in Mission Viejo and a former client of Mallory's."

"You're talking about Angel's food truck! I didn't know it had been renamed!" she said, glad to have something other than his sexuality to think about. It's a Wrap fit the menu better. It wasn't fancy, but she liked it so much more. It was as though he'd known she'd prefer sitting in the park during her lunch hour to being trapped at a table in a fancy restaurant. She spent a lot of the day trapped in a seat at a desk.

"I never met the couple because I was in Boston," she continued, "but Mallory called me about the case from the first day she met them. The woman wanted Mal's help in identifying her abducted son, without alerting his father, the abductor, to the fact that he'd been found out."

"Why not just call the police?"

"Not enough evidence for them to do anything. The woman was acting on instinct, based on a picture she'd seen at the day care."

"What did Mallory do?"

"She helped her! Without giving up any confidential information, or putting the child or his father at risk, in case the man wasn't guilty. Anyway, it all turned out well."

He was staring at her as though he couldn't get enough. Of her story, she had to remind herself, not of her.

"So...it was the woman's son?"

"Yeah. And Mal was the one who got the proof."

Flint Collins's full attention was a heady thing. Wiping everything else from her mind. And—

This wasn't going to help her father.

He'd pulled out his phone. Had it on his thigh. She couldn't hear any sounds coming from it, but realized, if she glanced at the screen, she'd see the newborn child he'd taken on that week.

Busy avoiding that choice, she wanted to ask if he knew anything about offshore accounts, but couldn't figure out a legitimate reason for wanting to know.

And wondered why he'd asked her out to lunch.

"How's everything going at home?" she asked instead. Not a Stella question. Unless he happened to mention her in the course of his answer.

He told her about Diamond Rose's first bath, complete with turning up the heat in the house. And her heart gave another little flip.

Because of the baby, she told herself.

What kind of fate was forcing her to spend time with a man who had an infant? And be attracted to him to...

"I've been trying to work up to asking if you'd like to join us for an evening," he said as they finished their wraps and threw away the trash, walking side by side as they made their way through the park to where they'd catch a cab back to the office. They'd spent all of twenty minutes together.

"Us?" she asked, concentrating on her step, keeping it steady. She had to do this. To pretend to be friends with him. And it wasn't like she freaked out anytime she was around an infant. She flew on planes with them. Ate in restaurants with them. She just kept her distance.

"Diamond Rose and me." He'd put his phone in his shirt pocket, his hands in the pockets of his dress pants.

She suddenly felt hot and waited for the chill that would sweep over her when the flash ended.

Maybe she really was getting the flu.

Could she at least hope so?

"I'd like that," she told him while hoping the thrill she felt was because she was one step closer to helping her father.

For the next couple of steps she warred with herself over whether or not she should say more—perhaps tell him she had baby issues.

But she didn't tell anyone that except the people to whom she was closest.

Besides, this wasn't a real friendship.

"When?" she asked as their arms touched.

"Tomorrow night? I can make lasagna tonight so we'd just have to heat it up. We could watch a movie."

What about Stella? She had to ask.

"I might be out of line here, but...are you seeing anyone? I...like to know what I'm walking into." No. Wrong. All wrong.

Now it sounded as if she was interested in starting a "seeing each other" relationship. Which she wasn't. She couldn't.

Could she?

In any case, she'd had no business asking.

"Not anymore I'm not," he said. "I was until recently."

"How recently?"

"Last week."

Oh. So, she was…some kind of rebound?

Strangely, that felt okay. Was actually growing on her. A friendship—maybe even a real one?—while he adjusted his life. Because even if he turned out to be her father's thief, Howard wasn't planning to press charges. Yes. This could all work. She could help her father, and maybe be friends for real. Someday. When this was all over.

They just had to make sure those erroneous trades never occurred again.

"Stella wasn't ready to take on a child," Flint said into the silence that had fallen, as though he thought she'd been waiting for more explanation.

She didn't mind knowing what had happened.

"She might come around," she offered, feeling inane.

He shook his head, his hair glinting like gold in the midday sun.

Another few weeks and the park would be decorated for Christmas.

What if their friendship was real? *Became* real? Would they still be friends by Christmastime?

If so, they could bring the baby down here to see the lights.

Her step faltered. If she kept her distance from the child—no physical contact—she'd probably be okay. Knowing from the outset that the friendship was, at most, only temporary.

And even if she wasn't okay, she'd do what had to be done. For her father. Her parents. She was all they had. Or ever would have, as far as blood family went.

"She gave me an ultimatum," he said after waiting for a crowd of schoolchildren to cross their path. "The baby or her."

She knew which he'd chosen. And felt she had to say something.

"Some women just aren't meant to be mothers." Wow. Hadn't meant for her own mantra to slip out.

But maybe it was best that he know, going in, that there could never be more than friendship between them. That she, like Stella, wasn't meant to be a mother.

Even if he turned out not to be guilty, even if they developed a genuine friendship, she was planning to set him up with Mallory. Mallory was perfectly suited to be everything he and Diamond Rose could ever want.

"She wants children," he said. "Just not the bastard child of an incarcerated convict."

The way he said the words—she looked at him—was he the one Stella hadn't wanted? The bastard child of a convict? Or had it really been because he'd wanted to bring his sister into their family?

"You don't sound all that bitter about it." Which surprised her. He had every right to be.

"I'm not. I'm thankful I discovered her lack of mutual respect before we got married and had children, rather than afterward. And to be fair to her, I'd failed to tell her that my mother was in prison."

They'd reached the curb.

He hailed a cab.

Chapter Eleven

By Friday afternoon Flint was feeling pretty good about himself. He'd met with Michael Armstrong, an attorney who'd come highly recommended by one of the clients who'd been with him the longest.

They could be as little as a phone call away from having the order dropped. Michael was certain he could negotiate a mutual agreement between him and the Wainwrights that would prevent either party from bad-mouthing the other, and that he could do it without a court order. Flint was willing to sign anything to that effect as long as they dropped the order.

Otherwise he was going to fight it. He had to. For Diamond Rose's sake. To let it stand unanswered meant it would be put into full effect. It would make him look guilty.

Michael was fairly confident, as was Flint, that the Wainwrights wouldn't want the matter to go to court.

While Flint was comfortable enough with the situation still open, after talking to Michael he felt one hell of a lot better going into the weekend.

The lasagna was already in the oven and Diamond Rose fed and asleep when Tamara pulled into his drive. He'd offered to send a cab for her. She'd preferred her own transportation.

He was pleased with the fact that she'd agreed to come to his house at all. She knew about his past. And had accepted his invitation anyway.

"Wow, this place is nice," she said as he opened the front door into a large entryway with a step-down living room to one side and a great room on the other. It had a wall of windows that opened up to a tiled patio and swimming pool beyond. The outdoor lighting was on and showed the pool, with the waterfall, at its best. He couldn't afford to be right on the ocean, but the pool had been a nice compromise. She turned toward the great room.

"I've got someone coming to put a wrought-iron gate around the pool," he said as he followed her through the room he'd furnished with a complete home theater arrangement, including big leather furniture with charging plug-ins. Stella had thought the room too big for intimate conversation. Too "masculine."

Diamond Rose, in her Pack 'n Play on the floor in the living room, was out of sight, but her monitor rested securely in the back pocket of his jeans.

He stood back as Tamara moved through an archway into the kitchen, which ran almost half the length of the house. One end held an informal eating area with bay windows and the other housed a more formal dining room set. A set his mother would have loved and had never seen.

He'd purchased the high-top suite for eight soon after meeting Stella.

"Dinner smells wonderful," she said, stopping to look at the pool out the kitchen window.

He wanted to tell her she *looked* wonderful. In leggings and a white shirt, gathered at the waist in back, that fell just past the tops of her thighs, with her amber hair loose and falling around her shoulders... He was sure he'd never seen anyone so beautiful.

And was getting way ahead of himself.

She'd turned. Was leaning against the counter, the window at her back with the landscape lighting a soft glow around her.

Maybe he'd pushed things too far, too fast. Having her over for dinner. It wasn't his normal approach.

But nothing about his life was normal anymore.

Nor was anything about this woman. The way she'd showed up in his life at the exact moment she had, preventing him from being fired long enough for him to make the trade that had, he was certain, ensured him his job. And then, when he'd been frantic about Diamond Rose, finding it impossible to calm her, in walked Tamara, who'd calmed her almost instantly.

He might not believe in karma and all the woo-woo stuff his mother used to spout, but he couldn't resist wondering, once again, if Alana Gold, in her death, was sending him her own version of karma. Proving that good was rewarded. That there was help beyond self-reliance.

That miracles really could happen...

"I, um, have to talk to you."

Little good ever came of those words.

He'd been about to get a bottle of wine. Stopped before he'd actually opened the refrigerator door.

His weekend took a nosedive. "What's up?"

"You told me about your ex and...I need to tell you something."

"You know Stella?" It was the first thought that sprang to mind. Was his ex-fiancée having him watched? He wouldn't put it past her. She was going to hang him out to dry for deceiving her by not telling her he wasn't from a nice, clean, *rich* family like hers. For daring to think she'd be willing to raise his dirty mother's orphaned child.

"No!" Tamara frowned, cocking her head to look at him. "Of course not. I just…need to be honest with you about something."

"Wine first," he said, grabbing the bottle of California Chardonnay. He opened it and poured two glasses, handing one to her without asking if she wanted it.

She took a sip, nodded.

Taking that as a win, he scooped up the platter of grapes and cheese he'd prepared and carried it into the dining area. Pulling out one of the chairs for her before seating himself perpendicular to her—where he could also glance across the L-shaped entryway and into the living room.

Tamara had said she needed to be honest with him. He had to listen.

And hope that whatever she had to say wouldn't be as bad as he was imagining. It would be a shame to have a second lasagna dinner drying out in the oven that week. Especially since he'd spent an hour the night before talking to a sleeping Diamond Rose while he'd prepared it.

"I—" Tamara looked at him, her expression…odd. He couldn't figure out why.

Glancing away, she took a grape, put it in her mouth, and he had an instant vision of a movie he'd seen once at a bachelor party. Tamara had a way of making a grape look even sexier than that, and she was fully dressed.

"I don't normally… I haven't ever…talked about this with anyone but my closest friends, so bear with me here."

He wanted to let her off the hook, to tell her that honesty was overrated. But after the week he'd had, the life he'd had, he couldn't do it.

No more stabs in the back, bonks over the head or officers at his door. He had Diamond Rose to protect.

He considered telling her that whatever she was struggling to say could wait. After all, they were just getting to know each other.

But he sensed that they weren't. She'd been more than a casual business introduction since the second she'd walked into Bill Coniff's office at the beginning of the week. Clearly she'd sensed something, too, or she wouldn't be about to share a confidence that only those closest to her had the privilege of knowing.

"I'm not ever going to have children." For all her struggle, she almost blurted out the words.

Did she somehow think he wanted her to? He then remembered the day before, when he'd told her that Stella had said it was either the baby or him.

"That's not really how I meant it to come out." She smiled but her lips were trembling. Flint had to consciously resist an urge to take her hand in his. To have some sort of contact between them.

"Before your... Before she wakes up—and before... Well, so you know going in... I can't do babies." Her face reddened and she was clasping her hands again, the way she'd done that day in his office.

"You were great with her," he said, assuming she needed reassurance for some reason. "The moment you picked he up, she stopped crying."

She shook her head, pushed her wineglass farther away. He had yet to take a second sip from his.

"You don't understand."

He was pretty sure of that.

"I—I can't have children."

"Okay. It's not a problem, Tamara. You figure I'm going to think less of you or something? We all have our crosses to bear." Thinking he sounded like an idiot, he continued. "I mean, I'm sorry for you, if it was something you wanted. I don't mean to trivialize that, but…"

Pulling her wineglass toward her, she took another sip. Her glass shook as she raised it to her lips and he just wanted to do whatever it took to put her at ease.

"I don't know what to say," he murmured.

She nodded. "No one does. Look, I wouldn't have brought it up, but…I've been through some…hard times. Not that I need to unload all of that on you when you've been nice enough to make me homemade lasagna, which I love. But the end result is…I keep my distance from babies. And I don't hold them. Ever."

But she had. Just three days ago.

He remembered her odd behavior then. The way she'd clasped her hands so tightly. Wringing them. Had gone for the door. And when she'd turned back, hadn't looked at Diamond Rose again. She'd been in some deep emotional pain and had done a remarkable job of covering it.

"In Bill's office, when the monitor went off, you heard that cry…" He let his words fade away, wishing he could do something to ease her pain.

She nodded. Took a piece of cheese. Bit off a small corner and played with the rest.

"Can you tell me what happened?"

With the cheese between the fingers of both hands, she shook her head, then let go with one hand to grab her wineglass. "You don't have to do this."

For some reason he did. Covering her cheese hand with his own, Flint said, "I want you to tell me."

How could he get to know her better without finding out? How could he help her if he didn't know?

How else could he understand?

Because, God knew, he wasn't just going to walk away. She'd been sent into that office on Monday for a reason.

She seemed to be weighing the decision. As though fighting a battle. Whether or not to trust him?

Then she glanced up and met his gaze. He felt like he'd won.

"I've been pregnant four times."

Flint's jaw dropped. Whatever he'd been expecting, it hadn't been that. She didn't wear a ring and had asked if he was involved with anyone. He hadn't even thought to ask if she was. He'd been a little preoccupied.

He wasn't generally a person who only considered himself. Alana Gold had taught him that through her own bad example.

He didn't regret asking Tamara to confide in him, but he was ill-prepared.

Questions bounced through his mind. All he came out with was, "What happened?"

"I lost them all."

Four small words. So stark. And carrying such an incredible depth of pain. He admired her for being able to sit there relatively composed.

He'd asked for this. He owed it to her to see it through. "Why?"

Her smirk, and accompanying shrug, held grief he was pretty sure he couldn't even begin to imagine.

"There was no obvious explanation," she said. "My husband and I both went through a battery of tests. Sometimes genetics aren't compatible. There're myriad physical causes. But nothing showed up. Which was why they said there was no reason we shouldn't keep trying."

So many questions. Things he wanted to ask. But this wasn't the time.

What did she need him to know?

"And you tried four times."

She nodded. Took a sip of wine. "Yep." She was staring at her glass and he wondered what she saw there. Wished there was some way he could take on some of her pain, help her deal with it.

Alana Gold had taught him well on that count, too. When he'd been able to keep her happy, she'd stayed clean. It was when she'd needed things he couldn't provide that they'd lost everything.

Tamara Frost had helped him. He felt deeply compelled to help her in return.

"Then what?"

Her gaze shot to his. "What do you mean, then what?"

He squeezed her hand, let it go. "Did they eventually discover a reason for what was happening? What was going wrong?"

She shook her head. "No." And when she looked at him again, there was a mixture of determination and vulnerability in her glistening eyes. "I couldn't do it anymore," she said. "I don't even want to be pregnant. I can't bear the thought of all those weeks of fear and hope, the unknown, not being in control. My own frenetic state of mind would create issues even if the fetus was healthy…"

"And your husband?" It seemed the appropriate time to ask that one.

"We're divorced, by mutual agreement. By the time we lost Ryan, we'd already drifted so far apart…"

"Ryan?" She'd named each lost fetus?

"He was viable," she said as though that explained everything. It didn't.

"I don't—"

"The others… I lost them at six, nine and eleven weeks. Still within the first trimester. But Ryan… He made it far enough to have a chance of survival. I could feel him moving inside me. I was showing. And I was sure that with him—"

She'd lost her last hope with the loss of her fourth child. Understanding came softly, but clearly. Because she was talking to someone who knew exactly when he'd lost his last hope.

Eight years before, when his mother had used the home he'd bought her to run a drug lab, implicating him in her criminal acts.

After that he couldn't help Alana anymore. Couldn't have anything to do with a future that involved her being out of prison and the two of them together. He'd visited her, because he loved her. Because she'd given him life. But he'd kept an emotional distance that had been necessary for his own mental health.

"There comes a time when you have to let go," he said aloud. Whatever the cause of the emotional pain, there came a time when you knew you'd reached the end of your ability to cope. You had to turn away. Say *no more*. "Ryan was your time."

Her gaze locked with his, those green eyes large, their gold rims more pronounced. "You get it."

He did.

And while he had no idea where it left them, with Diamond Rose sleeping in the next room, he knew for certain that their meeting had been no mistake.

She'd helped him.

He was supposed to help her.

Chapter Twelve

The baby cried.

Tamara sipped her wine, telling herself that whatever spell had bound her and Flint Collins had been broken.

He was still watching her.

"You need to go get her," she said.

He nodded. "She has to be changed and then fed," he agreed. "It'll take me about twenty minutes. You want to set the table in the meantime? The lasagna is due to come out in about thirty."

Could she do this? A flash of her father's worried face assured her she could.

"I can do that," she told him. She'd see if he had lettuce. She could make a salad. Salad went well with Italian food. And wine.

She had another sip.

Focus. That was all it took.

That and topping off the glass of wine Flint had poured

for her. Two was her limit. Or she'd have to hang around an extra hour before she drove. She found dishes. Set the kitchen table because of the gorgeous view of the pool from the bay windows.

No. Because there'd be no view at all of the baby sleeping in the living room.

She hadn't known that was where the playpen was until Diamond Rose started to cry. Then she'd had to fight to avoid looking at the room.

But…Flint needed to see the child. For his own sake and the baby's.

Gathering up the dishes and silverware, Tamara moved them to the dining room, placing them so he could see the living room and her back was to it.

Yes, that worked fine.

And she made salad. Cutting the carrots, peeling a cucumber, chopping onion, tearing lettuce. She did it all with precise focus. When Flint's voice broke through her concentration, soft and from a distance, she chopped with more force. The newborn cried once. Tamara replayed in her head the conversation she'd had with her father the day before.

Diamond Rose was a precious little baby who had nothing to do with her. Tamara wanted the best for her. Hoped to God that everything worked out so Flint could continue to care for his sister. If that was what was best.

And it seemed to be.

Flint was different from any other man she'd ever met. He had an emotional awareness she'd never seen in a male before—yet he was masculine and sexy and exuded strength at the same time.

In one conversation, and a sketchy one at best, he'd understood more about her emotional struggle than Steve had in all their years of marriage.

For the first time since she'd lost Ryan, she felt under-stood.

By a man who might be a thief.

And since her father wasn't planning to press charges, because of the hit his reputation— and then the company— would take if investors knew he'd been frauded, Flint should be free to raise Diamond Rose.

"She's back to sleep."

A piece of lettuce flew out of her hand and onto the floor when she heard his voice behind her. Focus could do that to a girl—take her right out of her surroundings.

"That's impressive." He was smiling as he pointed to her neat piles of chopped vegetables.

"You make your own dressing?" She'd found four jars, with varying labels, lined up in the door of the refrigera-tor. She'd chosen the creamy Italian to mix in before serv-ing their salads.

"I've been putting meals together pretty much since I could walk, it seems," he said. "By the time I was about eight, I couldn't stand the sight of peanut butter sandwiches anymore, so I asked my mom to teach me to cook."

"She was a good cook?"

"Yes, she was."

There was hesitation in his tone. And she wondered if there was more to the story. Like, when she was sober she was a good cook. Or, when she wasn't in jail she was a good cook. Tamara didn't know many of the details of his growing up, but she knew enough to fill in some of the blanks with at least a modicum of accuracy.

Within minutes they had dinner on the table and were sitting down to eat. He didn't mention the baby at all. She didn't ask, either. But it felt…unfair, somehow, doing that to him. Making him keep such a momentous change in his life all to himself.

A friend wouldn't do that. And posing or not, she had to be a good friend if she was going to find out more about him.

"It doesn't send me into a tailspin to hear about babies," she told him, spearing a bit of salad on her fork. "You can talk about her."

"I just want to make sure I know the boundaries first," he said. "I need to know what you can and can't handle."

"What I can't do is hold her." The words jumped out. "That's my trigger. The rest, I can manage. I can close my eyes if it starts to get me. Or walk away."

There. She relaxed a bit.

"But the other day...you picked her up so naturally."

"And I've been paying for it ever since." Wow...she was playing her part better than she'd ever suspected she could. She was being more honest with him than she was with anyone, including her parents.

Maybe because she knew he wouldn't be in her life all that long? Or because he was an outsider who wouldn't be hurt by her pain?

Maybe because she wasn't *completely* playing a part?

"Paying for it how?" he asked between bites of his salad.

"The first night I think I was up more than you were." And, based on what he'd later told her about it, that was saying a lot. "I have nightmares. And panic attacks."

She was tempted to say she had hot and then cold flashes, since she was having another series right now. But she'd had the first one before she'd known about Diamond Rose.

Speaking of which...

"Did you name her? Diamond Rose—it's such an unusual name."

"No." He finished his salad. "My mother did."

As he started in on his lasagna, he told her about the

names Gold, Flint, Diamond—and the rose. Expensive, beautiful, sweet.

And fragile, she added silently.

She'd taken her first bite of lasagna and was too busy savoring the taste to talk. She loved to cook. Considered herself good at it. He was better.

"It was the first time," she said out of the blue. She'd just swallowed that bite. Wanted to think about the second. Another sip of wine. Or the way Flint's shoulders filled out the black polo shirt he was wearing with his jeans. But she wasn't. She was still thinking about that baby.

"The first time you'd held a baby?" Leave it to him to catch right on. Did the man never miss a beat?

She nodded.

"In how long?"

"Since I lost Ryan, if you don't count the few times we tried in my therapy sessions, which I don't count because I never managed to hold the infant by myself."

Fork hovering over his lasagna, he paused before skewering another bite. "How long has it been?"

"Three years." Hard to believe it had been that long. That brought on another surge of panic. Her life was passing by so quickly.

"And how long since your divorce?"

"Two and a half years. He's remarried." And could be expecting a child any day or week or month.

"Are you two on friendly terms?"

"We talk." She didn't consider Steve a friend. He'd robbed her of her one chance to hold her son, having the baby swept away the second he'd been delivered, and asking the doctor to give Tamara something to calm her down, which had knocked her out. But their split had been amicable. Mutual. They remained…acquaintances.

She drank a little more of her wine. Had to wait a minute before sending anything more solid down her throat. Floundering, losing focus, she stared at her plate. Reminded herself what she was doing here.

"What about you and Stella? You think you'll remain friends?"

She heard the stupidity of that question even as she asked it—since the woman had ditched him because he was taking in his mother's child to raise. But desperation drove many things. Including stupid questions to fill the silence.

"I have no desire to. So, no."

Okay, then. That was clear.

But her father had said that Flint's spending habits had changed when the rich girlfriend came into his life. She had to get around to that somehow.

Or segue into offshore accounts.

She was drawing a blank.

Because she wasn't focused.

Maybe over dessert.

He knew how he could help her. Not the details, not yet. But Flint had a goal now. Find a way to repay Tamara, or the fates, for helping him out on one of the worst days of his life.

Not quite the worst. Because in another way, it might have been the absolute best. He wasn't alone anymore. He had a sister. A brand-new human being to raise.

He had family.

And it now seemed obvious to him that his payback was in helping Tamara heal enough to have a family of her own, too. To someday have a baby of her own to raise. There were other options if she couldn't give birth herself.

His and Diamond Rose's payback, really. They both owed her.

That infant sister of his already had a job to do. Because that was what you did when you planned to amount to something in life. You used the gifts you were given. You worked as hard as you could. You helped others.

The things he'd taught himself somehow. Or a message given to him subliminally in his crib.

His little sister's talents might not be clear yet, but for now, being an infant was all it was going to take.

The connection seemed unmistakable to him. Diamond Rose, who'd been screaming her lungs out, had instantly calmed when Tamara had picked her up.

Sign one.

Sign two. Tamara, who hadn't held a baby in years, who considered herself unable to hold one, had picked up Diamond Rose.

Still piecing things together, he had no idea how it was all going to work. What he should or shouldn't do. But he felt confident, as Tamara helped him with the dishes, that the answers would come to him.

He had the basics down anyway.

"I should be going," she said as soon as the dishes were done and the counters wiped. He'd put some of the leftover lasagna in a container for her. One serving was all she'd take, suggesting he put the rest in serving-size portions in the freezer, so that on nights when the baby wasn't co-operating, he could still eat a good dinner.

He'd been freezing portions for years, but didn't tell her that. He was too busy enjoying the fact that she was looking out for him, too. Stella had been mostly about what he could do for her, and he'd been all right with that. Even comfortable with it. And usually insisted on it.

"You want to do this again? Sunday maybe?" He felt confident asking. Some things you just knew.

"What time?"

"You name it. I'll be working at home all day."

She preferred afternoon to evening. He was fine with that, too.

Following her to the door, he moved closer, intending to kiss her good-night. Her expression stopped him before he'd made his intention obvious. She was worried about getting out the door without seeing the baby, not thinking about kisses.

He watched her walk to her car and only after she'd pulled out of his driveway and was out of sight did he close the door.

He really would've liked that kiss. To know her taste on his lips...

Probably just as well, though. He needed to get settled back into his career at Owens Investments and to learn how to be a dad before he took on any other committed relationship.

Friends was nice, though. Friends who helped each other...

Chapter Thirteen

Funny how things worked themselves out. Tamara hadn't had a chance to learn anything on Friday night that could benefit her father. Then, on Saturday, while having lunch with the office manager at Owens Investments—a woman ten years older than her whom she'd never met before the previous week, but instinctively liked—the way in was handed to her.

Maria had been telling her about the system they used to keep up with the fast pace their traders required of them, and in so doing had explained quite a bit more than her father had done about his business. Maria had given her a pretty clear glimpse into the life of a stockbroker. As her father had said, the risks were great, mostly because laws were commonly broken, although it could be hard to prove. Insider trading being one of the most difficult.

She'd asked if Tamara had seen a movie from the late '80s called *Wall Street*. She hadn't. Maria had highly recommended that she watch it.

That night she found it on her streaming app and on Sunday showed up at Flint's door in black-and-white leggings, a comfy oversize white top and zebra-striped flip-flops, with the movie rented and ready. All they had to do was type her account information into his smart TV and they'd be set.

"You've never seen *Wall Street*?" he asked as he brought glasses of iced tea and a bag of microwaved popcorn for them to share.

"No. It was out before I was born," she told him. And then thought to ask, "Have you?"

Of course he would have. He was a stockbroker. And Flint seemed to study everything about anything that involved him. Like the baby, for instance. Yeah, there'd been a couple of common sense things he'd missed during his research before he'd brought his baby home, but in just those three days, he'd become better prepared than most expectant parents she'd known.

"Only about a dozen times," he told her, taking a seat on the opposite end of the couch.

Relieved that he wasn't closer, that she wasn't going to have to let him know they were "just friends," she turned to smile at him, suddenly catching sight of the Pack 'n Play in the sunken living room behind them.

Suspecting that the portable bed was there because Tamara was where she was—in the living room—she felt a crushing weight come down on her. Disappointment, yes, but far more.

A baby was being ostracized because of her.

No, that wasn't quite true. A lot of parents kept their young children separate from the family's activities while the child slept. That was why there were nurseries.

But it wasn't what she would've done if she'd had a child. It wasn't what she'd planned to do.

"Do you keep her in there when you're in here watching TV at night?"

"I'm not usually in here watching TV. I spend any free time I have on the computer. Checking stocks. My job is pretty much a 24/7 affair when I don't specifically schedule time for other things."

Like watching an old movie with her?

He'd turned on the TV. Clicked on the streaming app.

"Where's your computer?"

He nodded toward a hallway off the great-room side of the kitchen. "Down there."

"And does she stay in the living room when you're 'down there'?" She mimicked him with a grin.

No response, which she'd expected. The question had been rhetorical. Of course he didn't keep his baby in other rooms when he was there alone.

With a fancy remote that had a small phone-size keyboard on the back, he was searching for the movie. On his account.

Stood to reason that he already owned it and she'd wasted the three dollars she'd spent. Oh, well.

"You can bring her in here, Flint." She wasn't going to be the cause of any child being on the outside of any gathering ever. "I'm not so fragile that I can't be in the same room as a baby. I fly on a regular basis, and you don't get to choose who you're seated by on a plane. I'll be fine."

She wasn't convinced she would be. But at least she knew how to keep up appearances. As long as she didn't pay attention to the baby, didn't let Diamond's presence pull at her. As long as she didn't even think about picking her up.

Or doing any nurturing in a hands-on way.

"If you're sure, I'll bring her in. But only if you're completely sure that's what you want. It's not like she's going to know the difference. She's out for at least another hour."

"Like she didn't know the difference the night you tried to get her to sleep in the nursery?"

"She's used to me now. We're doing much better." His grin did things to her in inappropriate places. Probably because she was so tense about getting information for her father. And being around a newborn.

She was challenging herself personally and professionally. So it made sense that her emotions would be off-kilter.

And she might've been fighting off a flu bug the previous week, too. Her system could be in recuperation mode. Busy rebuilding antibodies.

That thought was total bunk and she knew it. She didn't have the flu. Hadn't had it the week before, either. The man was attractive. She noticed. Not a big deal.

"I want you to go get her, please," she said as he cued up the movie. "Please."

She wouldn't be able to focus on her real reason for being there if she was busy feeling bad about being the reason that baby was in the other room all alone. She was a grown woman who could take accountability for her issues, her problems. Diamond Rose was a helpless newborn who had to rely on everyone around her to fill every single one of her needs.

Besides, Tamara needed Flint relaxed if she hoped to get information that could help her father one way or the other. She'd spent most of Saturday going through files and meeting with employees who'd come in on their own time to see her, in addition to the hours with Maria in and out of the office. Her father had told her someone was trading on various computers. He knew which ones, so now she did, too. She'd wanted to find out when they were in use most often, as part of her efficiency check, so she could give her father an idea of when or why they might have been freed up for other uses. She had dates now. Other specifics.

And she was slowly making her way through expense reports and comparing them to the provided receipts, examining dates, times, employee credit card numbers, clients. Looking for…anything in the past year. Flint's records had come first. She'd finished them very late Friday night.

He'd had a lot of fancy dinners, gone to shows, on cruises, to games, with a lot of important and wealthy people. And every single dime he'd claimed checked out to the penny.

She'd told herself not to let hope grow. She'd learned the hard way that hoping led to greater heartache. Still, she'd wished she could call and tell her father that things were looking good. So far.

But, of course, she couldn't.

Just when Tamara was hooked to the point of forgetting almost everything else, a little cough jarred her. Then a tiny wail, followed by another.

She looked at Flint, who was already headed over to the playpen. "She's got another hour and a half," he said as though babies watched the clock and knew they were supposed to be hungry at certain times. Focusing on the movie, which he'd paused on the screen—about the young man learning the Wall Street ropes from someone who was at the top of his game, but had gotten there by unethical means—she waited.

"What's the matter, Little One?" Flint crooned softly. The wails grew louder. He rubbed her arm. Felt her cheek. Continued to talk. Tried to get her to take a pacifier. She continued to cry.

Pick her up. Pick her up.

After a few more tries with the pacifier, he picked her up. The crying didn't stop.

For another ten minutes.

He walked with her. Talked to her about her eating schedule, explaining that it wasn't time yet. He changed her, which only made her angrier.

He left the room, taking her somewhere in another part of the house. Probably to give Tamara space. She could still hear the crying.

She couldn't just sit there, doing nothing. Poor Flint had to be getting tense. Frustrated. Especially with her there. Maybe she should leave and watch the movie another day. It wasn't as if her father had to have his answers within the next few hours.

Or that she was going to find them there that day.

The crying went on. She paced the room. Looking at bookshelves. Reading titles of DVDs. Noticing the lack of any family photos. Or personal mementoes.

Diamond Rose finally stopped crying and Tamara's entire torso seemed to settle. Until then she hadn't realized that her breathing was becoming shallow, the way it did at the onset of a panic attack. Hadn't felt herself tense.

And almost immediately the crying started again. She grabbed her purse. Had her keys and was at the door before she remembered she had to tell Flint she'd take a rain check on the movie. She couldn't just him let come out and find her gone.

Following the sounds of the baby in distress, she traveled a hallway he hadn't showed her yet, passing two rooms—a bathroom, the master suite—and eventually found him in a small back bedroom with a Jack and Jill bathroom leading into one of the rooms she'd passed.

Opening her mouth to tell him she was leaving, she

caught sight of his face. He looked scared. Honest-to-goodness scared.

"I'm sorry," he told her. "Nothing's working. She doesn't feel feverish, but maybe I should take her in."

His gaze moving from the purse on her shoulder to the keys in her hand, he nodded. "I'm sorry," he said, giving her a smile that seemed all for her, in spite of his crying infant, and went back to trying to comfort the child in his arms.

"Put her up on your shoulder," she said. "Pat her back. She might have gas."

He tried. It didn't work.

Tamara felt like crying herself. "Try rubbing her back."

That didn't work, either. Tamara had to get out of there. But she couldn't just leave him. His problems weren't hers, but he was trying so hard and she couldn't simply walk out.

"Do you have a rocking chair?"

He nodded, left the room, and she followed him. Into another room filled with baby furniture and paraphernalia. There was a mobile over the crib, but nothing on the walls. No color. No stimulation. Just…stuff.

A massive amount of stuff to have collected in less than a week.

Sitting in the rocker, he held the baby to his chest and rocked. Cradled her in his arms and rocked. She'd settle for a second or two and then start right back up again.

"Lay her on your lap," Tamara said. "On her stomach." Her purse was still on her shoulder. Her hand hurt, and looking down, she saw imprints of her keys in the flesh of her palm.

Flint pulled a blanket off the arm of the chair and did as Tamara said, settling Diamond Rose across his lap, continuing to rock gently.

"Rub her back," she suggested again.

The crying calmed for a second. Then another second. The baby burped, formula pooled on the blanket, and all was quiet.

Shaking, Tamara started to cry.

She had to get out of there.

In spite of the warmth seeping through the right leg of his jeans, Flint rocked gently, rubbing Diamond's back, while he wiped her mouth and pulled the soiled part of the blanket away from her. Her eyes closed, she sighed deeply and his entire being changed.

Irrevocably.

Almost weak with the infusion of love that swamped him, he knew he was never going to be the same. She was his.

He was hers.

Watching her breathe, he loved her more fiercely than he'd known it was possible to love.

And somehow Tamara Frost was connected to it all.

Tamara was gone when he finally made it back out to the great room. He'd known she would be. Putting Diamond in her Pack 'n Play, he flipped off the television still paused on a close-up of Michael Douglas with his mouth open, caught in midword. Then he gathered up the glasses of leftover iced tea, the half-eaten bag of popcorn and took them to the kitchen. Upon his return, he grabbed his laptop.

Settling back on the sofa, wanting to stay close to the baby, he did a search on medical degrees. They took an average of eight years to earn and then an average of four years of residency before a graduate could begin practice. A list of medical schools came next. He wanted the best. Decided on three and searched tuitions. Then he researched the average cost of living for a medical resident, did a calculation based on average cost of living increase each year, multiplying that by twenty-six, because, based on schooling, she'd be at least that before beginning a residency, and added the figure to his list.

His eventual total was about what he'd estimated when he'd been rocking his baby sister. But it was good to have solid facts.

He knew how much extra money he had to earn to fund Diamond's college account. She could be whatever she wanted. He was prepared for the most expensive, which was why he'd looked into medical schools. He checked the market next—something he did all day every day, using his cell phone when he didn't have access to his computer. Searching now for his own personal investments. There was always more money to be made.

And finding it was his talent.

He had all of half an hour before Diamond was crying again. Deciding it was about time, he tried to feed her. She drank for a couple of minutes and then turned her head. And kept turning it away whenever he tried to guide the nipple into her mouth.

So he rocked her. Laid her on her belly and rubbed her back. Walked with her out by the pool. Talked to her. Loved her.

And thought about Tamara. She'd fought her own demons that afternoon to help Diamond Rose. He couldn't remember a time other people had put themselves out on his behalf.

Except Howard Owens. He'd risked his own reputation to take Flint on eight years before. Flint hated that the man thought he'd been planning to stab him in the back.

Hated it, but wasn't surprised. That was the way his life worked. With his background, he was always suspect.

It was something he'd always known, even as a little kid.

And something he swore Diamond would never face.

Tamara had fought her own demons to hang around.

As he finally set Diamond down in a clean sleeper and with a full feeding of warm formula in her belly sometime after seven that evening, he pulled his cell phone out of his pocket. He'd changed into sweats and a long sleeved T-shirt and was sitting by the pool with a bottle of beer.

Tamara picked up on the second ring.

"I just wanted to apologize for this afternoon," he said as soon as she said hello.

"No apology necessary," she told him. "Seriously. I think what you're doing… Anyway, don't apologize."

There was no missing the wealth of emotion in her tone. He'd had a tough day with a cranky newborn, but he had a feeling Tamara's day had been immeasurably worse.

He did need to apologize. He'd been so certain he could help her—that somehow Diamond Rose would be the baby who'd help her heal from her loss, ease her pain—and with no real knowledge of the subject, he'd invited her into a hellhole.

He should just let her go.

He'd thought about it on and off all afternoon. And as he'd eaten his single serving of reheated lasagna for dinner.

He'd argued with himself and called her anyway.

There had to be *something* he and Diamond Rose could do for her.

"Maybe we should stick to having lunch for now," he offered, still at a loss.

If she even wanted to see him again. He wouldn't blame her if she thought he was too much trouble. He'd probably think so, too, if he were in her shoes.

Except he was beginning to understand that he had no idea how it felt to be in her shoes. Having children was a natural progression in life. Something most people took for granted. To be married and ready to start a family, to know you were pregnant, to be buying things for a nursery, making plans, and then to lose that child—he had no idea how any of that would feel.

And times four.

"Lunch would be good," she said, sounding a little less tense. "But dinner on Friday was good, too."

"Today wasn't."

"No."

"What did you do when you left?" Had she called a friend? How did she cope?

"I went to work." That he could completely relate to.

"Owens is closed on weekends."

"I have temporary clearance with security."

"Are you at the office now?"

"Yes."

He pictured her there. The building was quiet after hours. Peaceful. He did some of his best work when he was the only one on the floor.

Pictured himself there with her and actually got hard.

Either he was heading into the rest of his life or screwing up. At the moment, he wasn't sure which.

"You didn't get to finish your movie," he told her.

"You could tell me about it."

He heard invitation in her response and, settling back in his chair, beer in hand, he gave her a fairly detailed rundown of a movie he'd seen for the first time in junior high. He'd been in foster care, a six-month stint, and the family he'd been staying with had been watching old Charlie Sheen movies. The actor had just been hospitalized after having a stroke from a cocaine overdose. Flint's mother had been in jail at the time for possession of crack. The movie had a profound effect on him—establishing for him, very clearly, that ethics were more important than money.

But that money came a very close second. It had also given him his lifelong fascination with the unending opportunities provided by the stock market.

Not that he told Tamara all of that. With her, he stuck to the plot.

Until she asked him what it was that attracted him to the movie to the point of having watched it so many times. Then he told her about seeing it for the first time.

"Wow, that seems a bit callous to me," she said. "They knew why your mother was in jail, right?"

"I was certainly under that impression." He'd never asked.

"Did you say anything to them?"

"Nope." He'd known from experience that any questions from him would just lead to more lectures that he'd neither needed nor wanted. Or, worse, more scorn.

He was the bastard son of a drug user. Assumed to be like her, because how could he not be? He'd never experienced anything different. Not many good people were drawn to him.

"Did you know from the first time you saw the movie that you wanted to be a stockbroker?"

He sipped from his bottle. Chuckled. Pictured her in the converted closet they'd given her as an office and wished a glass of wine on her.

"I wasn't prone to lofty dreams," he told her. "I was curious about the market, but it didn't really occur to me that I'd have the opportunity to live in that world." She was easy to talk to. He couldn't remember the last time someone had been interested in him as a person.

Maybe some of that was his fault. He hadn't been all that open to sharing his life. Even with Stella. He'd shared his time. His plans. His future. But not himself.

He'd only just realized that...

"So when did you start believing in the opportunity?"

It took him a second to realize they were still talking about the stock market. He picked up the baby monitor on the table. Made sure the volume was all the way up. Diamond, who was just inside the door in her carrier on the table, had been asleep for more than half an hour.

"I had a minimum-wage job in high school, but I'd been earning extra money by going through trash, finding broken things, fixing them and then selling them. I'd made enough to buy a beater car and was saving for college. And I got to thinking I should look for things that were for sale cheap—you know, at garage sales—and then fix them up and resell them.

"I had quite a gig going until my junior year, when my mother got arrested again. I had almost enough saved to pay the minimum bail and went to a bondsman for the rest. I gave him an accounting of the books I'd been keeping with my little enterprise as a way of proving that I was good for the money. It's not like I had any real asset to use as collateral..."

He rattled on, as if he shared his story on a regular basis. Flint hardly recognized himself but didn't want to stop.

Talking to Tamara felt good.

"The guy was pretty decent. He paid the bond, without collateral, but told me he wanted me to check in with him every week, regarding my business intake. He helped me do my tax reporting, too. Supposedly it was just until Mom showed up in court and he got his money back, but I kept stopping in now and then, even after she was sentenced to community service and in the clear. He's actually the one who suggested I think about the stock market. He said I had a knack for making money. Turned out he was right."

He didn't hesitate to tell her the whole truth about this

aspect of his background, in spite of the fact he never did that. He guarded his private life so acutely.

"Did you ever go back and see him? After you made it?"

He hadn't made it yet. He wasn't even sure what "making it" consisted of these days. He'd thought that opening his own firm, having other brokers working for him, earning good money, would be making it.

"He retired and moved to Florida when I was a freshman in college."

And although Flint had given the guy his email address, had emailed him a few times, he'd never heard from him again.

"It was because of him that, years later, I started looking into offshore accounts," he told her. "He fronted money, which meant that he had to make money. He used to do a bit of foreign investing. He'd tell me about foreign currencies and exchanges and the money he'd make. He also talked about security.

"'Diversification equals security,' he'd say. If you keep all your assets in one place, and the place burns down, you're left with nothing. We like to think that our banks, at least the federally insured ones, are completely safe, and I feel that generally they are. But it doesn't hurt to have assets elsewhere, just in case of some major catastrophe—there can always be another crash like we had in 2008. It's not like it hadn't happened before that, too."

Okay, now he was reminding himself of Ross in an old *Friends* episode, going on and on about his field of paleontology and boring his friends to death.

"Sorry," he said, reining himself in. It felt as though a dam had burst inside him, which made him feel a bit awkward. But not sorry.

"Actually, this is the kind of thing I was after," Tamara

said. "Greater understanding of how the investment world works. But…I thought offshore accounts were illegal."

"Not at all. A lot of people use them illegally, because it's relatively easy to do. But they're not only completely legal, they're a financially smart decision. Especially for someone like me who invests internationally. You just have to report any earnings over ten thousand on your taxes."

"Do you do all your own taxes?"

"Yes." He did everything on his own, for the most part. He didn't like giving others the chance to make a mistake for which he'd be held accountable. "I meet with an accountant before I submit them, though," he added, "because the laws change every year."

Such a bizarre conversation. In a lot of ways, more intimate to him than sex.

And he'd started it.

"I'm sitting at the pool having a beer." He felt bad about that, considering his baby girl had sent Tamara running to work. "I wish you were here, enjoying it with me."

"I don't like beer."

"I have wine." It wasn't quite an invitation—he wouldn't do that to her, since there were no guarantees he could avoid a replay of this afternoon—but he had to open the door.

"Will it keep a few days?"

"Absolutely."

He asked her if she was free for lunch early in the week. They settled on Tuesday and Flint was grinning as he hung up the phone.

Chapter Fourteen

Sunday was about as bad a day as she'd had in a while. First with the aborted visit at Flint's in the afternoon and then with the confirmation that he not only had an off-shore account but that he did his own taxes. Things that someone with something to hide might do.

Neither fact made him a thief. But the circumstantial evidence pointing in his direction, along with a lack of anything pointing in anyone else's, was certainly enough to lead her father to that conclusion.

Over the next week and a half, she worked like a fiend as an efficiency expert, finding several ways her father's company could save money. She also searched for any discrepancy that could place doubt or lay suspicion on anyone other than Flint. She found a few. She always did. But nothing that wasn't easily explainable or a product of human error or laziness. Someone cutting corners, but not for nefarious reasons.

She lunched with Flint twice that week. Spoke on the phone with him several times. Getting to know the boy he'd been, who'd grown to become the man he was. Sharing more of herself than she had in a long while. She talked about how—although she now loved her job—when she'd been younger, she'd really wanted to be a stay-at-home wife and mother. Old-fashioned though that might be, she'd thought that, having grown up with a wonderfully successful career mother and an equally successful businessman father, the ideal would be a home with someone always there. Protecting everything they all worked for. She wanted to add the personal touches to her own home that her parents' place had gained at the hands of hired help. But then, she worked a job that could largely be done from home, if she wanted it to be, so maybe that's why staying home seemed doable. All of the records scouring, the line by line accounts she studied, she could do that while the baby slept…

And she told him about her job, too. How she'd entered the efficiency field due to years of learning to live a focused life. How the career fit her, fulfilled her. How great she felt when she found bottom-line savings for her clients.

He'd asked, once, if she'd ever thought about trying one more time to have a family of her own. Her answer had been an unequivocal no.

She didn't see that changing.

Her heart had closed up at his question.

As the days passed, her father was getting more worried. He'd talked about calling Flint in, confronting him. But he knew that could be professional suicide. If the meeting backfired and Flint set out to prove he was innocent before Howard could prove he wasn't, any actions her father might take would expose the fraud at Owens.

He'd risk having everyone in the company finding out

they had a thief among them. He'd not only tip the thief's hand, but he'd jeopardize the company's overall security. Once word reached the investment world that Owens had an unsolved fraudulent situation in-house, it could be the end of everything her father had spent a lifetime working toward.

Howard needed the matter solved quietly. And quickly.

Tamara went to Flint's for dinner the following Saturday night, more intent than ever on learning whatever she could to help her father. But she got so distracted worrying about the baby waking up—and then, when she did, Tamara made herself sit out by the pool for the twenty minutes it took Flint to change and feed her—that she was of little use to Owens Investments that night.

Flint had been pleased for her, though, saying she'd done well, staying put instead of running out. She'd wanted so badly to be in there with him. Changing that baby. Watching him feed her.

And that unexpected desire had scared her to death.

She'd warmed under his emotionally intimate look.

And run out. Sort of. She'd had one more glass of wine—her second—and left before anything truly intimate could happen between them.

She dreamed about him that night. It was a change from her usual dreams about crowds of people holding babies, with only her arms empty. Or the vacant house she'd walk into to find every room a nursery that had been abandoned. Or the one where she'd gotten to hold Ryan for a few minutes and then he'd had to leave.

Dreaming about Flint was a welcome reprieve. And yet a problem, too.

One she figured she knew how to solve.

Calling Mallory Harris, she arranged to meet her friend for dinner the Monday night before Thanksgiving. They had a favorite spot not far from the Bouncing Ball—one that Mallory's ex-husband, who owned and worked in the office complex that housed the Bouncing Ball, didn't like. The food was all organic and salad-based. According to Mallory, Braden preferred full plates of food that stuck to his ribs.

Tamara had never met him. She was part of the life Mallory didn't share with her ex-husband.

"What's up?" Mallory asked as soon as they had glasses of Chardonnay in front of them.

"It's been a while since we hung out and—"

Mallory was shaking her head. With her dark hair trimmed to fall stylishly around her face and over her shoulders, Mallory was softly beautiful, even in clothes as plain as the Bouncing Ball jacket and jeans she'd worn to work that day. "I could tell when you called that something was up. Now, out with it. Did you run into Steve?"

"No." Mallory knew about Howard Owens's suspicions regarding Flint. Tamara had told her when she'd asked her friend to take on Diamond Rose. But there was so much more her friend *didn't* know, that she needed to know.

Mallory was just right for Flint. And he was right for her, too. Tamara really needed them to get together.

She'd almost kissed him the other night. Had been thinking about him sexually more and more over the past several days.

In spite of the baby who was part of his life.

He was making it too easy for her to be involved with him. The way he'd taken on full responsibility for Diamond impressed her. Plus the fact that he expected nothing from Tamara but distance where the baby was concerned.

She was getting in too deep. And, because of her father, she couldn't get out. Or not yet, anyway.

She was even starting to think she might not want to

get out at all. Which wasn't fair to anyone. That baby girl of his deserved—and needed—a full-time mother. Not one who stayed in other parts of the house or in doorways when Diamond was around.

She had to admit that Flint hadn't, in any way, intimated that he saw Tamara as anything more than a friend. Perhaps one with momentary fringe benefits.

He wanted her, too.

That was part of her problem. He was going to be asking. She'd managed to put him off without actually saying anything so far, but things were escalating between them. At some point he'd ask.

She didn't trust herself to say no.

Unless she thought her friend wanted him...

"It's Flint," she said. "He's such a great guy and I'm worried about him," she said, looking straight into Mallory's pretty blue eyes. "He's in that big house all alone, keeping up an eighteen-hour-a-day workload, being mother and father to that baby girl and—"

"You've been to his house?"

Yeah, she'd forgotten she hadn't mentioned that.

She nodded, but continued. "His girlfriend ditched him when he refused to give Diamond Rose up for adoption."

"Why were you at his house?"

Was Mallory jealous? That would be a good thing, right?

"I just... My father told me he's not going to press charges if it turns out that Flint's the one who's been stealing from him. And while I'm not excusing theft or fraud, I've seen another side to the man and—"

"When were you at his house?"

"I think you should ask him out, Mal."

Mallory sat back. "Me? Why? I thought you were going to tell me you were falling for him."

"He's got a baby."

"Yeah."

"You think I'm kidding about not going down that road again?" Tamara quipped.

"I think sometimes love is stronger than the things we believe."

"I can't even be in the same room with her for more than a few minutes without getting a cramped feeling."

"Exactly how many times have you been at his house?" Malory asked.

"You need to go out with him, Mal. You'll see what I mean. He's perfect for you."

"You really want me to ask him out?"

"I really do."

Mallory nodded. "He and I—we've talked some."

"And he's gorgeous."

Neither one of them was the type who fell for looks first, but looks didn't hurt.

"But I can't seem to draw him into any kind of conversation beyond caring for his daughter," Mallory said.

Sister. Technically, she was his sister.

Who'd grow up as his daughter.

And she assumed he'd told Mallory that. Probably had to present guardianship papers. None of which changed the fact that, for practical purposes, Flint was Diamond's father.

"He mentioned that he's planning to attend your Thanksgiving dinner at the Bouncing Ball. Said he's always gone out for dinner on Thanksgiving, usually invited clients, but with the baby… He doesn't want Diamond Rose to spend any holidays without family."

Tamara would be at her parents'. She'd told him that when he'd invited her to accompany him to Mallory's dinner—since she and Mallory were friends and all.

Things were just getting too complicated. She couldn't not go to her parents. And she absolutely could not take Flint there with her, Diamond Rose aside, even if she wanted to.

"You're thirty-three, Mal. You want a family of your own. And there's no reason you can't have ten children if you want them. But you need to get started."

"You seriously want me to ask him out?" Mallory asked again.

"At least try to spend some time with him at dinner on Thanksgiving. Ask him to help. He's a great cook."

"He's cooked for you?"

Tamara ignored that. "I think the two of you are perfect for each other."

"Seriously?" Mallory repeated, leaning forward, looking her in the eye.

"Yes." She didn't hesitate. This was the right thing to do. "Unless... I mean, depending on... My dad is still afraid that he's the one who stole from him."

"What do *you* think?"

Shrugging, Tamara took a sip of her wine. "The whole way he is with the baby and all, which has nothing to do with this, but... I don't see it," she said. "At the same time, there's absolutely nothing popping up on anyone else."

"So what do you do now? Hire a detective?"

"I tried to get my dad to do that. He's adamantly against bringing in anyone else. The thief, whoever it is, hasn't done anything in over a month. Dad had some special notification put on one of his passwords, and the second anyone signs in as him, he'll know. But he's hoping it doesn't come to that."

"How much longer are you going to be at the company?"

"I'm about done there." Which was another reason she had to get Flint and Mallory together.

"So you won't be seeing Flint anymore."

"I don't see him much at the office anyway. We're on different floors."

"Do you see him outside the office?"

"Only as a kind of informant," she said, confessing what bothered her the most. "I ask him questions about the business, in my efficiency expert role."

"But he thinks it's more than that."

"Just friends." Tamara sat back and drank some of her wine. Thought maybe they should look at their menus so their waitress would realize they'd be ready to order soon. They'd sent her off the first time she'd asked. "I swear. Nothing's happened between us. I'm not kidding. I've been thinking all along that you and he belong together. You'd love him if you got to know him. And you already love his little girl."

Which Tamara could never do.

Even if she wanted to try, she knew she'd go into emotional shutdown.

"You're falling for him."

"I am not! How could I? I only met him a few weeks ago."

"I knew I was in love with Braden the first night I met him."

A love that had been blown apart, for both of them, by the death of their five-month-old son. They'd been divorced for three years and had found a way to build a good, solid friendship between them.

"And now it's time for you to find someone else to love," Tamara said. "To share your life with."

"Maybe the one it's time for is you."

Mallory just wasn't getting it. "Are you not listening to me?"

"Actually I think that's exactly what I'm doing."

"You want me to open myself to possible feelings for a man who might be stealing from my father? And who has a newborn?" How could Mallory suggest such a thing?

"I want you to be honest with yourself." Mallory's words fell gently between them.

"I am," she insisted. "It's not like I can bring him home to dinner with the folks, Mal. And even if I could, I can't take on his baby. He already had a woman leave him because of Diamond Rose and he just doesn't deserve another kick in the teeth."

She started to tear up, took a deep breath and then said, "His whole life, Flint has done nothing but try, and give, and work hard. And his whole life, people have done nothing but desert him. It's not even like he lets that get to him. He's the least victimized person I've ever met. He'd doesn't get bitter. Or lay blame. He just picks up the pieces and keeps trying. Giving one hundred percent to whatever he does."

"It sounds to me like you know him pretty well."

"I've been...investigating him." At work. At lunch. In his home. On the phone. She'd spent more time with him than any other person since she'd been home.

"Really? Is that all?"

It *had* to be all.

For so many reasons.

But there was one that could convince Mallory...

"How do you suppose he's going to feel when he finds out that I'm Howard Owens's daughter? And that I've been spying on him because my father, his one-time mentor and current boss, thinks he's a thief?"

"You're in love with him, aren't you?"

"I've never even kissed the man!"

"You want to."

"I imagine half the women he meets want to."

"Maybe two-thirds." Mallory smiled. And then immediately sobered.

"I wish I knew what to tell you, Tamara. I just know that you don't get to choose love. It chooses you."

"It chose you and you're alone."

Tamara realized how cruel that sounded but Mallory didn't seem offended.

"I am," Mallory said. "Because human beings are fallible. Love gave Braden and me a chance. We failed it. But you're right. More than anything, I want to be married again, to have a family. And yes, I'm thirty-three. If I'm going to have a houseful of kids, I have to get moving on that. And here I sit. You know why? Because I can't *choose* to fall in love. I have to keep my heart open and wait for it to find me."

"You could go out more."

"I've been dating."

"Ask Flint out. Like I said, maybe love will choose the two of you."

If it was half as powerful as Mallory believed, it would choose her and Flint. It should! The match was obvious.

"I'm not doing anything with Flint Collins with you feeling the way you do about him."

"I don't feel any way about him except for horrible. I'm deceiving him, and he's such a great guy."

"Aside from possibly stealing from your father."

"Aside from that," she said. In spite of the number of times she kept reminding herself of the facts, such as they were, she just couldn't believe Flint was a thief.

Not considering everything he'd told her. Everything she'd seen in him over the past few weeks.

And as far as Stella went, Flint had seemed fully over her a week after they'd parted. He'd chosen Diamond Rose rather than her without looking back.

He'd changed his entire life for that baby. Because that was the kind of man he was.

And because it had been his mother's dying wish.

Because the baby was his only flesh and blood.

But what about before that? Maybe the Flint she'd gotten to know over the past weeks wasn't the man he'd been a month ago.

He'd had no idea his mother was pregnant, so clearly he hadn't seen her in a while.

He'd been hell-bent on starting his own business behind her father's back.

And what about those foreign investments he'd made on his own behalf, the risks he'd taken?

Maybe she just hadn't been looking in the right place for information. Maybe it wasn't information she needed.

Maybe what she needed here was a motive. Did it have something to do with Stella?

Was she the reason Flint Collins needed to steal money? Had she made him that desperate? And if not, had something else? If Tamara could find the answer to that question, she might be able to end this whole episode in her life.

Problem was, after her conversation with Mallory, Tamara wasn't sure she wanted it to end.

Chapter Fifteen

Stella wasn't going away. Whether she was truly frightened of him now that she knew about his past or—more likely—just incredibly pissed off, she wanted a restraining order against him. No mutual agreement, nothing that could ever come back looking negative on her. All she wanted was him signing her damned paper, agreeing to release her family from any wrongdoing in perpetuity. And an order to stay away from her.

After almost two weeks of back and forth, trying to come to an amicable agreement, Flint's attorney called him the Friday after Thanksgiving and told him the only way to be free of the family was to fight them. In court. A date had been set for a hearing on the order for Thursday of the following week—on Diamond Rose's first-month birthday. Standing at the window in his office, watching the bustle of Black Friday shoppers on the streets below, he listened as his attorney highly recommended that he show up.

If he didn't, the order would automatically be put in place. Would become a matter of permanent record. In other words, if he didn't show up, he looked guilty.

Which meant that if he hoped to have any kind of long-term relationship with Tamara, even as just the close friends that was all she seemed capable of considering at the moment, he was going to have to tell her about the order.

It might be enough to push her out of his life.

He'd have to take that chance. He was done living with lies, hiding things because he was ashamed of them.

He was tired of being ashamed of his past.

The truth hit him so hard, he had to sit down. He was *ashamed* of who he was.

Almost as quickly as he sat, he stood again. The second he let life knock him to the ground, he gave it a chance to keep him there.

His much younger self had had the guts to stand up to the bullies on the bus and he sure as hell wasn't going to allow a selfish woman and her wealthy, powerful family to make him cower.

He had no reason to feel ashamed about anything. It was time to quit acting as if he did. Time to quit hiding the facts of his life.

Finishing with his attorney, agreeing to make the court date and authorizing him to go full-force ahead to have the order dismissed without cause, Flint hung up and called Tamara. She was working upstairs in her office, but she'd told him the night before, when she'd called after Thanksgiving with her folks, that she wouldn't be at the investment firm much longer. Her work there was almost finished.

She'd had a couple of offers. One local, one out of state. The out-of-state company was larger, but she hadn't yet confirmed either one. Hoped to be able to schedule both.

He hoped she'd be scheduling time for him, too.

"I hear there's an old-fashioned country Christmas-tree lighting at Pioneer Park in Julian tomorrow," he told her. "I've never been to a lighting, so I don't know what we'd be in for, but I was thinking it would be good for Diamond's first outing. Bright lights for her to focus on, and if she cries, we're outside in a noisy atmosphere. You want to come along?" He was taking a huge chance, maybe pushing her too fast. He went with his gut and did it anyway.

"I've actually been to that celebration before," she said. "Several times. It's nice. They have a lot going on. Santa. And other Christmas things. And...have you checked the weather? Do you know if it's going to be too cold to take her out?"

"The stroller has zip-up plastic walls and I've got a hat that completely covers her ears. And blankets."

He also had to tell her about the restraining order.

If they were going to move forward after her work at Owens Investments was done.

"So you hardly had a chance to talk to Mallory yesterday at the dinner, huh?" she asked out of the blue.

"There was another single father there, one she's apparently gone out with a time or two. While I like your friend, I had absolutely no interest in butting in where I clearly didn't belong."

"Would you have wanted to butt in if the other guy hadn't been there?"

Was she jealous?

Was it wrong of him to be smiling at that thought?

"If he hadn't, there wouldn't have been anything to butt into."

"Would you have asked her to the tree lighting if he hadn't been there? And the two of you had spent more time talking?"

"I just learned about it this morning," he told her. "I happened to see a sign on the way to work. If you don't want to go, you don't have to, Tamara. I'm not pressuring you. I'm just asking."

"It's not that I don't want to go…"

The problem was Diamond. He understood. So much more than she thought.

"She'll be in her stroller the whole time," he said. "And if there's an issue, I'll take her back to the car and handle it."

"Don't you think this seems more like a date?"

"It's whatever you and I decide it is. Just like our lunches. And dinners. Do *you* think it's too much like a date?" Maybe he was putting on some pressure, after all.

Maybe it was time.

"No. You're right, Flint. I'm making excuses."

"You don't have to go."

"I want to…" She sighed, hesitating.

"Then come with us."

"I'm scared."

"I know." He could support her. He couldn't take away her battle. Or fight it for her.

"Okay."

"You'll come?"

"What time?"

"It's about an hour's drive, so I'm guessing around five, being flexible in that I want to have Diamond freshly changed and fed right before I swing by to get you." He knew she owned a bungalow by the beach. He'd yet to be invited there. And he didn't even have the address.

"I'll meet you at your house," she said. "It's easier that way."

He'd prefer to deliver her safely to her door when they

got back, but let it go. She needed to be in control of her destiny. He was good with that.

And good with life in general, too. There would always be roadblocks. It was how he handled them that defined him.

Tamara had no idea what she was doing. Not really. Not deep down where it mattered. She'd told her parents, over a quiet Thanksgiving dinner the day before, that she'd befriended Flint for the purpose of spying on him for her father.

Neither of them had been thrilled with the news.

When she'd added that she liked him, and was struggling because of it, they'd looked at each other and frowned.

Her father had asked if that was how she'd known about the offshore bank account and, when she'd affirmed it, he'd asked her not to use a friendship to get any more information on his behalf.

He hadn't asked her not to be friends with Flint, although she figured from the concern on his face, and the hesitation in his tone, that he wanted to.

Instead, when she left, her parents had both implored her to be careful. They'd hugged her tight and she could almost physically feel their worry palpitating through them.

At no point during the day, not in a single conversation, had any of them mentioned a baby. Any baby.

And now here she was, sitting in Flint's car on the way to a holiday celebration, dressed in black leggings with black boots and a festive long black sweater with Christmas-tree embroidery. She wore Santa Claus earrings. Flint in his black pants and red sweater looked equally festive and she caught a glimpse of the baby's red knit hat when he'd loaded her carrier into the back seat. They resembled the stereotypical American family out to enjoy the season.

So not what they were.

It wasn't supposed to drop below forty degrees, but she'd dressed warmly.

At the moment she was sweating.

She hadn't turned around in the front seat, but she knew the baby was right behind her. Kept waiting for her to wake up. To need attention while Flint was driving…

"I have something to tell you." Flint's words brought her back to sanity fast. Was he going to confess that he'd siphoned money from his boss?

If he had, she needed to know. Needed all of this to be over.

And yet she didn't want it to end.

She felt trapped, with no way out. Or no way that would let her be happy when she got out.

For someone who had something to say, Flint was far too quiet. Maybe he wasn't ready?

"I have to be in court next Thursday to defend myself."

Everything stopped. It was far worse than she'd expected. He hadn't just stolen from her father? Someone else had pressed charges?

Where were her feelings of validation for her dad? Her rage?

All she could find was cold fear.

Disbelief.

"I told you about Stella—how I didn't tell her about my background…" He was continuing in the same calm tone. It took Tamara a second or two to catch up. There was an innocent baby right behind her. One who'd never have her own mom or dad, since her mother died without naming him, but had a brother who loved her as much as any parent could have.

"...she's taken out a restraining order against me. My attorney's been trying for two weeks to get her to sign a mutual stay away agreement, but she's more of a barracuda than I realized."

Focusing on the traffic along the freeway, taking herself outside something she wasn't handling well, Tamara juggled her thoughts.

"Stella claims you hurt her? That she fears for her safety?" She knew what restraining orders were for. Steve's sister'd had to get one against an ex-boyfriend.

Heaven help her, but there was no way she could believe Flint had threatened anyone, let alone a woman. He didn't deal with anger by attacking. He sucked it up.

She didn't have to see how livid he was to know that. She just had to listen to him, to see his tenderness, his unending patience with a crying child. And to know he'd given the mother who'd made his life hell a funeral, even though—as she'd later found out when she'd asked—he'd been the only one in attendance.

"The order actually reads that due to the fact that I hid from her who I really was, she fears for her and her family's safety."

"I thought you had to have proof of harm, or threat of harm, in order to get a restraining order."

"You only have to say you fear harm to get the initial order. The accused then has a chance to rebut the charge before the court and then the order's either granted or dismissed. If I don't go to court, it'll be automatically granted and become a permanent part of my record. Anytime someone did a background check, it would show up and I'd look like I'm an abuser."

"What a bitch." The words were out before she could stop them. She wasn't proud of them.

Flint's grin surprised her. "Thank you."

He didn't say any more about the situation and she didn't ask. He'd been honest with her, but she was lying to him every single second she was with him, by not telling him who she was. And she'd be breaking her word to her father if she did.

She felt like crap. She could blame Stella What's-Her-Name for wronging Flint, but she'd have to shoot recrimination at herself, too. Even after these weeks of getting to know him, she'd doubted him. The second he'd told her he was going to court, she'd assumed he'd done something wrong.

It could've been a simple traffic ticket he'd had to defend. That had never entered her mind.

And yet…she was drawn to him. To be with him.

So much it hurt.

Chapter Sixteen

Public restrooms. Something else Flint had failed to consider in his new life. He was a man with a baby girl and he had to pee.

They'd been at the festival for an hour, had a couple of chai lattes and, together with the coffee he'd had before they'd left home, his situation was becoming critical.

He could take Diamond with him. Just wheel her right in. It wasn't like she'd know the difference.

But he would.

He didn't want her in a men's restroom, sleeping there close to the urinals or…in there at all.

His only other option was to leave her with Tamara. Which wasn't fair.

Urgency won out over fairness. "Can you just hold on to this while I pop in here?" he asked as they approached the cement building that housed the facilities. Not giving her much choice, he pushed the handle of the stroller in her direction and made his break.

Three minutes later, when he rushed back out again, his hands still wet from a brisk wash, they were exactly as he'd left them. Tamara hadn't moved. Taken a step. She was standing there, her hand on the stroller, staring at the men's restroom door.

And when he got close, he saw the tears in her eyes.

"I'm so sorry." He took the stroller, wheeled them out of the crowd and off to a bench not far from the festivities but far enough to give them privacy. With darkness having fallen, a chill had entered the air, although it wasn't cold enough to warrant the shiver he felt running through her as they sat.

"I should've thought ahead," he said, not sure what he could have done differently. Even without the latte, he'd have had to go at some point. It was what people did.

And what he'd need to do again before the evening was over.

"This isn't going to work, is it?" he asked her, not ready to give up but not willing to hurt her any more, either. "This is too hard for you."

She shook her head and, in a season filled with hope, he felt his dwindling once again. No matter how many times that happened, he never got used to it. It never got easier.

He wasn't going to try to convince her, though. He cared about her too much to watch her suffer.

"I'm the one who needs to apologize," she told him, turning so that she was looking him in the eye. "I need to try harder, Flint."

She'd lost four babies. Heartache wasn't something that could be brushed off or ignored. On the contrary, broken heart syndrome was a medically proved reality, as he'd discovered when doing some research on her situation.

"You're doing great, sweetie. I just…" What? He just what? He'd called her "sweetie." As if they were a couple.

She was still looking at him, all wide-eyed and filled with emotion. So close. He leaned in. She did, too. And their lips touched.

Maybe he'd meant it to be a light touch. A sweet good-bye to go with the endearment.

Maybe he hadn't been thinking at all.

What Flint knew was that he couldn't let go. Her lips on his… His world changed again and he moved his lips over hers. Exploring. Discovering. Exploding.

He felt for her tongue. Lifted his hand to the back of her head, guiding them more closely together. Felt her hand on his thigh.

Laughter sounded and it was a little too close. An intrusion, shattering the moment. He pulled back.

"I'm not going to apologize for that," he said, breathing hard. He glanced at Diamond, her stroller right there in front of them, the wheels lodged against his feet. The baby had been asleep for almost two hours. She'd be awake soon. Needing attention.

And Tamara…

She was looking at the stroller, too.

"I'm not going to run," she said. Maybe that made more sense to her than it did to him.

"Okay."

"There are a lot of things against us," she continued. "And chances are they'll win out eventually, but I'm not going to run away."

If the park staff had chosen that exact second to light the huge tree across the way from them, Flint's world wouldn't have been any brighter. He could hear "A Country Christmas" coming from the live band onstage in the distance and, for the first time, understood what people meant when they talked about the magic of Christmas.

"I'm very glad you aren't running away," he said aloud.

* * *

"I want to hold her so badly it hurts."

They were in the car on the way home. Tamara had tried to keep her mouth shut. There was no future for them; she had to let him go.

And couldn't bear the thought of it. Of deserting him. Of him being deserted again.

"I'll help you try to hold her…"

She shook her head, arms wrapped tightly around her.

"We could start out easy," he said. "Just fix a bottle for her. Nothing else. See where that leads us."

Fix a bottle. She could do that. Maybe even do it without undue stress as long as she focused on something else while she completed the task. That wasn't how she usually did things; she typically focused on whatever needed doing immediately. But that wasn't what she needed here. She'd think about…what?

At the same time, she'd be paying attention to the amount of water to powder, of course.

"My dad bought Ryan a plastic baby fishing pole," she said, when fighting the inevitable didn't work. Babies always brought her to this place. "It's blue plastic with a red reel, and it has a big plastic handle that really turns and makes noise."

He glanced at her and then back at the highway.

Diamond had woken shortly after their kiss. He'd fed and changed her in the SUV while Tamara had wandered into a couple of nearby shops. After that, they decided to head out rather than wait for the big tree lighting.

"It's in the back of my shed." *Still in its plastic wrapping.*

"You never talk much about your parents."

Understandably, given the situation.

He didn't *know* the situation.

Guilt assailed her. She'd kissed him.

And she'd liked it.

Far more than she'd ever liked Steve's kisses.

What did that mean?

"Mom's a doctor." The darkness in the SUV made her feel safe. Secure.

Or maybe it was being with him.

"A cardiologist." Fitting. She was dying of heartache.

"And your dad?"

"He's into a lot of different things." He had investments in just about every field out there. "Computers, mostly," she said. She couldn't tell him the truth. But she wouldn't out-and-out lie any more than she had to.

She'd already told him she was an only child in one of their earlier phone conversations. They'd both been "onlys." She knew, from that same converation, that he didn't want Diamond to be.

"Have you told them about me?" he asked.

Oh, God, don't strike me down in my sleep. "Yes."

"And?"

"They're worried about my...well-being." She could be completely honest with that one.

"Surely they don't think you're better off alone."

"No, of course not. It's just been so hard...on them, too."

"Are they afraid of the possibility that you might get talked into trying again?"

Trying again.

Her chest tightened. The cords in her neck were taut. Her throat. What if she wanted that someday? Not simply to try again but...to try with Flint?

She shook her head.

She couldn't stretch the truth that far.

"I don't know," she finally said when she could.

"Do you think they want you to? Or hope you might?"

Looking out the car window, she thought about her mom and dad. "They've never said," she told him, but figured if they had, the answer would be no.

Just the thought of living through the months of waiting and worrying that would be involved—

Enough was enough.

And the three of them…they'd had enough.

The week following their trip to Julian was inarguably the best week of Flint's life so far. The only shadow at all was Stella's restraining order hearing and, in the end, it had been postponed. She'd asked for more time to prepare.

Not surprisingly, the judge had granted her request. Flint had had no say in the matter and only heard about the changed date when his attorney called to tell him he had to be in court the week before Christmas.

On the surface, not a lot had changed with Tamara. He still hadn't been to her home. She hadn't said why, but he could understand that it would be near impossible for her to have an infant in her most private space.

He would've been open to considering a lunchtime visit, but when she didn't suggest it, neither did he.

She'd wrapped up her work at Owens and while he'd liked knowing she was in the building, they hadn't crossed paths often enough for there to be a real difference in their time together. She'd taken the job in town, only a few miles from Owens, tentatively scheduling it for after the New Year. And on her last day in the office, he'd grabbed her out of view of all security cameras, telling her that knowing where the cameras were was a perk of spending so much time in the building—and then he kissed her. Soundly. So he could have that memory with him every single day he went to work.

She'd kissed him back fiercely. Telling him she wanted the memory to last.

They'd met for lunch four times that week. Twice they'd ended up in his Lincoln, making out. While it had been years since he'd even thought about kissing in a car, Flint was enjoying the slow pace of their relationship.

Tamara needed time.

He wanted her to have it.

If they went to her place, or his, they'd end up having sex and, as acutely as he needed that with her, he wanted it to be fantastic for both of them.

It wasn't going to be for her until she had some things worked out.

She'd been over for dinner twice and on Saturday afternoon to watch a movie. *ET* not *Wall Street*. One day at lunch they'd been talking about their favorite movies growing up and had decided to watch them all with each other. Her top three were *Mary Poppins*, *Annie* and *ET*. Other than *Wall Street*, his were *The Goose That Laid the Golden Egg*, *Rocky* and *Heaven Can Wait*.

Things were vastly different between them when they were around Diamond. The baby wasn't sleeping quite as much anymore. She'd happily spend time in her swing. Liked to be held for a while after she ate and before she went to sleep. She was also happy on a blanket on the floor for short periods, maybe ten minutes or so.

Tamara had mastered the art of bottle preparation. She'd taken over the sterilizing process, too, whenever she was there. She sat in a chair instead of on the couch with him when he was holding Diamond. And avoided looking in her direction at all other times.

Still, Flint took the week as a huge win.

She was trying.

And there was no doubt now that they equally craved their time together.

She came back on Sunday, bringing sushi for them to share while they watched a second movie. And then a third. They'd just finished *Heaven Can Wait*, a story about a young football player who'd left this world too soon, and she asked Flint about his mom. Not the bad stuff, she'd said, the good. She wanted to know all the things he'd loved about Alana Gold.

The things he wanted to pass on to Diamond.

If he was a guy who cried, he could have wept.

Over sushi, he asked her what she loved most about her parents. She'd liked that her mom never seemed like a doctor at home. She was just Mom.

Someone who worried too much. And was her greatest champion in the world.

"Dr. Frost," he said, anxious for the time to come when he could meet them. He'd been hoping by Christmas, but Tamara hadn't said anything.

"Her name's not Frost." The change in her tone was odd. Off. She looked like she had the day she'd picked up Diamond in his office.

Only different. Maybe worse.

"Your parents aren't married?"

"Yes. They are."

Sitting at the dining room table, with Diamond in her baby swing behind her, she dropped her California roll on the paper plate she'd brought.

He wasn't getting the problem. His baby girl hadn't made a sound. And Tamara couldn't see her to know she'd just smiled at him.

She'd been doing that a lot lately, this girl of his, smiling when she saw him.

"So your mother kept her maiden name?" he asked,

waiting to pick up another roll. He drank from the glass of wine she'd poured him.

She shook her head. "Frost's my married name." You'd have thought she'd admitted to some horrible crime, the way she'd said that. As if she expected him to be upset that she'd kept her ex's name.

A lot of women did that. For various reasons.

It was just a name.

"Okay."

Watching him for a second, she seemed to relax. She picked up her roll. And then another. Back to normal.

"So what *is* your maiden name?" he asked. He was planning to meet her parents at some point. He should know what to call them. Maybe even have their number in case of an emergency. They knew about him, so there was no reason he shouldn't have that information. "And do I call them Dr. and Mr. or—"

She'd gone completely white. Looked like she might be sick.

"Tamara? What's wrong, hon?" He stood, thinking he'd grab a cool cloth.

When she stood, too, he backed away from the table, giving her room to make it to the bathroom. But she wasn't going anywhere. She just stood there, facing him, looking... horrible.

"My parents are Dr. and Mr. Howard Owens."

Chapter Seventeen

She hadn't meant to tell him. Oh, God, she hadn't meant to tell him. They'd been sitting there, eating sushi and having a great day, and she'd been so aware of the baby, needing to help care for her, and the awful lie had been there between them. He'd called her mother Dr. Frost. Dr. Steve's-Last-Name.

The lie had been too horrendous to keep to herself.

"Say something," she said.

He was standing there staring at her, frowning at her, completely confused.

"I… Did you just tell me that Howard Owens, my boss, is your father?"

She'd thought she'd felt every acute stab of pain there was to feel. She'd been wrong. The grip on her heart when she looked at Flint was different than anything she'd ever felt before.

"Yes." And if, judging by the expression on his face,

he was this put out about that part of it, he'd never be able to accept the rest.

She hadn't expected him to.

"You were working for your father."

"Yes."

He nodded. "Bill knew that."

She could almost hear his mind buzzing as he started putting the pieces together. But even Bill didn't know the whole truth.

"And your father told both of you not to say anything to the rest of the staff."

"Something like that." Exactly like that, except that he, in particular, had been singled out not to know.

"So when you interrupted us that first day… You're the real reason I kept my job. You talked to your father—"

"No!" She shook her head. "I mean, I did say something, but he'd already decided to keep you on. He'd met with you by then. You'd already signed the noncompete agreement."

"Which you thought was a good idea."

"I did."

He nodded, his brow clearing a bit. She wished she could feel relief but she knew better. Her lips were trembling. Her hands and knees, too. Tamara slid back onto her chair.

"I can see why your father wanted you to do your work without anyone knowing you were his daughter. People would be more honest with a stranger who had no ties to their boss."

She wanted to nod. He was right—to a point.

She could sense that he was taking hope. Saw him working everything out in his mind.

It was an endeavor doomed to fail before he'd even begun.

The sound of the swing, back and forth, back and forth,

click, click, played a rhythm in her mind. Soothing her. She concentrated on that. Focused on it.

"Did you really tell them you're seeing me?"

"Of course."

There were no longer any creases on his brow.

"And they were okay with it?"

"They didn't tell me not to." That point was key. He had to know they hadn't rejected him—despite believing he might have stolen from them. She'd even go so far as to say, "They're supportive of whatever choice I make where you're concerned."

"But they're worried."

She'd already told him that much. She nodded.

"Your dad knows about my past. And about Diamond Rose."

Of course he knew. Flint had informed Howard about the baby himself.

He frowned again. "When I asked you to give me time to tell him...did you?"

"Yes."

His brow cleared. If she didn't know better, she'd start to take hope herself. As it was, she wanted to throw herself in his arms, beg his forgiveness and have wild, passionate sex.

She wanted to focus on him. On them. All the issues separating them be damned.

At the same time she wanted to run, but didn't trust her knees to carry her away from him.

"So...now that the cat's out of the bag," he began, "how about we pack up the girl here and stop over to see them? I know Howard generally spends his Sunday evenings during football season in front of the seventy-two-inch screen he had installed in your parents' family room."

"You've seen it?" She gulped. Buying time she didn't have.

"Of course not. He doesn't expose his employees to his family—and vice versa. You'd be the first to know that."

She nodded.

"So…give them a call. Let's get this over with." His tone was light. His expression wasn't, but it was filled with the warm light of…caring she'd become addicted to seeing from him over the past weeks.

She shook her head.

Flint sat on the edge of the seat closest to her then leaned forward, taking both of her hands in his. "I know there's a lot we still have to face, sweetie. Just as I understand why they're so concerned for you. Let me assure them that I know what's going on. That I have no intention of asking you to do anything if you aren't ready. Even if you're never ready. Let me set their minds at ease."

She couldn't do that. But how to tell this wonderful man—the man she seemed to have fallen in love with—that nothing was as it seemed.

She loved him? Nothing like going for the bottom line when everything was falling apart.

Mallory had been right. She'd known how Tamara felt before Tamara knew it herself.

She wasn't surprised by that.

"You owe it to me," he said next, his tone still light, grinning as she looked up at him. "I have to see him at work tomorrow, knowing that he knows but that he doesn't know I do." He rolled his eyes. "Whew. This is complicated."

He made her smile.

Which made her cry.

She loved him.

And she was about to hurt him so badly.

She loved him.

And she was about to lose him.

* * *

Getting over the initial shock, Flint was filled with undeniable energy. Ready to forge into the future. Taking Tamara in his arms, understanding her emotions as she finally told him a secret he'd had no idea she'd been keeping, wanting her to know that he understood and held no hard feelings. He rubbed her back. Buried his face in that glorious auburn hair. Inhaled her soft, flowery scent.

If ever he could have scripted a life for himself, it would be this one.

He'd known Howard Owens had a daughter, but he hadn't heard much about her. She'd gone to college. Gotten married. He'd never heard anything else.

He certainly hadn't known that Howard had lost four grandchildren before they were born. The man he'd thought unemotional to the point of impassive had gone out and bought his unborn grandson a fishing rod. Hard to accept that one—and yet he'd always admired Howard, had wanted to be like him. Other than the older man's penchant for playing it safer than Flint's gut told him to do.

And now…here he was, in an incredible relationship with the man's daughter. Howard knew, and hadn't told his daughter to run in the opposite direction.

"Flint…"

Sniffling, Tamara pulled away from him. Wiped her eyes. She wasn't smiling.

He stilled. "What's wrong?"

Tears welled in her eyes again as she looked up at him.

He didn't start to sink back to reality, though, until she took another step back. Bracing himself, he waited.

No point in reacting until you knew what you were reacting to.

"There's more. And I want you to know, right up front, that I don't care anymore."

Now he was confused. "Care about what?"

Was she telling him she had no feelings for him? He found that hard to believe. She had to be running scared because of Diamond.

A problem, to be sure. But they could work on it.

There had to be a way...

"Whether or not there's any truth to my father's suspicions. I *should* care. But I don't. I told him that on Thanksgiving Day." She stopped. Took another couple of steps backward, toward the great room where she'd left her purse.

He was watching her leave him.

He didn't get it.

"I told him I wasn't sure how much longer I could go without telling you..."

What, that she was Howard's daughter?

And what were Howard's suspicions? Flint had already admitted he'd been in the process of opening his own business. That had all been before Diamond. Before Tamara.

"What did he say to that?" he asked because he couldn't come up with anything else.

"He understood that I had to do what I had to do."

"But he didn't want me to know?"

She shook her head.

Okay, so all was not as he would've scripted it.

"He wanted proof, first."

Proof? Flint needed her back in her chair, across from him, eating sushi. He had no idea how to make that happen.

"He's not going to press charges," she said. "He told me so. Especially not if it's you. You need to know that..."

Press charges? What the hell?

No.

Grabbing the back of the chair with both hands, he

stood calmly. His life was what it was. Always had been. Maybe it always would be.

And he'd deal with it.

"Why don't you leave out all the preliminaries and tell me what your father thinks I've done."

"Someone's been siphoning money from the company."

"And he thinks it's me."

She nodded.

Her tears didn't faze him. The stricken look on her face didn't, either. He noted both, but was somewhere else entirely now. He was in his own world, where there was just him. Knowing that he had what it took to deal with whatever was in front of him.

First was finding out the facts. All of them.

"And you've known this how long?"

"It's why I was working at Owens," she said, exposing more and more of a nightmare he'd thought he'd already seen in its entirety. "As an efficiency expert, I'd have access to everyone and everything in the company. He wanted me to see what I could find out."

"You were his spy." His mind was working. The rest of him was dead to the world. Shock, maybe.

Survival, certainly.

"Yes." He respected the fact that she didn't spare herself. Didn't lie to him.

Ha! Irony to the hilt. She'd been lying to him since the moment they'd met.

A flash of that day in Bill's office came to him, along with a stab hard enough to stop his airflow. "Bill knew."

She shook her head. "Well, he knew who I was, but he doesn't know why I was really there. No one does, except my mom and dad and me."

She hadn't been sent to him by Alana Gold. Or for any

good reason. Her presence hadn't been a coincidence; he'd been right about that. But her purpose…

"He wanted you to look into me in particular," he said aloud. "Your interest in me—it wasn't real…"

Thinking of her there, in his home, with Diamond Rose, he wanted to puke up the sushi he'd just consumed.

He wanted her gone.

"I wish that was true!" Her words came out on a wail. "I wish to God my interest was nothing more than a way to ease my father's worry. Instead, I fell in love with you. When he told me he wasn't going to press charges, it was as though this huge flood of relief opened up inside me and I've been a mess ever since."

She fell in love with him.

Right. She expected him to believe that?

"I'm guessing you didn't find anything to convict me?" he asked almost dryly, although he was starting to sweat in earnest.

If he'd made a mistake along the way, and they were going to make it look like he'd purposely cheated the firm…

Who'd believe him?

"Obviously, I'm not a criminal investigator, but I couldn't find anything on anyone," she said. "But circumstantially, you're the most suspect."

Criminal investigator.

Sweat turned to steel. No way was he going to jail!

He would not lose Diamond.

His mind took over. "Circumstances meaning my past? My background?"

"Your offshore accounts."

The night he'd been talking to her about the *Wall Street* movie. He'd been falling in love. She'd been taking notes to betray him.

He'd think about that another time. If an occasion arose that required it.

"I know of four other brokers in the firm who have them. What else?"

"Your spending habits changed."

"I had a rich girlfriend I was trying to impress, and money I'd saved for a day when I had someone to spend it on."

She didn't deserve any explanations, but he was *not* going to jail.

"You were opening your own firm behind my father's back."

"I intended to do just as he'd done when he opened his firm. Once I knew the legalities were in place and it was actually going to happen, I intended to go to him with my plan. I was about a week away from that when I got word that my mother was dead. I'd planned to give Howard the opportunity to send a letter to all my clients, naming a broker in my stead, and move on. If any of them found me elsewhere and chose to follow me of their own accord, then I'd continue to service them. Instead, I heard from Jane in Accounting, that someone found out—I don't know who or how—and I heard that Bill went to your father with a version of the truth that made me out to be unethical."

And clearly Howard had believed that version.

She hadn't stepped back any farther. He was ready for her to do so. To keep stepping back until she was gone from his home. From his life.

He wanted to forget ever knowing her.

Forget that he'd ever thought her beautiful...

Her eyes flooded again. Like a sucker, he'd fallen for that compassionate look in her eye. And the fear she'd exposed to him.

But no more.

"Jane is the one who started the rumor. She found out what you were doing from a friend of hers who works at the office of the Commissioner of Business Oversight. She knew you worked at Owens, where Jane works. Jane's the one who told Bill. Why Bill spun the news when he told my father, I have no idea. A charity account was used to run the money through." She spoke as though she was giving testimony.

Jane had betrayed him! He'd thought the grandmother of four liked him.

"You were the only broker who knew the account number because, for a time, you donated your expense checks to it as a tax write-off."

"All three of the company directors, and your father, as well as at least one person in Accounting, not Jane, has access to that account."

She could keep throwing things at him. He'd done nothing wrong. Knowingly, at least. But it was clear to him that she was prepared to keep talking. He had to know whatever she knew, to find out what he was defending himself against. He was careful to keep his tone as level as hers. To converse. Not to shut her down.

"The broker who took the money used various office computers at all different hours of the day—always computers that aren't within view of security cameras."

A flash of memory from the past week visited him. The quip he'd made about knowing corners that were out of view of security cameras when he'd kissed her.

"You were spying all along?"

She neither confirmed nor denied that one.

Her list—and her father's—could be convincing. He was seeing the picture she was building.

And yet…

He was *not* going to jail. He would not abandon Diamond Rose as he'd been abandoned. He'd give her up first.

The baby, not three feet from him, slept obliviously. He was thankful for that. She didn't know. And if he had his way, she'd never know.

"Whoever it was signed in under my father's account."

"Then why don't you look at someone who knows his password?"

"He thinks you do."

"I don't. Go talk to Bill Coniff, since you're so fond of him. He has the password. Maybe he gave it to someone."

"How do you know Bill has it?"

"I've seen him use it," he told her. "A couple of times when we needed something critical and your father was out. I'm assuming the other two directors have it, as well."

"You've actually seen Bill sign in to my father's account?"

He saw where this was going. If he'd seen Bill type the password, then it would stand to reason he could retype it himself.

"I was on the other side of the desk. I didn't see him type. I just know he accessed the information we needed."

Tamara stared at him. They were done.

"Look, Bill's the one who told your father that I was starting my own business, spinning it to look like I was planning to contact my clients and steal my book of business. When, instead, upon hearing the rumor from Jane, he could have just come to me. Given me the chance to go to your father. And Howard believed Bill's take on what I was doing, without discussing it with me. And he apparently still believes I'm guilty of stealing from the company. Just as he's going to believe whatever else Bill tells him. Including that he gave me your father's password. Or that I was on his side of the desk and saw him type it."

He could see the evidence piling up. Bill would testify that he'd seen Flint use the password. It would be Bill's word against his, and even a kid could figure out who a judge would believe on that one.

Tamara wiped her eyes. Picked up her purse. "I'm sorry, Flint. I—"

"Just go."

"I'm going to do everything in my power to clear your name," she said. "That's what I've been trying to do—"

"You could've just asked me if I'd stolen money from your father's company."

She nodded. "If you ever need anything…"

He'd know who not to call.

Flint watched her walk out of his life and then calmly locked the door behind her.

Merry Christmas.

He allowed that one bitter thought and then got busy.

He'd do what it took. Just as he always had. He was going to *be* someone.

Not for Alana Gold. Not even for himself.

For Diamond Rose.

Chapter Eighteen

Four days later

Bill Coniff, who, it turned out, had a gambling problem, resigned from Owens Investments and quietly disappeared. After signing a full confession, as well as other documents at the behest of Howard's team of lawyers, making sure he couldn't malign Owens Investments, the Owens family, or ever again work as a trader in the State of California. In exchange Howard didn't press charges because it was best for the company not to have it out there that they'd had a traitor in their midst.

Tamara discovered that Bill hadn't originally planned to frame Flint; at first he'd truly been pissed that the guy was leaving. But not because of Howard. Because of himself.

As Flint's boss, he got a percentage of the money Flint made for the company. But then he'd figured out that How-ard knew about the siphoning of money thanks to an extra-long meeting Howard had with his accountant after the company taxes had been done. A meeting that Howard hadn't shared with his top three people, as he usually did. And, after which, Howard had asked the three of them about their use of the charity account.

Bill had known by then that Flint was leaving. He'd known, too, that with Flint's expertise, plus his background, he could easily frame him for his own wrongdoing. He'd seen a way out. And had been desperate enough to take it. And then Flint had changed his mind about leaving. He'd needed Flint gone. His chances of getting Howard to believe him would not only be much stronger that way, but he'd been afraid that, once accused, Flint would figure out for himself who was guilty. Bill had gambled on the fact that Howard would believe him over Flint if it ever came to a "his word against Flint's" situation.

As much as Tamara wished differently, Flint wasn't around to know about any of it, including Bill's leaving, or the agreement between him and Owens Investments.

Sometime after she'd left him that Sunday night, he'd packed up Diamond Rose and gone to Owens Investments, clearing out his office and leaving his key in an envelope under Bill Coniff's door. Howard had told her it had looked almost as though he'd purposely left behind a trail of his actions by staying within security-camera range anytime he could. He'd packed his office in the hallway, carrying things out and loading them into bags he'd brought with him, one by one. Showing the camera everything he was taking.

In tears, Tamara had asked for a copy of the tape. She watched it several times in the days that followed, sometimes staring only at Flint. And at others, finding herself looking at the precious baby she'd once held.

Once.

She started the job she'd accepted early and worked long hours so she'd be finished by Christmas. Focusing on the task and not on herself. She knew how to cope with grief.

And when the nightmares woke her, she lay in bed and replayed her time with Flint over and over—starting with the first meeting between her and her father in Howard's office, to that last horrendous half hour at Flint's house.

Working for her father, virtually undercover, to preserve the integrity of his business had not been wrong. Hanging out with Flint…that didn't feel wrong.

Falling in love, though? Completely inappropriate. And yet if Mallory was right, she didn't get to choose love, love chose her.

So what the hell? She'd been chosen to have a life of misery? Of unrequited love? First for the four children she'd lost? And now for Flint?

And little Diamond.

Even from a distance, that little girl had found her way through Tamara's defenses.

Tamara was crying too much again.

She spent a lot of time with her parents. Going over lawyers' paperwork with them as they moved immediately on getting Bill Coniff out of their lives. From start to finish had taken four days.

And now, here she was, on Saturday, two weeks and two days before Christmas—almost done with the current job and another beginning in the new year, with holiday functions to attend with her parents and shopping to do— walking up to Flint's front door like an idiot.

She knocked, having no idea what she'd say to him. She'd already said it all. She'd explained. She'd taken full responsibility. She'd also told him she didn't give a damn whether or not he was guilty. That she'd known her father wouldn't press charges. That he'd be okay. She'd told him she'd fallen in love with him.

Nothing she'd said had mattered. She understood that, too.

Knocking a second time, she told herself that her behavior was bordering on asinine. But she had to see him. To let him know he was off the hook—they'd found their thief. Just so he didn't worry that, on top of Stella's order, he had another possible court situation to face.

And she needed to know he was okay.

Maybe find out where he was working, so she'd know that he and Diamond were secure.

She'd already called Mallory, knew that Diamond Rose was still coming to day care on her regular schedule. Had been there the day before.

She knocked again.

Flint didn't answer any of her knocks.

With the garage door closed, she couldn't tell if he was home or not.

One thing was clear, though. If he was inside, he'd seen who was on his porch and definitely didn't want anything to do with her.

She had to honor that choice.

She just hadn't expected it to hurt so much and couldn't contain the sobs that broke out as she turned and walked away.

Flint heard from Howard Owens every day that first week after his last meeting with Tamara. He didn't pick up, leaving them with one-way conversations via voice mail. One way—from Howard to him. He didn't return any of the calls. Howard was requesting an in-person sit-down. He wanted Flint to stay on at Owens Investments. He never mentioned the theft, or his suspicions, not even on the first call Monday morning, when it had become known that Flint had cleared out. By midweek, his messages changed only to add that he'd put out the word to Flint's clients that, due to having just become a father, he was taking a week or two off. Howard was personally handling Flint's entire book of business.

Flint might have called him back to tell him to go to hell. If he'd been a bitter man.

Even when Owens implored him, he ignored the summons.

And when he sent his spy daughter to Flint's home to plead his case? Especially then. He was fighting for his very life. Something neither of them would know anything about.

It was possible he would've capitulated after a full week's worth of calls, but on the Tuesday after the truth about Tamara had come out, while Flint was home alone researching his next career path, he'd received another court notice.

Not from Stella this time.

Much worse than Stella.

Lucille Redding, Diamond's paternal grandmother, a woman no older than Diamond's mother, was petitioning for custody of his little girl. No one had told him Diamond's paternity had been discovered, let alone that there was a paternal family.

He'd called Michael Armstrong, his attorney, immediately. Faxed the petition over to him. Asked about the repercussions of taking his baby sister and disappearing from the country. Hadn't liked that answer at all.

Michael had told him to sit tight and let him do some investigating.

Flint had cashed in some of his more lucrative personal investments, moving the money to his offshore account.

He called his attorney again, filling him in on the news Tamara had given him on Sunday, assuring him that he absolutely had not taken any money from anyone in any kind of illegal capacity. Michael told Flint he believed him.

He wouldn't blame the guy for having doubts. But he was paying him to keep them to himself.

Instructed once again to sit tight, Flint packed a couple of emergency suitcases, one for him, one for Diamond Rose, just in case, storing them in the trunk compartment in the back of his Lincoln.

For the rest of that day he'd researched career options and tried not to hear Tamara's voice in the back of his mind. He played music. Turned it up louder. Left the news on in the background, watching the stock channel on cable.

She didn't love him. Truth was, she'd been so hurt, she was probably incapable of truly loving anyone, other than maybe her parents.

He'd put Diamond to bed in her carrier that night, keeping it on the bed with him, a hand on her, on it, at all times. If he hadn't read that it was unsafe to have the baby sleeping right beside him—read about the danger of rolling over in his sleep and suffocating her—he'd have snuggled her little self right up against his heart, where he intended to keep her forever. Safe from a world that would judge her just because of who she'd been born to. And where she'd been born.

As if she'd had a choice about any of that!

Michael called Wednesday morning just as Flint was pulling out of the Bouncing Ball Daycare.

Turned out that Alana Gold had had an affair with a twenty-eight-year-old male nurse, Simon Redding, an army reservist working in the prison infirmary. Simon had fallen in love with her and, according to what he'd told his mother, Alana had loved him, too.

Which was why Alana had refused to name him as her baby's father. She'd been protecting him from prosecution.

At his mother's insistence, Simon had volunteered for deployment shortly after he'd slept with Alana, to get himself as far away from temptation as possible. He'd died in Afghanistan just after Thanksgiving and his mother, honoring the love her son had said he'd felt, and knowing he could no longer be hurt by it, had tried to contact Alana. To visit her.

Only to learn that she'd died in childbirth. That the affair could have resulted in a baby girl.

She was requesting a DNA test to prove that her son was Diamond's father.

And, assuming the test was positive, would be suing for custody. She was married. To a colonel in the air force. Was a schoolteacher. Simon had been their only child.

They had the perfect family unit in which to bring up a little girl.

On Friday he'd received a court order to provide Diamond's DNA.

And as early as Monday or Tuesday, he could be faced with having to set up a time to make her available for a grandparent visit.

He wasn't leaving the house at all that day or the next. He and Diamond were going to lie on her blanket on the floor and watch children's movies. He was going to rock her. Feed her. Bathe her. Take pictures and video of all of it.

And come Monday, in spite of the fact that he had a pending restraining order against him, an ex-boss who suspected him of theft, no job and had been suspected of helping his convict mother finance the drug business that had put her in prison, he was going to fight like hell to keep Diamond and him together.

He could be a good father. And a good brother. Both at once. He knew that now.

No one was going to love her more than he did.

No one but him could raise her to understand the good that came from being Alana Gold's child. Or teach her about the good that had been in Alana herself.

Diamond wasn't just a convict's daughter. She was the daughter of a woman who, though afflicted with the disease of addiction, had loved fiercely. Laughed often. Who'd listened to understand. Who'd always, always, come back.

And who'd taught him how to live with determination, not bitterness. To stand instead of cower. To carry dignity with honor even when others tried to strip it away.

She'd made him the man he was.

It was up to him to teach Diamond all the value to which she'd been born.

Because she wasn't just going to *be* someone.

She *was* someone.

On the Tuesday of that next week, fourteen days before Christmas, Tamara joined Mallory at the Bouncing Ball after work to help her friend put up Christmas decorations. Saying that putting the tree up too early made the little ones anxious, Mallory always decorated for two weeks and two weeks only. If the day after Christmas was a workday, she came in Christmas night to take down the decorations.

Tamara had promised herself that she wasn't going to mention Flint or Diamond Rose. Nor was she going to look for any evidence that either of them had been there.

If Flint wanted her to know anything about them, he'd call her.

He'd have answered his door.

Her spying days were over.

Which made it a bit difficult when, after they'd hauled

the artificial tree out of the back of the storage closet, straightened its branches and were just starting to string lights, Mallory said, "Flint offered to stay and help do this."

Mallory knew Tamara wasn't friends with Flint anymore. Knew he'd quit her father's company. Why on earth was she...?

And then it hit her. Flint and Mallory.

Standing on one side of the tree, she passed the long strand of stay-cool lights over to Tamara, who wrapped the two top branches in front of her and handed them back. Mallory's tree always had lights on every single branch to make up for the lack of ornaments that she said just tempted little ones to reach out and touch.

Tamara had insisted that Mallory and Flint would be perfect for each other.

Had thrown him at Mallory.

Her pain at the thought of them together was no one's fault but her own.

"I figured Braden would be here," she said, bringing up Mallory's ex only because she'd promised herself that she wouldn't talk about Flint behind his back. But lying to herself was really no better than lying to Flint, although the truth was that she couldn't bear to hear Mallory talk about him.

Mallory passed the lights back to her.

She didn't know what she'd do if Flint and Mallory became a couple.

Move back to Boston probably.

Keep in touch with Mallory for a while by phone, wish her well from the bottom of her heart, then slowly fade away from them completely.

It was the right thing to do.

"Braden's always helped you in the past," she continued just because she'd already started the conversation. Taking off the section she'd just wrapped when the lights all fell onto the same branch, she tried to rearrange them.

"He's out on a date tonight."

Oh. She passed the lights back to her friend. "Is she someone new?"

"I have no idea. I didn't ask." Mallory's tone said she didn't care. Tamara wasn't sure she believed that. She'd never completely understood the relationship between Mallory and Braden.

"How about that guy you were seeing at Thanksgiving? What was his name? Colton something? Is that going anywhere?"

"No. My call. Not interested." Mallory returned the lights to her.

So it was Flint, then. Leaning down as they reached their way along the tree, Tamara covered a wider section of branches.

She should be glad to know that Flint and Mallory might find each other. She loved both of them and neither deserved to be alone. And yet...what kind of woman did it make her that she couldn't bear the thought of the two of them together?

"Flint's in a real bind, Tamara."

With the string of lights hung, Mallory plugged it in, making the room glow with the overabundance of multicolored twinkling lights. Tamara barely saw them.

"What's wrong?" she asked. Was it Stella? His court date wasn't until the following week. But the woman could have showed up somewhere he'd been and then called the police to report that he'd been near her.

"Please don't tell him I told you, but if there's anything you or your family can do to help..." Mallory bent to the box of decorations, hauling out plastic wall hangings. Tamara recognized the long faux mantel she was unfolding, on which Mallory would hang stockings for each of the kids, with their names on them.

"What's wrong?" she asked again, more tension in her voice than she'd ever used with Mallory before.

"He just doesn't strike me as a man who'd ever ask anyone for help, at least not that he couldn't pay for and…" Mallory was bent over the box again.

"Mallory!"

Her friend stood, a garland of bells in hand, facing her.

"It goes against everything in me to talk about a client but…he might lose Diamond Rose, and if he at least had a job…"

Heart pounding, Tamara could hardly breathe. Lose Diamond Rose?

She hadn't told Mallory he'd quit Owens Investments. Apparently he'd done that himself.

"My father's been calling him every day for a week, trying to get him to come back," she said. "He doesn't pick up and won't return his calls. What's going on?"

Flint could lose his baby?

Because of Stella's order?

"Her paternal grandparents have come forward, demanding a DNA test, and they're suing for custody."

Tamara fell into the chair closest to her. A tiny, hardbacked one. Mallory told her what Flint had been going through since she'd last seen him, at least the parts he'd shared with her. And only because he'd had to give Mallory's name to the courts, who'd be contacting her as Diamond's caregiver.

"Her father's younger than Flint." Tamara said the only thing she could focus on that didn't make her feel like she was suffocating.

Wow.

Oh, God.

"The grandparents are in their late forties, young enough to participate fully in her activities as they raise her. They've been married for twenty-five years, have professional jobs and not so much as a speeding ticket. Their son was a nurse and in the army reserves. His only apparent mistake in life was falling in love with Alana and having sex with her while he was working in the prison infirmary."

Mind speeding ahead now, Tamara stood as a list of supposed sins against Flint sprang to mind. She knew them well because she and her father had listed them as reasons to suspect him of theft.

She knew how easily that list could convince someone against him. And she and her dad hadn't even had the restraining order to include in the mix.

Add to that, he'd just left his job—walking away from all the people who'd been loyal to him for almost a decade, some more than that, who would've been able to testify on his behalf. Including his client list.

He had no one. No family. No girlfriend. No one to stand up and tell the court what a travesty it would be to take that baby away from him.

"He's a single man without a job," Mallory said. "I was thinking, if your father took him back, at least that issue would be solved... I didn't know he was already trying to do so."

And Flint hadn't returned Howard's calls. Because the one thing Flint had never learned was to rely on others. To allow himself to need anything he couldn't provide for himself. Or pay for.

Because he could never believe that anyone would help him.

He'd probably thought, in spite of Howard's assurances

otherwise, that her father was trying to get him to talk about the missing money. He'd have no way of knowing that Bill had admitted his gambling addiction, confessed everything. Some of it was confidential and couldn't be told, and the rest... Her father wanted to apologize to Flint in person, man to man. Eye to eye.

"I'm sure he won't value his pride over Diamond Rose," she said. "He can't. Especially once he finds out what's been going on." Apologizing to Mallory for abandoning her, she grabbed her bag and ran out.

She had to get to her father. To convince him to do whatever he had to—beg at Flint's front door if it came to that, or camp out in the Bouncing Ball parking lot until he showed up there—to give him his job back, whether he wanted it or not.

That was for starters.

What she could do after that, she hadn't figured out.

She just knew she had to focus. Get to her father.

And figure it out.

Chapter Nineteen

The last thing Flint had expected to see as he was coming out of the Bouncing Ball Wednesday morning was Howard Owens standing beside his Lincoln.

"I have nothing to say to you," he said, getting close enough that the fob in his suit pocket unlocked the door. He rattled off the name of his attorney, telling Howard to say anything he had to say to Michael.

He got in his vehicle and pushed the button to lock the doors behind him.

DNA tests were expected that day or the next. They could've been in as early as Monday. Flint was considering every night he had with Diamond as a gift at this point.

Living from moment to moment.

And planning for a future with his baby girl, too. He had to, if he was going to stay sane.

He had to, to give Michael something to present to the judge. Something that could stand up to practically perfect grandparents.

About to put the SUV in drive, he glanced out the windshield and stopped. Howard was standing there, right in front of the vehicle. Arms crossed.

Challenging him.

The man was in his fifties, graying, but every inch the fit and muscular man he'd been when Flint had first met him.

Flint couldn't be intimidated anymore. He'd had enough. He reached for his phone to call the police and then thought about having that on his record.

It would be his word against Howard's regarding who'd started the confrontation. Howard would bring up the suspicions of theft against Flint...

Leaving the vehicle running, he got out.

Stood face-to-face with the other man, his arms crossed.

"I'm here to help." Howard's gravelly voice didn't sound helpful.

"If she put you up to this, tell her that she can consider her conscience cleared. And while you're at it, tell her to stay off my property."

With a single bow of the head, Howard acknowledged the order. But didn't move. "You're a smart man, Flint."

He refused to let the compliment distract him.

"Too smart to risk losing your daughter without doing all you possibly could do to keep her."

They knew.

Glancing at the door of the day care, he realized he should've known. Michael had said he had to provide Diamond's day-care information. Tamara had recommended Mallory to him.

They were all in it together.

Like hanging with like.

Sticking together.

That was how things worked.

"She's my sister, not my daughter." It was all the fight he had in that second, while he figured out what Howard was after and then did something to circumvent whatever it was.

"She won't know the difference until after you're more father than brother to her."

Point to Howard Owens.

The admission was like a slug to his shoulder. Nothing more.

"Let me help you."

He stared at the older man. There'd been a real plea in his tone. He'd never taken Howard for an actor. Never knew he had that talent.

Stood to reason, though, considering his wealth and the business he was in, convincing people to part with their money.

Flint's business, too. His one real talent.

"Why?" he asked.

"Does it matter? You don't want to lose that baby, you need a job."

"I'll find a job."

"Not with almost a decade's experience, not with a book of business large enough to impress even the most jaded of judges, not one that's going to give you the security you've got at Owens."

"Until you fire me for fraud, you mean."

"We got our man," Howard said, giving him nothing more on that.

He wouldn't have expected anything different. Howard would be bound by a legal agreement not to discuss the matter.

"There'll be a next time."

"Probably not before your custody hearing." Howard didn't even blink.

"I don't accept pity."

"Not even for your little girl?"

He had him there, and Flint made a fast decision.

"Thank you, sir. I appreciate the offer. I'll move back into my office this morning. Would you like to send word to my clients that I'm back from sabbatical or should I do that?" The question was a real one, and issued with sarcasm, too. He wasn't dishing up a load of respect to the man.

"I'll do it. I have a few things I'd like to say to them on your behalf. And then you do what you damned well please. You're the best I have and I need you on board."

Now, that made sense to Flint.

He nodded, got in his car and drove off.

Later that week Flint got a call from Howard Owens. Sitting at his desk, he picked up.

"I misjudged you," the older man said.

"Yes."

"In the numbers business, the money business, we play percentages."

Flint more than Howard, and yet it was true.

"The percentages pointed at you," Howard noted.

"Years' worth of faithful and diligent service, coupled with high returns, don't rate well with you?"

"Most of the traders on staff have that."

Also true. "I'm your top earner."

"You were making plans to leave."

This conversation was going nowhere.

Or it had already arrived there.

He got Howard's point in making the call.

"Thanks for getting in touch," he said, his tone more amenable. He'd just received an explanation from Howard Owens. A collectible to be sure. Because of its rarity.

"I was wrong. I realize now that you were planning to do it right, Flint. I want you to know how much I appreciate that."

Damn. The man must've seen his bottom line drop significantly over the week of Flint's absence.

"Just glad to be back, sir," he said, determined to get busy and earn his future job security.

Which was all Howard had to offer.

He didn't kid himself about that.

A week before Christmas, just after Tamara had arrived at work Tuesday morning, Mallory called.

"He asked me not to say anything, and I haven't, but I think what you said about him is right, Tam. Flint doesn't ask anyone to help him and I'm really afraid he's going to lose Diamond."

"It's because he doesn't trust that anyone *will* help him," she said, having reached that conclusion sometime over the past week of thinking about him. About them. About herself, too. She took for granted that there'd always be people around her who would help her out.

Flint had never known a day in his life where he could take anything good for granted. Least of all the people around him.

"Tell me what's going on," she said. She'd called him a couple of times since he'd been back at Owens Investments, almost grateful to get his voice mail so that she could just say what she had to say.

She'd told him how sorry she was. She said she understood that the issues between them, including her aversion to motherhood, would always keep them apart, but that she wanted him to know she loved him and that if he ever needed anything, she hoped he'd call her.

She'd asked that he let her know about Diamond. Told him how deeply she believed the child belonged with him.

He'd called back the last time. When she'd answered, he'd simply told her to cease calling him and then hung up.

Very clearly she'd been warned.

He could keep her from contacting him, but he couldn't control her heart.

Love chose her. She most assuredly didn't choose it.

"The DNA must've come back positive," Mallory told her, "because Flint has to take the baby to court for a hearing this afternoon."

Tamara was just wrapping up her job with the box-making company she'd been working for since leaving Owens. She expected to be out of there for good by late afternoon.

"It's just a hearing, though, right? Nothing happens today, even if a decision's made?"

"From what I understand—and he's not too chatty with me since he knows I talked to you about him last week—it could go one of three ways. He could be given full custody, with the grandparents getting some kind of visitation rights. They could get joint custody. Or the grandparents could get full custody with him having visitation rights.

"I think he only told me that much because the outcome will affect Diamond's time here, as well as who can pick her up. He said he's going to request that in the event they get joint custody, the Reddings agree to continue bringing her here on a regular basis so her life has as much stability as possible."

Heart pounding, Tamara stood from the temporary desk she'd been clearing off. "You think there's really a chance they'd decide custody today?"

"He sure seems to think so because he said he'd let me know if she'd be here tomorrow. I guess he had an in-home study done over the past week, and I'm assuming the Reddings did, too. It's my understanding that they live somewhere in the area."

"So the case is being heard here in San Diego?" Tamara.

"Yes, I know that because I had to fill out a form, answering questions, and send it in to the court."

The hearing would be at the courthouse. She could find out the room when she got there. "Do you know what time the hearing is?"

"I know it's after lunch because he's picking her up at noon."

That was enough. "Gotta go," she said, thinking furiously. "Thanks, Mal."

"Just help him, Tamara, and then for God's sake, let yourself be happy."

She didn't really get that last part. But couldn't think about it, either. She was one hundred percent focused on devising a plan to change a course of life events and only had until noon.

You're going to be someone.
You're special. The best part of me.
Don't you ever give up.
You're going to be someone.

With the baby carrier on his arm, his tiny girl asleep and completely unaware of where they were, Flint walked into the courtroom just before two that afternoon.

He'd never met the Reddings, but knew instantly who they were when he saw the couple sitting at the table on the right, holding hands.

Her hair was brown, probably dyed based on the evenness of the color, her dress a cheery shade of rose.

Rose for Diamond Rose.

He was in full military dress.

Good move.

Flint didn't have a chance in hell in spite of his hand-tailored shirt and three-hundred-dollar shiny black shoes.

Much smaller than he'd expected, the room had only two benches for spectators behind the two tables facing the judge's bench. He'd been told the hearing was closed, but to expect a caseworker, probably Ms. Bailey, in addition to attorneys for both sides. Michael had also warned him that the Reddings could call witnesses on their behalf if they chose.

He'd been given the same opportunity, but had no one to call.

Certainly not Stella Wainright. He'd be back in court in two days for his hearing with her.

Merry Christmas.

He could feel the older couple staring in his direction as he pulled a chair next to him for the baby carrier and took his seat at the table. He didn't glance over.

It occurred to him that they probably wanted a glimpse of their granddaughter. All they had left of their only child.

He didn't blame them.

He just didn't like them. Or rather, didn't like that they existed.

Michael arrived and the hearing began shortly after. Flint had purposely timed his arrival so Diamond wouldn't be in court any longer than necessary. He'd tried to time her feeding so she'd sleep through the whole thing, too, but she hadn't been interested in lunch at one thirty. He hoped the little bit she got down would tide her over until he got her out of there.

Because he was going to get her out of there.

He had to believe that.

And he did, right up until he heard the voices of Grandma

and Grandpa Redding, heard their tears and the love they had for a child they'd never even met. Their own flesh and blood. The only grandchild they'd ever have.

Maybe Diamond would be better off with them, after all.

He had to get outside himself, his own sorry feelings, and do what was best for her.

Trouble was, he couldn't seem to get far enough outside himself to believe that she was better off without him.

Being the child of a convict... It was tough. Like Howard Owens had said, people went for percentages. And chances were, if you came from a life of crime, you'd be more apt to get involved in a life of crime.

People were always going to judge you accordingly.

Which tipped the scale even further toward a life of crime.

But that didn't mean you had to make that choice.

He *knew*.

And could teach her.

And while she was the Reddings' only grandchild, she was his only family, period.

He'd had his chance to speak. Had said some version of all that. He couldn't remember exactly what he'd said as he sat back down, but he could tell by the worried frown on Michael's face that he had to prepare himself for a best-case scenario of joint custody.

Which meant a life of upheaval for Diamond. She'd never have one place to call home. Or the same place. She'd never be able to come home day after day, week after week, to the same family. Or spend Christmas with the same people every year of her growing up, making memories they all shared.

He hadn't had it, either, not all the time. But he'd sometimes had it. Even when home had been a dingy trailer with a hole in the bathroom floor that looked down onto the dirt below, he'd preferred being with Alana Gold over the nicest of foster homes.

The Reddings had a couple of witnesses. A preacher. And someone else. Flint spaced it.

"If there are no further witnesses, I'm ready to issue my decision."

"Excuse me, Judge." Flint looked over as his attorney stood beside him. "I do have another witness to call—or rather a group of them. They weren't sure they were going to make it, but I just received a text that they're here in the courthouse. If I may ask the court to be patient for just another minute or two…"

The judge, a man of about fifty, not far from the Reddings' age, glanced over his glasses at the couple, at Flint and then at the baby carrier beside him. He seemed like a good guy. Flint didn't blame him for deciding, as he probably had, that the Reddings could give his baby sister so much more than a single man, son of a convict, could. In the obvious ways, at any rate.

"A child's future is at stake," the judge said after a long minute. "Of course I'll wait."

Agitated as hell, Flint scowled at Michael. "What's going on?" he whispered.

Michael leaned over. "You want to learn to trust that someone will actually help you, or just hand her over?"

He didn't like the man's tone. But sat straight, turning when he heard the door behind him open.

If Stella was pulling some prank, trying to play nice only to annihilate him…

Howard Owens walked in with a woman Flint had never met. The way her arm looped through his made him figure he was looking at Dr. Owens. Tamara's mother.

A fact that seemed more obvious when Tamara walked in right behind them.

In a pair of navy dress pants, and a navy-and-white fitted top, with her auburn hair falling around her shoulders, she looked stunning.

Just stunning.

He was stunned.

Because behind her, more people were filing in. Men, women, all in dress clothes. Rich men. Rich women. In rich clothes. A politician. The police commissioner. A college president. He knew, because he knew them all.

He'd talked to most of them that week, assuring them that their portfolios were solidly back in his hands.

"Your Honor, these people all know Flint Collins personally, have known him, and trusted him, for years. Most of them for more than a decade." Michael proceeded to introduce them, one by one, begging the judge's pardon for a few more minutes to allow each of them to relate just one piece of information about Flint's ability to provide Diamond Rose Collins with a secure and healthy home. The home her mother had chosen for her. Because she'd known her son.

Flint could hardly hear for the roaring in his ears. The tightness consuming him. He couldn't take it in. Couldn't comprehend it.

But before anything else could happen, before those around him could speak, his baby girl, maybe distressed by all the people gathering around them, started to cry. He shushed her quietly. Rocked her carrier. But the wails grew louder. He had a bottle, just in case. Was reaching for it, feeling heat rush up his body, when he noticed that someone was beside him. He caught a whiff of flowers. And then feminine fingers were expertly unlatching the carrier straps, Diamond was up, held in Tamara's arms, and the crying had stopped.

Tears in her eyes, Tamara faced the judge.

"I am in love with Flint Collins, Your Honor. These are my parents." She nodded to Dr. and Mr. Owens. "Flint felt he had to fight this on his own, but that's not what family's about. Yes, he had a challenging upbringing, which means he doesn't yet know how extended family works, and that's why we're here to show him. I've had the honor to be in this little girl's life since the day she came home to Flint, and I am fully prepared to be in her life until the day I die, just as any biological mother would."

Her words, a little hard to understand at times through her tears, were no less effective. Not where Flint was concerned.

Diamond lifted her head, throwing it back a bit, but Tamara's hand was right there, steadying her. She looked at Tamara and then laid her head down on Tamara's chest again, closing her eyes.

"If it pleases the court, I've got something to say," Howard said.

The judge shook his head. "I don't need to hear any more."

Just as quickly as Flint's hope had risen, his heart dropped. Until Tamara took his hand. When he looked at her she was grinning, for him only. Holding his gaze. Telling him something important.

He might not know a lot about family, but he wasn't a stupid man. He held on to her hand.

"After giving this matter consideration, I feel it's in the best interests of this particular child to honor her mother's legal wishes by giving sole custody to her brother, Flint Collins…"

The man's voice continued. Flint heard mention of the

Reddings working out visitation times with Flint. He heard some technicalities. And a comment about hoping to see them back in his court again for the young lady to officially adopt Diamond.

He heard it, but couldn't believe it. None of it.

"Court dismissed." A gavel sounded.

It made no sense to him.

He was going to wake up. Find out that he was still in bed, it was Thursday morning and he had to face getting up, knowing he might lose Diamond that day.

Except that Tamara's fingers were digging into his palm. People were gathering around him. Patting him on the shoulders. Dr. Owens came up to his side, opposite her daughter, put her arms around him and gave him a hug.

"Thank you," was all she said. Which made no sense to him, either.

He nodded, though. Because it seemed appropriate.

And as soon as he could, he turned to Tamara, put his arms around her and hugged gently, feeling how hard she was trembling. With an arm still around her, he took his baby girl in his other arm and knew he was never going to let go. Of either of them.

He'd done what he'd had to do.

He'd just become somebody he'd never known he could be.

Chapter Twenty

The tree was lit, Diamond had been fed and was asleep in her swing, steaks were ready to grill, and Flint stood in the kitchen, opening a bottle of wine.

Christmas Eve, and he wasn't working.

He'd put on the black jeans, the red sweater. He had gifts wrapped and under the first tree he'd had since he'd left for college, and he still couldn't quite believe he was going to have a family Christmas celebration.

The Reddings had been over. Almost every day since their court appearance. They'd agreed that when Diamond got older, if she wanted to spend some weekends with them, she could, but for now, they were content to settle for babysitting. And visits.

When his attorney, Michael, had called Stella's attorney and, with Flint's permission, started dropping names of those on the support team who'd showed up for Flint in court, the Wainrights had dropped the charge against him. And then, when Flint's attorney had pressed, they'd agreed to sign a settlement to stay away from Flint and any member of his family and never to speak ill of him. Even after he'd refused to sign a similar one for them.

Tamara was on her way over after going to an early service with her parents. And he and Diamond had been invited to Christmas dinner at their place the next day.

Not so sure about that, having dinner at the boss's home, he figured he'd handle it like he did everything else. Standing up. Moving forward.

But for now, he had something more important to do.

As soon as Tamara got there.

He had a plan.

Because she was born to be someone, too.

Life had a funny way of working itself out, Tamara reminded herself as she climbed the steps to Flint's door on Christmas Eve night.

She'd sat through church, hearing about a blessed birth and feeling sorry for herself because she hadn't been blessed with the ability to give birth.

And then, ashamed, she stopped that train of thought. She was truly lucky. She'd been given a second chance with Flint, and she wasn't going to blow it.

Her issues weren't going away. She'd been unable to sleep for two nights after her day in court with Diamond Rose. But she was going to fight. Every moment of her life, if that was what it took. She was going to be in Flint's life. And that meant finding a way to let herself love Diamond Rose without falling apart.

She'd talked to Mallory right before church. Her friend was spending Christmas on a yacht in the harbor with some friends, and sounded like she was having a great time.

As good a time as it was possible to have during the

holidays when you didn't have family of your own. But Mallory wasn't giving up on life. Wasn't letting the past prevent her future.

Tamara needed to do the same.

Flint opened the door before she'd even knocked. He'd obviously been waiting for her and she loved that.

She took the glass of wine he held out to her, but leaned in to kiss him first. Long and slow and deep. He was much more delicious than wine.

They'd yet to consummate their relationship, but she hoped to rectify that situation this evening. The lacy red thong and barely-there bra she'd worn under a festively red-sequined sweater and black pants were there to help.

But when she began to make her move, he stepped back.

"I want to try something," he said, leading her into the living room. "Have a seat."

He seemed nervous, which was saying a lot. No matter what Flint was feeling on the inside, he didn't let weakness show very often.

So she sat. And wondered if he was about to ask her to marry him. It was a little early, considering they hadn't even slept together, and yet…it didn't feel early at all.

Except that she was a woman who might never be able to be a mother to his little girl. And who almost certainly wouldn't be able to have any more children with him.

"Drink your wine," he said, taking a sip of his as he told her about his day. About running out of tape in the middle of wrapping and having to go out and get more, his baby girl right by his side. She listened because he wanted her to. Sipped wine for the same reason.

But she really wanted to know what was going on.

When she'd all but finished her wine, he set down his glass. "I need you to try something with me. If it fails… well, then it does, but I feel strongly that we should try."

"Is this like one of those times when you take a risk on an investment because you're sure it's going to pay out, and then it makes you a load of money?"

"Kind of like that, yes. The feeling is the same. But I'm going to need you to trust me."

Though he prided himself on his knowledge, gleaned from studying everything he could about a particular topic, he'd been gifted with acute instincts. She'd learned that much about him very early on. Believed it was those instincts that had guided him so successfully through a life filled with hardship. Aided by what he'd learned, of course.

Her mind was babbling again. His nervousness was contagious.

She didn't know where he'd gone or what he was doing. Maybe seeing to the baby, although she hadn't heard a peep.

Then she heard his voice, speaking calmly. "Lie back and close your eyes."

An odd request, but he'd asked her to trust him. And she did. Implicitly. She lay back. Closed her eyes.

"Take me back to the day Ryan was born," he said, coming closer. She opened her eyes and he turned away. "No, please, Tamara, close your eyes and tell me about that day. Everything you can remember. Even if it's just about running out of tape."

She didn't like this. At all. But the tape? He'd focused on the mundane for a reason, so she did, too. Because she trusted him.

She was safe with him. Emotionally safe. And so she did as he asked, sharing that day with him in the little things, things that hadn't mattered to anyone else who'd talked to her since her son's death. She remembered that she'd had chocolate for breakfast—in the granola bar she'd eaten. That she'd shaved her legs. She'd had a day off work. Had gone in for a haircut and had wanted to leave the salon. To be home.

Her car had half a tank of gas.

The weather was warm, balmy. The sun shining. She'd thought about picking a cucumber from her garden to have with cheese and crackers for lunch. Wanted to remember to call her mom.

He asked her what she was wearing that day, his voice so soft she almost didn't hear him. So soft, he didn't break her spell. And she told him about the pregnancy pants. Not leggings, but real pregnancy pants with the panel. Her friends had teased her, but she'd wanted them because she was actually showing enough to need them.

The maternity top had been blue with little white, red and light blue flowers.

She talked and talked. Remembering so much. Relaxed from the wine. And the goodness of the feelings that had welled up in her that day. The hope.

But it didn't stop there. In the same soft voice, closer, right next to her on the couch, Flint asked her to talk about the first labor pain she'd felt. What she was doing. What she was thinking.

One second at a time, through the little things, the thoughts she could remember, she went through that horrific afternoon with him, including every moment she remembered in the hospital, talking about the sounds, the voices she heard, other people's conversations.

A conversation about babies who'd been born at her gestational time period surviving and eventually thriving.

She took him with her through the pain of the birth, the silence when she'd expected to hear a baby's cry. The look on the doctor's face. On Steve's face. She'd known. They hadn't had to tell her, she'd known. Her precious baby boy hadn't survived the birth. Tears streamed down her face as she felt the hysteria building inside her. Steve told the doctor to give her something and—

Just before the darkness came... "Stop." Flint's voice was still soft. The command was not to be denied. She lay there, eyes closed, and waited.

"Do you want to hold him, Tamara? Just once? To say goodbye?" His voice. She started to sob. To sit up. To lash out and—

Gentle hands against her face. "Keep your eyes closed, Tamara. Stay with me. Trust me. It's okay to cry, sweetie. Just tell me if you want to hold him."

She was back in that hospital room, right before the darkness.

"Yes," she said. "Yes, I want to hold my baby."

"Here." Flint's arm slid behind her back, supporting her weight as he lifted her, straightening her a little. Something touched her chest and she reached up automatically, cradling it.

The weight was slight. He was only four pounds.

"He's in a blanket, Tamara, wrapped up and warm. He looks so peaceful. Don't be afraid to hold him tight. You can't hurt him."

Of their own volition, her arms closed around that bundle. She didn't think to question, to wonder what it was. She just held on for all she was worth. Crushing it to her. Aware that it had more give when she squeezed than a human body would, but she was holding him. Eyes closed, lying there against Flint, she was holding her baby boy.

She cried. Hard. And Flint held her. She lay there until Diamond's cries broke the spell. And then, when Flint didn't move, she opened her eyes, told him she was okay and urged him to go care for the baby.

He didn't bring Diamond in to her. She'd thought he might, but knew he'd made the right choice.

She was still sitting there, holding what she now knew was a teddy bear, weighted and stuffed with a gel-like pillow pad.

Her trials weren't over. She was well aware of that, and Flint was, too. His gift to her hadn't been a cure, hadn't been meant as one. Flint was too much of a realist for that. And it was clear he'd done a lot of reading she hadn't known about. Studying her situation. Giving her the gift she needed most of all. He'd given her what no one else had even tried. A chance to hold her own baby boy.

Mostly, Flint had just sat with her in her pain. Taking some of the weight of it from her.

Flint grilled the steaks. He picked at his dinner just like Tamara did. And when she said something about maybe heading home, he asked her to spend the night.

Not to have sex. Just to lie in his arms and sleep.

Diamond was old enough to spend a night in her nursery. He'd keep the monitor beside him.

He'd had it all worked out and was still surprised when she agreed.

Leaving a T-shirt and boxer shorts on the end of his bed, with a cellophane-wrapped toothbrush—compliments of the dentist—on top, he told her he'd get the baby fed and down and would be back.

"Just get in whatever side you'd like," he said, growing hard as he pictured her in his bed, and yet, not achingly so. Some things were more important than sex. "The remote is on the stand there. Find whatever you'd like to watch."

By the time he got back, she was asleep.

Tamara woke with something warm against her back. She couldn't figure it out at first and then memory came crashing back.

Flint. He was spooning her. In his bed.

She had no idea what time it was, but felt like she'd been sleeping for days. Deeply. It was still dark outside.

Diamond Rose. Had he fed the baby?

Listening, she heard a little sigh and then even breathing coming through the monitor.

It was a good sound.

A very good sound.

There were other good things, too. Like the arm looped over her side, holding her close. The…ohhh…pressed up against her.

It was growing.

In his sleep, or had she woken him?

She wanted him awake.

Turning her head slowly, she kissed his chin. Or what she thought was his chin. He moved and caught her lips with his.

He must've said something because she was back in a trance again. Letting him take her away, to a different place this time.

A much happier place.

With an incredible ending.

But when they lay together, exhausted and complete, she didn't feel as though anything was over.

"Marry me," he whispered in her ear.

"I want to, Flint, so badly, but I can't do that to you or Diamond. That little girl deserves to have a mother who can hug her all the time and let her know how much she's loved. Kids need to be hugged."

"She needs *you*," he said. And when she shook her head, he asked, "You want me to tell you how I know?"

She nodded.

"When it comes to Diamond, you've got a mother's instinct. That's what makes mothers special. It's not something you buy. Or even learn. It's something you have that makes a kid feel okay even when things aren't okay. It's what my mother had."

"I don't have that." He was romanticizing now. So not like him.

"When you came into my office that day, I couldn't do it for her. I didn't know what she needed. You did and you didn't hesitate. She quieted immediately. That was no mistake, Tamara. Surely you've been around crying babies in the past few years, but you've never walked over to pick one up and quiet him or her."

Yeah, but...

"Anytime I talked about Diamond, you seemed to know instantly what she needed. What I needed to do."

Well, that had just been common sense.

"And in court, I was going to lose her...we were going to lose her. And you swooped in and saved us. Not just by being there, but when she started to cry...she needed a mother to seal the deal and you became one. You are one. She looked at you, laid her head down and closed her eyes."

"I—"

He put a finger to her lips. "I don't have all the answers yet," he told her. "I don't have any more at all right now. I might not ever have them. But I know that you're meant for us, Tamara, and we're meant for you. It's all up to you now."

He knew what he was getting into and wanted to take it on. Take *her* on. Maybe even needed to. He'd never even told her he loved her. She imagined that didn't come easily to a man like Flint. But he'd showed her. In a million different ways.

Mallory had told her to let herself be happy.

No one could do it for her.

"Yes."

"Yes, it's up to you now?"

"Yes, I'll marry you."

She was done with letting her past prevent her future.

They made love a second time and still didn't fall asleep afterward.

Maybe he was waiting for Diamond's next feeding. A couple of hours had passed. She had too much on her mind to let sleep take over.

"I want to try again," she said, feeling sick to her stomach even as she said the words. "Not right now. Not anytime soon, but I want to have your baby. Our baby."

"We have our baby, Tamara," he told her, sitting up and pulling her against him. "Biologically she has two other parents, but she's all ours. And if at some point, we're sure you're ready, then we'll face whatever happens together."

Whatever happens. Because you couldn't control life. You could only control what you did with what you were given.

Which was why Flint had grown out of an environment of crime into a remarkable man.

Diamond's whimpers came over the baby monitor. Slipping into a pair of shorts, Flint went in to change her.

"I'll get her bottle." Tamara, wearing an oversize T-shirt of Flint's, was already on her way to the kitchen. She was the bottle-getter when she was in the house.

But when she went to the door of the nursery to drop it off, she didn't let it go.

She wanted to hold the baby. To sit in the rocker and know she could be a mom.

She started to shake.

"Bring her in with us," she said. "Just while she eats. I'll sit up to make sure we don't fall asleep."

Without saying a word, Flint did as she asked, setting the baby down in the middle of the bed, half lying beside her and reaching for the bottle. Tamara still didn't give it to him. Kneeling on the mattress, keeping her distance, she leaned over. Diamond Rose looked at her—that little chin dimpled, lower lip jutting out—and started to cry. With the baby watching her, needing what she had, expecting Tamara to give it to her, there was no thought. From her distance, Tamara guided the nipple to that tiny birdlike mouth as though it was the most natural thing in the world.

Because it was.

For a mom.

* * * * *

COMING SOON!

We really hope you enjoyed reading this book. If you're looking for more romance, be sure to head to the shops when new books are available on

Thursday 29th November

To see which titles are coming soon, please visit **millsandboon.co.uk**

MILLS & BOON

Coming next month

BEST MAN FOR THE WEDDING PLANNER
Donna Alward

They were just making their way to the lobby when Holly gave a squeal and picked up her pace.

'Dan!'

Adele was adjusting her purse strap, but when she finally looked up, her heart froze and her feet stopped moving. Holly skipped forward and hugged the man standing in a tan wool coat with one hand on the handle of his suitcase and a garment bag over his other arm.

Dan. Just saying his name in her head made her heart squeeze a little. Daniel Brimicombe. Of all the Dans in Toronto, he had to be the best man. It was too far-fetched to be even comical, but here he was, in the flesh, smiling widely for the bride. The man Adele had once planned to marry. The one who'd whispered plans in her ear in the dark.

The man whose heart she'd broken…and in the breaking of it, broken her own.

Best Man Dan.

Adele Hawthorne, wedding planner extraordinaire, solver of problems and manager of crises, stood rooted to the spot with her mouth dropped open and her hands hanging uselessly at her sides. This was one wrinkle that she hadn't seen coming.

Adele tried to unscramble the mess that was her brain. Dan hadn't noticed her yet, thankfully. She was still trying to recover, and it was difficult because he hadn't changed at all. Oh, sure, there was a slight maturity in his face but really…it was like it had been eight days rather than eight years since they'd seen each other. Dark, perfect hair, just a little stubble on his chin, and the way his coat fit on his shoulders…as if it had been specifically tailored for his build.

He'd always carried himself with that calm confidence. She'd envied it back then. Still did.

And then he adjusted his garment bag, turned around, and saw her.

His face paled. 'Delly?'

Her throat tightened. Damn. He'd used his old nickname for her, and that made it a hundred times worse. She wasn't Delly. Not anymore.

'You know Adele? Oh my God, that is so weird!' Holly seemed totally unaware of the shock rippling between Adele and Dan.

Dan recovered first, and the color came back in his cheeks as he smiled. The smile didn't quite reach his eyes. 'We knew each other in university. I haven't seen her in eight years.'

Eight years, seven months, and a couple of weeks, if they were going to be exact about it.

'Hi, Dan. It's good to see you.' It wasn't a lie. It was a huge mess, but it was good to see him.

Continue reading
MARRYING A MILLIONAIRE
Donna Alward

Available next month
www.millsandboon.co.uk

LET'S TALK
Romance

For exclusive extracts, competitions
and special offers, find us online:

📘 facebook.com/millsandboon

🐦 @MillsandBoon

📷 @MillsandBoonUK

Get in touch on 01413 063232

For all the latest titles coming soon, visit
millsandboon.co.uk/nextmonth